THE DAWN OF THE END

THE RISING SERIES
BOOK THREE

KRISTEN ASHLEY

ROCK CHICK
PRESS

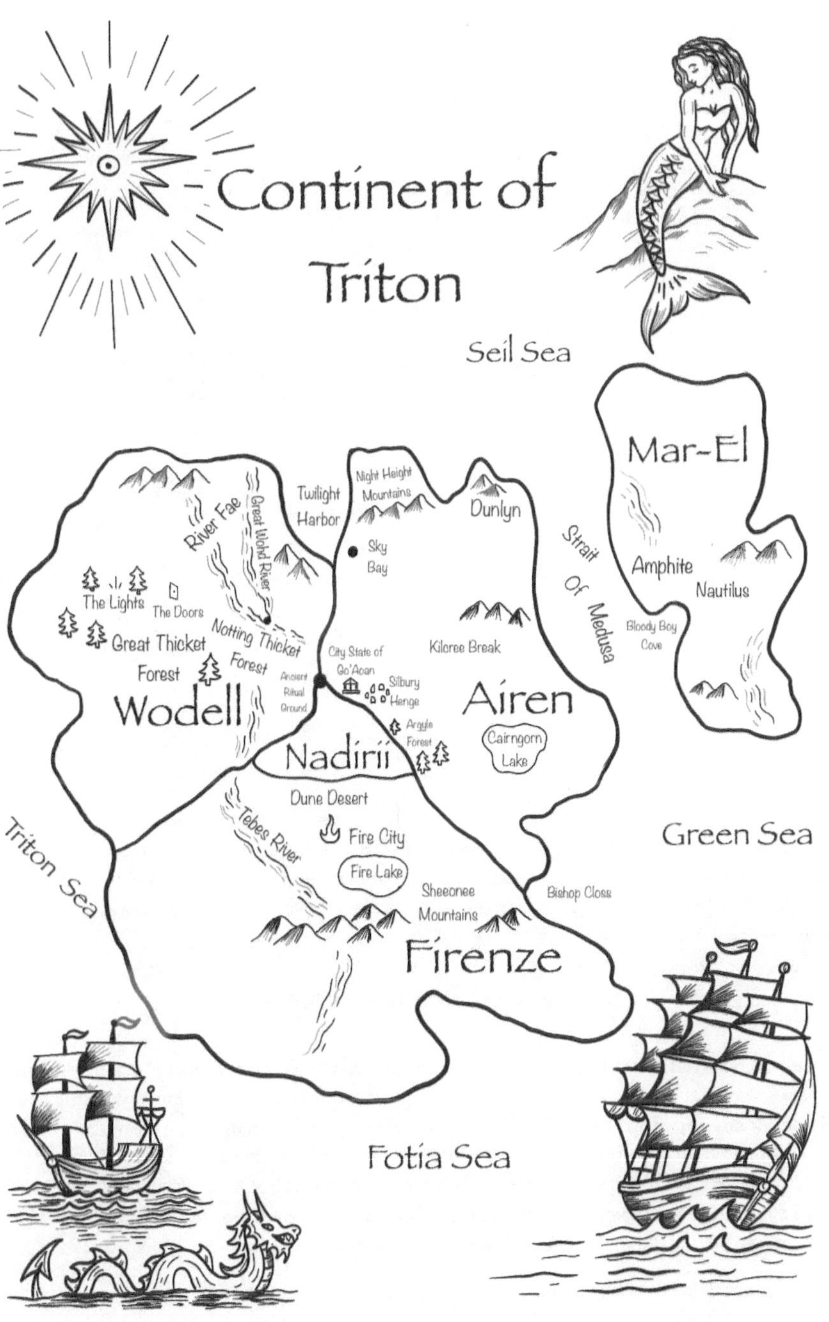

Continent of Triton
Seil Sea
Mar-El
Night Height Mountains
Twilight Harbor
Dunlyn
River Fae
Great Wind River
Sky Bay
Strait Of Medusa
Amphite
Nautilus
Bloody Boy Cove
The Lights
The Doors
Notting Thicket Forest
Great Thicket Forest
Kiloree Break
City State of Go'Aoan
Silbury Henge
Ancient Ritual Ground
Wodell
Airen
Argyle Forest
Cairngorn Lake
Nadirii
Green Sea
Dune Desert
Tebes River
Fire City
Fire Lake
Sheeonee Mountains
Bishop Closs
Triton Sea
Firenze
Fotia Sea

Cover Image: Pixel Mischief Design

Map Illustration: Megan Doherty

THE RISING

The Dawn of the End

A LOVE IS EVERYTHING SAGA BY

KRISTEN

NEW YORK TIMES BESTSELLING AUTHOR

ASHLEY

81

THE SCHEMER

Jellan
Underground Lair of the Beast
WODELL

He felt it, even in his weakened state.

The veil, it was growing strong.

The prophecy, it was advancing.

When he also felt he had company in this dark hole where they allowed him to go when they weren't using him or making him serve, Jellan curled deeper into himself, pressing his abused body closer to the stone wall.

He could tell them.

He could use his knowledge of the prophecy, his feel for the veil, to better his circumstances down in that dirty, cold, ugly hole.

"Hungry?"

It was *her*.

Marian.

The Mistress of the Beast.

His Beast.

1

That fiendish creature should be *his*.

Not *hers*.

The thing liked using him.

Perhaps Jellan could turn that around, gain control of...

She kicked him in the back, and Jellan tasted blood as he bit the insides of his mouth to stop from crying out.

He'd given them his tears. His pleas. His moans of agony.

They would have no more.

They would take no more from him than what they could force from him.

"I asked, *are you hungry?*" she demanded.

He needed to keep his strength.

"Y-yes," he answered.

He heard something drop to the ground close to him and turned carefully, battling the pain that seemed to infuse every inch of his body.

He could not make out what it was in the dark, a joint of some animal, not very much meat, lying in the dirt.

He took it up anyway, thinking he had to plan.

He had to *plan*.

And he had to have strength to plan.

He had power.

He was a Go'En priest, for Bedi's sake. A member of the Society of the Beast. One, if not *the* most powerful sorcerer in all of Triton.

He was born to master the Beast.

He was *made* to master the Beast.

He had to find a way.

He had to *plan*.

She started to move away, but he called to her, forcing timidity into his tone.

"C-can I ask you a question, Mistress?" he requested.

She turned, moved back to him, and he braced.

Like a woman, her moods were inconstant and sometimes volatile. He could not know if she'd kick him, call to the Beast and demand Jellan be used again or stroke his hair and coo to him.

In the end, he would lash her to the ritual ground, Jellan vowed it. He'd call the entire Society to have their way with her. He'd stand over and watch her take each cock and then he'd stand over her and watch her take each blade. And finally, when she was beaten and humiliated to the core of her soul and praying death would come fast, he'd give her that by drawing the final blade across her throat.

All of this looking right in her eyes.

All of this with the Beast at his back.

"What is your question, pet?" she asked.

So it was his benevolent mistress this time.

"I...the last quake, there was a demanding cry from the creature. I thought that he...I was not at that ritual, I thought that he—"

"Was calling to you?"

He nodded, gazing up at her but not meeting her eyes.

Fearful.

Submissive.

Beaten.

She needn't know he was none of that.

"He wasn't, he was calling out to me," she explained. "He sensed me. I'd been visiting him. And he was tired of your vicious shenanigans. Thus, he was calling me home."

"But, if he has no power down here, how does he make the earth quake? How did he call out like that? How does he pull you down? Me? The other women?"

"He has no magic, but he does have feelings. And just like everything with him, his feelings are stronger, more powerful, more sweeping than anything a mere mortal would have. They move the earth. When he makes the surface, if he should not get his way, they'll probably shake the heavens."

Jellan shuddered at that thought.

"But how does he pull you down?" he pressed.

"He doesn't. I did that."

He blinked up at her.

"I brought you," she went on, "and your *brothers*, our girls. That is *my* power. He reached to me, but my magic gave him that power. And my power brings him to the surface. But once there, the merfolk's binds on his magic are erased. And once we feel the time is right, we will surface and make all of Triton bow to us."

Not if the prophecy goes forward, Jellan thought. *Not if the lovers wed, consummate their love, ally all kingdoms, learn their gifts and how to use them. If they do, he will not be banished back to this under-realm, you won't either. He'll be slaughtered. As will you.*

"He...he would hum to me. After—" Jellan began.

She laughed an ugly laugh.

"This was considering what he'd do to you when I delivered you to him, not for any other reason, pet. Don't get any ideas in that silly, stupid, villainous, despicable head of yours. It was not your rituals he craved. Not your seed that stirred him. It was knowing I would come to him soon, and when I did, when I found my way to this place, to *him*, I could bring you to him."

So, the creature *did* want Jellan.

He wanted them both.

But he also wanted *Jellan*.

"You scheme," she said disinterestedly.

He stiffened. "I-I don't."

"You do and feel free," she allowed. "It will get you nowhere. But if hope keeps you performing to our standards…" She shrugged and let that trail.

Jellan thought for a moment before he decided to say quietly, "I honestly feel I could be of use to you. To you both."

"Oh, but you are."

"A *different* use," he stressed.

Abruptly, she leaned toward him.

He pressed himself to the wall.

"I like your use," she whispered, and he saw, even in the shadows, the flash of her malicious smile.

She then walked away.

And that was that.

So be it.

Once she was gone, as best he could, Jellan brushed the dirt from the joint before he gnawed on it, burrowing with his teeth to get all the meat, cracking the bones at their weak places to suck out the marrow.

He needed to keep his strength.

For she was right.

He did.

He schemed.

And he would find some way.

Some way to exact his vengeance.

Some way to be victorious.

He would make that happen.

No matter what it took.

82
THE HOPE

The Great Coven
Silbury Henge, Argyll Forest
AIREN

In the clearing of the forest, the first flash of light came before the first of the five standing stones.

The light was marine blue.

The witch Lena of Mar-el.

The next came and it was crimson.

The witch Nandra of Firenze.

The last was green.

Rebecca of Wodell.

And the witch who strode from the last flash did so speaking.

"I cannot be here, my queen is—"

"Rebecca," Lena spoke softly, "We are so sorry. But we had to call to you." She paused and finished, "Fern has been taken."

Rebecca gasped.

"The gentry of Airen did not even know of the changes that would be made once Cassius was proclaimed regent," Nandra said. "The moment he heard his son was to marry a Nadirii, Gallienus starting plotting. While they've been traveling, with great secrecy, the gentry allied their militias and created their strategy. When their spies noted the Firenz regiments camped close to Airen's southern border, they knew all did not bode well for the continuation of their regime with the heir to their throne soon to be wed to a Nadirii. Thus, they forged ahead with the first moves of their attack."

"And it was Fern?" Rebecca whispered.

Both fellow witches nodded, but only Lena spoke.

"Cassius had her guarded, but he could not understand the fullness of their desire to capture and imprison her. They sent great numbers to be certain this was so. His man, Otho, perished during the effort to try to spirit her away."

"Oh goddess, no," Rebecca breathed.

"This as well as more than thirty other Airenzian soldiers loyal to their crown prince," Nandra bit out.

"I did not feel the veil shift due to Fern—" Rebecca began.

"She is not dead," Lena told her. "She is only taken." She tipped her head to Nandra. "We believe they intend to try to use her powers. We also believe, as naught yet has moved forward with it, they do not know that she's raised an army of her own. Fern's army has just lost their commander...for the time being."

"They further do not know that all nations have allied with Airen to quell such a revolt," Nandra put in.

"I fear Wodell may not be able to join in that effort," Rebecca said sadly.

Her fellow witches both nodded, their expressions just as melancholy.

"There were two prongs to their attack," Lena went on, moving them from that subject. "Taking Fern and besetting Sky Bay. Cassius's men are holding the Bay, but they're under siege. They need reinforcements."

"I am sure this will be forthcoming," Rebecca murmured.

And it likely would.

"The Enchantments were attacked," Nandra announced.

Rebecca blinked.

"The Go'Doan fools," Lena mumbled.

"They didn't—" Rebecca started.

Lena shook her head. "They were trounced by the Nadirii. But they used a unicorn horn and Melisse to bring down the shield."

Rebecca's back shot straight and her eyes shot daggers. "A unicorn horn?"

"The creature will be avenged," Lena stated flatly, staring her sister right in the eyes.

This meant whatever glorious creature had been maimed for this vile effort *would* be avenged.

"And Melisse?" Rebecca asked.

"She holds to life, but barely. I have not seen good things," Nandra answered.

"I told her," Rebecca hissed, deciding to feel angry, rather than full of despair, for she'd had enough despair for one day.

"Melisse, like none of us, is perfect," Nandra replied.

"And this is why Ophelia isn't with us right now," Rebecca remarked.

"This is why, amongst other things," Lena responded.

Rebecca was confused. "But I have felt her strengthening."

"I as well, but I urge you, do not put too much hope in that," Lena advised.

They all knew.

What would be with Ophelia was not a possibility.

It was an eventuality.

"You have had much on your mind," Nandra said, unusually gentle. "And much occurring in your realm. But," she looked to Lena, bringing together their abbreviated circle, "there is hope. The veil strengthens. The lovers grow ever tied to one another. It is the first time I have felt real hope since the quakes began."

"This is true," Lena returned. "But something has occurred." She looked amongst her two fellow witches as well, saying, "You both must have felt it."

Rebecca shook her head.

"I felt something," Nandra told her. "Though I did not know what it was. Do you?"

"The sorcerer who rouses the Beast, his energy is gone," Lena said.

Rebecca, for one, had not felt *that*.

"Are you sure?" she asked.

"Can we be sure about anything we sense, see or feel through our craft?" Lena asked as answer. "But there is a great change, and it has naught to do with the fact that there have been less orderly quakes. The Beast is not gone, he is not asleep, he is...pacified. But he is the Beast. He has awakened. So he will not be pacified for long."

"I do not like the sound of that," Nandra muttered.

"I urge you, my sisters, in this time of despair, to hold on to hope," Lena said. "Much swifter than I ever would imagined with these four, I feel their power building. This means we must protect them at all costs."

"At all costs," Nandra agreed.

Rebecca thought of what was happening in her home.

So when she repeated, "At all costs," her words were full of sorrow.

As were the expressions of her sisters.

83

THE DOWN

Prince True
Crittich Keep, Notting Thicket
WODELL

The roads to Crittich Keep were lined with deathly silent Dellish citizens.

And not a one of them appeared surprised that Prince True rode his steed Majesty at a breakneck pace along the cobbles, his mantle flying out behind him, his face set in stone.

Though there were a goodly number of them who were astonished at just how brightly his eyes were glowing green.

But True was of no mind to the silent masses that lined the streets.

Only one thing was on his mind.

And this was why he'd thrown his leg over Majesty's rump to dismount before his horse even came to a full halt.

The instant he was on his feet outside the prison, he tossed his reins to a waiting guard who had to catch a still-moving Majesty and pull him back before he was yanked off his own feet.

True did not watch this.

His lieutenants Luther and Wallace—who had also dismounted on the fly—shadowing him, True stalked under the raised portcullis and through the high, double-wide, stone-arched door. A door that sat dead center in the long one-story section that separated the two tall, stark towers constructed of three-feet wide blocks of black Airenzian stone.

He was unsurprised that Aramus, Cassius and Mars awaited him just inside.

He was surprised that Frey Drakkar and Apollo Ulfr of Lunwyn were with them.

It was Aramus who approached first, his eyes moving over True's face, and thus his lips knew only to ask, "Which one do you want first?"

"Carrington," True gritted, prowling toward the inner hall without breaking stride, his mantle flashing behind him.

The men all formed a phalanx after him as True took a right turn in the hall.

He headed to where the prisoners of means were kept in spacious cells with cots with down mattresses, small tables with chairs, smaller irons for heating, with three square meals a day and views of the city from its thin windows.

The administration offices for the constabularies of all Wodell and their penal systems were also on the lower floors of that tower in the six-story keep.

To the left was where the commoners were sent. The cells smaller, filled with more than one man (or woman), with naught but blankets, no heating irons, chairs, mattresses or tables.

And the upper cells had views of the city's dump, cess-swamp, and the shanty village filled with vagrants, uncommitted lunatics, hopeless addicts of *ashesh* and *koekah* and other varied disenfranchised elements.

This would change, this separation of criminals.

Soon.

But not now.

Now was the time for something else.

"Where are the others?" True asked, his mantle caressing the corner at the winding stairwell as he swept into it to ascend.

"Down," Cassius answered.

True was unsurprised at this as well.

For it was as he'd ordered.

The Down was where the worst offenders were kept. Convicted murderers, rapists, and the abusers of the elderly, women and children were locked there in small cells with no light. Communication between prisoners or with guards was forbidden and only the barest necessities for survival were offered for as long as their sentence lasted, or their life ended, whichever came first.

If they survived, they were released into the Shanty, one class of the varied disenfranchised who existed there.

The Down was also where the ancient torture chambers were.

They'd been closed four generations ago after a public outcry became a riot that saw a goodly amount of the city burned, a larger amount looted, and Birchlire Castle had been in danger of both. This, after two young men, neither of them even twenty, were tortured to death for a crime it was eventually proved they did not commit. It was simply the fact that the lord of the manor didn't like them. Therefore, he'd accused them of a rape that one of his own vassals had committed.

The Down, after nearly two hundred years of being locked, was now open.

True would be going there.

Very soon.

But not in the now.

He stopped walking swiftly up the steps and started jogging, hearing the boots of the men behind him striking the stone treads in a quick cadence, following him.

He ceased doing this when he made the fourth landing, where Carrington was being kept.

But he did stride purposefully down the hall.

There was one guard at the top of the steps, two guards at the end of the hall, two at the door.

One of them moved immediately, putting his hand to his belt to procure the key and open the door.

True, with his assemblage behind him, stopped at it, and he caught the other guard not at work opening the door, bowing to him.

"If you bow to me again, twenty lashes," he spat.

The guard shot up, and the air in the hall went static.

"I-I'm sorry, Your Grace?" the guard stammered.

"You are a citizen of this realm and in service to it. You may salute me as your superior officer. You may salute me as a citizen of this land, and I am in a position of authority. But you do not bow to me. *Ever*," True replied.

The guard's eyes slid to his compatriot but then he looked back to his prince, nodded sharply, lifted his hand to his forehead and gave a smart salute.

True dipped his chin, turned his gaze impatiently to the other man who seemed frozen in his duties of opening the door.

When he caught True's attention, he swiftly went about finishing his task.

He threw open the heavy, studded door.

True strode in, and Carrington, writing something at the table, his iron lit, the room cozy warm, his clothing his own—well-tailored trousers and waistcoat made of worsted wool, shirt of fine linen, what looked to be a cashmere rug thrown about his shoulders (also likely from his own home)—stood from his chair, his lips quirking in a triumphant smile.

True wasted no time wiping it from his face.

His knuckles were split and two of Carrington's teeth were embedded in them before Aramus pulled him off and tugged him away, Apollo Ulfr needing to assist him with this effort.

Cassius stayed close to his struggling brothers while Mars took position before a prone Carrington on the floor and Frey Drakkar approached the traitor, staring down at him with distaste.

"This is not you, my brother," Aramus said in his ear, grappling to keep control of True at the same time Cassius and Mars were positioning to stop Wallace and Luther from assisting their prince in getting free. "Do not allow him to take away who you are. Keep hold, man." His grip under True's arms tightened. "*Keep hold.*"

It was the last that got through to True.

He stopped fighting against his friend and drew in a deep breath.

When Aramus sensed he had control, he let him go and he and Ulfr stepped away.

True took another deep breath and jerked his head side to side in an ineffectual effort to ease some of the tension there.

"Aramus speaks true, it's not you," Mars stated offhandedly. "But also, he cannot talk if he's unconscious, and we cannot torture him to any kind of success, again, if he's unconscious."

"Get him up in the chair," True bit out.

Wallace and Luther moved.

Carrington groaned as they did as ordered.

His face was a mangled mess. His jaw might even be broken.

True did not call for a physician.

He moved toward him and stopped.

True then bent his head to look down at his hand, dug out one, then the other, of Carrington's teeth and tossed them to the stone floor under the man's lax feet.

They made a quiet clatter as they skittered toward his boot.

Carrington's head was lolling on his shoulders to such an extent, he did not notice this.

"Do you know what they do to traitors in the necropolis of Firenze?" he asked.

Carrington's swelling eyelids fluttered.

But his split, bloody lips said, "Long live The Rising."

He said this with a lisp.

True was far from amused or even gratified by the sound.

Sensing this, Mars got close.

Cassius did too.

But Aramus stayed where he was and simply said, "My friend."

True drew in another deep breath.

"You'll be moved to the Down," he shared with his prisoner.

"Long live The Rising," Carrington replied.

True crossed his arms on his chest.

"I see," he whispered.

Carrington's head twitched at this in surprise.

True moved closer to him.

Carrington winced as his body braced.

Cassius and Mars stayed close.

But True only crouched beside the odious man.

"My mother told me you urged my father to tax the Go'Doan. With this show of loyalty to them, was that subterfuge?"

"There are many followers of Go'Doan in Wodell, *Your Grace*."

"And a tax against their religion would not be well regarded."

Carrington said nothing.

But if it could be credited, he smirked.

In other words, another plan to create dissension and reduce the popularity of the monarch.

True did not resort to his earlier method to wipe that smirk off his face.

"I'm claiming regent," he said softly.

Carrington's mangled face managed to show some shock before he blanked it.

"It doesn't matter," he replied.

"You did not wish that, but I see it doesn't alarm you," True remarked. "What will alarm you is that I will claim regent for only a very short time.

That time being as long as it takes for the papers to be drawn up and my father to sign his abdication."

Carrington jolted in his chair.

He hadn't expected that.

True felt no pleasure at his surprise.

None at all.

"These papers will be ready on the morn. They'll also be signed on the morn. And then I will have all clear rights, claims and powers over this land," True told him.

"That doesn't matter either," Carrington returned.

"You are so sure?" True asked.

"I am very sure, *Your Grace*," Carrington replied, a definite smirk now lifting his bloodied lips.

"Well then," True said on a sigh as he straightened from his crouch, "we shall see. But on the matter of you, there have been a number of changes."

Carrington lifted his chin. "I do not fear the Down."

"You won't be there long," True shared. "And I imagine you suspect that. Thus, I can understand why you would not fear it. However, with all clear rights, claims and *powers* over this land, I can make any number of decisions. Indeed, *all* of them. Including the one I make in the now. You are found guilty of high treason against the Kingdom of Wodell."

"I'll have my tribunal," Carrington stated calmly.

"You...will...*not*," True bit.

Carrington stilled completely.

Brilliant.

Now he had the man's complete attention.

"You studied extensively in Go'Doan. Do you remember what happened in olden times when a man was found guilty of high treason in Wodell?" True asked.

Carrington began to squirm in his chair.

He knew.

"Drawn and quartered," True told him regardless. "Hanged, almost until dead. Publicly. Then I'll have your cock severed from your body. Publicly. I will then have your bowels spilled from your gut. Publicly. And as you are there before all, spread open, spilling out, emasculated, I'll have your head. That's the last you'll experience. But now you'll know your dead body will be quartered, the parts taken to the four corners of this city, set out, and what is not torn away as naught but carrion will be left to rot. Your head, however, will be on a pike affixed outside the window to my mother's bedchamber."

"You cannot do that. That practice was outlawed—" Carrington began.

"We have not had an incidence of high treason since then, or at least not one instigated by someone not of royal blood. Now, we have. And as I will soon be the law of the land, I'm making it not outlawed any longer."

"I did not bear the bow that killed your mother."

Rage burned in him at the reminder of just *some* of the massive amount he'd lost that day, and True couldn't hold it in check.

He backhanded Carrington so hard, the man nearly toppled to the floor.

He then got it in check and shared, "As supreme ruler of this land, I've decided I don't fucking care."

True turned on his boot and moved to the door but stopped as both the guards there saluted him.

"Take him to the Down," he commanded. "Relieve him of his clothes. He wears commoners' prison garb. Broth and bread once a day. No butter. No meat. No coffee. No milk. Half carafe of water a day. Half a candle a day for light. No books. No papers. No exercise. No visitors. No talking. If a guard responds to him, relieve that guard of his duties, that being his employment with the Royal Penal Guard, and assign another who will not break this order. He does not leave his cell and put him in the smallest one we have. Am I understood?"

"Yes, Your Grace."

"And see to this immediately," True went on.

"Yes, Your Grace."

"Then send a guard to his home," True continued. "Strip it of all his possessions. Claim them for the crown. At the exact hour my mother lost her life this day, tomorrow, I want everything burned that can be burned. Anything of worth can be liquidated, the proceeds divided between the Royal Service Infirmary and Our Lady the Queen's Orphanage, after ten percent is deducted to be donated to the Temple to Wohden."

"At once, Your Grace."

"And last, you do not have to handle him gently," True finished.

The guard he was addressing smiled.

He was either loyal to True, loyal to Mercy, or what being one or the other actually meant.

Loyal to Wodell.

"You cannot do this!" Carrington called agitatedly as True began to leave the room.

He turned back. "This was your mistake, Carrington. For you put me right where I am. And *I can*."

With that, True moved out of the room, his group coming with him as Carrington shouted, "I will have a tribunal! You cannot prove a thing! I demand to speak to the king! You cannot prove—"

He was silenced abruptly. Clearly, True's final order had been carried out with due haste.

There was silence until they reached the ground floor.

As they made their way down the long hall to the opposite tower, Mars fell in step beside him.

"Farah," was all he said.

True felt his mouth tighten before he forced it to relax in order to reply, "You saw yourself it was a flesh wound. The arrow went through, easily broken at the head, the shaft removed without further damage. When I left, it had been cleansed, stitched, and her arm has been put in a sling. She was given a sleeping draught. The women are with her."

Cassius fell in step on his other side.

"Sir Alfie."

At that, pain raging along his spine, through his gut, in his heart, so intense in all places, it drove up his throat, True stopped dead and looked into Cassius's eyes.

Cassius read what he saw in True's and whispered, "Fuck, True."

"He will never walk again. I suppose, as the arrow struck the spine low, and he still has use of his arms, he has some hope of some semblance of a life, perhaps siring a child, getting himself around. But he's in agony. And when his pain fades, I am in no doubt he will ask for the Soldier's Poison. And I must make the decision if I'll grant it to him."

All the men got close.

But Cassius repeated, "Fuck, True."

True looked to Mars. "I was told my father dove under the pew."

"Do not think of these things in the now, my brother," Mars said quietly.

"Mars, did...my father...dive under...the *gods-damned pew*?" True gritted.

"Yes," Mars answered.

"He did this while Alfie rushed to protect her and any life he would accept was taken from him, but not in that moment. He does not die knowing he served his realm. He makes the decision to die, thinking he failed his queen."

"Do not think of these things in the now, *my brother*," Mars bit. "You will have vengeance. Your man will have vengeance. You will see to it. And if you don't, I will."

"As will I," Cassius said.

"As will I," Aramus added.

"You'll have my dragons," Frey declared.

"And you'll have my wolves," Apollo finished.

He looked amongst them.

Then he looked to Wallace and Luther.

Wallace looked grave.

Luther looked murderous.

True again turned and moved to the door that would lead them down.

They were at the bottom level, three floors under the earth. True knew this because he'd ordered them there. But even if he didn't know, the amount of guards at that landing and along the hall would have proclaimed it.

Nearly every one of the archers in the temple had been subdued after they'd let fly their arrows, either by wedding attendees, or by the palace guard that had been set to protect their king, queen, prince and his new princess.

One, however, had broken his neck after falling down a stone stairwell while attempting to flee.

Nineteen men were held down in that reopened torture chamber, the largest room of the lot.

And True made his way there.

The door was opened for him and the others quite a bit faster than the one they'd been through to visit Carrington.

What he saw when he entered the large, musty room was not the dust and cobwebs.

It was further not Gal and Brix, his gnome spies, who he had not seen since he and Farah had visited the Doors some weeks before.

It was also not Princess Serena of the Nadirii wearing her Nadirii tunic, leg casings and moccasins with the band proclaiming her royalty wrapped around her forehead. A broadsword was at her back, one dagger in her belt, her arse planted on top of a rickety table, legs crossed in front of her, currently engaged in daintily cleaning her fingernails with the tip of her other dagger.

He also did not see Mars's Trusted, Chu, standing near her wearing his Firenz leathers with the Trusted's black mantle edged in green and red at his back.

Nor did he see the dozen guards patrolling between the men who were stripped of anything but their underpants, on their knees spread wide on the cold stone floor, their arms tied at the back of their heads with a rough rope that also was tied around their necks.

He saw that there weren't nineteen of them.

There were twenty-one.

Mars didn't miss this either, thus he asked his man, "And who are our added guests?"

"They're the Go'Doan priests we caught with the missives I sent the message to you about. Sadly," Chu resolutely did not glance at True, "we deciphered their message too late."

Mars let his breath out his nose and the sound reminded True vaguely of an angry bull.

"You tried to warn us," True said to Serena.

She was watching Chu talk, but when he spoke, her gaze came to him.

"Your guard is good, True," she replied, shocking him by speaking complimentary words, the first he'd ever heard from her lips. "They wouldn't let me anywhere near, and I was in disguise, so they had no idea who I was."

"They were not good enough," True returned shortly.

"Do not do that," she said softly, shocking him again with her tone before she jerked her head toward the men on their knees on the floor. "These arseholes are sneaky as hell. It's going to take breaking one to know what we face. And further, it's important you understand you will not be the only one who lives the rest of your life with their failure. They will too."

They will too.

Was he talking to Princess Serena of the Nadirii?

He had no time to process what appeared to be a colossal change in her.

He simply lifted his chin and said, "Thank you. You tried to save my mother. And for that, I will forever be grateful to you."

She blinked, now experiencing her own shock.

She then looked to Chu, as if he could translate a foreign tongue she'd never heard.

Chu shook his head once, an indication they'd speak later.

She accepted that readily, sheathed her dagger, hopped off the table and crossed her arms on her chest, ready for True to get on with it.

True turned to do just that only for Gal to speak.

"We have failed you too."

He looked down at the gnome. "And how did you do that?"

"We did not discover the plot," Gal replied.

"Neither did I, or any of my men, or my mother, all of whom were aware there possibly was one, even if we couldn't imagine she'd be the target," True pointed out.

"We're better than all of you," Brix returned, and he was not bragging.

This was true.

"And although I'd like to see what happens next to these bastards," Brix jerked his head to the side, "I want more to get back to it. So you have our apologies for our failure. They are heartfelt. And now, we will help you seek vengeance."

True dipped his chin.

Brix glowered at him.

Gal sighed.

Both gnomes then strode out.

True watched until they disappeared, then he turned back to the traitors, ready to see to this grim business, when he heard Serena make a noise in the back of her throat.

His gaze went her way to see she was quickly drawing her broadsword.

"What is it?" Chu asked her, drawing his.

True pulled his sword from his belt and turned to the door as a commotion sounded from there, nearly drowning out Serena's answer of, "Magic."

"Do not stand in our way!" Elena could be heard shouting.

"Oh fuck," Cassius muttered, sounding harassed.

It then happened.

A great gust of wind swept from the hall, into and through the room.

Oh fuck was correct, for True had a feeling what was about to happen.

As it got stronger, True scabbarded his sword and braced his legs, and the indication he was correct came as Elena announced, "Do not forget, she is now Princess Royal!"

And then his very new wife came in.

And with her came the wind.

No.

A storm.

His hair whipped around his head, his mantle about his body, just as her hair, skirts and cloak whipped around hers.

She didn't even look at him.

Her one arm strapped to her chest from the opposite side, so the shoulder that had been pierced by an arrow did not have pressure, she brought the gale and her eyes shone like twin golden blazes.

He moved with difficulty against the tempest to try to get to her, starting to call her name, when she swung her free arm up in front of her and then to the side.

True's head turned when she did this, and he watched twenty-one men lifted right off the ground and tossed like they were wisps of parchment across the room, slamming against the wall and each other.

Her emotion was getting the better of her.

And as such, she had no control of her magic.

"Farah!" he barked, now moving swiftly to her.

She swung her arm the other way and only the prisoners, crying out in shock and fear, sailed across the room and slammed into the opposite wall.

"*Farah!*" he roared, making it to her and catching her by her upper arms, carefully on one side, but definitely with the aim to get her attention.

Her eyes shifted up to him and he fancied he felt their burn.

"Darling, calm," he whispered.

"We will have vengeance," she whispered back, her voice one he'd never heard before, not even when her own mother perished not long ago.

"My love, we will," he said. "But now you're injured, and you need to calm."

She pulled from his arms and turned to Mars.

"You will learn everything they have to tell," she demanded.

Mars looked stuck between amused and reciprocating her wrath when he replied, "Yes, I will."

Though, even in the circumstances, True did not fail to note Mars's expression was also partly exasperated, for his attention was partly taken by his wife standing behind Farah.

As were her friends, not only Elena, but Aramus's queen, Ha-Lah.

Mars focused on Farah. "I need you to take my wife back to the castle, little sister."

"I think not," Farah retorted. "She was the one who suggested we come. And she was adamant about it. She might be small, but when she's got something in her head, she makes it happen."

Mars's chin jerked into his neck as his brows rose and he looked to his queen.

He studied Silence. True studied Silence. Both men took in her determined expression and the mercurial shift of her silver eyes as the winds in the room died down.

True then looked to Mars only to watch him smile at his wife very slowly and very scarily.

"We will watch," Farah declared, and True's attention went back to his own wife.

"You will not."

"We will watch," Silence declared. "And if we have any ideas you can try, we will share."

"Oh, for fuck's sake," Cassius said to the ceiling.

"I couldn't stop them, my prince," Elena told him.

"Did you try?" he asked her.

She looked guilty and gave only a shrug in response.

"Do you want to watch, my queen?" Aramus asked his Ha-Lah.

Ha-Lah, however, wasn't looking at her husband.

She was looking at Serena.

And doing so, she answered, "I want to chat."

"I think this is a good idea," Cassius decreed.

"I don't," Serena put in. "I was hoping my job would be putting some balls in vises. Then squeezing."

"I think we have personnel covered," Cassius pointed out, gesturing to all the men standing in the room.

True did not have time for this shite.

Thus, he looked to Elena.

"Take them away," he ordered.

Her attention came to him and her face gentled.

"True," she said softly.

"Take them." He turned to Serena. "And you. Take them safe to the castle. And I'm trusting the both of you."

Serena looked to Chu.

Chu nodded.

Serena nodded back and moved toward the door.

True stared for a moment at her easy compliance before he turned to Elena to see her gaping at her sister.

He then gave his attention to his wife.

"Go," he said gently. "Go home. Please."

She gazed up at him for a long, heavy moment before lifting her hand and resting it on his cheek, any residual fury dying from her eyes as she studied his features.

"I will await you in our chambers," she whispered.

He wrapped his fingers around her wrist, brought her palm to his lips and kissed her there before he held that hand to his chest and urged, "Try to rest as you do."

She continued to study him as if hoping his expression would change and he would share this was all a hoax, all was well, and they could enjoy the rest of their wedding day—and night—as they had planned.

He could not do that.

All he could do was hold on to his own fury long enough to be sure his wife and her friends were away.

And only then would he unleash it.

Again.

"Go," he prompted.

Her eyes dropped to his hand. He noted when she saw his bleeding knuckles, but her gaze merely danced with gold fire before she gave him what he desired.

She pressed her hand into his chest, leaned in and touched a kiss to the underside of his jaw.

She then pulled away, looking deep into his eyes before she nodded and turned.

The women moved with her.

True looked to Wallace and Luther.

"They are safe to the castle, then you both come back," he commanded.

He got nods and his men followed the women.

When they were gone, True looked to Mars.

"Do you need your men?" he asked.

"They'd be useful."

"Are they here?"

"Outside."

True turned to a guard. "Get the Trusted."

That guard moved instantly.

"Chu," Mars called.

But Chu was already striding to the men that the guards were again arranging on their knees on the floor.

Chu did not look thrilled with his task, he did not look like he dreaded it.

He looked nothing.

Expressionless.

Emotionless.

As if what he was about to do meant naught to him.

True had noted this of Mars and his men when they'd been at work in the necropolis in Fire City after the last attack.

And then, as now, he thought if he was in the opposite position, that impassiveness would be the most terrifying of all.

Cassius coming to stand on his one side, Aramus on the other, Drakkar and Ulfr flanking either side, they crossed their arms on their chests.

Settled in.

And watched.

84
THE NIL

Queen Ophelia
Northwestern Border of the Veil of The Enchantments
WODELL

Ophelia stood at the side of the cot, staring down at her friend.

Melisse was deathly pale, and even unconscious, looked in pain.

Ophelia's mouth tightened.

"A word, Your Grace," a voice murmured.

She turned her head and looked up to the Go'Doan priest who may have saved Melisse's life.

G'Liam, probably named William by his parents.

He was the priest who gave her daughter the medication Ophelia now took to help battle the pain and fatigue of the illness that was slowly draining her life away.

It had taken some days for it to start working, but it did.

The sickness ate at her still, she felt it.

But she could now function with much more energy, and much less misery.

She inclined her head to the man, moved out of the tent and several feet away.

She saw her lieutenants, Julia and Lucinda close.

Agnes was supervising the lining up of the Go'Doan bodies that had fallen to the Nadirii in battle the night before so whichever ones could be identified by whoever might wish to claim them would.

Also, the corralling of the prisoners which they very much took and very much intended to interrogate.

"Her prognosis," Ophelia asked when they stopped.

"Frankly, I'm surprised she's still alive," he answered.

His attention was then taken, and Ophelia watched in some shock as his face softened with affection and his chin dipped to something over her shoulder.

She looked that way to see a Go'Ella, one of the acolytes of the Go'Doan, though this one not wearing the sheers of that caste, but instead, the same kind of apparel, though not see-through, and a lovely shade of pale pink, not white.

The woman ducked into the tent.

She was pretty, as many of the Go'Ella were.

She also had a certain serenity about her, which few of the Go'Ella had.

"My chosen one, Saira," Liam explained. "And if I see the changes in the Go'Doan I wish to make, she will be my wife."

At her age, there was little that surprised Ophelia.

But that did.

"I teach her what I know. She assists in my work," he continued astounding her. "You can trust her. She is very good at what she does, has much knowledge and experience. And if she had not been at my side helping me work on your sister, all would have been lost."

"She is a Go'Ella," Ophelia pointed out.

Aversion shifted through his expression before he replied, "She was and perhaps officially she still is. I have five other women who work for me, and officially they still are too, even if they are not."

Ophelia's brows shot up. "Who *work* for you?"

"Administratively, in what I do for the Education Ministry of the Go'Doan. Or as nurses in the work I do at the hospital. I do not consider them Go'Ella. I consider them colleagues."

And that astonished her most of all.

Thus, Ophelia studied him, perhaps his words, or the sense she felt that they were genuine, bringing to the forefront her realization if she was not as she was that day—her age, her condition—she would wish to lay with him.

More than once.

He was tall, handsome, self-possessed and unmistakably intelligent.

Alas, not only was she her age, and her condition, he was committed to another.

She brought them back to the matter at hand.

"And as Melisse is a miracle of survival at this juncture, you cannot say her prognosis."

"I can say I would prefer to have her in a situation where I could control her environs and the possible poisons that could get into her wound, which, it is my feeling, some actually exist in the air and not just the dressings or instruments used on the wound."

How fantastical, Ophelia thought.

"In other words," he continued, "I would like to see her in a hospital. But I do not think it's safe to move her now. Nor will it be tomorrow, if she survives. After that, I will reassess."

"But as she is now still alive, you must have *some* feeling of what the chances are my friend will get to *after that*?"

"If you asked me before I worked on her what the chances of her still breathing right now were, I would have said nil. But by some miracle, he missed her trachea by but a centimeter when he punctured her chest. However, she lost a great deal of blood, the wound is large, the weapon was a horn which I can assume was not drenched in spirits to kill possible poisons. So, my answer to whether she will still be with us in two days is, perhaps not nil."

Good goddess, she might like this Go'Doan.

On that thought, it was definitely time to move on.

"And your brothers who attacked my realm?" she queried.

"They are not my brothers," he replied calmly, lifted a hand when she opened her mouth to retort, and spoke on when she did not. "They are Go'Doan, trained priests. Yes. And it's my understanding some time ago, precisely thirty-seven years, a small faction of our kind approached the high priests, suggesting that the spread of our faith was not occurring fast enough. Peoples of Airen, Firenze and Wodell were doggedly worshiping their own gods, and The Enchantments and Mar-el would not even let our priests in to educate and heal. They felt more should be done."

Ophelia nodded.

Liam carried on.

"This was decidedly not a popular suggestion and their ideas to facilitate their desires were not only refused, they were remonstrated for even suggesting them and warned if they should do anything further, even discuss this with other priests, they would be cast out. Regrettably, this only served to make them even more zealous in their cause."

"And you know of this, so the Go'Doan know of this, so you must know the next question I will ask is why King Ares is dead, Sofia is dead, and Melisse is hovering on death and this was not stopped before it grew out of control."

He shook his head. "They were far from open about their recruitment, Your Grace. They were careful. They were also smart. Fervent, even fanatical, but not aggressive. They further took time to get organized. By the time they were large enough in number that there were whispers amongst the other priests, they had some hold and their aggression came in other ways. There truly are those priests of Go'Doan who have no idea they even exist. There are others who do who fear them mightily and for reason. And there are still others, like myself, who do something about it."

"And what do you do?"

"I'm afraid the number who is like me is small. So, I do what I can with what I can discover without getting discovered myself and I, or more importantly, my chosen one and the women I work closely with, finding ourselves targeted which could mean dire things, including the end of our lives."

Damn it all.

She could understand this was a deterrent.

It wasn't an excuse.

But it was an understandable deterrent, especially with this man and the way he looked at his Saira.

His hazel eyes intensified. "And the things I do are such as sending anonymous birds to Nadirii queens to warn them their realm is about to be attacked."

She would credit him for that.

But not much, because of what she asked next.

"And why didn't you save Melisse?" she snapped.

"I knew they had her, but I couldn't even begin to imagine that was part of their plan," he answered. "Not until too late. And then, I could only react, which," he gestured to the tent he had set up to care for Melisse, "Saira, myself and our group did."

It remained to be seen if that was enough.

"I cannot offer excuses," he went on. "And it is with grave remorse I share the fullness of our responsibility, for we were aware that things were well out of hand when King Ares was assassinated by G'Dor, who was one of the priests who had come forward with these desires for the future of our faith. He then left it, presumably at the time, because the others did not see things as he did. When he murdered Ares, we became very aware of just how far this had gone and those higher up who understood the situation was spiraling tried to handle things..." his pause was weighty before he continued, "*internally*. Clearly, they failed."

"Clearly, they did," she agreed crossly.

"And sadly," he kept on, "we do not know the extent of their operations."

This did not bode well.

"Are the Go'Doan prepared to condemn this faction and cast them out so they no longer enjoy the resources of the Dome City?"

He shook his head again. "I'm afraid I am not yet a priest of a level that is privy to the discussions of those who speak for our faith and make those kinds of decisions, much less am I invited to be in those discussions. But my understanding is, no. They simply deny it has anything to do with the true Go'Doan faith, condemn any acts made by the extremists and continue to try to stem the tide internally."

"I lost not a sister in battle to these men, who are not warriors," Ophelia stated, throwing a hand in the direction of the battlefield, such as it was. "However, if I did, I would be even *more* infuriated than I already am with my sister lying abed, her future survival unlikely, not twenty feet away. Not to mention having to ask my sisters to ride under the threat of any battle, this being that they may be harmed or killed. And I can share with you that a condemnation of the event without any teeth in it coming from the Dome City would not appease me in the slightest."

"I understand."

"Do you?" she asked.

He nodded. "I truly do. However, I am but one man. And the enormity of this issue is paralyzing those who might have some power to do something about it."

"This is not good enough. For we took prisoners. We will interrogate those—"

She stopped speaking when she saw Agnes galloping toward them on her horse.

Liam turned and they both watched as Agnes reined in when she was close before she swung off.

She wasted nary a second leading her steed to her queen.

"We've received a bird," Agnes declared. "The Rising launched another attack. They somehow infiltrated the temple during Prince True's wedding." She cast a filthy glance at Liam before she finished, "Queen Mercy was slain."

Ophelia took a step back, such was the blow.

"One of True's guard was severely injured," Agnes carried on. "Two others took arrows, but they will be fine. Farah also took an arrow. A flesh wound. She, too, will recover."

Without hesitation, Ophelia launched in at Liam.

"We regularly beat back those who wish to bring down The Enchantments. But *that*," she stabbed a finger in the direction of Notting Thicket, "*that* will not be abided. There will be no understanding thus no acceptance that these are not the actions of," she spiked her finger at Liam, "*your* people. *All* of you. If True does not wrest control, your temples will be overrun. Your priests will be in danger. You must communicate *immediately* with this *level* of priests you speak of who discuss these things and urge them *strongly* to renounce this Rising. If you do not, your home, your followers, your teachers and physicians, your entire *faith* will be in jeopardy."

He was shaken, she could tell by the paleness of his skin and his whisper of, "I did not know they had this planned."

"That doesn't matter. Now you do," Ophelia snapped. "Get thee to a goddess-damned *bird*."

He nodded, turned and did not dally.

He took off running.

Agnes's voice was much changed when she said, "My queen, we have also located the maimed one."

Ophelia's head turned to her lieutenant.

"The one who perpetrated this atrocity, has he been identified?" she asked.

"Yes."

"And he is alive?"

"Yes."

Ophelia nodded. "Let us see to this matter without delay."

"Yes, my queen," Agnes murmured.

Ophelia moved to her horse.

Agnes mounted hers.

And they rode.

~

THE STALLION'S mare was overly protective of him.

This was unsurprising.

She whinnied her warning angrily, butting under his neck to get in front of him and approaching hostilely as the once-proud stallion, shorn of his horn, apprehensively retreated.

Ophelia's blood boiled.

"Bring him to me," she bit, dismounting.

Her own mare shifted back as Ophelia stood where she dropped, not daring to approach either animal.

Enough had been done to them at human hands. They'd never trust another.

They would know they were avenged.

But they would never trust another.

She wondered briefly why they left The Enchantments at all.

She then made note to speak to her witches who spoke to the animals.

They needed to be warned about further wanderings.

When her sisters brought him, she saw he was as she'd ordered him to be.

The priest of The Rising who had perpetrated this atrocity was paralyzed by Nadirii magic, all but his voice, which was muted in its pleas and curses by a gag.

He was thus tossed like a doll to the ground before Ophelia, landing on his back.

At this, the mare nickered, and both creatures braced as if to bolt.

But Ophelia spoke soothingly.

"If I could heal you, I would. If I could give you back your sacred horn, your magic, I would perish from the earth myself to offer these returned to you. But I cannot."

The unicorns watched her cautiously.

"I can only avenge you, and after, use your magic for good."

The creatures continued to stare at her.

Ophelia did not delay.

She turned to Julia, who handed her the sacred piece, the magnificent horn that had been taken from the stallion.

It had, as she'd ordered, been cleansed of Melisse's blood.

Ophelia then took her position, standing over the villain, one foot to each side.

She looked down at him.

He stared up at her with wide, terror-filled eyes, his lips moving around the gag.

"You have achieved your aim. You lie upon the soil of The Enchantments," she shared with him. "And you die knowing you made your way onto that soil, but you did not make The Enchantments burn. You also die knowing the fullness of the depths of your failure. For you lived to bow others to your beliefs, and your death will serve only to strengthen the protections of a sisterhood."

She wished to give him time to consider that.

But she did not take that time.

For the unicorns, this must be done.

And she herself had things to do.

Thus, Ophelia lifted the horn up high above her head and felt the twirl of magic coil up her spine.

"Nadirii," she intoned, "means 'oppressed' in the old tongue. Nadirii," she continued, "means 'sisterhood' in the ancient tongue. You die by the hand of a Nadirii and this means you die by the hands of all the sisterhood. And you die tonight due to your treachery against what we hold hallowed. Nature. Magic. Both in one. Both in *the majestic unicorn*."

She then brought the horn down, embedding it where he had done the same in Melisse.

However, she did not miss his trachea.

His eyes grew ever wider as they filled with pain, and behind the gag he screamed with the last of the breath he had in what was left of his throat.

She took no joy from that.

Or comfort.

Ophelia simply stepped away and stood with her sisters as he whimpered behind his gag for several moment before his body started to disintegrate.

When it did, it did with coral particles starting from where the horn stuck from his chest.

Up they drifted.

Up.

More of them.

More.

Until all of him was naught but sparkling dust.

It spread high above and was absorbed by the magical shield that protected Nadirii land.

There was nothing left of him. No soul to raise or lower.

His essence would forever protect the Nadirii.

Until it was unneeded.

Then it would just...

Cease.

Ophelia looked to the unicorns.

"It is done," she whispered.

The mare dipped her jaw.

Then the stallion whinnied.

And they both turned and galloped away.

85

THE FAMILY INSIDE A FAMILY

Princess Elena
Hall Outside the Bramble Reception Suite, Birchlire Castle, Notting Thicket
WODELL

I was lost.

I'd heard from a castle servant the men had returned from Crittich Keep.

But I was avoiding Farah, Ha-Lah and Silence who were talking with my sister about all she'd been doing since Firenze (I did this because I regularly avoided my sister—it wasn't that I didn't want to know, it was that I knew they'd tell me later) and I was trying to find my way back to Cassius and my room.

But this bloody castle was humongous.

So, I was lost.

I was moving down the hall toward yet another set of stairs that led up to yet another turret when I noted movement to my right and looked that way.

I then stopped, for Silence was standing at the opposite end of a large room that was filled with tables that were still set elaborately for a royal dinner that had never been consumed.

And it appeared she was standing before a miniature version (but still necessarily large) of the very castle we were both in.

"Allo," I called as I walked into the room.

She started and turned to me.

She also gave me a small smile that she did not mean.

There would not be many smiles for a very long time and not only because of what happened that day at the wedding.

Much more had happened, it was just that what happened locally took precedence.

For now.

I wended my way through the tables to her, stopped when I arrived and asked, "Are you well?"

"I'm just..." she gestured weakly to the miniature. "It's a miracle. This cake."

I turned to the structure and stared at it in shock, realizing from close it *was* a cake.

An exact replica of the castle made of frosting tinted in the palest of pinks, yellows, creams, greens and blues. Flowers and leaves and bunting and ribbon adorning the windows, walls, arches and turrets. I could even see little candles that would have been lit in the windows and globes, had there actually been a reception.

"Aunt Mercy did this," Silence whispered, and my eyes darted to her. "For True. For Farah. For Wodell." Her attention went to the cake. "Who knew icing had power?"

I felt my heart squeeze.

"Silence," I said softly.

"She was not warm, but she was a good queen. I could have learned much from her and I sense she would have enjoyed teaching me," she said to the cake. She then turned to me. "Now I will not, and *she* will not."

"You will be your own brand of spectacular queen," I assured her.

Again, her gaze went to the cake as she mumbled, "I hope so."

I wanted to get to Cassius, check on the girls.

But watching Silence, I asked, "Do you want to go somewhere and sit, have some tea or a glass of wine?"

Slowly, her eyes came back to me. "I heard the men have returned. I mean no offense, my friend, but I wish to see Mars. He's been with him and thus I wish my husband to share with me how my cousin fares."

I nodded and smiled. "That's understandable." I then asked, "But before you do that, would you happen to be able to tell me where the hell my room is?"

A surprised laugh came from her, and even if it hadn't been a day since so much was lost, it sounded strange.

Out of practice.

She hooked her arm in mine and said, "Of course."

We walked. We chatted while we did. And Silence led me to a floor that was familiar before we bid our goodnights and she retraced her steps to find her own chambers.

As I walked down the hall to the rooms Cassius and I had that were across from the room Dora and Aelia shared, I tried to decide who to go to first.

Cassius?

Or the girls.

My decision was made for me when I arrived at the rooms, saw the door to the girls' room was slightly ajar, and heard Cassius's voice coming from there.

"They climbed, and they climbed, and they climbed..." he was saying.

What on...?

I approached the door, adjusted my body so I could see the bed that was set at the side, and froze stiff.

For Cassius lay on his back on the bed, Aelia down one side of his long body, her head on his chest, fast asleep.

But my Theodora lay down the other side of his body, head on his shoulder, and she was not asleep.

He had his head on pillows, his arms around both, and a book propped up close to Dora's waist.

And he was reading.

"And when they reached the clouds, they did not know if they could step off—"

"Cass," Dora interrupted him quietly. "She's asleep."

"I know, little bean," he whispered, and my heart squeezed yet again that day, but in an entirely different way.

I had not thought they'd grown close in their time together in The Enchantments.

Though Dora never gave indication she didn't like him. She answered when he spoke to her (and not in the cheeky way she did to me) and she watched him often and at least gave indication she found him intriguing (not as intriguing as she found Cass's man Ian, but still intriguing).

But that was not closeness.

However, with that day's events, I supposed you latched on to whatever you had that was real and breathing.

And lucky for Dora (and Aelia *and* me), Cass was both.

"I'm reading to you," Cassius finished.

"I'm too old for bedtime stories," she informed him.

"Indeed?" he asked with teasing disbelief.

"Yes," she answered firmly, my Dora, wanting to be a grown warrior and wanting that a week ago. "I'll listen if Aelia wants, but I can get to sleep without them. Ellie stopped reading to me *years* ago."

Those *years* being, maybe...one.

"Well then, if I tuck you in and turn out all the lights, will you go to sleep?" he queried.

"Of course."

I watched as Cassius bent to kiss the top of her golden head.

"This I'll do," he said after he did that.

I should leave them to it.

I was stuck in the vision of watching Cass kiss Dora's hair, thus, I did not leave them to it.

And I would be glad I didn't.

For after Cass tucked her in, Aelia beside her, and blew the lamp out by Aelia's side, he came back around to Dora's but grew still when she asked, "Will True be all right?"

Oh, my darling Dora.

Cassius stood immobile for a long moment before he replied gently, "You know he won't."

I closed my eyes tight.

"You know he won't too," I heard her whisper.

I opened my eyes wide.

How did she know Cassius lost his mother?

Did Aelia tell her?

Did *my* mother?

Half a dozen other big-mouthed Nadirii (namely, Jasmine)?

"Yes, Dora, I know he won't either," he confirmed.

"You have that. I have that. Aelia has that," she noted. "I love Ellie, and I'm glad she doesn't have that. But it makes us a little family inside a family, doesn't it?"

His voice was deeper, thicker, when he replied, "I guess it does, little bean."

"I don't like why we have that family, but because of that why, I like we have that family. Still, I don't like it that True became a member of our family today," she whispered.

"I don't either. We'll have to keep a close eye on him, you and me, while we're here. Yes?" Cass suggested.

Dora nodded. "Yes, Cass."

"Now sleep," he murmured, bent to kiss her cheek and that was when I skedaddled from my position, went across the hall and entered our room.

I was in the dressing room getting a handle on my emotion and wondering how appropriate it would be if I pounced on my prince the instant he walked through the door, and by "pounce" I meant the kind that led to making us both naked. Doing this to share how much I liked that he read bedtime stories and how much I loved how he treated Dora with care.

And I was still wondering when I heard him walk through the door to the chamber beyond.

Instead of making myself naked, I went there and again stopped still when I saw him sitting on the side of the bed, knees spread in that man-seated position that was annoying when you were sitting beside him in a temple pew but rather attractive otherwise.

His hands were turned up, wrists resting on his thighs.

His head was bent.

This I found an alarming posture.

But my alarm grew.

For suddenly, it was like he buckled.

His elbows went to his knees and his body folded, his hands clasping the back of his head.

Good goddess.

What was happening?

I rushed forward, got close, crouched low and reached out to his wrist, murmuring, "Cass."

"While at the Keep, a castle messenger came. I got a bird," he said to the area between his knees.

Oh no.

Not more dire news from Airen.

We already knew Sky Bay was under siege. Nero barely escaped it in order to ride across Airen unrelenting, with no sleep and little food, in order to deliver that message.

"Fern is taken."

"Shite, Cass," I whispered.

His fingers unlinked, but he only bent his neck to lift his head in order to catch my eyes.

His sky-blue ones were now unmitigated black.

My stomach clutched.

"Otho is dead."

I felt my heart spike, and my hands moved instantly to cradle his face.

"No," I breathed.

"And twenty-three men loyal to me besides."

"No." That word trembled from my lips.

"I'm sorry, my darling," he whispered, using an endearment he'd never used with me before, and I loved it, I just hated what drove him to using it. "We cannot assist True. We can't even attend Mercy's funeral. We must be away to Airen as soon as possible on the morrow."

"Yes, of course. Immediately," I said swiftly.

"I want the girls on one of Aramus's ships. I want them in Mar-el. It's the safest place for them in the now. And I know he'll order anyone guarding them to die for them if need be."

Mar-el?

Our girls that far away?

Across the sea?

Not easy to get to by horse?

I thought these thoughts.

"Yes, absolutely," I said. "I...I think that True will be busy, but perhaps Farah can have a chat with the girls in the morning, let them share how sorry they are, which I know they'll want to do, while I pack them, and then they'll be away."

"Is there any way I can talk you into going with them?" he tried.

My hands pressed into his cheeks, the bristles of his beard digging into my palms.

And then I said what I had to say.

"No."

He closed his eyes.

"Cass," I shook his head gently, "look at me."

He opened his eyes.

"I need to be seen at your side."

"Yes," he murmured tonelessly.

"Cass, I want to give you what you want but what you *need* is your princess by your side, her staff and her sisters at her back."

"I know it. I just don't like it."

"I know you don't," I said softly.

He changed the subject.

"We need to send a bird to your mother. I was unable to get her promise to ally with me should the revolt that's happening now, happen. But she needs to know where her daughter is, where her granddaughters are going, and the state of play at the former. She also has to help Fern, if she can."

I loved it that he thought of them as granddaughters.

Not singular.

I did not share that in the moment.

I nodded.

He suddenly sat straight, disengaging my hands and stating irately, "This is bloody worst fucking day since my first fucking wife died."

I drew breath in my nose and stayed silent.

"And I live with Gallienus," he went on. "So, no day is a good bloody day."

"Have you spoken to your father?" I queried carefully.

"He denies knowing anything about the insurgency. He also lies."

Undoubtedly, he did.

I bit my lip in order to bite my tongue.

He reached out, pulled me up so I had no choice but to take my feet and then he wrapped his arms around my hips, pulling me between his thighs and shoving his face in my ribs.

I stared down at his shorn hair, my hands out beside me, stunned motionless and unsure what to do.

There was a vulnerability to this.

Cassius Laird, fearsome general, heir to the throne of a tyrannical nation, was showing me vulnerability.

He'd lost a man, and he was hurting.

He was riding with his woman at his side to uncertainty, but certain danger, the outcome of which could no longer be assured, for who knew now what Aramus and Mars would do, knowing this Rising was sweeping all lands and just how far they intended to go to make whatever message they wished to make.

But True could not ride with him and that *was* certain.

Cass had undoubtedly just watched hours of torture.

His father was plotting against him.

And he'd come back to the castle, stretched out on a bed with two little girls, and read them a bedtime story.

I suddenly knew what to do and that was to smooth my hands over his hair.

In response, he shoved his face deeper into my flesh.

I wrapped the fingers of both hands around the back of his neck and whispered, "What can I do?"

There was no hesitation before his reply.

"You're doing it."

That felt...

It felt...

Beautiful.

But it was not enough.

I put my hands to his cheeks again and pulled him away, tipping his face up to me as I did.

I then bent to him and pressed my lips to his.

They opened.

I slid my tongue inside.

When I did, Cassius fell back, taking me with him, then rolling so he was atop me.

My part, I found just then, was done.

He took over.

And what he did was what I would assume he intended to do the first time we joined.

It was slow.

Very.

It was reverent.

Startlingly.

And it was life-altering.

Completely.

And much time after it began, as his finger rolled my clit while his now midnight eyes stared into mine, and he slowly moved in and out of me, the room around us taken over by night and blanketed with stars, my head arched back, and I climaxed magnificently on a silent moan.

Not long after, when the strength and velocity of his thrusts increased, he did the same, but I heard his deep sigh in my ear when he did.

As usual, when he was done, he nearly instantly rearranged us, so I was on top.

This, I figured he did so I did not have to bear his weight.

This, I knew he did so his hands could roam my bare skin.

What they were doing now.

"Apparently, we can make love silently," I muttered.

I felt his lips move where they were caressing my neck and I hoped it was in a smile.

"We're going to be all right, Cass," I promised.

His lips stopped moving altogether.

"The girls are going to be all right. It's all going to be all right."

He let his head fall to the mattress.

"We'll all be all right," I finished when I caught his eyes.

"I have never been all right, my lamb."

Goddess, I hated that.

Hated it.

I gave him a soft smile while tugging on his beard and saying, "Well then, that time is nigh, don't you think?"

He did not look convinced.

But he still said, "Yes."

And in that moment, with that single word, I knew precisely why he said this.

Precisely why he did anything he did.

Because in that moment, I knew *him.*

He read bedtime stories.

And he knew Aelia loved chocolate pots.

He also knew, if Dora told him she was too old for stories, he should not press that.

Further, even if his woman was a warrior, if he thought she was in danger, he took hold of her and carried her from a battle in order get her as far away from that danger as he could manage.

Because Cassius Laird, Prince Regent of Airen, had lived for one thing before, it was just that that one thing was now plural.

He lived to take care of his girls.

86

THE REVELATION

King Mars

Approaching the Mouth of the Stairwell of the Northwestern Turret
Birchlire Castle, Notting Thicket
WODELL

Mars was not in a good mood.

There were many reasons for this.

The current one, however, was that he could not find his wife.

She was not in their rooms.

She was not in any rooms in the northwestern turret.

And his palace in Fire City was large, but this castle was monstrous.

He did not fancy searching the hundreds of rooms in it to find his queen.

He fancied disrobing his wife, making love to her, then falling asleep so this loathsome day could be at an end.

"Good, there you are."

He heard these words when he'd descended the last step to the turret and turned around its corner, a corner that hid the mouth of the stairwell from the hall.

Ridiculous.

Offensively, you could not descend that stairwell and know what was in the hall below you.

Defensively, you could not turn and aim at it if it was chasing you.

Though you could hide behind it.

And it did not surprise him such was designed by King Wilmer's forebears.

He could not think on that in the now.

For his day just got worse, as impossible as that was for Mars to believe.

Because he apparently was going to have a confrontation with Silence's father, who they had, until that very moment, successfully avoided since Johan and Vanka followed them from the Arbor to Notting Thicket.

"I'm in no mood, Johan," he declared, not breaking stride, intent to move right past him.

"I'll take my treasure now," Johan said by way of retort.

Mars stopped as he came parallel, turned his head and looked down at the man.

"I'm sorry?"

"You said, in Fire City, that if I were to leave my daughter to her own life, the life she now has with you, that you would shower me with treasure," Johan explained. "I've decided I will happily do that. Therefore, you can have those chests of gems and coins you promised me sent directly to Bower Manor."

"I'm not providing you that treasure," Mars informed him.

"You bloody are," Johan spat.

Mars grew silent and stared down at him, making an effort to control his impatience.

It was then he smelled her.

Indeed, he fancied he could smell her perfume from ten kilometers away.

Not because it was strong.

But because it was hers.

Freesias.

His wife approached.

And not only could she shadow herself so others around her could not see (and she'd demonstrated this to him, even if he could always see her, he'd been in awe that others could not), she also informed him she could hear exceptionally well.

She'd further demonstrated that.

She'd make an excellent spy.

Though that would not ever happen.

"As I said, I'm in no mood, Johan," he repeated.

"I don't care what mood you're in," Johan returned.

"And you must trust me, you do not wish to discuss it now either," Mars advised.

"I don't trust you as far as I could throw you and considering you're a mammoth *lurch*, I couldn't even *lift you*."

Mars took no offense to the insult. He cared not what this man thought of him.

However, that did not mean he did not have reason to pause.

He had told his queen that he intended to see to it that her father left her and the family they were going to make in peace.

Therefore, he had no issue on his behalf with her hearing what might come next.

That said, he had grave issues on *her* behalf of what she might hear, even if he thought that she should hear it and understand precisely what kind of man her father was.

He just did not think that now, after she'd lost her aunt, and all the events of the day, it was the time for it.

"I'm telling you, this is not the time," Mars said low.

"A pouch of rubies. Chests of emeralds. Chests of coin," Johan droned. "That was what you said you'd pay me to step out of the life of my daughter."

Mars glanced at her as she was now walking down the hall, but she stopped when she heard her father's words.

He also noted that Johan had not realized she was there.

Mars made a decision, and thus, did not share with her father that she was.

He turned fully to the man and crossed his arms on his chest. "I did indeed say this. However, you did not do that. You played with her heart. You tried to undermine our very new marriage and drive us apart. Therefore, you can consider that offer rescinded."

"I won't allow you to rescind it," Johan fired back.

"It is not your choice."

Mars did not like the look on Johan's face, or the sneer on his lips, before Johan opened his mouth to speak.

"Johan, *stop*!"

Mars turned.

Silence turned.

Johan turned.

And all saw Vanka racing up the hall behind Silence toward Mars and Johan.

She shot a nervous look her daughter's way as she dashed by her and made her husband.

Johan was staring at Silence even as his wife curled both her hands around his arm.

"So now you know he tried to bribe me to keep me out of your life," Johan said to Silence.

"Johan, it's been a trying day, let's just go to bed," Vanka urged.

Mars narrowed his eyes on Silence's mother.

"I know it, Father," Silence replied, and he could tell by her voice she was moving toward them. "Mars told me he was going to do it."

"And I refused, and you still treated me in the manner you treated me at Cord Cottage?" Johan asked, sounding outraged.

When she was in arm's reach, Mars reached.

He then tucked his wee wife close to his side and he did this as she said to her father, "I treated you in the manner you were treated at the cottage because you were treating *me* in a very certain manner at the cottage."

"Don't talk in riddles," Johan snapped at her.

"I understood her," Mars stated calmly. What was not calm was when he finished, "And do not ever address my queen in that tone again."

Johan looked so angry, he could do something very foolish, like charge his much larger and much younger son-in-law.

"Johan, everyone's tempers are frayed after today's events. Please, my dearest, *let us go to bed,*" Vanka begged.

"I'll not be going anywhere until I'm assured I'll have my treasure," Johan said to his wife, but he did it scowling at Mars.

"Please, my love, *please*—" she kept trying.

"This conversation is moot. I'll not be paying that treasure and I'll not be saying it again that I won't," Mars returned.

Johan looked to his daughter with such hate, Mars immediately shifted her mostly behind him just as his gut seized.

Bloody hell.

Where did *that* come from?

Johan then looked up to him and whispered viciously, "Oh, you'll pay it."

"*Johan*," Vanka pleaded, now tugging on his arm in what appeared to be an effort to drag him away.

Mars shifted abruptly and looked down at his queen.

"Go to our chambers, *amore*," he ordered.

Silence blinked up at him. "But, Mars, I'm all—"

"I need you to go."

"Yes, Silence, go," Vanka encouraged, sounding desperate, even frantic.

Fuck.

Johan came around to their sides. "No, my dearest daughter," he said with sham adoration in his voice, "*please stay*."

Silence looked to her father, her head tipping to the side, her brows inching together.

Mars put a gentle hand to her cheek and forced her gaze back to his.

"Please, my wife, I beg of you, *go to our chambers*," he urged.

"Ha!" Johan hooted. "I made you beg. There it is. I bloody *made you beg*."

Mars shifted only his eyes to the side without moving his head.

Johan's gleeful expression faltered, and he took a step back.

"Mars," Silence called uncertainly.

He looked again to his wife.

"Go."

"What's happening?"

"Later," he bit out, trying to go gently, and unfortunately not quite succeeding. "Now, please, my Silence, *go*."

She studied him a long moment before nodding.

She looked to her father, to her mother who was again at her sire's side, and then to Mars.

"I'll meet you in our chambers," she said tremulously.

"I won't be long," he promised.

She nodded again, rolled up on her toes, Mars bent down, and she touched her lips to his.

She then lifted those long, Dellish skirts of hers and dashed away from him and up the steps.

He turned to his wife's parents and Johan was already opening his mouth.

"You won't speak until I give you leave to do so," he commanded.

"I'll speak when I bloody—"

Vanka emitted a strangled scream as Mars wrapped his hand around Johan's throat and squeezed.

He then bent his face to Johan's.

"You...won't...*speak* until I *give you leave*," he repeated.

When Johan's face started to get red, Mars released him and walked around the both of them.

He felt them following, sensing them rushing to keep up with his long strides, but he did not slow.

He made it to the end of the long hall, turned to them and assessed the distance.

He could not see Silence if she was hiding at the bottom of those bloody stairs.

He could only hope that hall was long enough they were too far away for her to hear whatever was said next should she be listening.

Johan and Vanka caught up with him, Vanka practically being dragged as she tried to stop her husband from finishing his approach.

Her face was agonized.

Fuck.

"Don't do this, Johan," she pleaded when the man stopped before Mars.

"Let me go," he snapped, shaking his arm.

She tugged on it. *"Please, Johan."*

"Bloody *let me go!*" he shouted, whipping around, and Vanka whipped with him, slamming into the wall.

Mars heard blood roaring in his ears.

That was it.

Enough.

Mars again took Silence's father by the throat, and it was Mars doing the slamming against a wall.

Johan emitted a grunt of surprise.

He then glowered up at Mars who had a firm hold on him, but this time he didn't squeeze.

"Release me," Johan demanded.

"Say your words and be done with it," Mars ordered.

"Release me!"

"You are not her father."

Johan's head jerked, not in offense, in surprise that Mars guessed accurately what this was about.

Vanka emitted a long whine.

Yes. He was accurate.

His queen's beautiful petite frame, ebony hair, pale skin, silver eyes.

She looked nothing like either of these people.

Even the mother.

"Bloody hell," Mars murmured. "Why didn't I see it?"

"Unhand me!" Johan yelled.

Mars let him go and took a step back.

Johan tugged his waistcoat down, then flapped his jacket more firmly on his chest, all this glaring at Mars.

"If you don't wish her to know, you'll pay me," he shared.

"And we don't," Vanka rushed in to say. "We *all* don't wish her to know."

"You need to keep your mouth shut," Johan snapped at his wife.

"Well, we don't, we don't wish—" Vanka stated.

"*You* don't," Johan retorted to his wife. "I no longer give a damn."

"She is Countess of the Arbor," Vanka reminded him. "She's yours in all but—"

"What counts," Johan spat. "*Blood*. I'm married to a fucking *whore*. You opened your legs—"

Vanka's face lost all color. "But you wanted a child so badly, my love, and we weren't—"

"I didn't want you to fuck *that horrid man* to give me one!" he shouted. "I told you to find someone worthy. *You did not find someone worthy!*"

"Quiet down," Mars growled.

Johan jerked his gaze to Mars. "I'll do what I want."

"And I will as well, including finding ways to keep you quiet that you will not like," Mars warned. "So *quiet down*."

Johan shook his head repeatedly while inclining his neck, making a pompous movement all the more pretentious.

"You told me you needed an heir," Vanka whispered, broken. "You told me to—"

"You didn't choose very well because we got strapped with *Silence*," Johan retorted.

Vanka continued to whisper. "I'm not a whore. You told me—"

Gods, this arsehole simply got worse and worse.

Johan turned to Mars and spoke over his wife. "If you don't want everyone to know you married a bastard, that your queen and the mother to your future children is spurious, then I'll have my gods-damned, bloody *treasure*."

"I have no care who begat my wife," Mars told him. "She has not changed in any way in my knowing you aren't her father."

Johan looked stunned.

Sadly, he recovered quickly.

"Are you sure those clans and tribes of yours who aren't so certain about your reign or the wife you chose will be as indifferent?" Johan asked snidely.

"No," Mars answered. "What I am certain of is that you will not breathe a word of this to a living soul. Not that first one. Not publicly. Not privately."

"I wouldn't be so certain," Johan sneered.

"You are not blood of her blood. You are naught. Naught to me, but more importantly naught to her," Mars returned. "I would have handled any necessary dealings with you with the understanding you are my wife's family at the forefront of my mind. Since you are not, I can do as I please."

"And *I* can do as *I* please," Johan retorted.

"Not if you aren't breathing after I slit your throat," Mars replied calmly.

Vanka gasped.

Johan's mouth fell open and he stared.

Mars shrugged. "You no longer matter. And as such, do as you wish, and I shall do as I wish. Though, be warned, if you do something I don't wish, I will do something you absolutely would not wish."

"You can't threaten me," Johan declared, but he'd lost his bluster and was now hanging on to bravado.

"It seems I can."

Johan started glaring at him. "Well then, I'll simply tell Silence."

"Did you not hear the part where I said you will not breathe a word to a soul?" Mars inquired politely. "But no worries. I'll be telling her. I assume she'll feel some relief that she is not of your blood. It will answer a great many questions she has."

Johan appeared extremely shocked and equally as offended.

"*She* will be relieved she's not of *my* blood?" he asked in full affront.

"You're a tremendously unpleasant man. You were an atrocious father. When she understands why, then yes. She will be relieved."

Before Johan could say more, Mars looked to Vanka.

"Do you know who her father is?" he asked. "She might wish to meet him."

"I was...he was..." she finished on another whisper, "a Zee."

"I do not wish to hear this," Johan spat at her.

"You began this conversation," Mars pointed out. "If you no longer wish to be a part of it, you're free to leave."

"You're detestable," Johan hissed at Mars.

"Interesting, you know how I feel," Mars drawled.

Silence's not-father's upper lip twitched into his nose repeatedly in a way that was odd and slightly amusing before he huffed off.

"Johan!" Vanka called after him.

"Find another chamber to sleep in tonight, *wife*," he replied without looking back.

Wishing to get to his own wife, Mars pressed a Vanka who was staring forlornly after her husband, "Do you know how to find this Zee?"

"No, I..." Her head dropped, she studied the floor, and it seemed to take some effort for her to lift her eyes that were bright with unshed tears to his face. "He's a Zee. He took what was offered. I-I found him comely. He..." She swallowed, shook her head then turned it, peering down the hall her husband had disappeared from, "He had the most beautiful silver eyes."

At these words, Mars took pity on her.

"If you leave him, you'll be welcome with us."

Her gaze shot back to his. "I couldn't leave my husband."

So be it.

He dipped his chin and made to move around her, but she caught his forearm and he stopped.

"Are you really going to tell Silence?" she asked.

"I'll endeavor to delay, as this night is not the time to share such news after the day she has had. But she did not leave us unaware that something was brewing, and if she presses, I will not lie to my wife."

"You are a...a good man," she said as if she didn't believe her own words.

"You are a weak woman," he replied.

She blinked and dropped her hand from his arm.

"But anyone is capable of change for as long as they're breathing," he went on. "I urge you to find your way to that. I would gather you'd be much happier, no?"

"He is a hard man, but he loves me," she said.

"A man does not whore his wife to another man to gain an heir if he loves her. You became pregnant. Thus, the issue with conception is clearly his. But even if it wasn't, you take life as it comes and find happiness in spite of lost dreams. You just build different ones."

"That's easy for you to say," she murmured.

"My father was murdered," he retorted. "He did not meet my lovely wife, whom he would have adored. He will not meet my children. He will not bounce them on his knee and tell them stories of their papa when he was a boy. Or how beautiful their mother was in her red dress when she was first introduced to his people. It is not easy for me to say, Vanka. And if you think that of anyone, that your choices were more difficult or more desperate or more limited than theirs in whatever circumstances they might have as compared to yours, and that is the excuse you make for making the wrong ones, you're far weaker than I thought."

With that, he moved beyond her and down the hall, wondering how he would delay in telling his wife about this when just hours ago she'd talked three level-headed women, one who had taken an arrow through her shoulder, into storming a torture chamber in order "to watch."

This made his lips twitch, something he stopped them from doing when he opened the door to their chambers.

He saw her first, coming his way.

He saw their wee monkey second, scampering much faster across the rugs to get to her papa.

Piccola climbed his pantleg and was cradling his neck by the time Silence arrived at him and demanded, "What on earth was that all about?"

"How likely am I to talk you out of your gown and into bed so we can fuck fast and hard and then pass out?" he asked in reply.

He saw a shift of interest in her eyes before she mentally set it aside and answered, "Not very likely."

Mars sighed, took Piccola from his neck and held her in front of his face. "Your mama is stubborn."

Piccola chirruped.

He held their monkey to his heart and looked to his queen. "She agrees."

Silence crossed her arms on her chest and said a warning, "Mars."

By the gods, she was the most precious creature on the planet.

He fought his lips twitching again, and did it thinking of the seriousness of this matter.

Then he said quietly, "It has been a difficult day for us both, particularly you, and your cousin, who you adore. Can we not let Johan's chicaneries make a bad day even worse?"

"How is True?" she asked.

"Beside himself with grief."

She worried her lips.

Then she said, "He told me, Father, at the party after our wedding, that you were never going to let me come to Wodell again. Was that a lie?"

By the gods, that man was foul.

"Yes."

She looked to the side.

"Silence," he called.

She looked to him.

"I will promise, after your aunt is at rest, and when the time is right, I will tell you the fullness of my conversation with your parents," he promised. "But for the now, let us find a good way to end a terrible day."

"Instead of making it worse?"

He decided not to field that one.

"Just tell me, did he hurt you?"

Mars was confused.

"Hurt *me*?"

"He called you a lurch. I don't know what that means. I've never heard it before. I just know he did not mean it nicely."

She was worried about him.

She was worried that conversation was unpleasant *for him*.

"You need to be naked in but one minute, wife," he growled.

Her eyes got large "Wh-what?"

"Never mind," he muttered, approaching her, "I'll make you that way."

Piccola, very used to the mood that was now in the chamber, scurried off Mars to head to wherever she scurried to in order to amuse herself while they engaged in activities she had no interest in for they paid her no mind at all, no cuddles and no coos.

And Mars took his wife's mind off the day, the night, and everything but them.

After he accomplished that, and did it thoroughly, they both passed out.

87

THE RULE

Prince True
The King's Study, Birchlire Castle, Notting Thicket
WODELL

"I will do no such thing."

"You will. The papers will be ready in the morn. The heralds ride out at seven sharp to share the king speaks at ten o'clock. By that time, the papers will be signed and recorded. You will make your announcement, then I will make mine."

"My wife's body is barely cold, and you make a play for my crown," he snapped.

It was unfortunate his father mentioned his dead mother.

Very unfortunate.

And Aramus was not there with him then.

Wallace, Luther, Bram and Florian—the latter two sporting bandages, Bram's under his shirt around his middle, Florian's over his trousers around his left thigh—were there.

And they did not lift a finger or even open their mouths to stop True from rushing his father across his study and pinning him bodily against the wall.

"Alfie took two arrows to protect her," he snarled into his sire's face.

"That is *his job*," his father spat back.

"You dove behind a pew to save yourself, leaving your wife an open target," True went on.

"It is not in this country's best interests to lose its monarch."

"Then why did you let this country's *true* monarch take *six arrows*?"

Wilmer spluttered in insult.

"You will sign those papers," True gritted.

"I will do nothing of the sort!" Wilmer shouted.

"You will either abdicate or I'll take your crown," True told him. "For on the morrow, if those papers are not signed, on the grounds of your incompetence, I'll declare war on the reign of King Wilmer of Wodell. I will lead my guard to your guard. And when I do, your guard will dismount and lay their weapons down in surrender. Alfie cannot ride. That means, in front of all, the two hundred royal guard that protects this castle will lay down their arms to five men."

"They wouldn't," Wilmer whispered.

"They will. I've asked each man myself and they've already vowed fealty to me. Now, do you want that spectacle to end your reign?" True asked. "Or do you want to share with your people that you are beside yourself with grief at the loss of your wife, beside yourself with mortification at your misreading of the true nature of your advisor, and you feel it's in the best interests of the realm in this trying time to abdicate to your son?"

"I will not be recorded in the Go'Doan tomes as the Dellish king who gave up his throne," Wilmer bit.

"Call out," True urged, stepping away from him. "Call out now, Father, to the guard outside your doors. Call out."

Wilmer, breathing heavily in anger, scowled at his son.

What he did not do was call out to his guard.

"You know they won't come," True said quietly.

Father and son stared at each other.

Wilmer broke the silence.

"I cannot believe you're doing this to me."

"I cannot believe you let my mother die."

Wilmer closed his eyes tight and turned his head away.

True drew breath in through his nose.

Much more calmly, he asked, "Now, do you agree to sign those papers?"

"I loved her," his father said in reply.

True's patience, already unraveled, frayed even further.

"That wasn't the question I asked," he pointed out.

Wilmer looked at him. "I am grieving, son."

"So am I," True returned. "The thing you don't entirely understand, Father, is that what we feel, what we experience, what befalls us matters not. Someone has to rule. Someone *always* has to rule. We don't get to retreat and take time to lick our wounds. We don't get to snivel and rail. We must *rule*." He paused to drive his last point home. "My mother taught me that."

Wilmer flinched.

"Now, we are under attack," True continued. "We must rout this Rising and set about doing it immediately. You allowed one of their own in this very castle to toy with you and loot our treasury to fund their efforts, a happenstance that not only lasted decades but ended with the queen being murdered. You want to retain the crown because you fear what will be written of you for posterity. I want the crown because I fear for the safety of *my people*. Tell me, Father, in those instances, *who should wear that crown?*"

"You cannot possibly expect me to make this decision through my grief," his father returned.

"Have you been listening to a word I've said?" True asked.

"True, be done with him," Wallace called.

"You haven't been given leave to speak," Wilmer clipped at Wallace.

"I do not need your leave for I do not recognize you as my ruler," Wallace shot back. "And not simply because *my* king does not make a man ask permission to speak his mind."

True studied his men, particularly Bram, who demanded to be standing right there even if he should be flat on his back in a bed.

The arrow Bram took had not hit anything vital, but it had still gone through his midsection.

They needed rest, all of them.

And they needed this day to be done.

"Let us go," True said wearily. "We'll finish this on the morrow on the backs of our horses."

The men nodded but hesitated as True moved their way, for they were preparing to flank him as they left.

"I'll abdicate."

All of them stopped and turned back to Wilmer upon hearing these quiet words.

"Say that again," True demanded.

Wilmer leaned his way, his face twisted, and he shouted, "I'll abdicate!"

True let out a long breath.

"And I will end this farce by sharing *this*," Wilmer pointed to the floor, "*precisely this* is what Carrington warned me about."

True felt his blood freeze.

The men around him shifted closer to him.

"He smirked at me when I made his cell this eve," True told his father. "Triumphantly."

Wilmer stared at his son.

"He was delighted she was dead," True went on. "He *planned her murder* and you can even speak his name?"

Red crept up his neck as Wilmer spat, "You have what you want. Go."

"I'll tell you this only once, Father. For her. Because she loved you. Because she put so much effort into propping up a fickle and wayward reign. Because she would wish me not to do it. Only for those reasons I do not send you into exile, never to have your feet touch the fertile Dellish soil again. But do not test that. That will be the only warning you'll get."

True had no more to say and refused to hear another word.

Thus, he turned on his boot and strode out the door with his men.

The minute the guard outside the door closed it, True turned on Luther.

"Get them to bed," he said, jerking his head to Bram and Florian. He then looked right at Bram. "And I don't want you out of yours for two full days."

"True—"

True interrupted him "Promise me."

"I'll want to visit Alfie," Bram said quietly.

Of course he would.

"He needs time too, brother," True replied in the same tone.

Bram nodded.

"All right, men," Luther said, starting to herd them, "the king has spoken."

Florian shot Luther a look.

Bram looked to True and shook his head.

But they all moved away.

True let out another long breath.

"You'll be wanting Farah," Wallace noted.

He looked to his man. "Yes. Though I hope she's abed, asleep, and recovering herself and not perchance leading some charge against a Go'Doan temple with Elena, Serena, Silence and Ha'Lah riding at her back."

Wallace's lips quirked only slightly before he said, "She's not abed, True. She's in a chair by Alfie's bed."

True closed his eyes and dropped his head.

But of course she was.

"We will rally him," Wallace vowed.

True opened his eyes and gave them to his friend.

"He'll want the Poison."

"We'll rally him, True," Wallace said through his teeth.

"His pride will not let him live a life where he has to depend on others, and you know it."

"Then we'll find ways he doesn't have to," Wallace retorted. "If his cock works, we will rally him."

"A man's manhood is not in his cock," True replied.

"Tell that to Florian," Wallace returned. "His manhood *and* his brain are in his cock."

True shook his head.

"And Bram," Wallace went on.

By the gods, True felt he might actually smile.

"And especially Luther," Wallace continued.

"Please be quiet," True begged.

"And Alfie," Wallace whispered. "Though, not the brain part," he finished on a mumble.

They held gazes.

Then True nodded.

"Get to bed yourself, Wally."

It was Wallace who nodded then.

True watched him go.

Then he lifted his chin to the two guards at his father's study doors before he turned the other direction to make his way to where Alfie had been taken.

It was in True's turret, as True had demanded his man be close.

They did not take him to the hospital because it was a longer distance from the temple where he'd been wounded.

But regardless, they had an infirmary in the castle that rivaled any hospital, so he'd been seen to as best as they could.

It was just that nothing could be done.

It was with these heavy thoughts, and a dozen others, that he passed the nurse that sat outside the door and entered his friend's room to see his wife indeed in a chair by his bedside, slumped down, head resting on the wing of the chair, fast asleep.

But his captain was wide awake.

"She needs her bed," Alfie rasped.

True made his way to Alfie's side, stopping just beyond Farah's chair.

He looked down at her, then looked to Alfie.

"You need to rest," he replied. "Shall I call for a sleeping draught?"

Alfie shook his head.

"Alfie—"

"Get your wife to bed, True."

"Alfie—"

His friend's face got hard.

"I will not make you make that decision. I would never do that to you. I will do it myself."

True knew exactly what he was referring to, and thus bent swiftly to his friend. "We will speak of this later."

"You claim king," Alfie stated.

"Yes."

"He will abdicate?"

True nodded.

"Then you must change the Soldier's Poison, my king. Do not make the soldier ask permission from his commanding officer. Allow him to do it himself."

"He always has that choice."

"There is no honor in that."

"Alfie—"

"Allow him to do it himself and have honor."

"The point of making him ask his commanding officer is why we're having this conversation, brother. You won't want to ask. You won't want to make me make that decision. And if you don't ask, I won't lose you. And if you don't ask, you will have the time to learn how to live life differently."

"You've already lost me."

"I'm standing right here talking to you."

"I'll never stand again."

True fought his flinch and straightened, declaring, "It is too soon."

"It is too late."

"You are my brother and I will speak true. To stop these thoughts and your pain, I would have taken that arrow for you, Alfie, doing it on my wedding day."

Alfie visibly ground his teeth for he knew True did not speak false.

"Do not make me lose you," True whispered. "I need you."

"I'm useless."

"Not even a little bit."

Alfie looked away, his head ticked, then he muttered, "Hullo."

True turned and looked down at his bride.

She was awake and watching them.

When Farah saw she had their attention, she said to Alfie, "I need you too. If you're not around, who's going to stop Wallace and Luther from bickering?"

To his shock, this made Alfie emit a guttural grunt of laughter before he started coughing and then taking deep breaths to handle the pain.

"Call for a sleeping draught, my darling," True murmured to his wife.

Farah rose and moved to the door to call the nurse outside.

"We will talk later," True said quietly to Alfie. "Much later."

Alfie stared at him a moment before he looked to the ceiling.

Farah came back to True's side as the nurse bustled about a table bearing clean dressings, vials, flasks and beakers.

"We'll leave you after you take that draught," True promised.

Alfie said nothing.

But when the nurse approached, he struggled, wincing fiercely, to pull himself up and took the glass from her himself.

The nurse's eyes darted to True and Farah pressed close to his side, but True did not intervene.

Alfie needed to learn he could do things for himself, and he might as well start now.

When he handed the glass back to the nurse and collapsed again to the bed, she snapped, "Well, I cannot say I very much like you possibly pulling out your sutures simply so you can drink down a sleeping draught."

Alfie blinked at her.

She looked at Farah, rolled her eyes and kept snapping, "*Men*. Worse, *soldiers*. Ulk."

She then stomped to the table, put down the glass, turned around, and asked True, "Aught else, my prince?"

It was then True saw she was rather comely.

And she had a lovely figure.

Though her disposition, especially for a nurse, was odd.

"Uh, no," he answered.

"How about you?" she asked Alfie. "Is there anything I can do for you?

Say, bring the tinctures over to your bedside table so you can mix your own draught when you need it?"

"Would you let me do that?" Alfie queried.

"Bloody *no*," she bit, threw up both hands like she thought he'd gone completely mad, then stormed out.

He felt Farah coming up on her toes beside him and then heard her whisper, "Would it be bad form to laugh?"

True watched Alfie's astonished face as he stared at the door the nurse closed behind her and he answered in a whisper, "Maybe we should make the hall at least."

She took his hand and squeezed.

She let him go in order to approach Alfie and kiss his cheek, but thankfully not do something that might upset him, like pull up his covers and tuck him in.

When his wife moved away, True bent and wrapped his fingers around Alfie's forearm and he did this tight.

"We'll talk more tomorrow," he murmured.

Alfie sighed and then nodded.

True led his wife out of the room and to the stairs that would lead them up to their chambers, both of them, prince and princess, soon to be king and queen, dipping their chins respectfully to a bloody nurse for fear of what she might do if they didn't.

On this thought, True was halfway to starting to laugh perhaps a little madly, and they were halfway up the steps, when his wife asked, "Do you know your mother's maid?"

"Helga?"

She looked to him. "Yes, that's her name."

"Yes," he confirmed unnecessarily. "What about her?"

Her face softened even as her gait stayed steady and her eyes remained on him.

"She is suffering, True. I've seen her twice today. It's clear she cared deeply for your mother. I know you are busy, and grieve yourself, but if you could find some time to have a word with her?"

Helga did care about his mother. As much as anyone could be with Mercy, Helga and she were thick as thieves.

He should have thought of her earlier.

"I will speak to her tomorrow," he said as they made the landing of their chambers.

"I knew you would," she murmured.

He walked them through the doors and closed them behind him.

"Did you learn anything during the interrogations?" she asked, not heading to her dressing room, instead standing before a sofa and watching him.

Ah, his fierce Farah.

"Darling, you took an arrow today," he reminded her.

"I know, but—"

"It would please me greatly if you would finally get some rest."

"I would rest easier if I knew those who took your mother received the treatment they deserved and will lead us to stop anything more happening."

He knew, in that moment, there would be times in their marriage where he would wish his wife was far less intelligent.

Fortunately, there would be vastly more times when he was grateful that she was so wise.

Thus, he settled in and shared, "Every one of them is Dellish." He then shook his head. "But they are most curious. It is clear they all embarked on their mission fully aware they would be captured, interrogated, and in the end, executed. I've never known a man, one who is not a trained spy, who enters a mission with this knowledge and does it willingly."

"This is most disturbing," she whispered.

"It is," he agreed. "But there is a dichotomy that might work in our favor. You see, at first, they did what it was clear they were told to do. What the men who were tortured by Mars and his Trusted in the necropolis were told to do. Say nothing. Except, in the case of the men at the Keep, the occasional 'long live The Rising.'"

"How does that work in our favor?"

True moved to her and carefully took her in his arms.

When he had her where he very much liked her, he explained.

"It works in our favor for they are not trained spies. They are not even trained soldiers. I think if Mars spent more time at it in Fire City, we would have learned more. As we had more prisoners, and more time, and some watched what was done to others and could only think the same or worse would be done to them, we learned that you nor I were the targets. Only Mother was. And this was why so many arrows went so many places. Ten arrows missed entirely. And what hit you, Bram, Florian, Alfie were not intended for those targets."

Farah said nothing for it was unnecessary to remind him that six *did* hit their target and some of the others did serious damage, even if it was not what was intended.

True did not touch on that either.

"They may have trained in their aim, but they were not trained archers," he continued. "And they may not have leaked vital secrets of this Rising, but all of them eventually talked. And we learned that they were all recruited through Go'Doan temples, or Go'Doan priests, but this Rising is clearly not officially of the Go'Doan religion. Indeed, they speak of the overarching faith in a sneering manner. Thus, it is a subset of the Go'Doan who have an aggressive mission that does not coincide with that of the Dome City, making it not truly Go'Doan at all."

"Then this is good," she noted.

"Yes, though we cannot tell who is of this Rising and who is Go'Doan, which will serve to make things difficult. We also learned that information within this Rising is highly compartmentalized, something else that will make things difficult. Their leader, the one who recruited them, called them to this mission, trained them, strategized it and carried it through, was the one who fled and died in the fleeing. He was a priest of the Go'Doan. They know not names of others. And the two priests taken, who likely know more, refused to say anything at all."

"And this is bad," she murmured.

He gave her a careful squeeze. "Not exactly. First, they are not soldiers. This is definitely in our favor. And it leads me to believe whoever is at the top of this is not trained in that manner, which could also be in our favor. I do not think they realize they declared war, in a sense, back at Catrame Palace, and definitely that declaration was made today. And you cannot win a war if you don't realize you're waging one."

"Are you sure they do not think this?"

He shook his head. "The only thing I'm sure of at this time is that this is not a house of cards. You can't pull one from the bottom and it all comes tumbling down. The hammer has to fall at the top. Thus, we must find our way to the top."

"It does seem this is true," she muttered.

He gave her another careful squeeze and a small smile before he went on, "Second, they are not Go'Doan, so although they recruit amongst the people of the realms in which they serve, if we can disseminate information, citizens can be made aware, or even come forward with information."

"This would be most useful."

"Yes," he agreed. "And last, it is far away, but it could be even more useful considering the lower downs know little, thus we need information about what is happening higher up. And Lorenz, Mars's captain in Fire City, has a priest who is formerly of this Rising, though this faction does not know this is 'formerly.' And he's willing to learn what he can of their plans and share it."

Farah brightened, but asked, "Can he be trusted?"

"I do not know. I know Lorenz trusts him and Mars trusts Lorenz. So I take heart in that."

She nodded before she said, "But it does not seem much to take heart in when so much is being lost."

"The priests of this Rising in the temple in Fire City fled after the attack. Some of them have been tracked down and they await Mars's return in the necropolis. But they do not await their interrogations. Lorenz and Guard are already interrogating them."

Her brows went up.

True kept speaking.

"Sadly, however, it seems, thus far, it's proving most of them are underlings, not those in authority. But it's clear with Carrington's placement in this very castle that these plans have been brewing for a long time. And we're getting a picture that perhaps there are some zealots higher up who are calling the shots and doing it poorly. And now that plans are being carried out, their followers are finding they're not quite as loyal as they believed, what with men in pieces in Fire City, or walking into the tar pits. Or what they will see happen to Carrington, which will be grisly, and the other traitors publicly hung."

"So you don't think they will feel some triumph at what they achieved today?" she asked quietly.

"I think citizens of this city still line the streets silently in mourning for their queen," he answered. "I think as gruesome as it will be, there will be cheers at Carrington's execution and the traitors will be led to the gallows with the Dellish spitting on them as they go. I think today, Chu capitalized on the fact nineteen archers expected to be captured, but their leader alone tried to escape. And Chu made it very clear to those in that torture chamber that they were sacrificed while their leader expected to get away."

"Oh my," she said quietly. "That was very clever."

"Yes. And Chu had further instigated a situation where there was no small amount of animosity of those underlings toward the priests who Chu also made it clear were higher ups who in some way got them in their present position but were saying not a word to get them out of it."

"That *is* promising," Farah noted.

He nodded. "Thus, I think anyone of this Rising will watch this and wonder how deep their loyalties lie. I cannot tell the future, sweets. I just feel all that was lost today in my marrow. My mother's life and Alfie's legs will not go unavenged in every way I can avenge them. That is what I know."

"And I will be queen on the morrow, the shortest reign of princess ever, most likely," she remarked, probably to lighten the discussion.

"You will be," he said softly. "However, the declaration may come tomorrow, but our official coronations will wait until after this current business is sorted. Mother's pyre burned, her ashes at rest. Carrington and the traitors dispatched. It will be a few weeks."

"I am in no hurry," she mumbled.

"Farah."

Her eyes focused on him.

He gave her all she needed to know for the now.

"Cassius has had news of not a small amount of unrest in Airen," he informed her.

"Oh, Gods, no," she whispered.

"I sense he has not told me the fullness of it in thoughtfulness to all that's happened today. But I'm also sensing he and Elena will need to leave."

She nodded again.

"Mars has promised his aid to Cassius, but he also knows this Rising has a foothold in his own realm. We might lose him too."

She bit her lower lip but again nodded.

"I suspect Aramus will back Cassius. Frey Drakkar and Apollo Ulfr have vowed to assist Wodell, but they did this before they knew the unrest in Airen. What I'm saying is, with Mother gone, it might well be you and me and my men who take this on."

"And the gnomes. The fairies. The pixies. And all the many people who love you."

He stared down at her.

"We suffered a grave loss today, True. *You* suffered a grave loss. And there is one thing I've learned about Wodell in the time I've spent here. Your people will not abide that. Not for them. Not for Mercy. But most of all, not for *you*."

She pressed closer and kept speaking.

"Cassius may go, and Mars may go, Aramus too, and I will be sad for their leaving, mostly because my friends will leave with them and because of why they all go. But we will prevail."

"I hope you are right," he said.

"I know I am," she replied.

He smiled down at her and then noted, "Now you have had what you requested, will you humor your husband and finally lie down?"

Her face grew soft. "I think maybe I can do that."

He was relieved, and not only because she damn well needed to lie down and get some bloody rest, but because there was one thing he had planned for their wedding day that he still fully intended to do.

It was the most important, even if it was arguable that it was what he was most looking forward to doing.

The other would happen when she had not but hours before taken an arrow through her body.

True bent to kiss her forehead before he released her and put a hand on the small of her back to scoot her toward her dressing rooms, saying, "If you need me, call."

"Servants are always at the ready in this castle," she murmured, clearly missing his fingers at her laces and moving in the direction he'd aimed her.

True headed to his own dressing room, wondering if Helga would wish to take on the new queen.

He'd assess her state the next day and ask when it seemed she would be open to such a request.

He was in his sleep pants and stoking the fire when his wife moved through her new boudoir into their bedchamber.

She wore a relatively demure, but very Dellish nightgown.

She looked beautiful.

But she said, "I had something else planned to wear for this occasion. Sadly," she indicated her arm in its sling with her other hand, "it will have to wait."

Sadly, indeed.

But there was that something that would not wait any longer, and as Farah moved to her side of the bed, True followed her.

"Love," he called when she pulled the covers back.

She turned and her head twitched slightly with how close he was.

"True, you know that I wish...have wished...have been waiting much time to—"

He turned to her nightstand, bent to it, opened the drawer and pulled out a long ebony box.

When he straightened, she was staring down at it with eyes wide and lips parted.

"I asked Elpis before we left Firenze to find one that would suit you. She brought me five," he told her. "I selected this one."

And with that, he thumbed open the box which inside had a Firenz marital chain from which hung diminutive emeralds, topaz and rubies.

"The emeralds might be of Firenze, but they also signify Wodell, in a way," he carried on.

Slowly, her gaze drifted up to his.

"The rubies are definitely of Firenze, your land, a part of you," he continued.

Her eyes started to grow bright with tears.

"The topaz," he grinned, "well, they just reminded me of your beautiful eyes."

"True," she breathed.

"Will you wear this for me, my bride?" he whispered.

A tear tracked down her cheek.

Then another.

"I didn't think—" she began.

"You are Firenz, this is your custom. I know it means much to you, so it means much to me too."

Another tear fell.

"Please, do not weep," he said quietly. "I had hoped this would bring you joy."

"It would be the greatest honor of my life to wear your marital chain," she replied.

To that he did not grin.

He smiled.

"Elpis tells me they are not slept in. Therefore, I shall put it on you tomorrow, hmm?"

Two more tears dropped as she nodded.

Then she bent her head and reached out tentatively to the chain, like it was the most precious thing to touch her fingers.

He very much liked she felt that way, for it wasn't even his custom, and he felt the same.

"Can I have a kiss now?" he asked throatily.

She looked up at him, still weeping, but dashed a hand along her cheek, the other, before she shook her head.

True was surprised at this response, for she had never, not once, denied his embrace.

"No?"

"No," she whispered, slid out from in front of him and walked right out of the room.

He stared after her.

She was not gone long.

And she came back with the fingers of her hand not coming out of her sling closed around something.

He turned her way as she approached him.

"Farah—"

"I shall say this fast." She stopped in front of him. "I was going to wait. But after that," she gestured to the box still in his hold, "I will not wait. Because of what this is. Because of what this day was meant to be. And because you deserve to have all of it the way she intended."

She intended.

Oh, shite.

"Farah—" That came out gruff.

"Your mother told me that a Dellish husband and wife give gifts to each other on their wedding day. She told me, without a doubt, you would adhere to this custom. And I am not surprised, as she would not be surprised, that you did. This is not my custom, so she helped me. And she...and she..." her voice broke as she lifted her hand, opened her fingers, and in her palm was a golden band set all around with emeralds, "gave me this to give to you."

The contradictory mixture of immense joy and colossal sorrow was such, True closed his eyes and dropped his head, doing so wondering how he managed to keep his feet.

But he had no problem wrapping his arms around his wife when she burrowed into them and he heard at the same time he felt her deep sob.

"I-I-I l-love that you will wear it and th-think of her at the same time you think of me," she blubbered. "Your queens."

His queens.

True took one arm from about her to set her marital chain aside then lifted his left hand between them, fingers extended.

"Put it on," he said hoarsely.

She did not delay in sliding it to the base of his ring finger.

"It's beautiful," she whispered, her hand wrapping around the side of his palm.

It was.

Outside his wife, it was the most beautiful thing he'd ever seen.

"I'll never take it off," he vowed.

He felt her eyes on his face, so he took his gaze from the ring and looked to her.

Her long lashes were spiky with wet, her cheeks drenched in it.

He cupped her beautiful face and slid his thumb through the evidence of the depth of her emotion. Emotion he loved just as much as, in that instance, for part of the reason she was feeling it, he hated.

"I am most happy to be your wife, True," she said softly.

"And I am most happy to be your husband, Farah," he replied in the same tone.

"Can I kiss you now?" she asked.

"Hell yes," he answered.

She got up on her toes.

True met his wife halfway.

88

THE TEST

Queen Ha-Lah
Guest Bedchambers, Southwest Turret, Birchlire Castle, Notting Thicket
Wodell

I wandered to my king after leaving him abed so that I could clean up after making love.

I saw in the lantern light that he seemed what he did not while his hands and mouth were on me, his shaft moving inside me.

Distracted.

As my husband had become wont to do, the instant he gave me his attention, he cleared his expression as if naught was pressing on his mind, and he gave me a lazy smile.

"My husband," I murmured, sliding in beside him only to be quickly claimed and pulled under him even as he shifted the covers up to his shoulders to keep us both warm. "You do not hide from me."

"Do not hide what?" he asked, lying poorly.

I simply stared at him.

He withstood it for an admirable amount of time before he sighed and rolled to his back.

I went with him, perching on his wide chest and looking down at him resting on the pillows.

"I am torn," he said to the ceiling.

I could imagine.

I'd been fully apprised of all that was happening...*everywhere.*

He looked to me. "I promised everyone everything."

"You cannot give everyone everything," I murmured truthfully, but drattedly unhelpfully.

"I do know that, my wife," he replied on a sigh.

I tucked my lips between my teeth.

"We all meet tomorrow, and I must know before then what I will do," he shared. "I have made my promise to Cassius. We've known each other for years. His rule is in jeopardy before he's even officially assumed it, and half the population of his realm is in the same position, have been for centuries, and if he's defeated, will remain thus. Mars may no longer be able to provide the support he promised as well, and with what happened today, knowing this Rising is at work in his land, I cannot blame him. Cass's capital city is under siege. I cannot *not* offer him my armadas now that the unrest has sprung forth to actual campaigns. Especially as they've started with Sky Bay, where my ships might be of service."

"Yes," I agreed.

"But True's mother was killed today and this Rising is an issue, we know, in at least two realms, and I cannot imagine the infiltration of it in Firenze and Wodell has not happened as well in Airen. Indeed, with the deviousness of this lot, they may even be operating on our island."

I hated to admit it, but he might not be wrong.

"Yes," I repeated.

His visage shifted to a scowl. "You are not being helpful, Ha-Lah."

"This is not true. I am," I refuted. "For I do not know these answers. I do not know what you should do. Both choices are the right ones, and from what Serena told us of the little she and Chu have been able to learn, I too fear for our own land. However, you are but one man and we are but one nation. Even the vastness of our armadas could not cover three realms as well as continue to protect our own."

I pressed closer to him when I finished what I wished to say.

"What I can do is listen to you as you speak of it, share what limited advice I may have, and in this way, help you work it out on your own."

"You have much more to give than that, my queen," he returned, and the manner in which he did made me grow still. His hand came to my cheek and he dropped his voice when he went on, "You have had many opinions in the past, and showed no reluctance in voicing them. But now, when we have been made very aware of what is at stake, you have little to say."

This was true.

But I was stung.

"It is not easy, what destiny has tasked us to do," he said carefully, his warm brown eyes on my face just as cautious. "So many see the castles, the grandeur, the riches, and think they have all the answers so it will not be difficult to live in luxury and rule. They do not see the decisions we make have ramifications, in some cases, for centuries. And thus, we must weigh them to the utmost of our abilities before we carry them through."

He was very right, and until that day, seeing Mercy seated in her pew, staring unseeing at the vaulted ceilings of that temple, arrows protruding from her bloodied chest and throat, I hated to admit it, but I couldn't escape it...

I had felt I had all the answers.

I as well had no problem sharing I felt as such.

And now, I was not nearly as certain.

I nodded to what Aramus had said.

My husband continued speaking.

"Thus, I understand your hesitance in providing guidance. When there seems nothing at stake, it is easy to offer your opinion. But when you realize just how much weight any decision carries, I fully understand why you would hesitate." He shook his head. "But this is not the time for hesitation, my Ha-Lah. Do we give all we have to one, while protecting our own shores? Or do we divide ourselves amongst many...?" He grinned. "While protecting our own shores."

At his encouragement, it took a moment, but I reflected, then I waded in.

"I do not think this Go'Doan faction has a hold in our realm, Aramus," I noted.

"I wish to agree, but with all that has happened, can we take that chance?"

I grew silent for I did not think we could.

I broke my silence and shared, "We are too long gone from our own realm, my king. These delays mean we will not be gone three to four months, but much longer. We've already been away three and with what's happening with Airen, we cannot know when Cassius and Elena will wed."

His eyebrows went up. "Abandon them all and go home?"

"No," I replied. "As we have seen, and from what Serena shared, the situation in Wodell and Firenze is insidious. What you could offer them is ships to sail their rivers, or provide presence at ports, perhaps men to bear arms, but what they need is spies. Our skin is not the same color as theirs, not to mention, none of our people, to our knowledge, practice this religion. Our people have no hope of successfully spying on this Rising."

"Mm," he hummed.

"On the other hand," I continued, "we can offer significant assistance in Sky Bay. Even if just to bring food and supplies. You can't lay siege to a city that is fed and watered and whose citizens that need to leave can do so, just aboard a ship."

"This makes sense," he murmured.

"And Firenze has the mightiest warriors of all realms. They do not need us. Not really."

My husband's head nodded on the pillow.

I got closer to him. "But we must go home. Our people must see in all that is happening across Triton, that you and I feel they are what they are. Our priority. And in so doing, we can send men to discover if this Rising has somehow taken hold on our own shores. Airen is but a day's sail away. Sky Bay, I do not know. Three days? Four?"

"Five," he informed me.

I nodded shortly. "Thus, if Cassius needs you, you can be there." I slid a hand up his chest and rested it at the base of his neck. "You can leave some men for True, but the war he must wage is not about swords, lances and cavalry. And you can leave behind some of our ships to patrol their rivers, guard their ports. This way, you can share your support for True and his people. Mars does not need it. Send ships to open up Sky Bay, if by some slim chance they have it blockaded. And we can go home with Cassius knowing you will personally come to his aid and can be there in a short amount of time if this is needed."

"That wasn't so hard, was it?" he whispered.

I blinked into his face.

And I did so understanding why he'd seemed distracted earlier.

"You were testing me?" I asked dangerously.

He grinned. "Not as such. I'd come to much the same conclusion. However, I intended to stay with Cassius while sending you home with some of my men to see to our people. Now, I agree it's best for us both to go home, at least for a time."

"But mostly, you were testing me," I noted, still dangerously.

His lips were quirking with amusement as his hands slid up my back. "My Ha-Lah."

"A woman lost her life today, Aramus. A woman. A wife. A mother. A queen. She lost it in this wretched web being woven around all of us. And you play games?"

"Yes, baby, if you must call it that," he said softly. "Because you are *my* woman, *my* wife and *my* queen. I had no mother alive to help you learn your role. You are proud and you are fierce, and I believe to my soul you were born to be queen. But that doesn't mean you cannot learn all the ways there are to be a good one."

I did not like that this answer was also a good one.

Aramus rolled me to my back, pressing into me and looming over me.

"I have often failed at being a good king. I will fail again, even if I strive not to. I have definitely failed at being a good husband, and I will do what I can not to repeat these mistakes or make others. But I fear, being human, I will fail again. What I know, through it all, as your king and your husband, is that I will need you at my side *not* hesitant, *not* worried about what your opinion might bring. Honest. Open. Sharing. Guiding. In the short period of time we have been true husband and wife, or moving in that direction, I have learned one thing for certain about you, Ha-Lah. Would you like to know what that is?"

"Yes," I mumbled.

His lips quirked again before he bent and touched his mouth to mine.

Lifting away, he shared, "Having you at my side, I do not know how I ever did this alone."

Immediately, I melted underneath him.

"Aramus," I whispered.

"Now, no less important is that we are in accord about what will come next for the both of us."

He was too clever by half, my husband.

"And thus, after a rotten day, we will rest easy," he finished.

Yes.

Too clever by half.

"Before we go, I must ask for you to give me some time, as much as I may have, with the Sisterhood of the Beast," I requested.

His brows drew together. "The Sisterhood of the Beast?"

"Silence, Farah, Elena and I," I educated him.

"Yes, I could put that together, my wife, but you've...*named* yourselves?"

His body felt like it was shaking.

With laughter.

This meant my brows drew together. "I don't know why it's amusing. For the Beast brought we sisters together, and together, we sisters will defeat the Beast. The name is fitting."

"It is. Right on the nose," he muttered, his words also shaking.

I decided to ignore his continuing humor.

"I wish to tell them my command of the seas and my kinship with its beasts."

Aramus did not find that particular morsel amusing.

"No," he denied.

"Aramus—"

"No."

"Your men know," I pointed out, for they did. We'd told them (and I'd shown them, covertly) along our journey to Notting Thicket.

"My men are *my* men. I know them to their bones. I barely know Silence, Farah and Elena."

"Well, I know them."

"Barely."

"Aramus—"

"Ha-Lah, no," he stated implacably. "I forbid it."

By the seas.

He did not just *forbid something*.

I stared at him.

He withstood it for such an admirable amount of time, it was I who broke the silence.

"We must know our own powers. We must know our own strengths. We must know the weapons we can wield. And in knowing, understand our weaknesses."

"This is not a weapon you will wield," he retorted. "It is a gift you have that you will not share...*with anybody* save those that already know, who are those I know I can trust."

"Aramus, you, the king of the seas, me, harnessing the powers of them, you must understand this is why we're destined to save Triton from the Beast."

"And should that need ever come about, and as days wear into weeks that are currently wearing into months, it seems it won't, if things deteriorate to a point of concern where they're needed, *then* we will unleash your powers and thus share them. Not before."

"What I wish to say is, Elena, Farah and Silence might have similar powers. Elena does not hide hers, but there might be more we do not know. And you saw yourself what Farah could do today. That was formidable."

"And the powers you don't know about, I can assure you," he pressed deeply into me, "absolutely *assure you*, my queen, their men have forbidden them to share for the exact purpose I do the same."

Mars, I could see this.

Cassius and True?

Not a chance.

"Aramus—"

"No."

Oh dear.

Now I was getting angry.

"Aramus," I said slowly, my new mood vibrating in his name.

"Ha-Lah, you will be at risk. This power will be coveted. I will protect you and the knowledge of it until I have no choice but not to."

You do not have to protect me. You don't because you don't understand just how powerful I am, as I'm mermaid.

I almost said it.

I did not.

As I had not in the weeks since that day long ago when I'd determined to do it.

Frey, Finnie, Apollo, Maddie, dragons, breaking camp, sailing, meeting Aramus's ships, weddings and assassinations had all gotten in the way.

My husband now knew nearly everything about me. And along the way, he'd put great effort into memorizing every inch of me.

That was the only thing of grave importance he did not know.

And the longer it took for me to tell him, the harder it was to do so.

For before, I worried what he would feel, being married to one of my kind.

But now, I worried how he would feel that I kept it from him for so long, through so much, including us falling in love, consummating our marriage (repeatedly), and moving from one traumatic drama to the next that befell our friends.

My husband broke into my thoughts by asking, "Is what I said understood?"

"I still wish to spend time with my sisters," I mumbled.

"I would not deny you this, my queen, of course not," he muttered. "But protect your secret. For if you don't, it will make it nearly impossible for me to do so."

I did not agree with this, but I did not wish to discuss it any further. The day had been trying enough. I refused to end it arguing (any longer) with my husband.

However, I could not stop myself from heaving a deep, beleaguered sigh.

This made Aramus's lips twitch again.

I decided I was going to ignore that too.

"There is one thing I have not yet shared," he told me.

I braced.

Aramus spoke.

"After Cassius received his dire news, he asked me to take his daughters to Mar-el for safekeeping. He needs to discuss this with Elena. If she agrees, they will be under our protection. Do you have issue with that?"

"Of course not," I answered. "However, wouldn't the most expedient choice be The Enchantments?"

He shook his head. "Cassius was vague about it, but apparently, Ophelia gave him the impression The Enchantments weren't safe. As it seems no realm on the mainland is, Mar-el is their only choice."

I stole my arms around him. "We will take good care of them. And should Elena agree, I will assure them both of the same."

My husband watched me as I said this, and he continued to do so with an unusual, but far from unattractive, expression on his face.

"What?" I whispered, somewhat mesmerized by his expression.

"We will have children," he said quietly.

A shiver drifted over my skin.

"Yes," I whispered.

"I look forward to that day. I look forward to watching my proud, fierce wife be a proud, fierce mother."

I actually trembled at that.

"Darling."

Aramus dipped closer. "We must keep safe for that to happen, my Ha-Lah."

Yes.

My husband was too clever by half.

"I will keep safe, if you promise the same," I said.

"I will keep safe, my queen," he vowed.

I smiled at him, pushing aside thoughts of what he would think of having a child, a future king of Mar-el, be half-mer.

My king dipped even further and kissed the smile off my lips.

Apparently, we were not done with this day for we were not done making love.

But it was Aramus who left the bed to get a cloth to clean up after we were through.

I was half asleep by the time he returned after that deed was accomplished and pulled me into his strong arms.

Then I was fully asleep.

And finally, the day was done.

89
THE NEWS

Queen Silence
Bark Parlor, Formal Receiving Rooms, Birchlire Castle, Notting Thicket
Wodell

I t was early.

True, and Farah, along with my husband, Cassius, Aramus, Frey Drakkar and Apollo Ulfr— who, in order to act as witnesses, had all been at the event that I hoped had just happened in the king's formal study —entered the room.

Each wore a severe face.

I did not think this boded well.

I took a moment to modulate my voice so I spoke (somewhat) calmly, instead of doing what I instinctively wanted to do, cry out.

"Did he change his mind?"

"He did not," Cassius answered, making his way toward Elena. "True is king."

The air in the room, which up until then included Ha-Lah, Elena, Serena, Elpis, Finnie, Maddie and me sitting in tense silence, drinking tea (though, Serena and Ha-Lah drank coffee), fell flat.

And then it rose up, almost as if there had been some drug infused with it, much like the smoke I enjoyed so much.

Thus, I came up from my seat on the sofa, my eyes fixed on my cousin, who did not look the slightest pleased with this turn of events.

As I made my movements, his gaze cut to me.

"Long live King True," I said loudly, and clearly, lifting my skirts at the sides, and falling into a low curtsy.

"You do not bow to another king," Mars said tightly, having made it to my side. "Indeed, you do not bow to *anyone*, even your own king."

I tipped my head back to look to my husband. "This one I do."

His mouth was as tight as his words.

True's voice sounded. "You do not bow to me, Silence."

I looked to him and said softly, "Yes, True, I do."

His jaw ticked as his eyes changed the most extraordinary green.

As for me, I felt tears sting my own.

"Arise, my cousin," he returned, also softly.

I rose.

"Do not do that again," Mars muttered.

I looked to him again only to see, with some surprise, he was not annoyed at me.

He was studying me warmly.

He then murmured, "Go."

That sting in my eyes grew stronger because my Mars had come to know me so well, and I loved that, but I did not note that as I also did not hesitate to move swiftly across the floor.

True opened his arms before I got there.

And I flung myself in them.

I held tight.

His arms wrapping around me, he did as well.

My cheek pressed to his chest, I whispered, "I love you, cousin."

His lips pressed to my hair, he whispered in return, "And I as well, cousin."

There was so much more I wished to say.

But none of it mattered more than that.

We held on for a long moment before he gave me a gentle shake and his arms loosened.

I took this cue, let him go and moved back to my husband, who claimed me about my shoulders, tucking me to his body, my front to his side.

"It is odd in the circumstances, but heartfelt, when I say congratulations, True," Elena said.

True inclined his head her way.

"Now what?" Serena asked.

Elena shot her a look.

But I had to say, I'd heard much about Serena of the Nadirii, though I'd had no dealings with her a'tall, until the last two days.

And I had noted that she wasn't warm and chatty, but she did not seem half as bad as everyone said she was.

She just acted like...a man.

Forthright, she didn't beat about the bush. She also did not appear to mentally nitpick every word she said before she said it in concern she might hurt someone's feelings when we were all adults and times were dire so we really didn't have any to dither about.

She wasn't rude.

She was a little abrupt, though I'd seen men be just as abrupt regularly and no one thought they were rude.

She was just...her.

I admired it.

Though I did not say, for Elena kept casting glances her way that said she didn't trust her and further said she did not wish to be in her presence.

And Elena was my friend, and as I had not had many friends, I did not know what to do in this type of instance.

But I thought the right thing to do was, if I didn't agree with my friend about something, keep quiet.

Thus, this was what I did.

"Father is reading through the announcement I've prepared for him, mine is at the ready, we take the balcony in fifteen minutes and then...it'll be done," True said to Serena.

"And then what?" Serena pressed.

"Serena," Elena hissed.

"Ha-Lah and I have discussed it, and we feel we need to return home. We've been gone too long," Aramus announced. He looked to Cassius and Elena. "We will take Theodora and Aelia with us." He looked to True and Farah. "We will send ships to your ports, three each to Seil Haven, Tradepoint, Mermaid Wharf and Welling Harbor. We'll also leave ships to patrol the River Dorian, Great Wohd and River Fae." Again to Cassius, he said, "And we'll send a fleet to Sky Bay with you, Elena and your men and with them we will send supplies."

Cassius nodded.

"If you need me, my friend, I will be there," he continued, his attention still on Cassius.

"I know," Cassius replied.

Aramus turned to True. "And if you need me, I will be there."

"I know as well," True said.

Aramus drew in a large breath and let it go as if what he said was a great burden he was relieved to let go.

And I saw that it was. He did not want to disappoint anyone he had made promises.

But I understood why he'd want to go home.

I understood this because, before leaving our chambers to be witness to an abdication, Mars had dropped this same cannonball.

We were going back to Fire City.

I had already decided not to argue this.

Treachery was afoot.

The King of Firenze needed to be home.

Further, we'd received word that Zosime had had her child, a girl, and I wanted to meet her.

I did not want to leave True (or Farah, but especially True). Not now.

But I was queen, and unlike many people thought, I could not have all I wanted.

Mercy had taught me that.

May the gods embrace her.

"Apollo and I have discussed how best to utilize our resources," Frey Drakkar entered the conversation. "And we've decided that I shall go with Cassius to Airen, but I will send my dragons to an unpopulated dune in Firenze, if that's acceptable?" he asked Mars.

My husband nodded.

Frey nodded back and turned to Cassius. "If they have not already seen them, once you know more about the situation, the element of surprise can be used to great success. However, we need to discuss this. Their power is mighty, and if not utilized strategically, there could be damage that's unacceptable."

"My gratitude," Cassius murmured with a chin dip to Frey.

"And I will remain here," Apollo put in, his gaze on True. "I've had occasion to communicate with a few alphas in this realm. From that I've learned, I have the same command of the wolves here as I do in my own land. And Frey and I believe we can put this to use in Wodell. At the very least, they can guard important places you feel may be targets or keep angry citizens from doing aught to these Go'Doan temples you fear may be the targets of misplaced ire. This would free some of your soldiers, who would be spread thin if they were to be deployed too widely. And a wolf, I have found, is a successful deterrent, even to those who have a great deal of belief behind their intended misdeeds."

"I would not be surprised," True replied. "And this will be most appreciated."

Maddie piped up, her eyes on me. "You do not speak to animals in this land?"

I shook my head.

She turned to Finnie. "How odd."

"You do?" Elena asked them.

Finnie nodded. "Women speak to some, men speak to others. Though only Frey commands the dragons and only Apollo commands the wolves."

"Men speak to animals?" Serena queried.

"Yes," Finnie replied.

"Sorcerers," Serena deduced.

"No, all men and all women speak to different species," Maddie told her.

How marvelous!

"How strange," Serena muttered.

"Back to the matter at hand," Frey interrupted. "We've received communications that Lahn and Tor are a day's sail away. Lahn will come with us. He and his warriors are unbeatable. In fact, I would not be surprised if in ancient times, they came from your land," he told Mars, then nodded as well to Cassius. "You will see many similarities in your peoples." He finished on a mutter, "Though Korwahkians are larger."

"Interesting," Mars murmured.

I agreed, for I could not imagine men *larger* than the Firenz or Airenzian.

"Tor will remain here," Frey went on. "With his experience, he could be useful in covert situations."

True inclined his head to Frey.

"Where will Chu go?" Serena asked my husband.

"He will come home," Mars answered.

Serena accepted this answer readily.

Elena and Cassius studied her closely as she did.

As if raised by her mention of him, the man himself, Chu, prowled in.

"Oh balls," I whispered at one glance at his face.

"What now?" Mars asked his Trusted.

Chu, to my surprise, looked not to his king, but to Serena.

"Two nights past, The Enchantments were attacked."

"This happens often, Chu," Serena dismissed on a shrug.

Chu, already looking grim, now appeared dour.

I would understand why when he shared, "They used a unicorn horn and had kidnapped a Nadirii in order to bring down the veil."

There were gasps, including one from myself, but before I'd recovered from my shock, I sensed an emotion much more intense had saturated the room.

Wrath.

And it was emanating from Cassius.

"What is this you say?" he hissed at Chu.

"I am sorry for the news," Chu said to Cassius but looked to Elena and his expression changed to one that made the skin at the back of my neck itch. "I am sorry for the news," he repeated softly. "The Nadirii who was abducted was your mentor."

The blood drained from Elena's face.

"She is alive, though gravely wounded," Chu went on. "The Nadirii received a warning prior to the attack, thus they prepared and easily defeated the aggressors. No other Nadirii warriors were mortally or critically wounded."

"We must go immediately to Mother," Serena declared.

"I must go immediately to Melisse," Elena whispered.

"Lamb," Cassius murmured, and Elena's head tipped back to look at her betrothed.

"Cassius," she said, but her voice broke pitifully in the middle of his name in such a way I felt a small break in my heart.

We all then watched as Cassius took hold of Elena, muttering, "Excuse us," and then he guided her out of the room.

I would not suspect that of Cassius, that thoughtfulness, that attention to Elena's needs and seeing to them without her being in a state to share them.

But I liked it very much.

After they left, Aramus asked, "Is this attack of The Rising?"

"Yes," Chu answered.

The feel of the room degenerated further.

"Were the communications from Ophelia?" Mars queried.

"Yes," Chu repeated.

"Were orders forwarded for Elena and myself?" Serena inquired.

Chu shook his head. "Not with the birds thus received."

Serena looked frustrated by this.

"I'm loathe to move forward, but my citizens have been amassing since the events of yesterday. I have an important announcement to make, and after what befell us, I cannot delay it," True mentioned.

"Not to worry, the Nadirii can take care of ourselves," Serena proclaimed. "Obviously," she finished proudly.

She was right.

Except, now…

"A unicorn horn was taken," I reminded her of a deed that was despicable in so many ways, it was impossible to describe them all.

It was also terribly unlawful in *all* realms.

"I cannot believe they have unicorns here," Maddie whispered to Finnie.

"I know, right?" Finnie whispered to Maddie.

"The Nadirii can take care of ourselves," Serena repeated.

"Perhaps all the birds have not arrived from Ophelia yet," True suggested. "We have some time before all scatter to discuss if this further news changes any plans. But now, we have no time. We must make our way to the balcony."

There were a number of nodding heads and all shifted to do just that.

However, I hung back.

My husband gave me a mild scowl.

"Go on, Mars. I'll be right there," I told him.

This did not improve his scowl.

I turned to Serena and requested, "Serena, if I could have a moment before we go?"

She seemed startled by this, but she stopped moving, indicating her assent.

I looked back to Mars.

"Just a moment, my king," I murmured.

He did not appear to like it, but he nodded and moved to and through the door.

I moved to Serena.

"I must ask a favor, and of course, you can refuse," I began. "Indeed, we may not have the time before we go our separate ways should you wish to grant it."

"What is it?" she queried.

"I wish for you to teach me some skills with, perhaps, a dagger."

She blinked at me.

"And, I do not know," I continued. "I am small, this may be useless, but some physical strategies. Should I, erm...find myself in the situation to, say, *use them.*"

"Smallness means nothing if you keep your head about you and do not mind punching a man in the throat or kicking him in the balls," Serena declared.

Faith! I thought.

"Oh," I whispered.

She studied me, still appearing to be astonished, but also something else.

Cautious?

Pleased?

"We will make time," she decreed.

I tipped my chin. "I would be most grateful."

"Farah and Ha-Lah too," she said.

"I think that would be wise," I replied.

"The men won't like it, will they?" she asked.

"I...do not know," I said hesitantly. "However, I think it best they do not know we intend to be trained thus in case they don't, feeling they can provide all the protection we need, and the situation arises that they..." I struggled against biting my lip before I concluded, *"can't."*

She gave a curt nod. "We will make it a priority."

She then moved to leave.

I fell to her side and she looked down at me, the astonishment back, her brows raised.

"I know you must have much on your mind, so truly, this is appreciated," I told her.

"I am Nadirii, Silence," she returned. "It is my sacred vow to be of service to all my sisters, be they Nadirii or not, for we believe all women are truly Nadirii."

I shot her a smile. "That's actually beautiful."

And this did not astonish her.

It flabbergasted her.

I did not have time to ask after that.

We'd moved into and down the hall, and my husband was waiting for me.

He claimed my arm, sent a dismissive look to Serena that still managed to convey some respect (I had to learn how to do that), and he escorted me toward the grand balcony.

"What was that about?" he asked.

"It's unimportant," I lied.

"What was that about, Silence?" he asked again.

"We'll speak of it later," I lied again.

He sighed.

Meaning he gave in...for now.

This pleased me, perhaps irrationally.

Thus, even walking, I leaned some weight into his arm.

"She is not to be trusted," he murmured his warning.

In my heart, I thought he was wrong.

But my mouth said nothing.

90

THE ANNOUNCEMENT

The People of Wodell
Grand Balcony, Southeast Corner, Birchlire Castle, Notting Thicket
WODELL

It was with deep astonishment that the citizens of Notting Thicket listened as their king announced his abdication.

Thus, there was stunned silence after Wilmer stepped away from the edge of the balcony, their new king stepped forward, and the heralds placed amongst the crowd who repeated the royal words so all could hear had ceased speaking.

And then their True spoke his first words as their king.

"I stand before you feeling no joy that I assume the mantle of your monarch," he began.

The heralds spread these first shocking words.

"If I had come about this responsibility as is customary, that being at the loss of my father, I would feel the same way," King True carried on. "I know this for I come about this responsibility after the loss of my mother."

A sorrowful, but assenting ripple moved through the crowd at this sentiment.

"I fear you do not know," King True continued, "for she was so very loyal, so very wise, so very adept in her service to this realm, just how much my mother gave to all of you. What I do know is that she would be proud she accomplished that. That through quiet toil, and in some important instances, great sacrifice, her service to our fertile green land seemed effortless."

Another sorrowful ripple shifted over the throng.

"I also know she has taught me well. I will serve you in mind and in heart. I will vow to you that I will make it my life's work to protect, defend and better the circumstances of *every* being in my realm," True promised. "I will listen to you and I will serve you. And please, make no mistake about what I just said. I will not *rule* you. I will *serve* you."

A startled, but enthusiastic, feeling began to swell through the onlookers.

"And in that vein, you cannot have missed," True said, "that we have an enemy in our midst. I can assure you that all efforts will be made to keep the peoples of this land safe. I can assure you I, and my father, and my lieutenants, and my soldiers will use every power at our disposal to root out this problem and dispel it from our borders. It is with grave disappointment that one of the first proclamations I must make as your king is that we are at war. We are at war with a party that calls themselves The Rising."

True took a moment to allow that to be heralded throughout, and the reaction it caused to melt through, before he carried on.

"Their goal is to subjugate all to their beliefs. I *will not* allow that to happen in my realm. My people are *free* to think what they wish, say what they will, believe what they believe and worship as their hearts guide them. And I will stop at *nothing* to defend your right to do all of that."

At these words, in the front, a cheer broke out, and as they were repeated, this cheer cascaded in a wave all the way to the back.

True allowed it to die down before he continued.

"To that end, I will share now, if you are of this Rising. If you have aligned yourselves with these oppressors who wear a false mantle of devotion. Consider this carefully. For I decree Henry Carrington guilty of high treason against the Dellish monarchy and the country of Wodell. He was the mastermind behind a fraud perpetrated on the entire nation, and he was complicit in the assassination of our queen."

An agitated murmur moved through the crowd.

"Henry Carrington will thus be drawn, executed and quartered on the morrow."

Shock swept the citizens.

But True kept on.

"Those who raised their bows against my mother, after they're fully interrogated, will be publicly hanged."

People shifted on their feet in dazed surprise.

True kept on.

"Anyone who collaborates with this Rising will share this same fate. People who abet this Rising, if proved in tribunal, will be imprisoned in Crittich Keep for twenty-five years."

A low hum started amongst the onlookers.

"Anyone coming forward, however," True continued, "with usable information about this faction will be remunerated with five gold coins, ten silver coins and five pewter coins. Twenty coins. Twenty being the number of archers who took aim at my mother, our queen."

The hum escalated.

"I will remind you, my people, we are Dellish," True told them. "We are wise. We are loyal. We are true to our own. Thus, no matter what you hear, this Rising is acting on its own remit. It has no alliance with any other realm or religion. If any citizen of this land causes harm or commits foul against anyone or anything, including people or property, this will be punished. Information and known associations with this faction are to be reported to a representative of the crown. Anything else will be unacceptable and punishable by royal edict."

The buzz increased, as did the shifting.

"My queen and *your* queen, Farah, and I will be officially coronated after we rout this wickedness from our land. But in the meantime, we will serve you faithfully and tirelessly in all things, not simply this current blight that threatens our people."

The crowd took in their new king, his queen (incidentally, wearing a lovely forest-green gown with gold trim) with her arm dressed close to her chest standing at his right side. Their lovely Silence, queen of another land, standing at his left, her impressive husband at her side. Cassius of Airen, Elena of the Nadirii positioned to the King of Firenze's side. The King and Queen of Mar-el next to their new queen. Important personages from another continent altogether gathered as husband and wife on either side.

Their old king stood behind True looking as normal.

Hazy, confused and bored (all at once).

Even so, with all that was said, and all that now was, it was the most impressive thing any of them had ever seen.

And most of them had stood on the wedding parade route just the day before.

"We have suffered an egregious blow," True declared. "I mourn my mother as my mother and as my queen. Her loss will be felt, for my children will never know her. Her loss will be felt, for I cannot turn to her for what she has given me the whole of my life, great wisdom and astute guidance. And her loss will be felt simply because I loved her."

The crowd again grew silent and morose.

"But we are Dellish," True stated, his voice rising. "We are strong, and we are proud. No matter what, we carry on. And we will *carry on!*"

A bubble of pride started growing amongst the spectators.

"And as such, I will end with sharing from the heart that it is my deep honor to be your king. It is my destiny, but mostly it is my privilege. And because of this, you have my vow now until my last breath, I will serve you fair. And I will serve you..." He drew in a visible breath and then bellowed, *"True!"*

A shout began at the front and rose in strength and volume as it exploded to the back.

And it did not die down as True, their *king*, bowed *to them*.

The crowd grew frenzied when he turned to his new bride and touched his lips to hers only for him to pull back and her beautiful face, still tipped to his, warmed with her smile.

King True then nodded to his people, turned, tucked his queen's hand in his elbow...

And they strolled from the royal balcony.

91
THE END

Princess Serena
Stand Hall, Birchlire Castle, Notting Thicket
WODELL

"Of course that would be your decision," she hissed at her sister.

Elena appeared wounded.

But fuck that.

She was going with Cassius to Airen?

When their Sisterhood was under attack?

Melisse had been injured?

"I should have known you'd be one of those. One of the weak ones who'd grow addicted *to cock*," she spat.

"Enough," Cassius growled, and Serena's gaze sliced to him.

"You may lead her around by her twat, but not me," she hurled at him.

He appeared like he was preparing to attack.

Which meant Serena braced to defend.

But Elena put her hand on his chest and he visibly relaxed.

Disgusting.

The both of them.

Utterly pathetic.

"We can only wait long enough for a raven to return sharing Melisse's condition," Elena said. "And any further news from Mother," she went on with her ridiculousness. "A day, at most two. But you must understand why I have to go with Cassius to Airen and do it without any further delays."

"I think I've made it damned clear I *don't* understand," Serena retorted.

"I will be their queen," Elena repeated what she'd said earlier.

"You *are* Princess of the Nadirii," Serena returned.

Elena tossed out both hands, the exasperation in her gesture also suffusing her features.

"Do you think this decision was easy?" she demanded.

"Yes, though you've made the wrong one."

"Melisse would not agree," Elena shot back.

Serena went in for the kill. "You've no idea what Melisse would think, and won't, as you intend to abandon her."

Her words struck true, she saw, for her sister's pale face turned ashen and her body jolted with the invisible blow.

"This is getting us nowhere," Cassius cut in. "It's clear you understand naught but selfishness, and—" His words stopped when his eyes jumped over Serena's shoulder and his lips spread thin.

Serena turned and she felt her stomach tip.

Shite.

Nero, Cassius's man, was approaching.

She needed to exit this conversation and this location.

Immediately.

She turned back and caught only the fact that Cassius's eyes had narrowed on her.

Thus, her alarm grew, and she needed to do something about it.

"As usual, we'll never agree so there's no point wasting further energy on it. Thus, I'll bid you farewell and to enjoy your time in Sky Bay," she said to her sister.

"They're under *siege*, Serena," Elena retorted. "*Another* reason why their prince regent and his future princess must not delay in returning."

"Cass," Nero came up to their sides and broke into the conversation, as men, Serena had no doubt, felt it was entirely their right to do, "I received word from Mac I go with you, not Aelia."

Shite, shite, *shite*.

"What the fuck?" Nero finished on this terse demand.

"This is my decision," Cassius confirmed, but his gaze was on Serena.

She shifted her features at the same time shifting to leave.

"She's going to a fucking island across a fucking sea. When circumstances warrant, and I'd say these circumstances warrant, Otho and I are her personal guard. We've always been her personal guard," Nero stated. "And we've lost our brother. Which means now *I'm* her personal guard. Therefore, I'd like to bloody well know why I'm clearly no longer my princess's personal *fucking* guard."

"Because you killed Theodora's mother," Cassius declared baldly. "And Theodora travels with her."

"I'll leave you to it," Serena muttered swiftly.

"I'm sorry?" Nero rumbled disbelievingly.

"Serena shared with us in Fire City that you killed Tiana, Dora's mother," Cassius stated before she could make her exit.

"Cass, maybe now is not the time to—" Elena began.

"Fucking hell, you *cunt*," Nero gritted.

To her.

Serena's body turned to stone.

"Nero!" Cassius bit.

"By the goddess," Elena whispered.

"Why would you say something like that?" Nero demanded, again to her.

"I think our conversation begins and ends with the word you called me," she returned, her heart beginning to race for some inexplicable reason.

"I don't think it does, seeing as Theodora will be princess of my realm and I'm her for-all-intents-and-purposes new father's lieutenant, tasked with keeping all royals safe, a task I promised my sword and my life to, and your lie makes that impossible," Nero returned.

"Lie?" Elena was still whispering.

Serena tried to save her deceit, wondering for the first of any that she'd concocted why she'd committed it.

"With Trajan, you warred against my sisters repeatedly. You can't possibly know who you killed or did not."

"I disagree, since I've never killed a single Nadirii," Nero retorted.

The atmosphere all around them grew weighty.

Shite.

"Though I took issue with a prince I did *not* support warring against them for reasons I also did *not* support, and when forced into his service, the only thing I could do to share that was be a very poor soldier with absurdly bad aim with arrow, sword, dagger and fists," Nero shared. And he was not done. "Added boon, he was so disgusted with my service, he released me from it. That said, I'm rethinking my position about refusing to kill a Nadirii right about now."

"What you said was a lie?" Elena asked.

Serena turned to her sister to see Elena staring at her, stunned.

"Not to my knowledge." Another lie. "It was reported to me Nero brought Tiana low." And yet another one.

Yes, Serena was wondering why she'd instigated this deception.

Elena stared at her.

And then she breathed, the words dripping with hurt, "It was a lie."

"Elena—" Serena began.

Her sister's eyes suddenly glowed amethyst, something Serena had always hated, but in that unfortunate moment, she understood it was not hate.

It was envy.

And in that moment, regrettably, she saw that glow was rather arresting, although she bizarrely wished she was not the cause of it.

"You're *despicable*," Elena spat. "I can't even stand to look at you."

Her heart squeezed.

She actually felt it *squeeze*.

What on earth?

"Go about your business," Elena snapped. "I no longer care what you do, what you think, where you go. And you never gave me much reason to enjoy your company, but I shall refuse it until I can find some way to stomach the sight of you. Further, not that you care, I shall still inform you, even if I should manage to best that gargantuan feat, you've lost me. Whatever little part of my heart I held safe for you regardless you did naught to deserve it, it's lost. Gone. Never to be recovered. Mark this, not ever, Serena. Not...fucking...*ever*."

Sister stared at sister.

And another first for Serena.

She greatly wished she had something to say.

But she did not.

"I mean, truly," Elena whispered. "Using the loss of Tiana? And using...*Dora*?" she asked.

She did not expect an answer.

With that, Elena didn't even glance at Cassius or Nero.

She stormed away.

Serena turned to watch her go, her mind scrambling to find words to say, for all of a sudden, she couldn't bear the idea of parting with her sister in this manner.

But she remained mute.

For what she saw behind her, she felt the odd and not at all pleasant sensation of her clenched stomach entirely evacuating her body at the same time something depressed her chest.

And that something felt the size of an entire Nadirii treehome.

This was because Chu was standing there.

"Chu," she whispered.

"I fear you don't care you just lost your sister," Cassius said behind her. "But I'm seeing that matters not. For you're about to lose something that, to you, is even more dear." He then murmured, "Let's go."

"Cass, I'm not even close to—" Nero refuted.

"*Let's go,*" Cassius repeated.

Serena wasn't paying them all that much attention.

Her gaze was riveted on Chu.

Though she did sense Cassius and his man leave.

Her gaze still did not leave Chu.

When they were alone, he asked calmly, "Did you speak this lie?"

"I—"

"You spoke it," Chu declared expressionlessly.

She took a step toward him.

He lifted his hand her way.

She stopped.

"To hurt her. To hurt them. To hurt your sister, her man, their family, you spoke these words," he stated. "And you did it for no other reason than to cause harm."

"Please, let me—"

"This is our end."

At his decree, she snapped her mouth shut right before her body locked in an effort to contain an abrupt, excruciating, head-to-toe pain.

Chu walked away.

And he did not look back.

92

THE SPY

Tedrey
Go'Doan Temple, Fire City
FIRENZE

"You can speak in front of him."

"But, Fenn—"

"I will not repeat myself."

Tedrey sat next to his old lover—nay, his renewed lover, G'Fenn, ostensibly a Go'Doan priest, in reality a Rising general, and he did so quietly as he studied the priest standing across the table.

He was tight-faced and wished to be tight-lipped.

They did not trust Tedrey after the time he spent with Lorenz, the captain of Mars's Trusted, and knowing he still spent time with him, as he was living with him.

However, Fenn knew Tedrey, or thought he did, and as he did, his old/new lover had been easy to convince that Tedrey was still a devout soldier for the cause.

Or, more to the point for Fenn, a devout worshipper of Fenn's cock.

"We have received word," the priest before them said tightly. "Prince True is now *King* True and he's announced they will publicly execute not only our agent in Birchlire Castle, but *all* those who participated in the assassination of Queen Mercy."

"*King* True?" Fenn asked quietly.

"Wilmer abdicated," the man answered.

Tedrey sat still and watchful, and he did not hide he was the latter.

Considering this news, appearing watchful would not cause anyone concern as to why he was openly very much just so.

"This is unexpected," Fenn murmured.

"That's the least of what was unexpected, Fenn. For the birds take days to arrive and thus it is without a doubt that by now, our agent has not been executed, but drawn, *butchered* and quartered," the soldier spat.

"By Vicee," Fenn breathed. "They have not practiced that in—"

"Centuries," the man finished for Fenn, and Tedrey tried to recall his name, he just couldn't.

Too much on his mind.

He had to get better at that. Lorenz (and Faunus) had taught him that things such as names were important.

"The rest will be hung, if they have not been already. *And* True has offered a reward to anyone who brings forth news of our cause or those who have committed to it."

"We have expected that and prepared for it," Fenn dismissed.

"We did not expect and prepare for one of our most loyal soldiers and nineteen of our followers to find a humiliating death in front of the Dellish throngs of Notting Thicket," the man returned.

Fenn had no reply to this, and Tedrey could understand why.

Honestly, if he was still truly committed to the cause (something he now knew he never really was, he was blindly committed to Fenn), knowing what befell those men would make him reflect long about the depth of that commitment.

Execution in Firenze for traitorous acts was expected.

The same in Wodell?

No.

The barbarity of being drawn and quartered?

Absolutely no.

"I must think on this," Fenn muttered.

"They have several of our people here in Firenze that they've captured, Fenn. Not followers, *priests*. Our *own*. And they will walk into the pits. That is, after they're tortured, which they're being right now. Make no mistake."

"They will say nothing under torture."

The soldier seemed stunned. "*That* is your only concern? These men will lose their lives. *Our brothers* will *lose their lives*. They have five, that I know. They might have more. We've lost touch with them—"

"We did because they fled."

"They fled because we bungled the attack here in Fire City and further failed them by putting G'Seph in charge of them."

"And then they demonstrated they are weak and that their faith in our mission is unsound," Fenn returned. "No man who committed to The Rising should have given up so easily."

"Listen to what you say," the man hissed. Lacking patience when the conversation began, he was running out now. "If this is true, are you so certain they will not share under torture?"

"They know little."

"Pieces can be fit together, Fenn," the priest retorted. "The attack in Fire City failed, and all who participated in it are dead. Some of the priests who masterminded it are in the necropolis, waiting for Mars's return to be *further* tortured then executed. The assassination of Mercy succeeded, but the men who performed it will hang. However, they were captured, and they were not priests, so who knows what they will share under interrogation. The Enchantments did not fall and our losses there were grave. However, they took some alive, and no doubt the Nadirii are hard at work doing whatever they can to learn what those men know. And those bitches have *magic*. Rewards have been offered for information. If a few talk, and that leads to another few, and another, where will we be?"

He did not allow Fenn to answer.

He carried on to say, "And we don't even know if we continue to have access to our treasury—"

"Enough," Fenn bit.

But Tedrey was trying very hard not to straighten to attention in his chair.

Treasury?

What treasury?

"We cannot recruit if we cannot pay," the soldier informed Fenn.

Pay?

Pay who?

"We're done speaking," Fenn decreed.

"We cannot possibly be done," the priest refuted.

"For now, we are *done speaking*," Fenn insisted. "I must think."

"We must retreat, regroup, take stock. Like we did after we lost G'Dor.

What we *should* have done after our attack on Catrame Palace failed. But Seph pushed."

"Seph has been dealt with," Fenn reminded him.

"Not quickly enough. Now we must pause before all is lost."

"And perhaps we will, *if you give me time to think*," Fenn snapped. "Not to mention, I must understand what the others are thinking and that will take the time you ask, for we have to wait for bloody *birds*."

"Mars returns, and this is not good news for us. They have not forgotten." The man cast a meaningful glance at Tedrey. "They are sniffing about our acolytes—"

"The Go'Ella know nothing," Fenn reminded him.

"Are you so sure?" the soldier queried. "Are you sure they have not overheard anything? Are you sure no loyal soldier said something stupid during pillow talk? Are you? Because I'm not. At this point, I'm not sure of anything."

Fenn made no response.

The soldier looked to Tedrey.

"Do *you* know anything, considering you're so very *close* to the captain of the Trusted?" he demanded.

"I know what I've shared, what you've just shared," Tedrey replied. "That they have not forgotten. That they have already connected G'Dor with The Rising, and although they have no evidence, they are operating on the fact that we infiltrated their land years ago. They have five priests, I know of no more, and they are interrogating them, not waiting for Mars. Though, when Mars returns, they will walk to the pits."

"Other than that, you have nothing," the man stated his question.

"Other than that, so far, no. However, I do remain in his confidence, even if he understands why I felt the need to return to my faith. That said, he hardly shares with me everything they do to protect their realm."

"And he knows you're not of The Rising," the soldier pressed.

Tedrey faked preening.

"For some time, up to the now, I live with him, his wife, let him *fuck me*, his wife watching, and no. They think I'm a teacher and a priest. Nothing more."

"You're certain?"

At that, Tedrey faked annoyance.

"I'm sure, but even if he suspected, I've said nothing and *will* say nothing," Tedrey assured testily. "I want no noose around my neck. I want no pitch filling my lungs. What I want is our sacred gods revered throughout all lands. *I* managed to survive the last campaign. *I* managed to get close to the *captain of the Trusted Ones*. I am here. I did not flee. *I* withstood the abuse of our last general, and *still* I am dedicated to our mission. So, it would please me if *you* did not question my faithfulness. For it has been tested, *sorely*," he threw out both hands, "and here I sit."

He felt Fenn's admiring gaze but did not break his own from the man before them.

"With that, I think we're finished," Fenn decreed.

The man glared at Tedrey, he shifted his glare to Fenn, then he stated, "I'm on record as feeling we should hold, for a time, examine what has happened, what was gained, what was lost, and only move forward when we have a solid plan that has a much larger hope of succeeding than the last three."

"We killed Mercy," Fenn pointed out.

"To what gain?" the man asked. "I *still* don't know the point of that except to agitate a slew of Dellish *against us*."

Fenn at first had no response, and Tedrey knew why this was as well.

Mercy's death was Fenn's plan.

And if it carried on seeming as it seemed, faulty, it would be Fenn who would have to answer for it.

They couldn't possibly recruit more followers through assassinations and subsequent executions.

At least, not in Wodell.

Now, in Firenze...

"Mercy's death was meant to further destabilize that regime," Fenn muttered, not sounding as keen about that strategy as he once was.

"And instead, our agent was found out, Wilmer has stepped down, and we were counting on him to pave our way with his incompetent rule. Thus, in the end, what we've done is put a strong, *beloved* leader on the throne," the man pointed out.

"Again, that was unforeseen," Fenn returned through his teeth.

"A good deal has been unforeseen, Fenn," the priest retorted. "Too much. Those who follow us will begin to think we've no idea what we're doing. And frankly, I don't blame them."

The two men scowled at each other, but Fenn did not deign to reply to the soldier's last comment.

"I'm on record," the man repeated.

"So noted," Fenn sighed.

More scowling was shared before the priest sent them both a dismissive glance, turned and stomped out of the room.

Fenn sighed again.

Tedrey weighed his next words before he stated quietly, "He is not wrong to be angry."

Fenn's, "I know," came out on a resigned breath.

"Mars returns, Lorenz shared that with me," Tedrey told him something he'd already shared. "He should be home in but weeks. He's likely already on his way."

"Yes," Fenn murmured.

"We need cohesion, Fenn," Tedrey urged, ever attempting to appear loyal to the cause, but in truth, wishing to delay further offenses in the hopes of saving lives. "Our operations are in disarray. Perhaps a summit? The generals amassing to come to an agreement on a plan that can be carefully crafted before its carried forward?"

He kept his gaze keen on Fenn. His hope, in bringing up what he would say next, Fenn might share some things that Tedrey was not privy to, he dropped his voice and carried on.

"At the very least we need time to allay what are sure to be the fears of our followers, not to mention, recruit more. We've lost a good deal. I know not how many we have, but the loss in the attack on Catrame Palace alone numbered at least a hundred. I have heard murmurings about how those losses meant others in Firenze abandoned the cause. And that was *before* all that happened in Wodell."

Fenn said nothing for long moments before he replied, "I must send birds. And I must think on what I'll say in those birds."

He was not going to share how many followers had been recruited across the realms.

Tedrey felt but hid the frustration that nagged inside him.

Fenn's eyes were still on the door the priest had closed behind him.

He turned them to Tedrey.

"You may suckle me before you go back to your Trusted," he declared, saying this like he was bestowing an honor on Tedrey.

This, most of all, took much from Tedrey.

He had no desire to even touch Fenn, much less do that to him.

And this was worse, for the moment Fenn had seen the scars Seph had left on Tedrey, he had not returned the favor of release, further sealing Tedrey's understanding that he had decided irretrievably wrongly in his chosen one.

He thought Tedrey's fixation with him was such that he would accept crumbs, when Tedrey had learned that the giving and receiving of true affection was akin to being offered an entire, multi-layered cake.

However, he managed to arrange his face in a semblance of passion that Fenn did not see through before Fenn pushed his chair back and Tedrey took his knees between the man's legs.

As Fenn liked, Tedrey himself parted Fenn's robes and exposed his hardened shaft, dipping his head to hide his distaste for it.

He then began to take care of that unpleasant business.

He hoped Fenn would not read his hurry as he performed his task. But he needed to get this done.

He had things to report.

As much as it seemed a desecration, a betrayal, regardless of the fact that Faunus had demanded he do thus, he closed his eyes and thought of Faunus as he did this, for he needed to think of his warrior in order to be able to fake any kind of enjoyment in the duty.

When he was finished, he hid his gag as he swallowed and allowed Fenn to stroke his hair and then his cheek as Tedrey released his cock and looked up at him.

"Such a pity," Fenn murmured as he stared down at Tedrey.

Tedrey stiffened.

"Perhaps, some other time, I will...see to you in the dark," Fenn offered.

"I would wish this," Tedrey lied.

Fenn gave him a tolerant smile.

"Go, my Drey," he bid.

Tedrey tried not to appear like he was rushing as he did just that.

And he did the same as he made his way through the streets of Fire City to the home of Nyx and Lorenz.

He also did this knowing he was followed.

Lorenz and Faunus (*and* Saturn) had drilled into him a variety of skills regarding how to observe without appearing to be observing, how to sense someone was watching when they wished to appear not to be doing so...

And how to know when he was being followed.

He did not breathe easy until he smelled the honeysuckle that grew abundantly at the side of Lorenz and Nyx's manor.

Nyx greeted him as he walked through the back door.

She then proceeded to pretend she was not waiting anxiously for him to arrive, for Nyx very much did not like the danger he was putting himself in, and she did this by saying, "I'm off to spend some time with Zosime."

"She's off to cuddle and coo at Guard's new daughter, whom she has become obsessed with, and even though she wants one of her own, she seems to have forgotten she needs to be in her husband's bed to make one," Lorenz, who'd appeared down the hall, noted.

Nyx shot him a killing look, and it was Tedrey hiding his anxiousness, for it seemed from the moment he started his role as a spy, there was growing discord between them.

She then kissed Tedrey's cheek, slid beyond him and out the door, closing it soundly behind her without a farewell to her husband.

Tedrey looked to Lorenz.

"If I'm—" he began.

Lorenz shook his head and interrupted him. "It is not the first time I've done something that vexes her. I will be at her side the entirety of my life. Thus, I suspect it will not be the last." He tipped his head to the doorway at his side. "Come, let us have wine."

He then disappeared into the parlor.

Tedrey followed him.

There was already a carafe of wine laid out along with some bowls of olives and almonds.

Lorenz poured and they settled before Tedrey shared, "I have some things to report."

Lorenz leveled his eyes on Tedrey before he said in a quiet voice, "We are friends, and as such, I must remind you that you do not need to buy my attention or regard by providing information practically the moment you enter my house. We can chat, as friends, before you do what you perceive as your duty."

"I know, however—"

"With recent events, it has become even more clear with the lengths to which these insurgents are willing to go that you take a grave risk with what you're doing."

Ah.

The reason why Nyx was vexed with Lorenz.

From the beginning, she did not like Tedrey was intent on doing what he was doing.

However, now...

"This is my choice, Lorenz," he reminded his friend.

Lorenz sighed before he nodded that Tedrey proceed.

"They have a treasury," Tedrey announced.

There was a slight titch in Lorenz's eyebrows, but other than that, only the charged feel of the room betrayed his keenness for this information.

"Fenn and one of the soldiers of The Rising were arguing. It was mentioned," Tedrey told him. "Fenn seems open about discussions in front of me. However, he covered this quickly and did not allow it to be discussed. That said, not only was it mentioned, it was noted that they might no longer have access to it and something about not being able to recruit if they could not pay."

"The Dellish coin," Lorenz murmured.

"Sorry?" Tedrey asked.

Lorenz took a drink of his wine before he sat back in his chair and stated, "Carrington. The traitor counsellor to Wilmer. He's been stealing from their coffers for decades. They could not trace where that currency went. Carrington is likely now dead. If he's hidden it, and not shared its whereabouts, The Rising will not have access to it."

Tedrey nodded.

"And any crusade such as this needs funding," Lorenz continued. "Not to mention, for the most part, soldiers expect to be paid. Since learning Carrington was embezzling, we suspected it was for these reasons."

"Of course," Tedrey muttered.

"This is good, Teddy," Lorenz noted. "I can send communication to True. He can focus efforts. This mention means there's coin left. If he finds it before they do, he can return it to his realm's reserves. He can then start his reign with a success that will be popular and make him appear crafty, wise, resourceful and strong. Not to mention, not having coin, especially the vastness of what they had, will significantly weaken their cause."

Tedrey felt a thrill at this, a thrill that settled as warmth in his stomach.

He did not know Prince...no, *King* True. But Tedrey was Dellish from birth, and he was surprised that it meant something to him that his country and its ruler could grow stronger in some part because of what Tedrey had learned.

And if that coinage was found, it would be a blow to The Rising, possibly a grave one.

Yes, that warmth settled in his stomach.

"Faunus has requested to come visit," Lorenz drawled, overly casually.

His friend was very good at a great number of things.

He was very bad at matchmaking.

So bad, Tedrey nearly smiled.

Knowing he had to say what he had to say next, he did not.

"It is not safe. I'm being watched. You know this."

"I do," Lorenz agreed. "However, I am a general and he is a soldier. It would not be unusual he was to attend me at my home."

"Lorenz—"

His friend lifted his hand and dropped it. "If you feel it is a risk you cannot take, then I understand. But Faunus worries about you. I tell him repeatedly you are doing well, but he is deaf to the words. He wishes to see with his own eyes you're handling this as you are handling it." His voice dipped. "He cares for you, *amico*, greatly. You did not ask my advice, but I share it with you regardless. I would give him that."

Tedrey wanted to give Faunus that.

He wanted it very much.

But he needed to do what he was doing.

He had wrongs to right and doing something solely for himself was not the road to take to achieve that aim.

That said, if Faunus was worried...

"Perhaps, when I feel I have won over more than Fenn. I am not trusted by them, Lorenz. With the way Fenn stopped discussion about this treasury, I see I do not even have his full trust. They follow me. They watch me. They are not comfortable speaking in front of me. They are in disarray. There is discord and not a small amount of anxiety around the capture and execution of Carrington and the defeat at The Enchantments. Seph moved forward with a great amount of hubris, but it was Fenn's plot to assassinate the Dellish queen and attack The Enchantments as it was done. If I can ingratiate myself in this cadre in Fire City, as they plan for future campaigns, the information I would be privy to could be crucial in thwarting them."

"And if that should happen, you would be the first suspected," Lorenz pointed out.

"This is the risk I knew I took from the beginning."

"And it causes no harm to remind you that you're taking it, and further, that you can abandon it at any time and you still would have my protection, a place in my home, my family and my heart."

Tedrey felt his eyes get itchy.

In order to give him privacy to control his emotion, Lorenz looked away, bringing his wineglass to his lips, and muttering into it, "Just know that."

Tedrey had to clear his throat before he replied, "I do."

Lorenz took a drink, swallowed, turned again to Tedrey and inquired, "I wonder what that father of yours would think of you now?"

Tedrey's entire body strung tight.

"It is not the manner of a man what he does with his cock," Lorenz stated, finishing with, "No?"

"No," Tedrey whispered.

"You are more man than many men I know, Teddy. And most the men I know are soldiers."

To hide his increasing emotion, it was then Tedrey looked away.

"Let us see if we can find some food," Lorenz suggested. "I grow hungry and intend to end this enmity with my wife tonight and do it in a way we both will be most fatigued. I need sustenance."

With that, he got up, and raised his brows to Tedrey until Tedrey also rose.

And even if they both were not needed to perform this task, they both went to find a servant to order some dinner.

It would be much later, when Tedrey was abed, and he did not hear the noises of passion emanating from his friends' chamber down the hall, that he lit a lantern and did what he often did, what Lorenz had, some weeks ago, suggested he do.

Something, with the things he was doing now, he did nearly every night.

He opened the beautiful, leather-bound journal Lorenz had given him. He took up the lovely, silver pen Lorenz had also given him.

And he shared his fretful thoughts with the page.

93

THE CITADEL

Princess Elena
On the Seil Sea Outside Sky Bay
AIREN

"I think it's over," I noted when the deafening blast of cannon fire stopped and did not start again.

"I hope it's over," Finnie muttered.

"I do too," Circe said, shaking her head in such a manner it looked like she was trying to clear water from her ears.

Circe being *Dahksahna* Circe, the Golden Warrior Queen of the Korwahk nation of the Southlands.

We'd met just hours before we'd all boarded one of Aramus's ships and headed right back from where she and her husband Lahn had come from.

King Noctorno and Queen Cora remained in Wodell.

Lahn was, right then, where all the men were.

Up on the deck with swords at the ready in case we were boarded.

As far as I could tell, we had not been boarded.

The air was acrid with the scent of cannon powder. I could hear faraway shouts that I suspected were the cries of men who were aboard the ships we had (I hoped) sunk that were blockading Sky Bay by means of its only wharf, Twilight Harbor.

But there were no cries of men closer to (say, on our deck) that would make me believe anything but that we were safe, and we'd been triumphant.

I did not look through a porthole to ascertain if I was correct in this assumption, for we were in a cabin that did not have a view to the action (I'd already checked).

I also did not look because I was fuming due to the fact we were in a cabin at all.

I could use a sword, very well.

Finnie, I'd learned, was also proficient.

And Circe was known as the Golden *Warrior* Queen, for the goddess's sake.

That said, from the ferocious scowl her husband sent my way when I was arguing the need for the women to stay belowdecks (which I had to admit, was a scowl of a level of ferocity that caused a trill of trepidation to skim over my skin, and I didn't not feel such a sensation often), I did not fight Circe's quarter.

Or Finnie's.

Just my own.

I also lost.

"From what you've told us," Circe said, and I stopped lounging on the daybed in the cabin, fuming, and instead lounged on the daybed and looked to her (still fuming), "you face many battles. Perhaps it's best you conserve your energy for ones that are worth it."

"I'm sorry?" I asked.

Circe cast her gaze to Finnie, who took over.

"They are…I mean, the men in this world are…" She faltered as I adjusted my thinking to take into account these two had long been of this world, but they were not *of this world*. They were of an entirely different one that, along our journey, they'd shared much about.

Including fantastical stories about things called "cars," "computers," "smartphones," "sushi" and "fluffernutter sandwiches."

All of which they very much missed.

But love kept them here.

Love for their husbands and then love for the families they had made with said husbands.

And I was thinking, in my present mood, that was the most fantastical part by far of any of their tales.

"Well...*men*," Finnie finished weakly.

"They are men," I agreed.

"That is to say, they're more *men* than most *men*," she went on. "Yours included."

I stared at her.

She, also lounging on the daybed (as was Circe—Jasmine and Hera were outside the door, guarding it, and at least *they* were allowed to perform duties they'd trained since girls to do), leaned my way to reach out a hand to circle my wrist. She left it there, squeezing what I suspected she thought was reassuringly.

"You will, as the years pass, get super freaking pissed at him," she said.

To this, I blinked at her.

"As in, *angry*," she explained her strange vernacular, something she'd needed to do quite often during the few short days of our voyage.

"Right," I bit off, not surprised about that in the slightest.

"And you will, as the years pass, need to decide what is important and what is not. What he is simply being bull-headed about, and what actually means something to him. And you will come to understand something that is very difficult to come to terms with," she said.

"What's that?" I asked, curious even if I did not wish to be.

"That you will on a regular, but hopefully not frequent, occasion do things that will make him super freaking pissed...*at you*," she educated. "And he'll have a right."

"That's the worst," Circe mumbled.

I'd already, in a way, discovered this.

I said nothing.

"I don't know Cassius very well," Finnie went on. "But I've noticed the closer we get to his homeland, the more tense he becomes." She shrugged. "This might be that his capital city is under siege. It might be that dissidence is brewing across his land. It might be all that happened in Wodell. The way things are going in this place, it could be a hundred different things. But I get the sense he's tense...*for you*."

Now that surprised me.

"For me?" I asked.

"This country he's taking you to, *his* country, from what I understand it's not only not at all what you're used to. But much more, especially to him, you're in danger here," Finnie stated.

Oh dear.

This was very true.

"And he doesn't like it," Circe put in.

I looked to her.

This was true as well.

"I mean, like…he doesn't like it *doesn't like it*, as in, he'd go just about anywhere else happily, including knocking on the fiery gates of hell and asking if they'd let you two in to have lunch, instead of coming home. Coming here. But mostly, bringing *you* here," she carried on.

Completely true.

"And since he's in love with you—" Finnie began.

Wait a second.

"Hold on," I interrupted. "He's not in love with me."

This time, Finnie stared at me.

She then cast a glance to Circe, who was also staring at me.

Circe felt her gaze, looked her way, and they both stretched their mouths in expressions that were not lost on me.

"He's not in love with me," I reiterated.

"Um…okay," Circe muttered.

"Okay" meant "all right," I'd learned.

And in this instance, she didn't mean it at all.

"He really isn't," I said quietly. "He was married before. He lost her in childbirth. He loved her dearly and he still does."

"No doubt," Finnie agreed. "He's still fallen in love with you."

I felt my lips part.

"And knowing this, knowing he's lost someone before you, would explain a good part of why he does not wish to take you somewhere he thinks is dangerous for you," Finnie concluded.

"But," I whispered. "He's not in love with me."

They looked to each other again and seemed to come to some accord that I did not understand, and not simply because I was reeling due to the fact they thought Cassius had fallen in love with me.

Not to mention feeling equal measures of terrified and experiencing the bubbling of sheer glee at this possibility.

Finnie took my mind from these thoughts when she squeezed my wrist a bit tighter but held on.

"After we explained it to Aramus and Ha-Lah, we discussed this. Frey, Apollo, Lahn, Tor and among us women, all decided that the best thing we should do was to keep it from you." Another wrist squeeze. "All of you. Too much pressure, and you're all already under too much. More would not be good. But right now, I wonder if that's wise."

"I always wondered if it was wise," Circe stated. "I mean, I haven't been around them as long as you, but anyone can see it's already happening, or has happened, so what's the big deal?"

"I know, right?" Finnie said to her.

"Right," Circe agreed.

My voice pitched higher when I asked, "What are you two talking about?"

"The prophecy," Finnie answered on yet another squeeze, but this time she let my wrist go and sat back.

"The prophecy of us defeating the Beast?" I queried.

"That very one," she said on a nod.

"What about it?"

"It's not about alliances," Finnie said.

"It's about love," Circe said.

Love?

"It's always about love," Finnie noted.

"Always. People need to get that. It'd make every world I know, and I know more than most, a better place," Circe added.

At that, they both burst out laughing.

I wasn't quite sure I knew what they found so amusing.

Because...

Love?

"What do you mean...*love*?" I asked.

However, I would receive no answer.

The door flew open and we all jumped.

Cassius prowled through, looking in a record-setting foul mood.

Frey then came through, appearing relieved (yes, we had been triumphant).

Lahn came after Frey, and even though all the men were tall, he had to tuck his chin in his neck and even bend a bit at the waist to get in the door, that was how large the man was.

He definitely looked like he could be Firenz (or Airenzian). Dark. Forbidding. Big.

But he was all that multiplied by about fifty.

I was not surprised he was known as the most powerful warrior in the Southlands *and* the Northlands. Indeed, I would imagine many wet themselves before turning to run just being confronted by the idea of battling with him.

That said, he was ridiculously attractive.

Not as good-looking as Cassius (my prince's tattoos, shorn hair, those blue eyes, there was no compare).

But Lahn was not hard to look at.

Then again, neither was Frey.

"We dock," Cassius veritably barked, making me jump again at his tone and tear my eyes from my assessment of Frey to look at him. "The men will deal with distributing the supplies. We're away to the Citadel. Prepare yourself but do not concern yourself with your belongings. They will be fetched."

And with that, he stalked out.

I stared at his back and then at the open doorway he'd disappeared through.

Both Jasmine and Hera filled that doorway, Jazz with her head turned, undoubtedly glaring in the direction of the departing Cassius. Hera had eyes to me.

"Quickly, for I'm getting that if there are delays, his mood will deteriorate," Finnie said, and I looked to her, wondering how Cassius's mood could possibly deteriorate from where it was now. "Woman to woman, long-time wife to a sister who's learning the ropes."

The ropes?

"Have a mind," she continued. "This is not a question of your skill or abilities and what he feels about them or how you disagree about you using them. This is about where his head is at and that is not a good place. In other words, my friend," she leaned closer, "in choosing battles, this is one to set aside and instead channel your energies into looking after your man."

I studied her.

Then I looked to Circe, who nodded.

My eyes moved to Hera, who dipped her chin.

Jazz's attention was now in the cabin and even she indicated her assent, which was a shock (then again, her ongoing affair with Mac was getting serious, I'd noted, not to mention Cassius was not a man to dislike, when he wasn't being an ass, and she'd learned that).

I then took in Frey and Lahn.

Lahn just stared at me with his dark, intense eyes.

But I sensed he agreed.

Frey was the only one who spoke.

"My wife is no fool and our marriage remains strong over decades solely because of it."

"That's not true, my handsome husband," Finnie replied. "You've nurtured our marriage too."

"Only as taught by you," he returned.

Well then...

That was sweet.

"We best vacate the premises before they jump each other," Circe suggested to me, and it was then I felt the current between The Drakkar and his Ice Princess, not to mention saw the heat of his gaze on his wife, and I moved to exit the daybed, considering it was *their* bunk.

As I left the room, Jasmine and Hera positioned close to my sides.

"That doesn't mean going forth into that wasteland not fully armed," Jazz muttered under breath.

"Absolutely," Hera agreed.

I drew in a good deal of air.

And we all headed to Cassius and my cabin so I could prepare myself to meet this part of my destiny.

Fully armed.

But with a focus on the needs of "my man."

Dear goddess, help me.

Sky Bay was *not* a wasteland.

I noticed this immediately when I came up to the deck.

I noticed it more as I rode at Cassius's side through the black paved streets with my lieutenants and his men surrounding us so close, our legs and boots brushed.

It was austere, yes.

But the architecture was astonishing.

I thought the height and breadth and grandeur of Birchlire Castle was a spectacle, a visual feast. And when I had been there, I'd thought the golden domes and white-washed buildings and avenues of Go'Doan were a marvel, blinking blindingly clean and beautiful in the sun.

But everywhere you looked in Sky Bay was like that, and even more.

It seemed all of it, from the carvings in the black stone, to the domes and steeples atop the buildings, to the buttressed dormers, looming gargoyles, massive stained-glass rose windows, even to what appeared to be a colossal *working* clock atop a multi-storied building that looked like a temple (but Cassius had bit out that it was a bank), there was nowhere to look that did not hold some interest.

And in most cases...beauty.

It was true, it was not the beauty I was used to. The bright, sunshine dappling through the green leaves of The Enchantments or the rolling patchwork of Dellish fields and the quaint thatched villages there.

But it was no less beautiful.

Simply its own kind.

Indeed, even the thick, gray smoke drifting from the chimneys contributed to the overall mood.

Which, for some unknown reason, made me want nothing but a warm cup of something at hand where I was curled somewhere comfortable with a throw covering my legs, a good book in my hand and nothing on my mind but just *relaxing*.

As I would do on my deck in my treehome.

Or I wanted to be under the covers with Cassius, doing something far more active.

And these I did not feel were bad things.

But I would soon note, as we drew closer, the most beautiful of all, the beacon of this magnificence shone (in its way) from the Citadel that seemed carved (exquisitely) in the southwestern ridge of craggy peaks that surrounded the entirety of the city, making it somewhat of a bowl that had a break at the harbor.

Cassius's home, the Sky Citadel curved along its side of this range that guarded the Bay, and even from afar, I knew the iron crosses over the windows and hostile wrought notions shooting from its towers and fencing its battlements were extraordinary.

Honestly, I could not wait to get there and discover every inch.

I did not speak of any of this.

Cassius was clearly in no mood, and because of this, the rest of us adopted his mood.

But regardless, every turn we made, my mind was taken with something new to discover.

For instance, on some streets, right through the middle, were cut *waterways* on which narrow boats were shunted up (or down) as a way to transport people, and a goodly number of them, so that the streets of the populous city did not get clogged with horses and carriages (and all the congestion and smells that came from them).

And down another street, I witnessed some sort of conveyance. It took up one side of the street. It was long (it had *eight* windows down the side), was on *rails*, and seemed to be propelled by men pedaling large apparatuses at the back.

This, too, was a way to transport large numbers of people distances that would take a great number of horses, carriages, or a good deal of walking up and down (sometimes steep) avenues.

It was, no other way to describe it, *extraordinary.*

Even through this, it was not lost on me that the streets were not clear of people and the return of their king (Gallienus rode before us with his own guard) and prince after a time away and a return heralded by a sea battle could not have been missed.

But although it couldn't have been missed, it didn't seem to matter.

This was the only thing (at first) that made me uneasy.

For there were very few women and what women there were, were not dressed in finery, out for a stroll on an overcast day. They were dressed drearily, and in some cases tattily, busy going about doing what they were doing.

And this busyness seemed fretful, and in some cases, frantic.

They didn't stop to watch our procession (not the women, or the men). The women scurried on their way, heads bowed, but clearly paying attention, for they were careful to steer clear of any man who might need their share of the path.

And I did not have to watch long to see that any man, dressed finely or not, received right of way.

But the men, they might glance our way, but other than that...

Nothing.

What made that uneasiness start to shift to worry was when my wonder at my surroundings began to wear off and the fact that I sensed there was absolutely no joy or even liveliness started to drift in.

Indeed, the air was void of it.

It was incredibly odd, especially in a place of such beauty, apparent prosperity and obvious ingenuity.

I did not, by far, expect it to be the happiest place on earth.

It was, after all, a city whose women rose up and slayed the men who were their masters, then fled to become the Nadirii Sisterhood.

But this was unexpected, disturbing.

Further, it didn't appear any of the citizens were suffering under siege.

No one looked haggard. And still, although the harbor had been freed very recently, there was no response.

There was no cheer that their monarch and his son were amongst them, had secured the harbor, the four ships docked there bringing supplies.

There were no jeers either.

Not even at the sight of me riding alongside their prince caused a reaction.

A Nadirii in their midst (actually, three of us with twenty more riding at our rear).

I received some glances, many (from men, obviously, the women didn't even look our way) baleful.

But other than that...

There was nothing.

Yes, this was troubling.

When we finally made it to the tall, austere iron gates that guarded the switchbacked lane that led up to the Citadel, all my admiration at all that was Sky Bay had leaked from me.

So much, I felt actually drained.

I wanted to race up the jagged lane, drag Cassius off his horse, into that castle, be certain Jazz and Hera and Cassius's men made it in with us, and barricade the doors against that air, that mood, that atmosphere.

And then take Cassius to bed, not for enjoyable activities.

To hold him tightly to me, absorb his strength, the depth of his need to protect (which had to be the depth of his ability to love, which was bottomless) and infuse him with anything light and sunny and cheerful and good.

Anything.

Even just a whisper.

He had often called his home bleak and miserable.

He did not mean the look of it.

He meant this.

The fact that the very air seemed permeated, heavy, even clogged with despair.

I did not race up the lane.

I had to stay alert.

There were soldiers, shoulder to shoulder, lining each side of that lane, wearing their black battle leathers and slate-colored wool mantles, staring at us under their shining black helmets with long, lethal-tipped lances pointed to the sky and held tucked to their shoulders.

We could be felled in a trice.

But not a one of them moved, nary an inch. I didn't witness one so much as twitch.

What I did was wonder why they weren't fighting the radicals that were laying siege to the city for that lane was long in its rise up to the fortress. There were easily hundreds of them.

However, they just stood at attention for their king and their prince, their leathers, lances and helmets pristine.

Odd and not a small amount of unsettling.

I noted Cassius didn't feel that way.

But upon glancing behind me, I saw Frey and Lahn, both visibly alert and openly taking in the lines of warriors, absolutely did.

At the top, dead center in a large, stately courtyard paved in smooth cobbles and dotted at the sides with some shrubs that were not pleasing-to-the-eye hints of nature in this dark stone landscape, but precisely trimmed in squat cone and pyramid shapes, sat an enormous fire pit that raged with orange flames.

Not a tinkling, peaceful fountain.

Perhaps it was an ode to ancient times when Airen and Firenze were one and they were ruled by the Fire King.

Perhaps it was once a fountain, but some ruler along the years preferred something threatening and severe, not welcoming and tranquil.

I did not have the chance to ask after this (not that I would). I also did not have the chance to grab Cassius and drag him somewhere safe so we could hold onto any happiness we might have left lingering in our souls.

Out of the high, wide, arched double doors to the Citadel that were open (both of them), three women drifted down the steps that were lined with servants who also stood motionless, uniformed and at attention.

These were the only women I witnessed wearing what might amount to finery in Airen, though I vowed to my goddess I would never wear such.

Thick, leather, what only could be described as *engineered* corsets over silk blouses confined their ribs. The blouses were buttoned all the way to their throats, the collars stiff and uncomfortable-looking. Their skirts were wide and appeared heavy, with a variety of deep ruffles, bunches or ruching (or all three) that made them seem like they weighed stones and stones.

And their faces were painted to extremes. Thick kohl around their eyes, stark and unnatural red at their lips, white powder on their skin and clownish rouge at their cheeks.

Indeed, there was so much paint on their faces, I could not tell if they were aged sixteen or sixty.

They wore tangles of strings of pearls and gold chains that fell about their chests, dangled from their ears and bound their wrists.

This demonstration of wealth was not only ostentatious (most specifically because of the absolute lack of such adorning the women in the city), it also seemed more like manacles and yokes than gilding.

It was a shock to the system, for seeing it, I realized there was no color in this place. Not anywhere. Not here, at the Citadel, not down below, in the city.

No flowers. Even if it was late in the season, mums, sage, goldenrod, roses, sunflowers and asters still bloomed.

No colorful awnings.

No bright pottery or brightly glazed tilework.

There was not even color in the fabrics, not in the uniforms of the servants, not in the clothing of the women (the corsets were all in shades of brown or gray, the blouses white or cream, the skirts, black or gray).

My thoughts were turned when the women all rushed directly to Gallienus before he even dismounted and fell into such low curtsies, their skirts looked like pools of dark silk on the cobbles.

His wives.

All three of them.

Nearly prostrate before him with their heads bowed.

I felt bile chase up my throat and heard Jazz choke down hers.

"Welcome to my home," Cassius drawled, and I looked to him in alarm.

With one look I knew more than I already knew.

He hated it here.

Abhorred it.

And here we were.

Here *I* was.

And he did not want me here.

But here was also where he was raising his beloved daughter, his Aelia.

He did not want that either.

And I could now understand why.

I stared into his eyes, seeing the sky-blue was gone. They were dark as night and blinking with miniscule stars.

This, how they looked when he felt deeply, in the haze of passion or in a blaze of anger.

And looking into those eyes, I sensed something gathering along my spine.

Not my magic.

Something even more important.

Vital.

Fundamental.

I needed to save him from this.

I needed to save him and Aelia and Dora from this.

I needed to protect them from this nightmare, deliver them from it.

And the only thing I could do in order to achieve that was to transform it.

At first in mind.

And then in reality.

"It's the most beautiful thing I've ever seen," I only partly lied.

His chin jerked into his neck.

"The whole city. Those…I don't know what they're called, carriages on rails," I went on.

"Trains," he said.

"Trains," I repeated. "And the canals. And the rose windows. The steepled roofs." I looked up to what seemed like the interminable towers of the Citadel, doing so gazing past gargoyles in shapes of everything from lizards to bats to trolls to griffin to dragons to, well…gargoyles to see intimidating wrought iron finials spiking into the sky. "And this…" I searched for words. "It's just extraordinary."

It appeared my words only served to make Cassius even more aggravated, and he underlined this by stating, "Elena, do not lie."

"Right," I gave in a little. "So, I would hope in the spring you'd let me, or, say, some royal gardener plant some ivy, because really," I flung a hand toward the castle, "there needs to be more green and it'd look lovely climbing up the walls."

Cassius blinked.

"And a few more shrubbery wouldn't hurt," I went on gamely.

He simply stared at me.

"And I might switch the fire pit out to a fountain."

He spoke then.

"There's a vein of natural gas that feeds that flame."

"Oh," I mumbled, turning my eyes to the fiery display. I drew in breath, and with it fortification, and turned back to him. "Let us discover the inside."

He raised his brows. "Would you like to meet my stepmothers?"

Actually, I wouldn't.

I turned my gaze to the women who were all now on their feet, shuffling back, still with heads bowed, as Gallienus dismounted.

I looked to Cassius and chirped, "Of course."

As I had never, in my entire life, chirped, and Cassius had not known me my entire life, but he'd come to know me well these past months, thus, he knew that, his eyes narrowed.

I dismounted.

Hera and Jasmine, already off their mounts, instantly got close to me.

"Ellie—" Jazz murmured anxiously.

She was not an anxious person.

But even the strongest warrior would be infused by harmful feelings just breathing this Airenzian air.

"We're going to do this," I murmured back.

"Do what?" Hera asked.

"I don't know," I admitted. "But we're going to figure it out."

"Mm-hmm," Hera mumbled dubiously.

I couldn't be dubious.

I had to *do this*, whatever it was, and I couldn't wait until spring to do it by planting ivy.

I glanced at Finnie and Circe, who were approaching us accompanied closely by Frey and Lahn, and I gave the women big eyes.

Finnie's gaze jumped beyond me, where I sensed Cassius approaching, then to me and she nodded.

Circe just gave me a sour expression, but then again, she'd already experienced an Airenzian city, so she understood it was sour indeed.

Cassius took hold of my elbow.

I drew in another fortifying breath and moved with him toward where Gallienus was standing impatiently, not close to his wives, who all were lined up, their heads still bowed.

Had he embraced them, and I'd missed it?

Had he even said words to them at all after being away from them for months?

"My father's beloveds," Cassius said drily when we'd arrived at them. "The Ladies Royal, Horatia, Cornelia and Domitia," he introduced with arm extended and moving to each one as he said their name. "Ladies, my betrothed, Princess Elena of the Nadirii."

"My pleasure," I said.

Heads still bowed, they only nodded, and it was just Domitia who looked over her brows toward me with some curiosity, and I saw, from closer, she seemed the youngest of the three (by far).

"Speak when spoken to by a princess," Gallienus spat at them, and at his words and tone, I tensed.

Cassius tensed.

All our people who had gathered around us tensed.

"Do not do one thing that you do not wish to do or are not comfortable doing," I decreed sharply.

That got me all three pairs of eyes examining me (though they did this under brows).

Horatia, the oldest (I guessed), peered at me with some measure, and I assessed her instantly as a problem.

Cornelia was gazing at me with some surprise, but a good deal of reserve, and I decided she needed further assessment.

Domitia stared at me in shock (yes, even over her brows).

"And do not bow your heads to me. We are equals. We are sisters," I educated.

"You are a princess and they are—" Gallienus started.

"Queens," I finished for him.

I heard a gasp, presumably from Domitia, but nothing from the others.

"They are known as Ladies Royal. We have no queens in Airen," Gallienus informed me.

"My bride will be a queen," Cassius put in.

"Your choice, not mine," Gallienus said to him.

Cassius, as I'd noted he often dealt with his father, dismissed him and turned to the women who all still had their heads bowed.

"Elena told you to raise your heads," he said, his tone gentling.

"We obey the command of our king," Horatia announced, and both the women at her side shuffled a bit.

Yes, a problem,

Gallienus subjugated them.

Horatia ruled them.

"Then it's important you know that, during our travels, your king did not abdicate his throne, but he abdicated his authority and I am now Prince Regent, ruler of this land and this Citadel. So, when I tell you to raise your heads, I mean for you to *obey me*," Cassius returned in a much less gentle voice, and I suspected he spoke as such because he knew precisely what role Horatia played in this sick farce.

Both Cornelia and Domitia raised their heads, each wearing expressions that were masks of shock.

Horatia lifted her gaze much more slowly and her expression was composed.

Too composed.

She said nothing but her eyes were working.

Definitely a problem.

"And it's important to note, as Prince Regent, my intended will be Princess Regent," Cassius shared.

Domitia's mouth dropped open.

Cornelia's gaze shifted into the distance beyond us, her face frozen.

Horatia's eyes went slightly squinty.

"This will become official on our wedding," Cassius continued. "But you should behave as if it is official now."

Gallienus made a sneering noise.

Horatia looked to her husband.

The others looked toward the ground.

"And the wedding will be going forward," I proclaimed gaily, gaining all the women's attention. I forced my voice to remain light as I said words I did not wish to say. "So perhaps while Cassius discusses the state of Sky Bay and this dreadful siege, we can talk about happier things, like how the wedding plans are coming along."

"These affairs are handled by the steward," Horatia snapped. "*He* is seeing to the planning."

"Well, since I'm here now and it's *my* wedding, *I* shall be taking over supervising the arrangements." I was pleased with myself I got that out without gagging, and since I was on a roll, I kept going. "So let us all get briefed and after," I looked up to Cassius, "you can give me tour of your home."

"This is not going to work," Cassius said to me.

"What?" I asked mock-innocently.

He studied me.

Then he lifted a hand, his fingers curled in, but his thumb extended, and with it he stroked my cheek.

Another gasp (again, I suspected coming from Domitia), as Cassius murmured, "No, it will not work, my lamb. But it will at least be amusing to watch you try."

"I've decided to be married in pink," I proclaimed abruptly, sounding slightly strangled as I forced out those words. "Yards and yards and *yards* of *frothy* pink."

I heard Jazz make a noise like she was very much being strangled.

Cass just stared at me.

Then he threw his head back and roared with laughter.

I watched, stunned immobile at how beautiful he looked laughing, and how exquisite was the sound of his laughter.

He had not, not once in all our time together, laughed with that abandonment anywhere near me.

It was gorgeous.

Still doing it, he caught my face in both his hands, dipped his head and kissed me thoroughly.

I vaguely heard another gasp (also likely Domitia), but mostly I just smelled and tasted Cassius and his kiss.

He lifted away minutely and whispered, "Yes, it will be amusing to watch you try."

I smiled at him.

He shook his head, let me go, looked over my shoulder and queried, "The sergeant-at-arms is waiting to attend us to share his briefing?"

"Yes, sir," a male voice barked efficiently.

"Let us go," he sighed, looked down at me, lifted his hand again to glide his thumb along my cheek, and then he stepped away.

I instantly turned to the Ladies Royal and quickly claimed Domitia and Cornelia by linking arms with them, stating my preferences immediately, and casting Horatia into a position she was going to have to get used to.

No one ruled a sister.

Be they king or bully.

"Let us go, have some wine, get to know one another and talk about adventures and weddings," I bid as I moved them toward the doors.

As we walked, I sensed something even more unpleasant than the air we were breathing and cast my attention in the direction from whence it was coming.

There, I saw a comely maid standing amongst the other servants, staring daggers at me.

I did not have any experience with such.

I still knew why that emotion was aimed at me.

Cassius had had her.

And she was feeling proprietary.

Shite.

My heart pinched, my eyes locked with hers, and I realized Circe had been right, though at the time she didn't know how right she really was.

I had to conserve my energy.

For I had a number of battles on my hands

And none of them would be won with staffs and arrows.

I was not adept at the tactics that would bring these kinds of victory.

Nor did I have Melisse (who was, thank the goddess, upon news from the last bird we received, still with us) close to guide me.

I was on my own.

I was also (effectively) Princess Regent of Airen.

Thus, I was going to have to learn.

And do that quickly.

94

THE SUMMIT

Queen Farah

Queen's Dressing Room, Birchlire Castle, Notting Thicket
WODELL

"Sling."

At my husband's voice, my eyes, aimed at the mirror, shifted from watching Helga work at the laces at the back of my gown, upwards, to my husband's face as he approached me.

"I'll return shortly, my queen," Helga murmured, dipping, and then quickly, and silently, gliding from the room.

"True—" I began.

He stopped behind me, dropped his head and touched his lips to the exposed skin of my neck where it met my shoulder.

I fought a shiver.

His green eyes then lifted to mine in the mirror.

"I miss doing your laces," he murmured.

I did too.

I also missed him *undoing* them, and more, wished we had moved on to him undoing them for more purpose than to help me prepare for bed in order to sleep.

Before I could reply, he repeated, "Sling."

"My arm is stiff," I told him.

"It's healing," he told me.

"It's annoying," I shared.

"I can imagine," he replied. "You're still wearing it."

"I'm fine. *It's* fine. It's time to move it and—"

"Farah, three more days, and then we'll assess."

"One day," I haggled.

He smiled at me in the mirror and said softly, "Two."

I did not wish to wear that bloody sling two more days.

Yes, there was still pain.

But I'd examined my wound closely just that morning (and the morning before, and so on). The skin was knitting nicely. There was no longer any swelling. There was barely any redness. In fact, I could likely have the stitches removed entirely in two days.

And then, perhaps, I could do something I very much wished to do.

Consummate my marriage with my king.

I stared into my husband's eyes and saw the fatigue he could not hide.

He did not sleep very well on the whole. A soldier's lot, these terrors in the night that drove rest away.

But lately, since his mother had perished in such an ugly, quick, public way...

And I had been injured.

And Alfie had been wounded so severely.

And now, he was king, taking his throne in troubled times where he had to make terrible decisions.

It seemed he barely slept at all.

"Two," I agreed.

He put his hands to my waist, turned me, and I saw he was still smiling when he settled me facing him.

I rested my hands on his chest and was heartened by the softness that invaded his features, the contentment that faded the weariness in his eyes at my touch.

"Ophelia arrived this morning," he informed me.

"Good," I replied. "Did you see her?"

"I did. We spoke at some length."

"She is well?"

"She looks better than she did in Fire City."

"Good," I repeated.

"She brought many prisoners. They will be detained in Crittich Keep," he shared.

I nodded.

"However, that business sorted, she doesn't wish to delay. As discussed, she and the Nadirii will be launching a rescue effort to release the Airenzian witch, Fern, from her confinement. Thus, later this morning, we will have the summit. Her, her lieutenants, me, Father, Apollo, Tor, Rus, Tint, and the representatives of Go'Doan. However, she asked to speak to Serena immediately. They're talking now." He gave my waist a squeeze. "Do what you will this morning, but I ask you to meet me at ten o'clock in my formal study."

I was surprised.

"You wish me there?"

In return, he appeared surprised at my question.

"Of course."

"But, I—"

"You're very wise, Farah," he said over my words. "And I learned many things from my mother, one of the most important being, if you have wisdom around you, no matter the gender of the person who wields it, you utilize it."

I veered closer to him, putting some weight into my hands at his chest.

"And you are queen, my queen, this country's queen, and as such, you will have a voice," he went on.

One could say Mercy and I did not have a very easy start.

And we did not have time to change that when she made it clear she wished to do that.

Even so, this was not the first time, and I knew it would be far from the last, that I wished she was still among us so she could witness what she had wrought in her son.

"I will be there," I promised him.

True slid his hands around to the small of my back, pressing my hips lightly against his, asking, "And what will you do in the meantime?"

"I will visit with Alfie."

He drew in a breath so deep, it pressed his chest against my hands.

"I will escort you to do that," he said as he released it.

"He will be happy to see you," I lied.

"Liar," True whispered.

I pressed my lips tightly together.

True visited with Alfie as often as he could.

With more time to do so, I visited with him more frequently.

What could heal for Alfie was doing just that.

What could not heal was the problem.

It was not that he was angry with True.

It was that Alfie didn't wish to see anybody.

True's gaze moved over my hair and face and down my gown, which was Dellish, thus heavy. A flaxen velvet with an embroidered trim in gold, red and green at the deep vee of the chest and the wide hem at the bottom. The sleeves poofed at my shoulders and upper arms but were dotted with pearl buttons down my inner arms from above the elbow to my wrists, these buttons closing the material tight against my skin.

I did not much like the heaviness of the gown, the tightness of the sleeves and bodice.

In this cold clime, I did like the warmth of it.

And I very much liked the belt at my waist made of square, golden disks and the silk underskirts of a warm olive green felt lovely on my legs.

Therefore, I focused on those last.

"I…" I hesitated, drifting a hand in the direction of my hair, which was free, something I had noted nearly everywhere was not the fashion of the Dellish, before I finished, "Don't really know."

True chuckled and called, "Helga!"

Mercy's maid, now my maid, who was offered this position by True, and took it, though I was not certain she did so for any reason outside her need for employment, came bustling in.

I watched her covertly as True shifted to my side and asked, "Is my wife ready to face the day?"

"I…her…um…" she stammered, her attention acute on his face in a manner it was clear she didn't want to turn it to me. "Yes," she concluded, but it sounded like a guess.

"True," I called quietly, my gaze to my maid. "Will you give us a moment?"

I felt him look at me, but I didn't take my eyes from Helga.

"Of course," he murmured.

Only then did I tip my head back, fortunately just in time for him to touch his lips to mine.

He left us, entering our chamber and closing the door behind him.

I faced Helga.

"Am I ready to face the day?" I repeated my husband's question.

"Yes, of course, Your Grace," she answered.

I did not believe her, and I determined it was time to do something about this.

Therefore, I set about doing that.

"I speak sincerely when I say that I do not wish to hear what you think I wish to hear. I wish to hear your honest answer to whether or not I'm ready to face the day," I said carefully.

She fidgeted.

"I know you loved her," I announced.

Her eyes widened.

"I know you grieve her," I continued.

She clasped her hands in front of her and held them tightly.

"I will never replace her. That would be impossible. There was only one Queen Mercy for this land, and for you, in your heart," I went on.

I took a step toward her and kept speaking.

"But I would wish that you and I could build our own rapport, over time. That you would trust me. That we—"

"I would trust *you*?" she interrupted me, then immediately rushed on, "Begging your pardon, Your Grace."

"How about, in this room," I lifted both hands, "I am Farah and you are Helga, and you are free to say what you will, and me the same?"

She stared at me.

"You are a servant of this castle, a servant of your queen, and always a servant of your king," I carried on. "But we share many intimacies, you and I. I have no friends here. No allies. None but my husband and his men. I would be honored if you could find your way to being one of them."

She was silent, and she was this way for so long, I was about to open my mouth to speak in order to end this so I could get to my busy husband, when she blurted, "You did not flinch at the executions."

Oh dear.

"Helga—"

"I went. I watched. I watched *you*. Many did. And you did not flinch."

"In my land, we execute traitors," I said warily.

"In this land too. We hang them. Though I have never witnessed this for this has not happened in my lifetime. But Carrington..." She shook her head and whispered, "You did not flinch. You watched that entire sentence carried out and did not flinch, nor once look away."

"It is my culture that we deal severely with those who would endanger the king or his queen," I explained.

"I would have humiliated him," she suddenly hissed, leaning my way. "I would have walked him through the streets, naked. Allowing our people to throw excrement at him. Tear at his hair. Scratch his skin to shreds."

By the gods.

"The people," she continued. "They saw you watch without emotion."

Oh no.

Was she saying...?

"Do they think that I have some unhealthy sway over True and this is why Carrington met that particular end?"

I feared this, but I couldn't believe it to be correct, for as True suspected, the people had cheered the grisly entirety of Carrington's sentence *and* the end to the traitorous archers.

"No," she stated, leaning back. "His mother was murdered on his wedding day. His bride injured. His treasury sacked for decades. His father is considered widely to be an imbecile, and for some, that word is kind. Our land had been floundering for many years, the people felt it, and they did not like it. They thought it was our king. Now they know it was him as played by Carrington, which is not only no better, it is worse."

I could not disagree with anything she said, but she was not finished.

"There is much talk of the ships being built in the north, the men finding jobs there. It is sweeping the realm, how shepherds, farmers and foundry owners must learn how to raise more sheep, grow more crops, craft more pewter to load on those ships. There is hope in our land, for once, now True is our king. So, no. It would not be met with surprise that our new king showed mercy to a traitor, any of them. It is King True's way. But that would have been met with disappointment."

This was a relief.

"Then I don't understand why you mention that I had no reaction to the executions," I noted.

"Because my queen, my Mercy, my..." Her voice broke, and I held myself carefully in order not to go to her as the emotion ravaged her face. She drew breath into her nose sharply, straightened her spine, lifted her chin and finished, "My queen Mercy, she...would not...have *flinched*."

I felt my own spine straighten and warmth gathered in my chest.

"I miss her," Helga whispered.

"Of course," I whispered back.

"You should bind your hair," she said, still speaking quietly. "I will roll it so the back is long, but it is away from your face. It will be Dellish, but it will be lovely, and it won't take long."

"I would like that," I replied.

She nodded.

I moved to the door to the chamber, opened it, and poked my head through.

True was standing, appearing impatient, something he wiped clean the minute he turned his gaze to me.

"Fifteen minutes?" I asked. "My hair needs to be rolled."

His lips twitched.

"I'll meet you in your study," I told him, "then we'll go together to Alfie."

"I have work at my desk here, darling," he replied. "Take your time. I'll wait for you."

I smiled at him.

He tipped his head to the side before he turned toward the desk that was in the sitting room, off our chamber.

I closed the door and moved toward Helga.

I sat on the chaise.

She fussed about me.

"Our king appears," she began hesitantly, "tired."

"He does not sleep well," I shared unhesitantly.

"I can imagine," she muttered.

"It is all that is happening, but it is also a soldier's burden," I told her as she gathered my hair.

"I have heard of this," she murmured.

"I had not, and I cannot tell you how frustrating it is that there is nothing I can do."

She clucked and rolled my hair.

I said no more.

But I was pleased.

I'd never had a maid.

However, I was thinking I would enjoy this acquisition greatly.

And not simply because her hands in my hair felt *sublime*.

~

"There's no bloody point to it."

"How about you let me be the bloody nurse and you be the bloody patient?"

"How about you be bloody somewhere *else* and leave me bloody *be*?"

"You'd like that, wouldn't you?"

"Yes, since I requested it, one could take from that I'd bloody like it."

"Well, we can't always have what we like."

"Don't I know *that*?"

At these loud words emanating from the open door to Alfie's room, I looked to True, True looked to me, and we both hurried our steps to and through the door.

There we saw Alfie's nurse was at the side of the bed, a bed where the sheets were bunched at his hips, his long legs bared, and the nurse was maneuvering them, bending one at the knee, then pushing it up to straight toward the ceiling.

What on earth?

"Let me alone!" Alfie demanded, his voice just as loud, but thickening oddly.

"I...*oh!*" she cried, set his leg down carefully, this right before she jumped away from his bed.

They both noticed us at the same time, the nurse whirling our way, her cheeks blooming a deep pink, Alfie scowling down his body at us, both his hands darting to cover his groin.

Oh.

"This is fucking *joke*," Alfie growled.

I swiftly looked away, lifted my hand toward the nurse and suggested, "How about we let these men have a chat?"

She rushed to me, beyond me, and out the door.

I glanced at True, who looked in danger of bursting with laughter, something that heartened me greatly, for I had had a few chuckles from him since we lost his mother, but not laughter, before I ducked my head and left the room, closing the door behind me.

The nurse was pacing the hall, and I realized, embarrassingly (as there had been a number of them), in the days that had passed since the incident, I had not learned her name.

She was one of three who attended Alfie, the only one he didn't seem to be able to abide.

And now I was understanding why.

"I'm very sorry, I have not ever asked your name," I said to her.

"Bronagh," she choked out, still pacing, but she interrupted this to dip an awkward curtsy, only to take up pacing again.

I studied her a moment before noting, "I would assume, as you were given this duty, attending a personage as important as Sir Alfie, that you've had some amount of experience in your profession."

"I-I studied at the Go'Da. In the Dome City. I-I did advanced studies in the healing arts. And I," she swallowed...hard, "I've been at the Royal Service Infirmary for five years."

"So I would assume," I gestured to the door, "that has happened before. No?"

She ceased moving, her eyes floated to the door and she stared at it, not answering.

In fact, she stared at it seeming of a sudden caught in a daze.

"Bronagh," I prompted.

She started and looked to me.

"I fear, my queen, that I must ask to be released from my duties attending Sir Alfie."

I felt my brows inch together. "So, this has never happened before?"

"Not with...not with..."

She was unable to finish that.

"Not with?" I urged her to go on.

"A, uh...well, erm, not with...it isn't...that is to say..."

After what we just saw, I was worried Alfie would demand True leave his room, king or not, and do it quickly, so I needed this conversation to carry on, even more quickly.

"You can speak freely with me," I informed her.

Her eyes, huge in her face, a pretty face, with freckles, and they were pretty eyes, a warm brown, came to me.

"He's very handsome," she breathed.

I found myself yet again pressing my lips together, this time for a much different purpose.

I released them to agree, "Yes, he is."

"I have never really...that is, with any other patient I have not—"

"Been attracted to them?" I inquired.

Her cheeks reddened again.

I moved closer to her and said softly, "It is not a surprise you'd be attracted to an attractive man."

"It isn't appropriate I go on attending him if I have, erm...*feelings*. That is to say, these types of *feelings*."

It was me who was trying not to burst with laughter at her emphasis every time she said the word "feelings."

But I still managed to speak softly when I queried, "In your experience, has that happened with another patient before, Bronagh?"

She waved her hand in front of her face. "It is a natural reaction, for men, in some instances. And also natural for them to have their own feelings for the nurses attending them, and thus, such happens. It isn't real. It's something else. Simply physical. Or gratitude they are confusing with something different."

"Is this real, what *you* feel?"

Her face remained red, but her eyes flashed. "He's most irritating."

He probably was.

True tended not to be irritating, ever.

Mars, however, could be irritating often, and I'd noticed that this trait only served to make him more interesting to the gender not his own (though, whenever he was being irritating to me, I just found it irritating).

That said, it was a vast understatement that Alfie was currently not in the best of moods.

But of his three nurses, one of which was much older than him, the other was of the same age as Bronagh and also quite lovely, it was only Bronagh who he seemed to be irritating *to*, not simply being irritable.

I took a moment to consider this situation.

I then made a decision and shared it honestly.

"Alfie is important to me. I cannot say I know him well. He is a man who is reserved. I can tell you, what I know of him is a privilege and he's very important to my husband for a number of reasons, some of them quite personal, as they are good friends. So, what I will say next, you must understand, you are free to do what you wish, for I'm acting from a place of selfishness. But I feel you are the best person in this realm to attend Sir Alfie."

"It isn't appropriate," she whispered.

"I must say, right now, what has befallen Alfie, I do not care. He is a man of action. He does not see a life ahead of him worth living if he cannot carry on just so."

Stark fear struck her expression and her gaze this time shot to the door.

Right then.

With that, I knew I had made the correct decision.

Her attention came back to me when I carried on speaking.

"Therefore, he must be shown life is worth living for any number of reasons, including pretty fair-haired nurses with lovely brown eyes and beguiling freckles he finds most irritating because he, too, finds her attractive but he feels he can't do anything about it."

She blushed again.

I grinned at her.

Bronagh did not grin.

"He does not like me," she shared miserably. "He's always fighting me."

"He does not fight his other nurses."

Those brown eyes again grew round. "He doesn't?"

I shook my head. "I cannot say he jokes with them, for he does not. But he also doesn't fight them, curse at them or act stubborn around them."

"Oh," she breathed, yet again looking toward the door.

"What were you doing with his legs?" I asked. "For his other nurses have not done that to him."

She turned to me. "It is not common practice...yet. But my professor at the Go'Da, with injuries like Sir Alfie, with much evidence he is quite correct, including my work with other such patients, contends that exercising muscles a patient cannot use will keep them, if not strong, then supple, movable, toned." She shook her head. "If this is not done, they become stiff, the knee difficult to bend, and in the end, the muscle wastes away."

"Then you must carry on."

"He has feeling there."

I stared at her, my heart flipping in my chest.

"In his hips. Even his legs. I have touched his hips and he...he...winces. Not from pain. From me touching..."

"I understand," I murmured when she trailed off and did not carry on.

She then carried on.

"As the swelling has gone down, I've even noticed him flex the muscles in his thighs."

"By the gods," I breathed.

She shook her head swiftly. "Do not hold hope. Please, Your Grace. It would be foolhardy. His injury was severe. But it was low on his back. I do not think he will ever walk again. But I've known men who have had such injuries who regain some mobility in their legs. Control of certain functions. Important ones, my queen, for life and dignity. And he...he...there is some small hope, for he has those."

"Then you must *carry on*," I urged.

"The patient must help," she told me.

I twitched my shoulders. "Leave that to me. True and me."

More likely True, Wallace, Luther, Bram and Florian and *maybe* me.

But we'd see to that.

Absolutely.

"It is not to his benefit if I cause him distress," she advised.

"The kind of distress you will cause him, Bronagh, might be the only thing that keeps him alive."

She let go a gust of shocked breath.

"Please," I whispered. "It might take much from you, and I do not know how it will end, but please. For my husband. For Alfie. Please, do not give up on him."

It took her a moment to reply.

But I felt my shoulders slump in relief when she said, "I will do that for you, my queen, and my king and...and..." her eyes brightened, "for Sir Alfie."

I nodded to her and smiled. "Thank you."

"It is my calling."

I hoped it would be much more than that.

"Regardless, thank you."

Her gaze drifted to the door and she mumbled, "I hear he doesn't shout at his king."

"He shouts at nobody but fair-haired maids with beguiling freckles."

She could not hide the hope as her eyes turned to me.

And I could not stop my smile.

The door opened and we both jumped from it like we were doing something we felt guilty about.

True closed the door behind him and trained an evaluating gaze to Bronagh then to me before he said to Bronagh, "I think he needs a rest from...whatever it was you were doing."

She bobbed a curtsy and replied, "Of course, Your Grace."

"We don't curtsy in this castle any longer, Bronagh," True, apparently having asked after her name (so very True), reminded her.

"Right." She bobbed again and muttered on another blush, "*Gads.*"

True shot her an understanding grin before he turned to me.

"I'm sorry, love," he murmured, taking my elbow. "Alfie isn't up for more company."

"Of course," I murmured in return.

We started moving away.

When we were some distance from Alfie's room, True shared, "He wants me to sack Bronagh."

"Of course he does. He's determined to let this beat him, and I don't blame him. I could not imagine. What I could imagine is that I'd likely be the same. However, she's the only one of all of us who has the skills to make sure that doesn't happen."

"He barely knows her, Farah, and what he knows he shares he does not like."

"Hmm," I hummed.

"I'm sure you can understand that was humiliating for him, sweetling," he muttered.

"I'm sure the quick glance I saw was impressive, *il mia vita*," I returned. "And Bronagh undoubtedly felt the same way."

A short, sharp bark of laughter erupted from my husband.

"He is a man without the use of his legs, but he's still very clearly *very much* a man, and Bronagh did not miss this," I went on.

True let my elbow go only to slide an arm around my waist.

Though he did his speaking.

"You're being entirely inappropriate, my queen."

"Bronagh agreed, though I talked her out of that."

True stopped us both from walking and looked down at me.

"Pardon?"

"Let's see how this plays out, shall we?" I suggested.

"Farah—"

I curled into him, lifting my hand that was free of the sling to touch the tips of my fingers to his lips.

"He must be shown every reason to carry on with life. Even if it's bickering with a pretty nurse."

True wrapped his fingers around my wrist and pulled it down to hold my hand to the base of his throat.

"I worry this is a faulty play," he said gently.

"I fear in this instance, *caro*, we all, but mostly Alfie, have nothing left to lose."

Although he did not like the reasons behind it, my husband saw the wisdom of this, I knew it when he bent to kiss my forehead.

I would wish for the feel of his lips to mine.

But for now, I would take that.

He then turned me to his side, our arms still around each other.

And as such, we walked to his study.

"You must understand, our hands were tied," the Go'Doan priest said sharply.

"I understand no such thing," Ophelia returned.

"I am sorry what befell your lieutenant," the priest replied, fashioning his features into a semblance of the emotion he was purporting, something which was not lost on anyone at that table, specifically my husband, who I could feel anger emanating from.

True was not irritable.

He was also not quick to anger.

But this priest, called G'Aron, was a foolish choice for the Go'Doan to send to attend this particular summit.

Mars and Silence had left some days ago, after Mercy's funeral, after the executions.

However, he had left his mother, the relict Queen Elpis behind to sit in his stead.

Cassius had left his lieutenant, Severus.

Aramus, his man, Tintagel.

Serena also sat that table, looking both miles away and wishing to be anywhere but there, what she had been now for days, if I saw her at all (for most of the time, she was not in the castle, whereabouts unknown and unreported, though it wasn't my business anyway).

With Ophelia were her lieutenants Lucinda, Julia and Agnes.

King Noctorno of Hawkvale and Apollo of Lunwyn sat with us as well.

And the Go'Doan had sent two Go'En, their high priests.

G'Aron, who I assessed to be perhaps in his fifth decade on this earth (late into it). A man who was prideful and had clearly been given the directive to deny all responsibility, try to convince everyone the Go'Doan had nothing to do with this Rising and create as much distance as possible between the two.

And G'Ry, an elderly man, my guess being in his seventh or even eighth decade of life, who was quiet, watchful, often grunted unintelligibly when Aron said things I was coming to understand he didn't agree with, but who mostly looked confused as to why he was even there.

They weren't taking this seriously.

Then again, it was not their lands under attack.

Last, at the table was another priest, his name G'Liam. He was a man who arrived with Ophelia, not the contingent from the Dome City.

And he made it clear he looked upon Aron with great distaste, not simply the things he said, but whoever Aron was in the order of their faith.

Wilmer, I was not surprised to learn, had opted out of attending this meeting.

"But I will again assert the actions of these fanatics have nothing to do with the Dome City," Aron concluded.

"You knew from the moment G'Dor murdered King Ares this was an issue and you did not breathe a word to anyone, anywhere," Ophelia retorted.

I did not look at Elpis.

But Aron shot a vicious glare at Liam that promised reprisal, for Liam had shared this information with the Nadirii queen.

"If even a *hair* is harmed on his head, the Nadirii will ride through the Dome City and *lay waste* to your gold and white," Ophelia spat.

I felt True's attention shift from keen to critical at this assertion, along with my own and that of everyone at the table.

A Nadirii dropping the gauntlet for a Go'Doan priest?

Only then did my eyes shift to Elpis, who was staring at Ophelia.

She felt my gaze, looked to me and appeared astonished for a moment that she held it.

This was not a surprise. I had been cold to her after my own mother's death.

But now, much had been lost.

It was not time to nurse grudges and nurture rifts.

It was time to hold all that was dear as close as you could get it.

She was once like a second mother to me.

Losing my own as I did and all that came before, I did not know if we would get that back.

I just knew I no longer intended to nurse grudges and nurture rifts.

Her face softened as she read these were my thoughts before she raised her brows.

I bit my lip.

She tipped her chin nary an inch to share I should pull myself together.

I did just that and stopped biting my lip.

"We do not hang those who transgress in Go'Doan," Aron returned.

Oh no.

"We also do not slaughter them publicly," he went on.

True's attention was no longer acute.

It was infuriated.

I caught myself from reaching my hand out to take his.

But when I thought True would speak, instead, Noctorno did.

"I would caution you to remember that tragic events have very recently passed and there are those at this table who have suffered much because of them. There is no one here who believes the people true to your faith are behind them. That is not the issue. The issue is stopping those who are perpetrating these acts from doing anything further."

"Right now, for the Go'Doan," Aron retorted, his attention turning to True, "the issue is that we've received alarming reports that violence is freely being practiced against our priests here in Wodell as well as our followers in this realm. From children throwing stones at priests to our temple being burned to the ground in Ramsay. Thus, I must repeat my request that you send soldiers, as soon as can be arranged, to guard our sacred sites and keep safe the men who speak our faith but also tend to your ill and educate your children."

"And I'll happily do so," True replied casually, though I knew from a thread in his voice that there was nothing casual at all about this.

Aron appeared astonished and sat back, saying, "Well then."

"When you give me the names of all known members of this Rising in Wodell, Firenze, Airen, the Dome City or anywhere," True carried on.

Aron sat forward and snapped, "You can't possibly ask that."

"I just did," True pointed out.

"These men can be reconditioned," Aron retorted.

"From what we know, these men conspired to kill my mother, my wife's mother, Queen Elpis's husband, Ophelia's lieutenant, and at Catrame Palace, at the very least, my cousin, but with the number of attackers, it was clear their intent was to wreak havoc in the royal houses of five realms. And I know I don't need to remind you, three of those assassinations were successful, and one of them nearly so."

"So you wish us to betray our fellow believers by handing them over to you so you can butcher them?" Aron demanded.

"If it makes you feel better, you have my promise, and I'll sign my name to it on parchment, that they will be interrogated...*humanely*," True added this last when Aron opened his mouth to interrupt. "They will then sit tribunal, and if found guilty, they will not be executed, but instead take residence in Crittich Keep for forty years, or to their death, whichever comes first."

"I cannot sentence a Go'Doan priest to that," Aron spat.

"You fail to see," Apollo entered the discussion, "that you walked into this room after the cards have been dealt. You turned your back to the game at a time when you were the only one who knew it was being played and you held all the trumps in order to win it. In the interim, the rest were forced to the table. Now you've decided to enter it. Thus, sir, you not only have no cards, you most assuredly have no trump."

"I have human decency," Aron rejoined.

"The men recruited to this cause and killed in Fire City, outside The Enchantments, those hanged for treason here but days ago and those sitting right now in Crittich Keep were Firenz and Dellish. These people send you their sick. They send you their children. Or they are lost and alone. And through their need and their gratitude, they have been preyed upon, and in the end, used. Have you no decency to extend to them?" Ophelia asked.

"We have decency enough to extend safe harbor to Airenzian females who seek to escape their oppressors and we send them to you," Aron retorted.

"A need that will no longer be necessary as Cassius has been made Prince Regent and his first order of business is to free the females of his realm of that tyranny," Ophelia deftly rejoined.

Aron stared at her in amazement.

Apparently, that news had not yet made its way to the Dome City.

"Aron, my brother," Ry put in quietly before anyone else could say anything, "perhaps you and I can have a word outside the doors for a moment."

"We're in negotiations," Aron returned.

"I believe he missed the point of my trump comment," Apollo muttered to Noctorno.

Noctorno, who had requested I call him Tor, shook his head at Apollo in apparent disgust.

"But a moment," Ry pressed.

Aron's voice dropped. "I'll remind you of your remit here, my brother."

"I don't need reminding," Ry replied.

Aron glared at him pointedly, saying without words he felt he did.

"I would have a chat with your colleague," Noctorno advised, sitting back in his chair and leveling a contemplative stare on Aron.

"With respect to your throne *across the sea*, I don't even know why you're here," Aron said to Tor.

Tor opened his mouth.

But True spoke.

"He was asked *by me*. He is a guest *of mine*. In *my home*. Where *you* are *sitting*."

Oh my.

True was talking through his teeth.

I'd never heard him do that.

My hand veritably itched to reach toward his.

I looked to Elpis.

It was barely perceptible, but she shook her head.

I sat still.

"Hawkvale is now allied with Wodell in many matters," True went on. "King Noctorno is here as my counsel. He is *welcome* here. But it is Lord Apollo whose skills guard your temples, Aron, for he has sent his wolves, which he commands, to do just that. Therefore, we've noted a rapid decrease in reports of such issues at Go'Doan temples. Indeed, since Apollo sent his beasts, we've received not a one. Though it should be noted, he can also call them away."

Aron looked to Apollo.

True kept speaking.

"I would be careful of making enemies as you sit here trying to turn attention from the careless decisions of your leaders that have led to grave tragedies and loss of life. I have warned my people they'll be punished if they take their ire out on the Go'Doan, and if they are caught doing so, this will hold true. But it is not *me* who created this problem by not dealing with it. It is the *Go'Doan*. You forget we have been made fully aware that *you* have been fully aware that this has been an issue for some time. Indeed, since the death of *a king*. And you did nothing. Now, we all must clean up your mess and instead of arriving and casting your lot to share in that effort, you antagonize us and make demands."

Aron opened his mouth, but True was not finished.

"I would suggest you have words with your colleague. If you do not, this summit will end, you will be escorted back to the Dome City, and five nations will be forced to take things in their own hands without the Go'Doan having a voice in how we do that."

"I would ask you where G'Jell is," Aron, for some reason at this crucial juncture, demanded.

"I would ask *you* where G'Seph is," True retorted. "However, I won't, for I know. He is in Crittich Keep, without his hands, after being run down by the Nadirii when he attempted escape after he assisted The Rising in their mission to breach The Enchantments in order to burn them down. We've been told by prisoners he was a general in that cause. We *know* he was a high priest with much responsibility bestowed on him from the order of

Go'Doan. So perhaps neither of us knowing where G'Jell has disappeared to is good for Jell. For now."

Aron looked ill, his gaze shifting to Ophelia. "You took Seph's hands?"

"The Rising took his hands," True told him.

Aron now looked shocked. "They did?"

"They also murdered my mother as she sat in our temple on my wedding day. A temple where *I* worship, as did she," True reminded him. "Thus, it seems they're capable of a great deal of barbarity."

"But if Seph is of them, he's...well, *of them*," Aron pointed out.

True sat back and sighed, his eyes moving to Apollo and Noctorno.

"Why don't we let him chew on that for a while and take a break," Tor suggested.

I could use a break.

"Aron, during this break, I'd be keen to have a few words with you," Ry said urgently.

Aron was staring at the table, clearly thrown.

Ry rapped on the table with his knuckles and Aron jumped.

"My brother, a word out of doors," Ry prompted.

Aron finally saw the wisdom of this, rose, and the two Go'Doan left the room.

"I think we could get further if we conducted discussions while tearing their fingernails out by the roots," Elpis suggested, as any good Firenz queen would do.

I fought a smile.

Severus looked surly.

Tor, Apollo and Tintagel looked amused.

True grinned wryly at her.

I leaned toward my husband where he sat at the head of the table.

"Would you like me to order food? Tea?" I asked.

"We have water, my love, and if anyone needs anything else, they know how to pull the cord to request a servant," True answered.

I nodded and righted myself in my seat, turning to Ophelia.

"I hesitate to ask, but how is your lieutenant?"

"She's now in hospital and she's recovering," Ophelia replied. "She can speak and she's keen to get home."

"I'm glad for it."

Ophelia nodded to me then shifted her attention to True. "I must warn you, True, I not only tire of this, I have no time for it. By now, my daughter is in Airen and Fern has been imprisoned for weeks. The state of that realm is precarious. The Nadirii need to ride."

True glanced at her other daughter then her lieutenants and offered, "Would you like to leave a proxy?"

Ophelia turned to one of her women. "Julia?"

Julia extended her head. "My queen."

Ophelia gave a short nod and looked to Liam. "You will ride back to Melisse with a guard."

"I'll get back to her fine, Your Grace," he replied.

"You will ride back to Melisse with a guard," she repeated.

He also inclined his head.

Ophelia stood from where she sat to True's left and looked down at him.

"Serena may or may not sit this table, it is her choice. We have agreed another mission for her, True, but I must request you continue to extend your hospitality to her while she completes it."

"May I ask what this mission is?" True queried.

"You do not need to ask, she's been told to report directly to you," Ophelia shared.

True's gaze shifted to Serena, who still looked remote and, it had to be said, downright bored.

His attention went back to Ophelia when she spoke again.

"Ignore Aron. Work G'Ry. He has sense," she declared.

"He might have sense, but I fear he has no authority," True replied.

"Their error for sending a priest who would appear to be an elder who they have no regard for and think is just an arse in a seat that will make a new king mistake him for a person of note, thus doing their duty to a summit they have no interest in, for they're scrambling at home to look for ways to cover *all* their arses."

True's lips twitched again.

"He may have no authority to them, but they sent him," Ophelia continued. "Thus, he's their representative here, and as such, any agreements he makes hold."

"Of course," True muttered.

"Now I will speak to Sir Alfie and go," she declared.

True tensed at this declaration, and I did the same.

"Ophelia, I don't—" True began.

"Son," she said softly, "do you not think I have stood by the side of many a warrior's bed and explained to them there are mountains we face in this life that seem insurmountable, until we reach the peak?"

True relaxed, and I did as well.

"I will have a care," she promised, but she did not leave, and her gaze stayed locked to True. "Your mother was a great woman. Her loss is felt."

And with that, her two lieutenants in her wake, the Nadirii queen left the room.

I controlled my lip quivering at the same time felt that itch in my hand to reach to True.

I looked to Elpis.

She nodded.

Thus, I took my husband's hand.

His fingers closed tight around mine.

The door opened and I tried to pull away.

He disallowed that, and holding hands, we both looked to Ry, who stood in the door.

"It would seem we need to send birds," he announced. "I apologize for the delay."

"You have until tomorrow morning at ten," True returned.

"But, Your Grace, birds cannot—" Ry started.

True stood, and as he had my hand, I stood with him.

"Tomorrow, ten," he repeated. "Now we all have things we wish to do. We'll use the ensuing time to do them."

And thus, he guided me out of the room at his side, and I walked with as much dignity as I could with my arm in a sling.

Two (and a half) more days, and I could be free of it.

Two (and a half) more days, and that daily reminder of what befell us on our wedding day could be gone for me and for True.

Two (and a half) more days, and I could pounce on my husband and make him truly mine.

Two (and a half) more days, and I could share things with True that might exhaust him enough to make him sleep an entire night, but at the very least they would take his mind from things that weighed heavily.

Two (and a half) more days.

I couldn't wait.

95
THE ABYSS

King Aramus
Throne Room, Keel Castle, Nautilus
Mar-el

When the hinges of the tall doors down the long hall groaned in protest, Aramus, sitting on his throne atop his podium, had the desire to shout in frustration.

Along the journey home, he, with his queen, had drafted (and redrafted, and then again, and more) the language he would use for the changes he would be making in his realm.

And in doing so, he, with the encouragement of his queen, made one adjustment to what he had promised the rulers of the other realms of Triton.

That being, not only would bounden be released after five years of service...

No new ones would be taken.

Even by pirates.

This would not be popular for some, but True had been right, the time not only had come, it was long past.

Not to mention, regimes that allowed just that were breeding grounds for causes like The Rising.

And he would not have that in Mar-el.

Therefore, upon arrival, he was ready.

Thus, he set his secretaries to putting pen to paper, and he signed his signature at the bottom.

He then ordered the royal heralds ready to ride, for the bounden holders would be given advance notice to the changes in the law in order that they could begin preparations immediately for said changes.

He then had the paperwork drawn up to make just those changes in the law.

At the same time, Aramus sent ships to ports and soldiers across the land to provide presence, and if necessary, quell resistance when the letters were received and when the new law was officially heralded.

This had taken days.

It was now done.

However, in all of this, he had forgotten how it was when he was away on a long voyage and what he came back to on his return.

Copious missives, grievances, arbitrations, decisions that had to be made, orders carried out.

The good news was, although the last tidal was extreme, it did not cause significant or long-lasting damage, though there were two losses of life.

The bad news was, for the last three days, his arse sat that throne as his people came before him in an endless stream with a variety of complaints, concerns, and in a few rare, but exceptionally annoying cases, demands.

Through this, to the now, his men, save Tintagel, loitered around the base of his podium, already displaying impatience to get off land and back to sea, to some adventure, to anything but this ridiculous, time-wasting lunacy.

He had never liked this part of his role.

His father hadn't either.

His men didn't either.

However, in all that had occurred, he'd forgotten just how much they all found this trying.

Thus, he could feel his men, too, radiating exasperation when the doors began to open but minutes after Aramus had demanded everyone get out so they could have a rest from the incessant chatter.

However, when the heavy doors opened enough that Aelia could slip through, dancing, followed by Dora, who, even not of Elena's blood, had the Nadirii princess's economy of grace, and finally his wife entered, Aramus not only relaxed.

He found himself confronted with the only thing at that time that could set him to smiling.

His girls.

All three of them.

Three beauties.

Thus, he smiled.

"Uncle Aramus!" Aelia shouted. "I touched *a shark!*"

Aramus stopped smiling.

"You *what?*" Xi growled.

Suffice it to say, Aelia as Aelia was, Dora a budding warrior fascinated by those who had already bloomed, thus hero worshipping all his men, along their voyage, the two girls had earned themselves five new uncles.

Five new *protective* uncles.

"*A shark!*" she shrieked, as Aramus rose from his throne and walked to the edge of it to stare down at her as she arrived at the bottom and danced around his men, such was her excitement.

He then looked to his queen.

"Wife, explain," he demanded.

"It was a little baby one," she said.

He did not feel much better at this knowledge, even having it knowing she could likely communicate with the creature.

It was still an animal with animal instincts.

Undeveloped thus *unrestrained* animal instincts.

"It was caught in a tidepool," Ha-Lah shared.

"Yes, and we released it," Dora bragged. "It was *amazing.*"

It was in this moment, for the first time, he wished he had not encouraged Cassius to take Nero with him rather than sending Aelia's personal guard with Aramus.

He had felt Cass would need all his men about him.

And he had felt he and his men would be entirely prepared to protect them.

He had forgotten about his stubborn wife.

"As I promised my friend that I would give my life to protect those of his daughters," Aramus began slowly, his eyes locked to his queen. "I'd prefer not to have to explain why one of them got their hand bitten off by a baby shark."

"It wasn't going to bite us, Uncle Aramus," Aelia informed him. "I think it wanted to play with us."

"You promised Cass to protect us with your life?" Dora breathed.

Ha-Lah gave him big eyes.

Aramus tore his from hers, ignored what she was communicating, and looked down at the girl.

"Yes," he answered.

"Aramus," Ha-Lah murmured.

"He made you promise to protect us with *your life?*" Dora asked.

"Yes," Aramus told her, for he felt she should know how Cassius felt about her.

"*Aramus,*" Ha-Lah hissed, for she felt she should not be frightened, when that was not a concern as he'd let nothing happen to any of his girls.

"But...you're a king," she said.

"And you're a daughter, and when you have one, you'll understand which is most important," Aramus shared.

She stared up at him with her lips parted.

"All right, well, we came to save you from your citizens for a spell while we had luncheon with you, but if you're feeling unable to rein in the honesty, we should let you eat alone," Ha-Lah stated irritably.

"Perhaps *we* should have a moment alone," he suggested to her.

"Perhaps we should take that moment later, after dinner, when the girls are down," Ha-Lah retorted.

When the girls are down.

Would he and his queen have girls?

He'd like girls with her ringlets and those crystal eyes.

Therefore, he decided, they'd keep going until she gave him just that.

At least two.

Or, perhaps, three.

"My queen, I did not say—" he began.

"We'll discuss it later," she interrupted.

"Ha-Lah—"

"Don't worry, Auntie Ha-Lah," Aelia singsonged, dancing to his wife, taking her hand and tugging on it. "Nothing will happen to Uncle Aramus or you or me or the boys," she threw her other arm out to indicate "the boys," in other words, his men, "*or anybody.* I mean, Uncle Aramus is *the king of the seas.* And *you* control its *beasts.*"

Aramus's vision turned white.

"Shh, Aelia!" Dora hissed.

She'd told them.

And she'd told them to keep it a secret.

But...

She'd told them.

"Everyone out," Aramus ordered.

"Uh-oh," Aelia whispered.

"*Out!*" he thundered when no one moved.

"Let's go, minnows," Nav murmured, beginning to herd the girls.

Ha-Lah looked as if she was going to assist in that endeavor.

Therefore, Aramus stated what he thought was the obvious, his eyes pinned to her, "Not you."

"Uh-oh," Aelia repeated.

"It was a secret, dummy," Dora snapped under her breath.

"I forgot," Aelia replied.

Dora took her hand as they made their way across the expanse, and Aramus heard her mumble, "It'll be all right. Auntie Ha-Lah will make it that way."

Aramus was not certain of that.

"My king—" Ha-Lah began.

"In a moment," he gritted, turning on his boot, stalking to the stairs behind his throne, and by the time he was down them and arrived at his wife, the doors at the end of the hall were closing behind the others.

"They're girls," she said the minute the noise of the closing doors finished ringing around the room. "They're no danger."

He looked down at her. "I see I have failed impressing on you—"

"Husband," she said softly, leaning into him and putting a hand to his chest. "It is not an issue."

"Aelia shared it openly."

"Yes, to *you*."

"In a way she would do the same to anybody."

"And if she did it to anybody, she is young, those anybodies who do not know of what she speaks will not understand what she's saying."

"I see that is all right with you," he noted.

"I love that you wish to protect me, but—"

"*Sirens damn it, Ha-Lah!*" he thundered, and at his sudden loss of control, she dropped her hand and took a step away. "Mercy died before our eyes!"

"Aramus," she whispered.

"Do you not understand what is happening across realms?" he demanded.

"Darling—"

"Do you not understand, that at this very moment, there are bounden holders throughout our land receiving news they very much will not like and that they may wish to share that with me in unpleasant ways, doing that using *you*?"

"It will be fine," she assured in a pacifying voice.

"I know you wish me to believe that so I do not worry, and you are correct, it will be fine. But that will take *time*. And in that time, I must protect my throne. I must protect my reign. I must protect Cassius's daughters, my men, my citizens. But most important of all, *I must protect you.*"

Her face softened at his words, but she began, "I have power—"

"And Fern of Airen has power, and she's been abducted and imprisoned."

She opened her mouth to retort.

But Aramus was not done.

"And Melisse has power, but she was abducted and impaled with a unicorn horn."

It took her a moment to get there, but she eventually did.

"Perhaps I made a poor decision, sharing what I did with Aelia and Dora."

He was heartened that she was able to admit that. She could be proud and stubborn in that way.

But even if a part of him worried he should not push it, the stakes were too high.

He had to do just that.

"And as all my men, save Tint, were at the foot of my podium, what tidepool were you visiting, *alone* with two little girls?"

She did not quite hide her guilty look.

"Ha-Lah," he growled, so angry, he was unable to go on.

"It was on the castle grounds," she assured him.

"You go nowhere without a guard," he informed her.

Her brows rose. "In my own home?"

"In it, especially around it, I do not give a fuck. Unless you're with me or my men, you have a guard."

"Aramus, obviously as we were at a tidepool, I was close to the sea. I could—"

"I wasn't opening this up for discussion."

"We seem to have this conversation frequently," she snapped.

"Yes, we unfortunately do," he returned just as crossly.

They stared at each other.

Or, more aptly, she glared at him while he glowered at her.

A part of him, the part that loved her spirit, wished to soften his stance, or at least any ensuing words.

Another, stronger part of him, forced him to drive his point home.

"It is your lot as queen," he pushed.

"I did not agree to it," she returned.

He withstood that blow and retorted, "You did not, it is true. But then you did when you fell in love with me."

She looked away, the elegant sweep of her jaw and line of her neck tense in her anger.

He gave her the time it took to understand she had no choice but to concede that point.

She took that time, returned her gaze to him and nodded tersely.

But she asked, "It will always be this way, won't it?"

"I'm sorry, my love, but yes. It will. But I will point out, as it seems you haven't noticed, that it is not just you. I go nowhere without my men and they are my friends, my brothers, but, baby, they are also my guards."

He saw that had not occurred to her as the flash of understanding blazed in her crystal-blue eyes.

"All right, fine," she muttered her concession.

"It has been a trying day, you walked in with those girls, and there was nothing that could make me smile. Except you walking in, with or without those girls."

The anger leaked from her expression.

"Though it gives me great joy to watch you with Cass and Elena's daughters," he told her. "It makes me yearn for our own."

And that made the warmth suffuse her face.

She moved to him again, lifting both hands to wrap them around each side of his neck.

And only then did Aramus relax.

"I see you're becoming very adept at handling your quick-tempered, stubborn wife."

"You aren't quick-tempered and stubborn. You're independent and spirited."

She began laughing quietly. "Yes, I prefer those words too."

He grinned down at her.

A shadow crossed her eyes just as she moved a hand to stroke his beard.

"You do know," she said softly, "I will be fine."

"I do know that, baby," he whispered in return, "for I will make it that way."

She held his gaze a moment, before she nodded.

"Shall we have luncheon?" he suggested.

"Yes, let's," she agreed.

He bent his head to kiss her, his intention a light peck.

She came up to her toes and pressed into the kiss, thus it ended anything but a light peck.

They then strode to the doors with their arms wound about each other.

For his part, Aramus did this hiding his thoughts, which were centered on the fact he was rather rabidly concerned for his wife's safety.

This was, on the one hand, logical.

On the other, a quarter of Keel Castle's grounds were bordered by ocean, which was at his wife's command. But regardless, there was a dock, which was guarded on land and at sea.

The rest of the castle grounds were protected by a fifteen-foot wall, which was manned with soldiers. There was a gate to get to the lane to the castle that was staffed with guards and a portcullis to enter the courtyard that was manned by more. And the castle itself had yet another cadre assigned to it.

And there were a further one hundred in the guards' quarters that could come at any sign of trouble.

She was safe there.

She was safe in her home.

She was certainly safe by the sea, for she could make herself that way.

In foreign lands, that was one thing.

But as she put it, in her own home, was entirely another.

So why was Aramus so utterly terrified she was not?

He knew the answer to that, he was in love with his queen and times were rife.

He also knew there were other answers to be had, and he'd put it off, for a number of reasons.

But in times this rife, now that he was home, he needed to seek them.

From olden times, the King of Mar-el had a secret weapon.

It was just, due to its perils, he had to be very careful about using it.

∿

"I do not think this is a good idea," Ore said as Aramus dismounted at the neck of the abyss.

He looked up at his brother still on his mount and saw Oreti's eyes aimed at the opening, and they were not narrowed only against the stiff sea breeze.

He was not surprised at Ore's reticence. The abyss did not look welcoming. Indeed, the entire area was craggy, bleak and uninviting.

Aramus did not refer to that.

"No matter what you see, or hear, or feel, you do not descend this chasm behind me," he ordered.

"Cap," Xi murmured.

"No matter what," Aramus said.

"Who thought I'd want to be back in that throne room listening to landowners griping about fence placement disputes," Nis muttered.

But Bond dismounted.

Aramus turned to him.

"No matter what, Bond," he warned.

Bond got close and dropped his voice.

"My king," he began, and Aramus braced, for none of his men addressed him in this formal manner.

His next words explained it.

"As you are aware, I do with honor what my father did before me. I am in direct service to my king. And as I've taken up that mantle, it is my duty now to share what my father told me. This being that your father told him that if you were ever to come to this place, I should do what I could to talk you out of walking that path."

He said this, pointing to the narrow path that ran the side of the gorge.

"Rest easy, my brother," Aramus replied.

"The royal missives are being received, and thus far, there are no reports of unrest. With the end of bondage in the Southlands, which are known to be barbaric, and we are not, they must have known that this would happen here and be waiting for it."

"It is early days."

"True, but we are prepared."

"Bond—"

"And we began operations even before we left Wodell to ascertain if that Rising was attempting a foothold on our shores, and thus far, there's no murmur of it."

"This doesn't—"

"Aramus," Bond got closer. "The quakes have ceased. We have not felt one for some time."

Aramus understood his friend had to do this.

So, he fell quiet to let him do this.

"We all saw her murdered, my brother," Bond stated quietly, coming finally to the meat of the matter. "But if told Queen Mercy would die for her country, she would not have shirked that honor."

"She did not die for her country. She was made a martyr."

"Queen Mercy would not have shirked that either. The only thing she would have changed is not allowing her son to see it."

Aramus clenched his teeth, for he was right.

"We can keep her safe," Bond asserted.

He was now referring to Ha-Lah.

In a low voice, Aramus shared, "The Nereus men do not love like normal men love."

"Yes," Bond muttered.

"My father with my mother, it was legend."

"Yes," Bond repeated.

"My grandfather with my grandmother."

"Aramus, I know."

"It is the gods who bring them to us, it is the women who force the fall."

Bond fell silent.

Aramus had to choose his next words wisely, for his men did not know what was within that abyss.

Only the King of Mar-el knew.

And his heir.

"I can no longer go on not knowing what I've come here to know," he felt it safe to say.

"I wish you to rethink your ability to do that," Bond urged.

Aramus stood quiet and closed his eyes.

But all he could think was just how angry he became at the thought of Ha-Lah in any danger.

How much she chafed at that.

And how much danger the both of them faced along with all their friends.

Indeed, everyone on the continent.

He opened his eyes.

"I must descend."

Bond drew in an audible breath before he nodded.

"I did my best," he said.

"You did, my brother," Aramus murmured.

He then clapped his friend on the shoulder, and without looking at the others, he turned to the mouth of the abyss.

He was a large man, the path was narrow, the fall so far, he could not see the bottom, just hear the whoosh of surf all the way to the top.

But he did not hesitate taking his first step, or his next, or the ones after.

As his father told him, the farther he descended, the deeper the darkness that surrounded him.

However, unlike others, who, if they tried to take this journey, would eventually find themselves blind and either have to turn around, or end up falling to their deaths, he could always see the path before him, a magical light guiding the way of the king who was proclaimed thus by the gods.

But his father had not told him, for his father had never found reason to take this descent, about the sound of the angry sea at the bottom, and how, step after step, the volume increased, so as to become a din, a thunder, a *roar*.

And as it churned, it splashed, so much eventually the mist felt like rain.

Aramus was soaked to the skin by the time he could see the tempest whirling at the base. The water was agitated to the point it was all white, the chasm wide, the swirl violent, the knowledge immediate that if he should fall into that foam, he'd be sucked deep, perhaps his drowned corpse taken to the earth's core.

It was humid but chill, wet, dank, dark, and as he wound his way around and around the abyss, again and again, he wondered if he'd been descending ten minutes or if time had warped and he'd been gone ten years.

A man could go mad down here, he thought, just as he saw the lanterns.

Orbs of green and blue glass, glowing from within, perhaps twenty feet in front of him. They hung at odd intervals, and only very dimly lit what appeared to be a circular opening to a cave on the side of the cliff path.

As his father had warned him not to do, Aramus did not hasten his step. One stumble on this slick rock, and it would not be Ha-Lah who would be lost to him due to the fates.

It would be he who was gone forever.

Carefully, he made it to the orbs and stood outside their murky glow.

"It is I, King Aramus," he called against the crash of water behind him, feeling a complete fool.

"And it is I who receives The Head."

The Head?

"Enter, King of the Sea," the voice bid.

Dodging hanging orbs, Aramus did that, and even though he went through no door, the moment those orbs were behind him, the thunder of the swirling sea became naught but the sound of gentle waves lapping a shore.

Aramus did not like that.

He also did not question it.

He further did not like that beyond those orbs there was nothing but pitch dark.

He did not question that either.

"It has been long," a voice came from the shadows.

Aramus knew not how to respond.

Thus, he simply said, "Yes."

"Did your father tell you of me?" the voice asked.

It sounded old, but strong. Wise, but elusive. He could not even pinpoint from where it was coming.

And in those shadows, he could see not a thing.

"Yes," he repeated.

"So you know, you do not descend without peril. And you do not learn without sacrifice."

Shite.

"I know," Aramus confirmed.

"*The unicorn and the balls, the shadow and the cock, the sage and the heart, the crystal and the head,*" the voice sang eerily.

And nonsensically.

"May I sit?" Aramus requested.

"Do you wish to sup with your bride?" the voice asked.

"Yes."

"Then no, my king. I think your visit should be brief."

Aramus forced himself to breathe evenly, but deeply.

Then he began, "There is much happening."

"Oh, I know. I know. Know, know, know. I know everything, Sea King."

Aramus had no reply.

"So what do you give me to get what you wish of me?" the voice asked.

"What do you want?"

"Your first child."

Aramus took a step back, his hand instinctively moving to the saber at his belt.

"I see this is not to your liking," the voice noted.

"My father told me the sacrifice would be mine to make. That would be mine. But it would also be my wife's. You may require of me. You do not require of her."

A disturbing chuckle before, "And I see your father was thorough."

"Yes, he was. You are our secret. You are our protector. As such, you have my respect. And with that respect, I must share I do not have time to play games."

"Not I," the voice replied. "I have all the time in the world."

"I can imagine that would be a boon," Aramus muttered.

"No, my son, it is a curse. It is the worst curse of all. That and loneliness. Think of that, an eternal lifetime of loneliness."

"The kings would visit, if they did not have to sacrifice."

"The gods would frown, if they did not get their due."

"Are you a god?"

"I was."

Aramus felt his neck begin to itch.

His father told him of the riddles, the games. That you did not seek the seer without a vast store of patience. That you needed to guard against getting caught up in the enigmas, or you could be lost to that abyss forever.

And you did not seek the seer unless you were willing to pay the price.

He drew on his store of patience and asked, "Do you still have power?"

"If I did, would I be in this pit?"

"The Beast rises," Aramus told him.

"No, he has risen. He has visited the surface, but returned to his lair. Though he will come to stay. And soon."

At that, Aramus felt his chest seize.

"The dragons will be an interesting addition to that battle," the voice mumbled.

Indeed, even in this pit, the seer knew all.

"Do we prevail?" Aramus demanded.

"Is this what you wish to know, Sea King?"

"Yes, but most of all, I wish to know my wife will be safe."

"The mermaid queen."

Aramus stood stock still.

When he did, a sinister cackle rent the air before, "Oo, that surprise. So delicious, that one was free."

"Mermaid queen?"

"Ah, lovers," the voice said like a shake of the head. "So foolish. Ages pass, and they remain fools."

"My wife is a mermaid?"

"Secrets, secrets."

"Tell me, is my wife a mermaid?"

"You know, of all I have witnessed on this earth, the cruelties vastly outweighing the kindnesses, that is something I never did understand. How things so extraordinary could be treated so abominably. And it is everywhere. Do you know, on the parallel world, they kill *baby seals* simply so women can wear their fur?"

"Sir—"

"And they contain creatures in cages so that humans can gawk at them?"

"It would mean much to me—"

"Magnificent beasts who by rights have the breadth of the seas to call their own, they imprison in small pools and force them to perform as entertainment?"

Aramus shut his mouth.

"We do that too," the voice whispered. "We did that to the Mer."

"I know," Aramus whispered back.

"Cut them in half, hallowed out their fins, so they could be worn by humans of means on parade."

He didn't know that.

And knowing it, Aramus's stomach turned.

"Mermales slaughtered by the hundreds so mermaids could be captured, forced to reside in tanks and perform such acts on human males." The voice dipped. "Such debauched acts."

Aramus clenched his teeth.

"Triton and Medusa created them together. An act of love, was the Mer. A gift to this earth, their beauty, their brand of magic. And that was how they were treated."

Aramus had no words for there were none.

"This is why she hides."

Aramus closed his eyes and dropped his head.

She was a mermaid.

His wife was a mermaid and she had not told him.

"You are not being overprotective. You are the Sea King. You are sensing her specialness. And you are moving to shield it."

Aramus opened his eyes and looked into the dark.

"In sharing that, will you take something from me?" he asked.

"I am glad we are here for I prefer that to be a surprise."

Aramus had a feeling he would not like that kind of surprise, but for the sake of time, he didn't fall into discussing it.

"Will she be safe?"

"You do not wish to sacrifice what that answer would buy me."

"Will you keep our realm safe?"

"I have enjoyed our visit, Sea King. Do not end it by offending me."

"Your power has not been called on for centuries and you allude to being stuck in this place, unable to leave," Aramus pointed out.

"I will admit, in these troubled times, I do have concerns my power is a bit rusty."

And Aramus used more patience.

"The Beast—"

"Ignore the lore. It is faulty, magnified over the years in the mouths of tellers that are liars. His power is not manifest, it is insidious. But it is perilous. In other words, he is not what you think. Even those who think they can control him do not know all he is and all he's capable of. And he has allies. Ones you would not ever expect."

"What is he?"

"You have much to contend with before you concern yourself with him."

Aramus was quickly coming to the end of his supply of patience.

"You are not telling me anything I do not already know."

"And this, Sea King, your father could not know for he never deigned to attend me. You come with nothing and you leave with what I want to give you, no more."

"I would protect my queen and I would protect my people."

"Do you know the most destructive force on earth?"

"Tell me."

There was a pause.

And then, "*Water*."

Aramus made no response.

"Fire, wind, nothing decays, nothing rots, nothing sweeps away all in its path, like *water*. A fire can burn the trees covering a range of mountains, but not touch the stone. However, over time, the rains will beat even stone back into the earth."

Aramus brought matters in hand.

"I come here worried for my wife and my realm and those of all of Triton and I leave here with more reason to worry."

And reason to be infuriated with his queen that she had kept something so vital from him for absolutely no reason.

"And is this not something crucial I give to you, Sea King?"

It was vastly irritating, but he was not wrong about that.

"The payment too dear, I will not come again," he warned. "And you have given me nothing to earn due."

"I have given you everything you need to know."

Aramus did not see it that way.

Until he thought...

Water.

"She commands the seas," he whispered.

"She could sweep Sky Bay into the ocean on a whim," the voice replied. "You add to her the air, the fire, the earth..." the voice trailed away.

The air, Elena.

The fire, that had to be Silence.

The earth, undoubtedly Farah.

His heart grew light.

"We prevail," he stated.

"Evil has its own brand of magic and not one of you has faced true evil."

Aramus's heart no longer felt light.

"In all your might, all your magic, there is only one weapon you can call on, Sea King. You think you know it. You think you have it in hand. You think you can harness it. And that, my Head, if you fall into that trap, will be your downfall."

Aramus remembered what Frey had told him.

"Love," he said.

The voice did not reply.

"It is not us, the men, the warriors who defeat the Beast. It is the women who have the power. Our job is to protect them," Aramus surmised.

"Climb," the voice ordered.

"The couples are all falling in love," he shared, again feeling not mild relief.

"Ah, the arrogance of a monarch."

"What does that mean?"

"You are right. Love. Now leave me and climb."

"What does 'the arrogance of a monarch' mean?"

"That you think it is only you, and the others, and the alliances you make, and the emotion you feel for each other, who might defeat the Beast. There will be sacrifice, Sea King. But it will not be to me," he declared, and Aramus felt his stomach drop. "Now leave me and *climb*."

Without him moving his own body, Aramus found himself standing outside the orbs with the roar of the surf pounding in his ears.

It was only then that Aramus remembered the last of what his father told him of this place.

When he was ordered to climb...he *climbed*.

He turned, and eyes to feet, making certain each step was sure on the slick rock beneath him, he moved as swiftly as he could.

And as the magical light that guided his way started to dim, he did not hasten his steps. He put his left hand to the wall, trailing the stone, some of it coarse and jagged, biting his flesh, and he put one foot in front of the other.

And then again.

And again.

He did not panic as the light kept fading. Panic and haste were killers.

His father had told him, he needed his head about him when he approached the abyss, when he descended into it, when he spoke to the seer and when he left the abyss.

Like every king should be at all times in all things.

When a new light started illuminating the path, he allowed himself a moment to look up.

And saw the moon.

They had left after luncheon. His journey down the chasm was long, but it was not miles.

There should be no moon, not yet.

Time had warped while he was down there.

Even knowing this and how concerned his men surely were, he did not rush to the top.

He called out, "Ahoy!" but took his time, and when he saw his men standing at the edges, gazing down, relief swept through him like a tidal wave.

"Sirens-damn it!" Xi clipped. "You've been away hours!"

Oh hell.

Aramus cleared the top, thrilled to be on solid land, and Nav noted, "You're soaked to the bloody skin. What happened down there?"

At the same time Bondi asked, "Did you get what you were looking for?"

He did not.

But he got something.

He nodded to Bond, moving to his steed, and said, "Let us be away. My wife will worry."

He was not certain all she had to worry about, though in that moment, the thought of her worry (for she would be as she did not even know he was away from the castle) was outweighing his.

And as he rode across the black rock of his realm, he knew a part of him understood why she would hide.

It was simply that the other part of him, her husband, the man who loved her, did not.

He was buoyed when he saw Keel Castle in the distance, it's gray stone, ocean-blue tiled turrets, the swirls of colonnades cutting through the grounds leading to it.

He and his men rode around, heading direct for the magnificent gate which was fashioned of chalk-colored stone, much different than the rest of the castle.

It was a colossal five-story-high statue of a woman, her eyes black holes, the expression on her face impassive, her hair that hung all the way down to the ground carved long and thick with curls and waves, threaded with seaweed, kelp and coral.

Great fins swept out where her shoulders should be. Out and down, through her hair, pointing at each side to the gate that would be at her womb.

And at her chest was a pendant in which was a trident, the weapon of Triton, the sea god, her husband.

It was a statue of their goddess, Medusa.

Upon seeing them, the guards at the gate opened the doors and Aramus and his men rode right through.

After they rode up the lane, through the portcullis and the arched opening under the guardhouse beyond, into the cobbled courtyard, men who were no longer bound to service (for he himself had freed his own) moved forward to take the reins of the horses.

Aramus dismounted but he saw his queen racing out of the trefoil arched doors to the castle proper, her skirts drifting out behind her in her haste.

"Aramus! Where have you been?" she demanded as she ran down the steps. "You've been gone *ages*, and no one knew where you went. I've been worried *sick*."

He moved to her and stopped when they met, taking in her face, which was a mixture of anger and concern.

Her beauty was unparalleled, this was the sole reason why she was his wife.

But somehow, over the centuries, this had led to the kings of his realm to discovering sunken treasure for that beauty was small compared to the beauty within.

And she was mermaid.

"Well?" she spat. "I put two very anxious girls to bed—"

"You should have told me."

She clamped her mouth shut, her eyes rounding before they filled with fear.

She knew he knew.

His men filed around him, making their way into the castle silently, eyes averted from the couple, as the servants led their horses away.

He should not do this on the castle steps. It was the last place he should do it.

It simply did not seem like he could stop himself.

"What gave you any impression that you could not tell me?" he asked.

"Tell you what?" she queried in return, and he was not angry, he was also not *not* angry.

But at her question, he was beginning to feel *angry*.

"Do not," he whispered.

"We should go inside," she whispered back.

"I am very aware, most especially considering a conversation we had but hours ago, that *you* are aware of my intense desire to protect you."

"You did not know all I was."

He said nothing.

"Now you know, don't you?" she asked.

He said nothing, but he nodded.

"How do you know?" she inquired hesitantly.

"That is not for you to know," he returned.

"Aramus—" she began.

"I love you," he stated.

She gazed up at him, eyes again wide.

"Do you not understand what that means?" he demanded.

"I—"

"You could fall in a vat of boiling oil, your skin melted off, and if you survived, I would love you. You could fail to give me children, and I am an only child, my father was as well, the current heir to the throne a distant cousin. A young boy I do not know the man he will become, but I would leave my realm to him and have only you for my life, and I would love you."

"My husband," she whispered.

"And you are as you are, and *I love you.*"

In the firelight of the torches that lit the courtyard and doors of the castle, Aramus saw the bright of tears hit her eyes.

"And I have told you that, I have shown you that, and you did not trust me with this part of you?" he asked.

"I wanted to, but the longer I delayed, the harder it was to tell you for this very reason," she shared. "I did not know how to explain why I didn't, and I knew the longer I didn't, the more it would hurt you." She paused and finished, "And worry you for you desire so to protect me against, well...*everything.*"

Aramus did not reply because he *was* hurt.

He was also angry.

However, he could understand, for his Ha-Lah, this was not easy.

His queen said nothing either, just studied him apprehensively.

"There are more of you," he eventually stated.

"We—"

"Have legs," he interrupted her to point out.

"We developed the ability to...yes, have legs."

"And pass."

"Pass?"

"Pass as human."

She looked away.

"How many are there?" he demanded to know.

She turned again to him, but her gaze darted around the courtyard as she said, "We should speak of this inside."

"No one will harm you," he proclaimed, and watched her body twitch at his grand tone. "Not only because you are queen, but because if anyone harms a Mer, they will hang from a yardarm, their blood draining from their throats."

And yet again, her eyes grew round.

"You have the protection of the king, and when I say *you*, I mean you and all of your people," he decreed. "I will speak with Cassius, Elena, Ophelia, Mars, True, and I will demand that the Mer have protections in their realms and any who hurt the Mer will be punished severely. I cannot decide that punishment for another ruler. But if I do not feel it is enough, I will renege on opening passage of the seas *and* binding their citizens if they should try."

"Aramus—"

"And once we ascertain there will be no unrest due to the abolition of binding in this land, I will outlaw the hunting of whales and dolphins, squid, octopi and sea lions."

The bright of tears returned to her eyes.

"And after that has been established, and any revolt that might come of it quelled, we will reintroduce the Mer to our lands and our seas and they will be under the strict protection of the king."

"A-all right," she forced out.

"Now, how many are there of your people?"

"I do not know, but there are...quite a few," she answered. "The rest live solely in the depths of the seas, somewhere I've never gone."

He nodded.

"Aramus—"

He did not let her finish for he was not done, and he had left the most important for last.

"We will keep nothing from each other, not again," he declared.

"I hesitate to say this, for I agree with you, and I must share that it has been very difficult for me, trying to understand how best to tell you what I so wanted you to know. It becoming worse now, when you know, but it was not me who told you."

"I do not hesitate to say that I find it difficult to feel sorry for you, my queen."

"Yes." She nodded swiftly. "I understand."

"However, is that what *you* hesitated to say?"

"No, I simply..." She now shook her head. "You say no secrets, but you told me it is not for me to know how you learned about me."

"That is a secret that has been kept for centuries. Only the King of Mar-el know of it and only the King of Mar-el *can* know of it. It is not a part of me. It is not who I am. The knowing and not sharing of it does not put me in danger or hold something of import from you. My men know nothing of it. No one does. But me. And when we have our heir, he or she will know of it, for that is the only way it can be. And this is all I can and will tell you and it is not keeping a secret, my Ha-Lah. It is keeping a legacy."

She studied him closely before she nodded.

They then stood on the steps of their castle, staring at each other silently.

She broke it.

"Are you angry with me?"

"I am angry," he shared. "And you were right, I am also hurt."

"Darling," she whispered.

"But I understand."

Her shoulders sagged with relief.

"No more secrets, my queen," he said softly.

She nodded, her lips trembling, but she said through them, "Can I embrace you?"

"There will never be a time you cannot do that, so from this point on there will never be a time you should ask that again."

At his words, she moved the short distance that separated them, pressed to him and folded her arms around him, laying her cheek on his chest.

She held him tight.

Aramus wrapped his arms about her and did the same.

"I'm so sorry I didn't tell you, Aramus. I really wanted to. I'm *so* sorry I did not," she said into his chest.

He bent his head so his beard tangled in her curls and his lips moved against them when he replied, "It is done. Behind us. Think naught of it any further, my Ha-Lah."

She nodded, her cheek moving against his chest.

"Do I need to look in on the girls so they know I'm all right?" he asked.

He lifted his head as she tipped hers back and said, "Yes, though I believe Aelia is asleep. Dora is not. You worried her with what you said earlier."

"She should know Cass's feelings for her *and*," he stressed when it looked as if his wife would open her mouth to interrupt, "after witnessing the death of Mercy, know she's protected at all costs."

"She lost her mother, my love," she reminded him quietly.

"And thus, she must know that in times of strife, when danger lurks and much is uncertain, she will be protected at all costs."

"She is fond of you, me, the men, she shouldn't be thinking about losing any of you."

"In time, she will have no choice but to lose us all. The only choice all of us have is to hope that time is long."

Ha-Lah pressed her lips together.

"It is young for her to learn of death, of mourning, of how you heal but don't. Of traitors and plots and deception and danger. But she is a princess of *two* realms, Ha-Lah. And she is not five, she's eight. She's old enough to know."

"Aelia was there too."

"Aelia bounces through life in a bubble of cheeriness. Cassius has worked hard to build that around her. Nothing touches her and won't, until the time Cass decrees it should."

"I wish to say at this time that we will be discussing if eight years old is the appropriate age to share about plots and deception and danger when it comes to our children."

For the first time in hours, Aramus smiled.

His wife's face softened when she saw it, and he shifted her out of both his arms and held her with only one at her shoulders, turning her and moving them up the steps.

"I will look forward to this discussion."

"I'm thinking thirteen," she stated.

Aramus almost laughed.

He was not going to shelter any child of theirs, of royal blood, of *Mer* blood, until they were thirteen.

They would learn to be alert and cunning and prepared.

"We'll talk of it then," he said.

"When they're thirteen?" she pushed.

He started chuckling, doing it replying, "When they are *here*."

The doors opened for them and they passed through.

When they were shut behind him, and he was moving her to the wide staircase that wound about the edge of the central turret, the supports of the railings made of stone carved in lacy versions of coral, Ha-Lah murmured, "Thank you."

"I'm sorry?"

She stopped them before they took their first step and looked up at him.

He looked down at her.

"You had every right to be angry, to lose your temper and rail at me. This time, Aramus, you had every right. So, my darling, thank you. Thank you for not shouting down the castle when you had cause and thank you for understanding why I did something hurtful and foolish. And last, thank you for loving me the way that you love me."

In that moment, he did not want to check to see if Dora was sleeping soundly, and if not, show himself to her so she knew he was safe.

He wanted to throw his wife over his shoulder and carry her to their bedchamber.

But he needed sweet Dora to rest easy.

Therefore, instead, he simply bent his head, pulled his wife again into his arms, and he kissed her.

Thoroughly.

When he pulled away, and he knew she was of a mind she would not be averse to him throwing her over his shoulder and taking her to their chamber, he grinned at her and took her to check on Dora.

And then, he took her to their chamber.

96
THE CREW

Princess Serena
The Shanty, Notting Thicket
Wodell

Princess Serena, who had not bathed in days, and was wearing the rags of a dead woman, lolled in the crumbling doorway of a building that used to be a home, but time and neglect meant there was no door and beyond there was no roof.

She had a large, heavy, chipped jug of grog on the step before her, a ragged blanket pulled over her head, and her shaded eyes aimed across the alley.

There slouched a troll, a big one. She had not seen many in her lifetime, but of the ones she'd seen, this one was *large*.

He had a vague blueish-green tint to his skin, much of which was on display since he only wore breeches, boots and forearm shields.

He also had a mass of filthy black hair on his head, matted into ropes.

He further had a pronounced underbite, to the point his lower teeth were exposed, and that lower set, unlike the upper ones, had large fangs.

All his teeth were yellowed with inattention.

She worried this mission would last so long, without cleaning it, her hair would get the way of the troll's, and she'd have to have it all shorn off.

She then stopped worrying about that, for she could be bald. Scarred. Skin and bones. Hairless, sunken and weak.

And there would be no one to care.

Perhaps, her mother.

Perhaps, her lieutenants.

Perhaps, Silence and Ha-Lah, who, in the short time they remained before being off to the realms they essentially helped rule due to the men who doted on them, she had taught a few hand-to-hand defensive moves and some minimal skills with how to use a dagger. And both had been kind to her.

But not her sister.

Not Chu.

Never again her sister.

Never again Chu.

He and she had ended.

No.

He had ended them without allowing her to say a word.

As for her sister, since it had happened, it had often come to mind how Serena did not want what she had when she had it, but when she lost it, she missed it.

As she'd been doing, she forced her mind from these things and again took in every facet of that slumped, immobile troll.

As far as she knew, trolls did not leave Airen.

They did not go to Firenze because they detested the heat. Their bodies ran hot, this why the troll in her sights wore only breeches and boots even in the chill that had finally settled into Wodell.

They also did not wander into Wodell, unless by mistake (and this could happen, for they were not the smartest of creatures). This was due to a war centuries ago, when the fairies, pixies and gnomes united in an unusual alliance to drive them and their blundering, heedless violence and gluttony out in order to claim the green land for themselves.

And they could not breach The Enchantments as they not only weren't very clever, the Sisterhood forbade it for they were thoughtlessly destructive, quick to temper, did not know their own strength, and easily caused harm to human and charmed folk alike.

Thus, they resided only in Airen where many were captured and kept as pets whose sole purpose was not to receive affection from their owners, but to act as much larger and better coordinated guard dogs.

So why was that troll there?

She understood she was in the Shanty. And in the days she had been there, staking her claim to this crumbling doorway, being seen amongst the downtrodden, vagrants, criminals, addicts and lunatics, behaving uninviting, unfriendly, and faking being consistently drunk so they would not question her addition to the ranks, she understood that no one raised an eyebrow to a befuddled and constantly inebriated troll.

But Serena did not buy it.

She was noting a way about the Shanty.

A few left to go do jobs during the day, these jobs mostly being begging for money in the city, earning it for the sole purpose of buying drink or drugs (or both).

A few left to go to jobs during the night, these jobs likely nefarious or women and men who sold their bodies for the sole purpose of buying drink or drugs (or both).

The rest simply *stayed*.

Only the city guard came in, not frequently, but regularly, mostly to collect any dead. Those being the ones who had taken in too much *ashesh* or *koekah*, been too long at the drink, or perished of exposure to the cold.

The guard carted the corpses away, literally, in open carts, with no ceremony and no emotion.

And she suspected, but did not see, that they took them directly to the cess, which was adjacent to the Shanty, and dumped them in.

She could not think that True knew of the depths of misery in this place.

If he did, she had to believe he'd do something about it.

However, she could not think on that now either.

She could not think of True and his plans for his realm, knowing he was a man who would do something about this place, and how something settled inside her, knowing that. Settled for a land not her own. Settled knowing it had gone through an era of weak rule, but now found itself led by strength.

She could not think on Ha-Lah and Silence, off to their homes, the danger they were all in and how Serena would need weeks, nay, months, of training them so they could properly defend themselves if they were called upon to do so.

She could not think on how she could not fathom why she cared about that.

She could also not think on how it felt, spending time with them during the little she had. And even if they sensed all was not right with her, they did not goad her to anger or bitterness, as her lieutenants (and she had to admit, her mentor) would do. They did not press her to internalize it, feed on it, use it to make her a better witch, a craftier warrior.

They ignored it but did so seeming to endeavor to handle her with care, not knowing how to do that for they did not know her.

But they tried.

She could not think that if Chu had not ended things, if Elena had not been so hurt and angry she'd also ended things, Serena might have found...

Teaching Ha-Lah and Silence...

Their keenness to the task, their easy way of laughing at themselves when they did something wrong, but striving to do it right the next time...

She would have found it...

Fun.

She could not think on any of that.

She had to be in the now.

And in the now, she had to know.

She had to know why that troll was there, sprawled in the doorway, the area about him littered with empty bottles of spirits.

For his doorway was not crumbling, no longer the entry to nothing beyond.

His doorway was sturdy, with well-oiled iron hinges and a shiny-new lock at its latch.

And what lay beyond was dark, the windows boarded from the inside, and it was one of the few buildings in all the Shanty that was stout.

She sipped her grog, sparingly, for she'd not only had no baths, but also little food. She did this as Chu had taught her. She needed to embody her disguise, and in doing so, losing weight and being haggard, for doing this was much better than trying to *look* haggard.

Mostly, she spilled it upon herself not only to appear intoxicated, but the smell also assisted in her pretense.

There were many empty bottles around the troll. He belched often (and loud). He snored often (also loud). And he had a large, but dwindling, stack of crates filled with similar bottles ensconced in the entryway of the building. These crates, and the bottles within, full.

Serena often wondered if it was the building, or those crates, that he was intent on guarding.

But in the days since she'd claimed that doorway, wandering from it for spells, none of them long, and always coming back, it was rare she'd seen him take a drink.

Was he conserving, as his master had not come to visit in many days?

Or were those spirits a ruse?

It was time to find out, she decided.

Listing up, dragging the heavy vessel with her, protecting it as she'd seen others in the Shanty do, she began to approach him as he lay there sleeping (perhaps) and pretend she was checking his bottles for dregs she could consume.

However, what she wanted was to see if her movements would make him alert.

He was across and just down the alley from her perch.

She was not even halfway there when her jug was knocked from her hand.

It went crashing to the cobbles, splitting at the bottom, the grog spilling out.

"What—?" she snapped, but stopped speaking when the small, empty coin purse at her belt was snatched away at the same time something thudded in her back.

She vaguely noted the troll was lifting his head.

She mostly noted two gnomes laughing and sprinting away from her, one carrying her coin purse.

"Oy, scoundrels!" she shouted, for not a soul in the Shanty would allow their purse to be taken.

Definitely not at the sacrifice of their drink.

"Give that back!" she yelled.

Remembering at the last moment to make it cumbersome, stumbling a bit, she gave chase.

Down one alley and around a corner to another one, the gnomes' short legs moved fast, but not faster than her.

However, she started to feel uneasy for gnomes had other abilities to aid in escape, including the fact they could leap high and long. Further, they could swing with great coordination from vines, ropes or outcroppings, as long as they had something to catch or somewhere to land.

They could disappear over a rooftop in a trice.

And they were not doing this.

Had she been found out?

And if she had, were they leading her into a trap?

The charmed folk could (and had) argue for millennia, but one thing was certain. Whichever one was first in creation, the pixies, fairies and gnomes were more Dellish than the Dellish, for they'd been there far longer.

And they had their own gods they worshipped.

She could never imagine any of them being involved with The Rising.

She had a dagger in her worn boot and a strange star that had caught her eye in a shop in the Thicket. It was crafted of six short, sharp blades of steel attached seamlessly to an inner circle. She'd practiced throwing it, and she was not yet adept at it. However, she knew it would cause great harm if thrown correctly, for example, embedded in the back of a thigh.

A gnome was a small target she feared she did not have the skill to hit, and if she did, the harm that star would cause would be much more egregious than to a full-grown human.

But should this situation deteriorate, she had it in a pouch attached to her other belt that was worn inside her tattered dress, against her skin.

Both gnomes turned down another alleyway, and alert and cautious, Serena followed them at the same time scanning for possibly more who might be involved in this caper...or whatever was happening.

They went down yet another alleyway and she began to get concerned.

She had wandered the Shanty somewhat copiously, but she did not know it. Not close. It was not huge, but it was a maze. A mishmash of wynds and closes. She could easily get trapped in a dead end or so lost, it would take ages to find her way back.

The gnomes again turned, taking another alley, and Serena was wondering if she should leave it at the fact she gave chase, find another bottle of grog (for she had another purse inside her belt with some coin alongside a parchment signed by True that she could show to the guard at Birchlire to be allowed back in, no matter her state when she returned).

She didn't finish wondering.

The gnomes ducked into a doorway, disappearing inside an abode, and when she stopped outside it, deciding she was not going into those murky depths and wind up in a trap, a voice called out, "Princess Serena, you'll want to walk in here and hear what we have to say."

She stared into the depths just as a match was struck and a lone candle was lit on a table at the back wall.

One of the gnomes was standing on the table, the other one climbing the rickety chair at the side to do the same.

She did not move.

When the other one was also on top of the table, he turned to her and stated, "Approaching that troll would ruin everything we've been working to achieve in the Shanty. But worse, it might save The Rising."

At these words, she walked through the door.

The gnome that lit the candle lit another one beside it before he hopped down to the seat of the chair, then to floor and moved across the room, disappearing in the shadows.

"Close the door," the one still on the table ordered.

Serena was not keen on taking orders, or closing herself in with the unknown, but these were gnomes.

Not that they couldn't be dangerous in their own ways.

But they were known to act as spies.

Not to mention, there were very few charmed folk in the Shanty at all.

For unlike her kind, for the most part, theirs took care of each other.

Thus, she did as told, her hand wishing her dagger was not in her boot, but at her belt.

The room started to illuminate, albeit dimly, as the other gnome lit several candles along a mantel over a cold fireplace.

"I am Welbrix of The Doors," the one on the table said. He swept an arm to the one who was sliding down a rope attached to a hook in the mantel. "That is Galbdor, also of The Doors. You can call us Gal and Brix. We are spies for Prince True."

So they *were* spies.

Serena did not move or speak.

"And we think that troll guards the treasury of The Rising," he went on to state.

"This is what I think as well," she felt it safe to tell them. They were gnomes. They were also, as noted, spies. And finally, it was not a secret all gnomes (and charmed folk, and simply Dellish), adored True. "And thus, it'd be good to overwhelm that troll, breach that door, and put that coin back where it belongs."

And it would be good.

It would cripple this bloody Rising.

She knew it.

Her mother knew it.

And that was her mission.

She'd had a hunch that the missing currency was here, in the Shanty. True's people had been searching for it everywhere.

But not in the Shanty for no one went to the Shanty.

She'd worked toward that instinct before her mother made the Thicket for the summit, and instead of riding with the Nadirii, she'd been allowed to stay in the city to work toward seeing if she was right, or wrong, and in either instance, reporting to True about what she'd found.

"It would, but if we did that, we wouldn't be able to identify and gather the evidence to try and then convict The Rising recruiters that scour the Shanty for soldiers and now also search it for their coffer of pilferings," Gal put in after climbing back up to the seat of the chair.

She watched him make the table and stand by his mate.

When he did, she asked, "Recruit?"

"You're too focused on the troll, and you should be. He is a drunk, but he's functioning. If our guess is correct, he has been kept in his whiskey and food and promises of whatever it was he needed promised *by* the insurgents. He will not allow that door to be breached without a fight," Brix told her.

"Recruit?" she repeated.

"In the interrogations of the archers who sought to murder our queen, it was discovered that fourteen of the nineteen were enlisted from here," Brix pointed to the table, meaning the Shanty.

"They turn gratitude for treating their ill or offering opportunities to their children to allegiance to this Rising," Gal took over. "But that is dangerous and could leave them exposed if not handled delicately. Especially now, as rewards have been offered for knowledge of just this thing. In our last meeting, True told us there have already been nine arrests across Wodell of priests of the Go'Doan who've been reported on by the people."

Nine arrests.

It wasn't much, but it was something.

"However, they were smart enough to diversify," Brix went on. "Therefore, they recruit from places like this. The disenfranchised. Those who have nothing to lose, thus anything offered would be more than they could dream."

She hated this was clever.

For it was bloody clever.

"As far as we can tell, there are four of them," Brix shared. "Four priests that work the Shanty. They, like you, come in disguise. Perhaps at some earlier time, they were better at it, but in the now, although they wear rags and muss their hair, they wear good boots and they do not smell as if they have not seen soap for a decade."

Goddess damn it, once she'd spotted him, she'd been so focused on that troll, that door, its hinges, its *lock*, she hadn't noticed this.

"They haven't been discovered so they grow arrogant," she mumbled.

"Perhaps," Gal replied. "Perhaps it's that this area is not patrolled by the city guard or *any* guard, and their generosity, which we have observed is not much, but it's more than anyone here normally experiences...food, liquor, blankets, *koekah*, *ashesh*, *taibac*, smoke, they are grateful and would do anything. Or perhaps they do not disguise themselves too much, so the population of the Shanty can identify them as personages who can hold any promises they might make."

Serena found a wall and leaned against it, crossing her arms on her chest, her gaze never leaving the gnomes.

"And they're still at work even after True's announcements?" she queried.

Both gnomes nodded, but Brix spoke.

"Once we reported our findings to him, our king has sent in others, like you, but they are men here setting themselves up to be recruited by this Rising. If this is successful, it will be a way to understand their inner workings."

Thank the goddess, this was clever too.

"And that troll?" she pushed.

"He must be guarded, but as far as we can tell, and word has it from an operative in Firenze, with the death of Carrington, they've lost their knowledge of where their treasury is. We had not seen it, but I believe that troll, that door, and what lays behind it, was known only by Carrington."

Which could be why she had seen no one get near the troll.

"Until they find it as it is hardly hidden," Serena drawled.

"And thus, it needs to be guarded," Gal replied. "And he must not be approached. He must not be provoked. There might be others about, keeping an eye on the Shanty and doing it much better concealed, or searching themselves. We cannot bring attention to that door."

"Have you seen that troll with anyone?" Brix asked.

She shook her head.

"Has he left his post?" Gal asked.

She again shook her head. "He pisses by the door, and I would not round the corner of that building. There has to be a mound of his shite there."

Both gnomes curled their lips.

"He has also not been approached," Serena continued. "But it was not yesterday Carrington was taken. If Carrington was keeping him stocked in whiskey and whatever else he needs, by now, even a troll will become concerned Carrington no longer comes. Which brings another issue, for I've never seen him enter either. But if he knows what's inside, and hears his comrade is no longer among us, he might help himself. I've noted those in the Shanty don't concern themselves with affairs of state. They concern themselves with where they can find some *koekah* to sniff up their noses. I would not be surprised he does not even know of the executions. But Carrington not coming, he'll find out."

"Just what we need, more issues," Brix muttered.

"Or we could be wrong and he's just a drunk troll in a doorway in the Shanty," she carried on. "We need to know what's behind it or guarding it is a waste of time when we have none of that."

Gal looked to Brix.

Brix shrugged.

They both looked to Serena.

"We form a crew," Brix declared.

Serena felt a frisson over her skin.

A crew.

She and Chu had been a crew, of a sort.

A highly functioning one.

It was much more fun working something like this with him.

It was *much* more fun, returning to their lodgings after a day of working something like this and doing that with him.

Life was just much more...

Everything...

With Chu.

But she had lost him.

Through jealousy and hate, she'd lost him.

"One of us provides distraction, the others breach that building," Gal spoke into her thoughts.

Hmm...

She had a feeling she knew who would be the distraction.

"To keep my disguise, which I will need to do in case we're wrong, I would have to fight pretending to be unskilled and inebriated," she said. "Trolls are mighty, even when they're deep in their cups, and they don't know their own strength. He could harm me greatly. And trolls have cocks and he's a *he*. If I bring myself to his attention, he could want something else, and not giving him that, and I will *not* be giving him that, I would need to expose my skills to fight him."

"Can you pick a lock?" Gal asked.

She could not.

Damn it.

"You could teach me," she tried.

They looked at each other again, but neither shrugged this time before they looked to her.

"True wants men planted in their ranks," Brix shared. "We must wait for that. We cannot give any indication we know they're operating in the Shanty. Once we have men covert in The Rising, we can launch the operation to distract the troll and get inside."

"And what if The Rising finds this troll and his door before we do all of that?" she queried.

"Then we will have no choice but to tip our hand. In the meantime, you've established yourself here. You can help us patrol. We can divide the space, gather information, keep watch on the inhabitants, and meet here to share what we know and adjust our tactics, if necessary," Gal said.

"Team up," she murmured.

"Yes," Brix agreed.

Serena looked to the mantel with its five glowing candles.

She wanted a bath.

She wanted a bed.

She wanted a decent meal.

She wanted to know how her sister fared in Airen, if she was safe.

She wanted to know how her mother fared at all, for she'd seemed better, but Serena sensed that was borrowed time.

She wanted Chu.

In all of that, there was only one thing she could have.

"Do you know any news from Airen?" she asked quietly.

"Why would we care—?" one of them started.

"Her sister," the other whispered.

"Right."

"No, but we can find out."

She drew in breath through her nostrils and released it, looking back to the duo.

Two gnomes.

Her crew.

"He's become used to me being there," I said. "I need to return. I'll leave in the morning, ostensibly to find more grog. One of you can take over then. Instead I'll come here, sleep a bit and then patrol. Is there a pallet somewhere in here?'

"Over there." Brix pointed to the darkness opposite the fireplace.

"We don't light the fire, just the candles. People in the Shanty might have candles, but none have fuel. The windows are boarded. No one can see the candles. But they could see smoke from the chimney, and it would bring attention we do not want," Brix explained.

She nodded.

"We will get extra blankets," Gal promised.

She did not care.

She cared about nothing except crushing this Rising, then doing whatever she could to help defeat the Beast (should it ever arrive), and then going back to The Enchantments.

And with peace in all realms, she would train warriors in skills they would no longer need to use and...

That was it.

And that would have to be enough.

No war. No death. No fights.

No love.

Just...breathing.

"I'll get back," she mumbled, making a move to do just that.

"Are you all right?" one of them, she thought it Gal, asked.

She had always thought she'd been all right.

But she'd been shown herself in a looking glass and she realized she'd never been all right.

You could not be when you spent your life drowning.

Drowning in jealousy and hate.

Now she didn't have that to sustain her.

And she did not have the other, the other that she was given that was true sustenance. The kind that made you feel light and free, not burdened and empty.

The other being someone telling you sad stories under the moon in the desert or holding you at night when they slept.

Serena had been wrong back then.

It was not unbearably sad the lady of the chalk fell through the nothingness, alive and holding her dead lover in her arms.

Now she knew what was unbearably sad was having no lover at all for you lost him because of your own ugliness and spite.

She knew what was truly sad was having been given something, losing it, and then having nothing.

"I'm fine," she said, hand on the knob of the door.

"We'll look in on you in the night, and I'll find a way to signal that I'm taking over in the morning," Brix called to her back.

"And I'll get some blankets and food in for when you're here in the morning," Gal added.

They would get her blankets and food.

No.

She was wrong.

She did indeed have nothing.

Except, for the now, she had this crew.

It did not make her feel better.

But it was better than nothing.

She lifted a hand, opened the door, moved through it, closed it behind her.

And headed back to her doorway.

97

THE CONSUMMATION

King True

Bedchamber of Sir Alfie, Birchlire Castle, Notting Thicket
WODELL

"We now have eleven priests arrested," True told Alfie.

"Eleven is good," Alfie replied. "Are they in the Down?"

True nodded. "Being interrogated by Bram and Wallace." He felt his lips twist before he went on, "They learned much from Mars and his men, but they do not have the taste for it."

"Torture brings unreliable information, True," Alfie muttered.

"This is why Florian and Luther are interrogating them a different way. Though we do know they're of The Rising."

"And how is this?" Alfie inquired.

"They say naught but 'long live The Rising.'"

This time, Alfie nodded, before he asked, "And what from Go'Doan?"

"They still await a bevy of birds, sending them and receiving them. Ophelia is long gone. Apollo's wolves guard their temples. But in some places, their priests are prisoners to them, the people so agitated, they fear showing their faces." True shook his head. "It is not that there's naught I can do. I could send soldiers. And it leaves a bad taste in my mouth that I do not. But it is the only bargaining chip I have with them."

"No more temples have been burned down or priests harmed, they have something with these wolves," Alfie replied, and a softening came to his eyes. "You have to do what you have to do, True. And this you have to do."

True turned his gaze away and slouched into his chair.

He could not say he ever looked on with relish to the day he'd be king.

But if he'd known how tedious it was, how rife, there had been times since his mother's death when he thought he might have wished to escape it altogether.

Though if he'd done that, he would not have found Farah.

"News of Airen?" Alfie asked.

"Nothing from Ophelia. But upon return, Cassius wasted no time. He and a good number of men sailed down the coast, marched inland and attacked the besiegers from behind. It was not what they were expecting. Especially with Nadirii in their midst. They were trounced. Slán Bailey is now as populated as Crittich Keep."

"This might be a quick victory, but it will not be a quick fight," Alfie warned.

"I believe he knows that but now the focus is on freeing Fern and, well... the wedding."

Alfie looked astonished. "He's prioritizing the wedding?"

"He isn't, Elena is."

Alfie now looked shocked. "Elena?"

"Apparently she's keen to have done with it," True said, his lips twitching.

Alfie began to look amused.

And seeing his amusement, True's day, which was not better than yesterday, not worse, but not good, was made good.

"I can imagine she is," Alfie muttered, but stronger, asked, "Has he heralded he's prince regent?"

"Yes, after they brought down the siege."

Alfie said nothing for a moment before he asked, "That's it?"

"No, he also heralded across the realm the new laws pertaining to women and sent word that all gentry must disband their standing armies. He offered all soldiers released from local militia posts in the Airenzian army or preferential consideration for merchant ship crews."

"Well, all I can say to that is it is a bold move, not to dole out the bad news over time but to hit them with it all at once," Alfie remarked.

"Cass leans toward the bold," True replied.

"And?" Alfie prompted when True said no more.

"Nothing."

"No word?"

"No," True told him. "Nothing."

"They prepare to strike," Alfie murmured.

"Indeed," True agreed.

"That's going to get ugly," Alfie predicted.

"Cass has a trump. Frey's dragons."

"And is he willing to lay waste to his realm by using them?"

"I do not know. Though if it was I, I'd be willing to sacrifice something to make an example."

"Indeed," Alfie murmured his agreement.

"It would be good this Rising was dealt with and we could go help."

"Give it time. I sense they're suffering. If Serena and the gnomes can find this treasury and you can get a few men placed in their ranks, perhaps things will go much more swiftly."

True nodded.

"Firenze?" Alfie kept on, and True was even more relieved.

He seemed keen to know.

Indeed, True's relief came because Alfie seemed keen about anything.

Not listless, most the time, or irritable, which was what he was around Bronagh.

"Mars and Silence have not arrived in Fire City yet, but they'll be there soon," True told him.

"And Mar-el?"

True felt his neck muscles tighten when he shared, "Aramus abolished binding altogether. Those taken will work the remainder of the five years, but no more can be taken, and the others who are past that have been freed. There have been uprisings. Not many, but he's been busy. I know no more as I suspect he does not have time to send many birds."

"He is doing right, it will settle, and then it will be past," Alfie said quietly.

He hoped so, but it was his experience it was never that easy.

True nodded yet again.

"In school, I was quite a keen student of history," Alfie noted abruptly.

"You had told me that," True reminded him.

"I do not think I told you that, at one time, I did not fancy becoming a soldier. I fancied going to the Go'Da to study history in order to return to Wodell to teach in one of our own universities."

"No," True murmured. "You had not shared that."

"I do not know a single time in history where this much change swept Triton all at the same time," he declared.

True regarded him closely.

"We have not had any quakes in some time, True," Alfie remarked. "And I do not wish to add to your plate, but this change…"

His voice trailed away.

"We know nothing of the Beast. Not really," True said. "But I see what you're saying. It's unprecedented, all that's happening. And if there is some force that does not wish peace and prosperity—"

"But feeds from war and greed—"

"It will rise to put a stop to progress."

"It is a supposition," Alfie said.

"It is also a supposition to think the quakes have stopped because the last one was the worst and he no longer rises, he's risen. And he lays in wait. But I must admit to my mind turning to that and doing it often."

True and Alfie stared at each other.

The door opened and Bronagh bustled through.

Alfie looked to the door.

True kept his gaze to his friend, and thus saw Alfie's face change instantly from speculative and concerned to inhospitable and annoyed.

True turned to her when Bronagh stopped at the foot of the bed and put her hands to her hips, regarding Alfie while noting, "I see you're your usual chipper self today."

"I see you unfortunately did not fall off a cliff since your last post," Alfie returned.

True drew in a sharp breath.

Bronagh's pretty face went stricken before it looked like it would crumble.

"Alfie," he whispered.

But Alfie was looking like he'd give anything to rise from that bed on his own power, not to walk, not to ride, not to fight.

But to take his feet in order to properly apologize.

"That was—" he began.

Bronagh quickly hid her emotion behind efficiency and interrupted him to query, "Are you in pain?"

"Bronagh—" Alfie started gently.

"Are you in pain, sir?" she demanded.

"No," he said.

"You will call if you're in pain. I'll be outside the door."

And with that, she turned and scurried to and through the door, closing it behind her.

"Fuck," Alfie muttered.

True considered carefully what to do next.

And out of necessity, he made a quick decision.

"That was not my captain," he stated.

Alfie looked to him. "True—"

"I don't know who that man was, but he was not you," True informed him flatly. "I cannot begin to imagine the many things plaguing your mind and your body. But the Alfie Henriksson I know would never speak like that to a woman. Indeed, to anyone."

"She draws up ire in me, I know not where it stems," Alfie admitted.

True stood, looked down at his friend and shared it openly.

"It stems from the fact you're attracted to her. You feel the same from her. And you're convinced it can go nowhere. Thus, you wish to drive her away. I think she is one of the very few who have some inkling of what you're going through, and what your life could become, if you fight for it. And she comes here every day and looks at you like she looks at you so that tells me what your life could become, and who you could have in it, if you fought for it."

Alfie's face hardened. "I haven't been in this bed even a month—"

"I don't care," True cut in. "The Alfie Henriksson I know wouldn't care. He fought battles that were useless and unwinnable out of loyalty to me and the belief one day it would be over, and the future would be better. Now he has a battle that is crucial to win, *and* it's winnable, and he falters."

"Fuck you, True," Alfie spat.

"Good," True whispered and bent to him. "Shovel it at me, I can take it. But her," he kept bent and pointed toward the door, "maybe she can't, but you don't want to find out if that's the case."

He decided that was enough, straightened, and without another word to his friend, he walked out of the room.

Bronagh did not meet his eyes when he was in the hall, and True gave her that, turning to make his way to his and Farah's chambers.

It was not late, it was not early. Not long ago, he and Farah had dined with a number of men and charmed folk, for even if True had an insurgency on his hands, the Beast possibly risen and lying in wait, his friends in their realms dealing with serious and dangerous issues, he had not given up on his idea for the future of Wodell.

He could think of no other future than one where they quelled this Rising and defeated the Beast.

Which meant there *was* a future, and he had to plan for it.

And that meant, when (not if), they recovered the coin Carrington stole from them, he would utilize it to build a parliament building, adjacent offices for its members and staff, and to hold elections throughout his land.

Emissaries from various provinces and clans of charmed folk were astonished by this idea, but receptive to it. Tremendously so.

This meant there was much to plan, much to do, his people needed to be educated about this idea and understand that they were not losing their king. He was not shirking his duty. He would continue to be the last word in his realm and deeply involved in its governing.

But they would have a say.

He was pleased at the response to this idea.

He was also tired just thinking of implementing it.

Exhausted.

He did not sleep well in the norm.

But since his mother's death, he had barely slept at all.

If he could have his greatest wish, he would take Farah somewhere remote and private, maybe the Royal Cottage on the sea outside Welling Harbor and hole in. No meetings. No conferences. No summits. No strategy sessions.

Just his wife and himself, a bed, perhaps a few books, the waves lapping the shores...and sleep.

He could not do that.

He might not be able to do that for months, or with all he had planned, even years.

But he wanted nothing but to do just that.

Helga had said she'd needed a word with Farah after dinner, therefore Farah had followed Helga, and True had gone to visit with Alfie on his own (and in the end, that had been a boon, for he would not wish his wife to see Alfie behave that way, and he might not have said what he needed to say after he did).

Now, he hoped she was in their chambers and did not mind going to bed early, for he wanted nothing but to curl into her soft warmth and get as much rest as he could before the bad dreams chased it away.

This was his thought upon entering their chambers, seeing their sitting room dark, but their bedchamber brightly lit.

"Farah," he called, making his way there.

She didn't answer.

He called her name again.

"Farah."

He took not a step into their bedchamber, for he stopped dead in the doorway.

This, because his wife sat cross legged at the end of the bed.

And she did it wearing naught but her wedding chain.

Her dark hair was long and falling down her chest, mostly covering her bared breasts. Her hands were clasped loosely in her lap, covering her sex.

Her eyes were on him.

True was struck still, his mind scattering, his eyes not knowing where to go. Thus, they roamed the entirety of her, drinking in her beauty.

That was, he was struck still, except one part of him which had been called to stiff attention.

"I think," she broke the silence, her beautiful voice floating across the room, "it is high time we truly became husband and wife, no?"

In normal circumstances, he would shout his agreement.

Her injury.

The death of her mother.

The death of *his* mother.

"Farah—"

"I am cold, True," she whispered before adding a verbal invitation to the one she'd been issuing since the moment of his arrival. "Come and warm me."

The fire was blazing on its iron in the grate.

The room was awash with light as every lamp was lit.

But he could not have his wife feeling cold.

He moved her way.

She adjusted her position, coming up to her knees, exposing her slightly rounded belly, her bare hips, her sex.

True moved faster.

Her arms came out his way.

He walked into them, watching her head tip far back, as his bent down...

And he took her mouth.

Her lips opened under his, her arms rounding him.

He slid his tongue inside, diving both his hands into her thick hair.

But at the taste of her, the knowledge she was bared to him, the invitation she had offered, the wanting of her for so long, and not having her, he could not hold himself in check.

He leaned into her, taking her to her back in their bed.

He was atop her, the scent of her all around, the taste of her on his tongue, the feel of her softness squirming beneath him, all of this unraveling him.

She started tugging at his clothes.

He did not stop her, his hands roaming the silk of her skin.

Some vague sense of chivalry permeated, and he tore his mouth from hers, murmuring, "Your shoulder."

"It has been fine for days," she breathed, tugging at his frock coat.

True shrugged it off and tossed it aside.

When he dipped back in, he went for her neck.

Gods, but her perfume was extraordinary.

Spice and Farah.

He ran his tongue along her neck as he ran his hand up her side.

She was struggling with the buttons on his waistcoat.

"Your clothes must go," she demanded.

She was right.

They must.

Immediately.

He wanted his skin against hers.

He pushed up to his knees, straddling her.

She pushed up to her behind, and both of them went after the buttons on his vest, fingers bumping into the other's.

He caught her hands.

Her hair tumbled all around her shoulders as she tipped her head to catch his eyes.

"How about I do the waistcoat and you do the shirt?" he suggested throatily.

She grinned and lifted her hands to the buttons on his shirt.

He saw her hands were trembling.

His hands were not.

His were impatient.

He had to stop to take off the vest, but he did not bother with all the buttons of his shirt. Once a few were loose, he pulled it over his head.

And felt his cock kick when her heated gaze fell on his chest.

"You are just...*so beautiful*," she breathed before she pressed her lips to his skin, running her tongue along an indentation in the muscle there, on her way down.

It would be later when he both wished she did not do that, at the same time he was glad she did.

For he had thought, when this happened, when he had deemed she was ready, and that would be when it could be about naught but them, their touches, tastes, joining, with nothing bearing down on them, he had wanted to take his time in giving her pleasure.

But when she touched her tongue to his flesh, he heard an odd sound in the room, like a gentle breeze moving through leaves.

And he lost his mind.

True had no memory of the loss of his boots, his socks, his trousers. He did not know if he removed them, or she, or the both of them.

But he would never forget the first time he drew her nipple into his mouth, feeding it there with a sweep of his tongue, and the sound of her whimper, the pucker of her hardening flesh against his lips, when he suckled it deep.

He would also never forget doing much the same to the other.

He would further not forget her nails raking through his scalp and down his back.

And he would not forget the whisper of her lips on his throat or the moist trails of her tongue along the boxes of his stomach.

He would not forget the smell of her sex tingeing the air.

And he definitely would not forget the cast of the room turning green before he closed his eyes when he first tasted the nectar between her legs.

She writhed against him as he took her with his mouth, thus he wrapped her legs about his shoulders so she would be able to find purchase.

And he drank from her.

Deeper and deeper, until her movements grew needy and her noises desperate, her fingers that were fisted in his hair alternately pushing him closer and tugging him away.

He wanted to bring her to climax in that manner first, to assure it and to prepare her to take him, but the pushing at his head became tugging as she breathed, "No…I can't…I don't want to be…not before you, without you. True," a fierce tug, "come inside."

He should have fought it, but in that moment, the want in her tone, the desire in his body, he could not.

He swept over her, hazily taking in the beauty of desire softening her features, heating her amber eyes, and he covered her, careful of his weight even if she'd assured him her wound was healed.

"I am not small," he had the presence of mind to murmur.

"I noticed and I don't care." She had strength in her tone, and in her fingers, which were clenching greedily at his arse.

Gods, his beautiful wife.

"Farah—"

"Make me yours."

He dipped closer, gliding a finger along her hairline, it coming to him that they should slow this, be present in it, not lost to it.

"Farah—"

"I want to belong to you," she whispered, and he grew still. "I *yearn* to belong to you, True. Please, *il mia vita*, it seems I've waited eternity. Please, my husband, make…me…*yours*."

This was her wish, and his, he would give it to her.

To them.

True took hold of his shaft, found her with the head, and slowly, he eased inside.

He watched as her eyes closed in ecstasy when they became one.

And his body locked as her slick heat tightened around him.

She rounded him with all four limbs.

He stared at his wife, his queen, now his lover, just his love, her hair all over the pillows, vines of ivy creeping through the locks, and he did not notice this oddity.

He moved inside Farah, finally making her his, finally giving himself to her.

"Yes," she whispered.

"Yes," he grunted, struggling not to climax, she felt that good, smelled that good, her pleasure *looked that good*.

She tightened further around him…*everywhere*.

He gritted his teeth and moved faster.

"Gods, *yes*," she whimpered, her hips finding his rhythm.

"Look at me," he demanded, his voice guttural.

He watched as she forced her eyes open.

"You're mine," he declared, the movement of his hips slipping out of his control, thus they hammered into hers, fast and hard.

"I'm yours," she gasped.

"You're mine forever, Farah," he growled.

Her nails dug in at the base of his spine and the back of his neck.

He gloried in the bite of her claiming.

"I'm yours," she whimpered, her movements frantic, her sex grasping, clutching, *seizing*.

Gods.

"And I am yours," he told her.

Her dazed eyes focused on him and they grew wet.

"You are mine." Her voice sounded like it would break.

"Forever, my beloved," he said.

"Forever, True," she whispered, her arm wrapping all the way around, her fingers holding tight to his side, her hand at his neck cupping it.

He bent to kiss her as he shifted a hand over her hip, between them, over her belly and down.

He pressed at her nub as he thrust deep inside and slid his tongue in to claim her mouth.

His wife instantly climaxed against it.

Giving her that, True let himself go, continuing with finger and tongue to offer her more, take her higher, make it last as long as he could, until he had to clamp on her hip to hold her steady as his world went a dense green, his balls drew up and he shot inside his bride.

Glorious.

He had his face in her neck and felt her fingers trailing the small of his back, just above his arse, when the climax released him.

He managed to ascertain he still had his weight in his forearm, but that was it.

He could not move.

Which was fine, for he did not want to.

"That was a terrible trick, but I could not wait any longer."

Farah's words made him move.

He lifted his head to gaze down at her in confusion.

"Pardon?"

"Sitting on our bed in the nude in hopes of seducing you," she explained.

He nearly burst out laughing.

In his effort to contain this, his body started shaking violently, so much, his cock almost lost its place.

He liked where his cock was, therefore, he got a handle on himself.

"I do not believe I've complained," he pointed out.

"I should have had a conversation with you. But you've been very busy. So distracted. I thought when the sling was gone, we would...and then we didn't. For *days*. And it was meetings. And you going to Crittich Keep. And visiting with Alfie. And behind closed doors with Bram and Wally and Florian and Luther. And—"

As she spoke, he realized how agitated she was.

And as she spoke, and his cock slid out, losing the heat of her, he saw the vines that had overtaken the bed retreat.

"We created a garden," he noted, cutting off her words.

"I...sorry?"

"Your magic, my world," he said, shifting his eyes to the side.

She turned her head just in time to watch two vines of ivy slink away.

"Oh," she breathed.

He looked to her and grinned at her when she turned again to him.

He then sobered.

"I have been derelict in my duties to my wife," he declared.

She moved a hand from his back to lay it on his cheek, murmuring, "True. It isn't that. It's—"

"A dereliction of duties to my wife," he somewhat repeated. "I did not sense you were ready."

"The best way for you to know I was ready was for me to tell you, not trick you into making love to me by essentially throwing myself at you."

"Farah, please rest assured, and I wish you to take this in and know it completely, I am quite all right with you meeting us in our bedchamber, your beauty openly exposed for me, every night for the rest of our lives."

She stared up at him.

Then she dissolved in laughter.

True again grinned down at her.

"Though next time," he said through her amusement, "know you have my permission to actually throw yourself at me, rather than waiting for me to come to you."

She kept laughing and did it harder.

True kept smiling at her.

She got hold of herself (mostly) and then moved her other hand so she could frame his face in both.

When she had a hold on him, she declared, "We are husband and wife."

They were.

Thank the gods.

He felt his body settle further into hers.

"Yes, darling," he agreed.

"I am truly yours," she said.

His voice was thick at knowing what this meant to him, hearing what it meant to her, when he replied, "Yes."

"And you are mine."

"Yes, Farah."

The tears sprang to her eyes.

"None of that," he whispered, shifting his own hand to her face in order to rub the pad of his thumb along her cheek.

"They are happy tears."

"All right. Then I'll allow it," he muttered.

She gave him a watery smile.

And then she gave him the new meaning to his life.

"It will all be much. Too much. Who you are. What you must give to your people. Overwhelming. Onerous. Sometimes monotonous. Also, frustrating. I know there will be victories. Successes. Advancements. Celebrations. But I practically grew up in Catrame Palace. I know what the duty you face is. I saw Ares assume that mantle every day, and he was a great king, but he was also human. I could not miss sometimes he did it with reservations, or fatigue. But here, True..."

She explained "here" by again wrapping her arms about him, her legs tensing where they were still curled around his thighs.

"Here, for both of us, is sanctuary," she finished.

Sanctuary.

Gods, just the word from her lips in their bed, her body beneath his, made him feel he was there.

Thus, yes.

She was right.

This was *sanctuary*.

"I will listen," she said. "If you wish it, I will give my advice. If you must rail, I will keep quiet and be your sounding board, allowing you to release it. If you must fume, I will give you nothing but patience and my ear. But this," she squeezed him again, "is where you come, and know you are understood. You know you have unwavering support. You know it is yours, it is ours. And that is all. The world does not enter here. It is just you and me. It is us."

He felt his throat close and he feared his eyes, too, were growing wet.

He loved her.

He could not do this without her. Not navigating the loss of his mother. Not the taking of the throne. Not dealing with Alfie. Not living the rest of the days of his life.

She was not his support.

She was part of him.

He had fallen in love with her beauty and strength, and now the rapture of her body.

But it was simply that he loved her.

He had for some time.

And now, with her words, he knew he would never stop.

"What?" she whispered, gazing up at him.

One could argue, after the first time they made love, declaring his feelings as they were right then was the perfect time to do so.

But True would argue that it was not.

He wanted to share this with her when there was nothing to question the pure sentiment behind it. Not caught up in the afterglow of a climax. Not having it mistaken for gratitude for her attention or support in times of mourning, in times of trouble.

He wanted to look over a breakfast table, into her eyes, and just say it, so she knew, apropos of nothing—and everything—that it was true.

"My husband...*what*?" she prompted.

"That went quickly, and I was not as gentle as I would have wished to be. Are you sensitive?" he queried.

"Are you asking if I wish you to ravish me again?" she queried in return.

He shot her another grin, wondering who it was that was ravished, for he felt that it was he.

He had no complaint about that either.

She lifted her head and kissed the curve on his lips before dropping back down and answering, "I am delightfully sensitive, and if we do not make love again, my king, it would be very vexing."

He rolled off her, onto his back, taking her with him so she was atop.

"I would not wish to vex you," he murmured, eyes to her mouth.

"Then don't," she whispered, head descending.

She kissed him.

He returned his wife's kiss.

Then they set about not making her vexed as True again let himself be ravished.

And he returned the favor.

~

IT WAS THE NEXT MORNING.

They were both in dressing gowns, at their breakfast laid out in their sitting room.

Farah was spreading marmalade on a triangle of toast.

True was watching her.

Her hair was tousled, a glorious mane adorning her shoulders.

Her face was relaxed, and for the first time since he knew her, carefree.

He had, at times, been able to make her happy.

He had never, not once, seen her look carefree.

"Farah," he called, and she lifted her gaze from her toast to his eyes. "I love you, my darling."

She grew still as a statue, her eyes glued to his.

"Finish breakfast, sweetling," he urged, his lips curved. "As ever, we have a busy day."

She did not move.

True reached for his own triangle of toast from the caddy.

"True."

He looked to her just in time to see one lone tear trace down her cheek.

She no longer looked carefree.

Her eyes were shining with gratitude, happiness and...

Love.

He had been right.

Over breakfast was perfect timing.

"Here," he whispered. "My study. A meadow. The moon. Anywhere, my love, it is yours, I am yours, and that is all."

"I would experience it all again, if it brought me to you," she whispered tremulously.

True reached to her cheek, running his knuckles through the wet, then opening his hand to slide his fingers into the side of her hair.

"I love you, True," she said.

And he had her love.

"I am blessed," he told her his truth.

"Not as much as I," she returned.

"No, Farah, I am far more blessed."

"You are wrong, True. It is I who is the most blessed. By far."

He started laughing.

She smiled brightly at him and began laughing too.

She stopped and said, "A meadow. The moon. I am yours and that is all."

At her words, he used his hand in her hair to pull her to him as he leaned to her.

And their love was sealed with a kiss.

Over the breakfast table.

98

THE TRANSFORMATION

Prince Cassius
Bedchamber of the Prince Regent, Sky Citadel, Sky Bay
AIREN

Cassius woke to an empty bed.

He instantly growled.

He did not like waking to an empty bed, but it seemed every day since they arrived in his home, just this had occurred.

His soon-to-be bride only woke beside him in a bloody tent on bloody campaign.

A campaign, incidentally, during which she was miraculous.

It had not been a difficult battle to win, defeating the besiegers, but she was outstanding with bow and arrow and superb with staff.

But her talents with a sword, he had not, until then, witnessed.

And they were exemplary.

Though she should use a bloody shield.

And even if they had argued, as he had not wished her to come along, but at looks he received from Frey, and Lahn, and to his surprise, Mac, he had allowed it, he was glad in the end.

For victory sex with Princess Elena of the Nadirii was gods-damned *magnificent.*

But now he was abed, awake, hard, and his woman was gone.

Doing what, he did not know.

But his intended had been busy since they made the Citadel.

It made him anxious.

And in times like this, it made him frustrated.

He threw back the covers, tossed his legs to the side, stood and started to prowl to his dressing room.

But he stopped dead.

He then blinked.

There was a new rug on the floor.

It was not black with charcoal gray edges.

It was cerulean.

And the space beyond it that all his time in this bedchamber held nothing, now, facing the bed, sat a button-backed chesterfield couch covered in azure velvet.

Next to the couch was a low table, the base fashioned out of what looked like thick silver wire, on its top, a stack of books ready at hand should you wish to read.

And in the corner was a tall, healthy green plant with long, fat, glossy leaves.

Slowly, he turned and froze when he saw a squat, round silver vase erupting at its rim with a poof of velvety pale purple roses on the chest at Elena's side of the bed.

And on the chest by his, a childish drawing Aelia had done while in The Enchantments that his daughter had given him, and he had kept, now stood in a frame.

"What the bloody hell?"

These things had to have been there last night.

However, he had come upstairs with his intended after she'd been at the wine with him and their friends for some hours (something she arranged every night—it was a constant celebration, no courtiers to be found, just Elena, him, people they cared about and a goodly amount of spirits).

She had been kissing him, thus he had been kissing her, and his mind had been elsewhere as they entered the room and fallen in bed.

He turned again.

The couch was long, it looked comfortable, and it was handsome.

On this thought, he continued stalking to his dressing room, threw on his leathers, pulled on his boots, and moved out.

He strode down the hallway, his mood deteriorating as he did so, and he did not meet a single servant to ask where his betrothed was.

But he stopped dead on the stairs down to the entryway.

He did this, for now, under the enormous daunting candelabrum, stood a wide round table of gleaming rosewood, under which was a circular rug with an ombre pattern of midnight blue in the middle, expanding out to sky blue at the edges.

And on the table was a large crystal vase filled with a massive spray of brilliant purple, pale yellow, rich cream and delicate peach gladiolus.

He stared at the blaze of vibrant color in a room that had not had a vibrant anything in *centuries*, the shock this delivered to his system so extreme, he was unable to move, even when he heard angry words coming from the Great Hall.

"I must again inform you I take my orders from my king…and my prince," a voice Cassius knew was the castle steward declared.

"And again, I must inform *you* that I will be your princess and then your queen," Elena retorted.

"The running of this citadel has always been left directly in the efficient hands of the steward, that being *me*, including all decisions therein taken, be they about food, spirits, cleaning, maintenance, heating *and decorating*," the steward rejoined. "Even the king's wives have no say in such matters."

"I am not called to the king's bed when he has gathered enough energy to perform," Elena returned, and Cassius's gut jolted, for he had the unusual desire to emit a bark of laughter. "I am in the *Prince Regent's* bed, thankfully, and *he* has no problem bestowing the right of decorating her own home *to his bride*, that being *me*."

Cassis resumed descending the stairs as the steward pronounced, "We do not have flowers in the royal foyer."

"You do now," Elena replied.

"And those red cushions will be removed from the davenports in the informal sitting room immediately," the steward went on as if she did not speak.

Red cushions?

"If they are, I'll have you beheaded," Elena threatened.

Yes.

It was happening.

In this place. This terrible place where his mother died. His wife died.

And he had lived what felt like a walking death.

He was fighting back laughter.

He moved beyond the gleaming rosewood table standing on its richly colored rug (and he wondered where she'd procured them), heading toward the Great Hall, succeeding in the endeavor of quelling his laughter, though with some effort.

No further effort was needed as he heard the steward sneer, "You do not have that power, female, and you never will."

"Elena, find Mac."

Both turned to him at hearing his voice.

"Your Grace." The steward dropped into a graceful bow.

He halted ten feet away from them, eyes to the servant, but his words were aimed at Elena.

"Elena...*Mac*," he growled.

"Cass, I think that—"

His gaze sliced to her.

She quieted.

"Go...find...*Mac*," he bit out.

"What are you going to do?" she whispered.

"Go," he whispered back.

Her eyes blazed amethyst as her mood set to stubborn.

"Not until you tell me what you're going to do," she demanded.

"He's going to the dungeons," Cassius drawled.

Elena's face paled.

The steward shot up straight and stared at him with fright.

"Cassius, we were just having a discus—" she began.

"Get Mac."

"It is not that important," she retorted.

"It is my will that women will be treated with respect in my realm, Elena. And obviously, this will start in my own, gods-damn, *bloody home*. If I allow my own steward to speak like this to you, all is lost. He is a servant. You will live here your whole life, raise our children here, and die here. Thus, this is his place of employment, but it is *your home*. He does *not* get to tell you that you can or cannot have flowers. And he does not...*ever*...speak to you in that manner. Now, go...get..." he leaned her way, "*Mac*."

"And you can speak to me that way?" she attempted to make her point.

"Yes, because you have my respect, you have my regard, you have my cock, and you can speak to me any bloody way you feel like doing it, and you do, and when you do, I listen to you," he returned, making his point.

"This is true," she murmured.

"By the gods, Elena, just go find Mac." He finished this time with, "Fucking *please*."

"Well, since you said please," she mumbled as she made her way to him. She kept mumbling when she was close, doing it to say, "We'll be discussing this dungeon situation later."

"No, we won't," he replied.

She rolled her eyes before she left the room.

He moved his to the steward.

"Sire—" the man started.

"Quiet," Cassius ordered.

The steward quailed.

Cassius took a few moments to gather his patience before he spoke.

"You were in the courtyard when I brought your future queen to her new home, were you not?"

"Yes, sire, but—"

"And thus, you heard me say that she was to be considered your Princess Regent, did you not?"

The servant shakily nodded his head.

"I understand it will take some time, maybe decades, before the men of this realm understand the wisdom of the decisions I have made and the bounty I have bestowed on them in the making," Cassius stated. "However, even understanding that, it is necessary...nay, *crucial*, that the example is set forth for the people of my land in my own home. And it will not be tolerated when it is not."

"Yes, sire, I—"

"What's happening?" Mac asked from behind him.

"You're arresting the Citadel steward for gender sedition," Cassius shared, not taking his attention from the man in front of him.

"Is there such a thing as gender sedition?" Mac queried, now at his side.

Cass turned his head and looked at him.

Mac's lips quirked.

Mac then turned to the steward and rolled his hand at the man. "Right then, come along, old chap. Let's get you in chains."

"But, may I—?" the steward began.

"I will hear your words in two days," Cassius said.

Visible relief swept through the man.

Mac moved to him and caught his upper arm, beginning to escort him from the room, but he stopped them when Cassius spoke again to the steward.

"It would be a shame, when you know what you do better than anyone in this city, to lose your knowledge and skills. Think on this, sir, in your two days, and how we will proceed after our chat."

The man nodded fervently.

Mac pulled him away.

Cassius turned to watch but stopped watching when a beautiful woman with golden hair and flashing violet eyes came to stand in front of him in order to glare at him with her hands planted firmly to her slender hips.

And he was reminded how annoyed he was at not waking with her at his side.

"Was that necessary?" Elena demanded.

"What else have you done?" he inquired.

"Sorry?"

"Flowers in the foyer. A sofa that's in the bloody way in our chambers. Aelia's drawing. Truly, Elena, red pillows in the sitting room?"

"It's a shock of color," she muttered. "It works splendidly."

"My warrior," he said softly. "I appreciate the effort, but the gloom of this place cannot be dispelled by gladiolus."

"Then you did not see them properly, my warrior, for it can."

He looked beyond her to the stunning floral array.

The entrance hall was massive, the chandelier above it almost sinister in appearance.

But he could not deny that those spikes of lively blooms transformed the space.

He looked back down to his future wife.

"I would prefer to wake to you at my side than wake alone as you're off arranging flowers," he shared.

The ire swept from her face, she took her hands from her hips and leaned into both at his chest, her lips curled up at the ends.

"I thought I exhausted you last night," she said softly.

"I thought it was I who exhausted *you*," he returned, curving his arms about her.

Her expression grew serious.

"I cannot falter in my mission, Cass," she said. "I must attack it with great fervor and no respite. For you. And for our girls."

Their girls.

He slid a hand up her spine, and when it reached the area between her shoulder blades, he pressed in, bringing her closer.

"We have more important battles on our hands," he reminded her.

"No, we don't," she disagreed.

"Elena, they're but flowers."

However, should she stop in these pursuits, he would be certain to have that drawing of Aelia's remain where it was.

And fresh roses put by Elena's bedside daily.

"I have had a home all my life," she said, bringing his attention back to her. "You have never had one. Thus, I understand. You do not know how important it is, Cass. But when I show it to you, you'll understand. You'll understand there is nothing more important. But for the now, you will just have to trust me."

He did not understand, she was correct.

However, he was not allowed to continue what had become a rather pleasant discussion with her in his arms, her gaze gentle on his face.

This because a scream rent the air.

They both grew solid before they both flew into action.

When another scream came as they reached the top of the steps, and it was coming from the west wing, his father's wing, and not the east, his, Cass's stomach dropped.

"You stay here," he ordered, still sprinting at the same time trying to push her back.

"Not on your bloody—"

Her last word was drowned out by another scream, this coming from his father's chamber, but Horatia was scurrying toward them, both her hands up their way.

"It is a matter between husband and wife," she said hurriedly when Cassius was forced to stop rather than bowl her over.

His head jerked toward his father's door when he heard a thud.

He moved, Elena moving with him, to round Horatia, but she shifted to block them, putting her hands to Cass's chest and pushing.

"It is not your concern, my prince," she stated firmly.

"You'll get out of my way," he ordered.

"You have control of a kingdom, but you must understand, you'll never have control of a man's bedchamber," she returned.

She was bloody wrong about that.

Especially when it came to what was happening right then in his father's.

He did not take time to discuss that with her.

"You'll get out of my way," he repeated as another thud that came with a sharp cry of pain could be heard from his father's rooms.

Horatia shook her head, increased her pressure on his chest, opened her mouth, but the only sound that came from it was her own cry of pain, but also surprise, as Elena rounded him, caught her by the hair, and used it to yank her to the side, where, arms flailing, she went flying.

"He said, you'll get out of his way," she snapped to his father's wife.

Cassius did not wait for what came next between the two women.

He went to his father's door, but when he turned the handle to let himself in, his shoulder slammed into it instead of it opening, for it was locked.

"Open this!" he shouted at the panel.

"Be gone!" his father shouted back.

"*Open!*" he barked.

He heard a noise within the room he could not decipher, except it was coming from a female and it did not bode well, and then he put his shoulder to the door with intent.

Elena did the same at his back.

Both of them pounded on it with all their might, and it shook in its jamb, but did not yield.

"What on earth is happening?" he heard Antonius ask.

"This is *profane!*" Horatia screeched.

"Back," Cassius growled.

Elena stepped back, as did Cassius.

Then he lifted his boot, and with all the strength he had in his leg, kicked at the door.

Wood shrieked, and the door flew open.

At what he saw, at Elena's horrified gasp, his blood ran cold, but his lips moved.

"Get her gone," he ordered.

"By the gods," he heard breathed and knew Ian had joined him.

"*Get her gone!*" Cassius yelled.

"Cass," Elena called.

"Fucking hell."

And they had Nero.

He turned in time to see his men dragging Elena, stunned inert, away, Horatia glaring at him, and Cornelia cowering off to the side, her back to the opposite wall.

He took hold of the door and threw it to, keeping his hand up to hold it shut for there was no longer a latch.

Then he turned to the bed where his father was, on his knees, a bloodied Domitia on all fours in front of him, receiving his cock.

"I'll be done in a minute," his father sneered at him.

He was doing this...*this*...in retribution for all Cass had done.

This.

He had done this.

Horatia was correct.

This was profane.

Cassius walked into the room.

Toward the bed.

"What—?" his father started.

Domitia had her head turned away from him in shame.

"I might not wish my son as audience," Gallienus noted.

Cassius snatched up a woolen throw from the end of the bed, then gently placed his hands under Domitia's arms and pulled her away.

"What the bloody—?" his father shouted.

He carefully put her to her feet on the floor, wrapped the throw around her and murmured, "Go. Now. Elena will take care of you."

He saw it out of the sides of his eyes and caught the fist coming his way in his palm, his fingers wrapping around it tightening in a crushing grip.

His father made a noise of pain.

"Go, now," Cassius whispered to Domitia.

She kept her gaze averted from him, but he could see her eye already swelling, her nose and lip bleeding.

Blood was also coming from her ear.

"I thought the law now said I could say no," she whimpered.

Cassius's chest caved in.

"You thought right," he replied.

She glanced up at him, and he could see blame in her hesitant gaze.

"Unhand me!" his father ordered.

Domitia flinched at the sound and rushed away, limping.

Cassius's blood now burned.

"Unhand me!" his father shouted.

"Ian! Tone! Nero!" Cassius called, turning to look his father in the eyes.

Gallienus tried to get free of Cassius's grip, but he just held tighter.

Gallienus ceased struggling and yelled, "Unhand me!"

"Cass," Ian murmured.

"Arrest this man for rape," Cassius commanded.

The room went static.

"Cass, are you sure?" Ian asked.

"*You can't arrest me!*" Gallienus shrieked, attempting to gather the sheets around his hips with his free hand.

Cassius looked to him. "Would you like to lay a wager?"

"This is preposterous," Gallienus spat. "Unhand me!" He jerked his hand in Cassius's hold.

Cass let go and he fell to his arse in the bed.

"Arrest him," he said.

"I'll do it," Nero said, moving in.

"*Do not touch me!*" Gallienus screamed, scrambling to get away. "I am your king. I am your monarch. I am your ruler. I rescind the Regency. I take back my reign!"

Cass did not watch.

He turned on his boot, saying, "Ian, help Nero. Tone, come with me."

He went to the door where Horatia was still standing, glaring at him.

Cornelia was not to be seen, and he hoped she was with Elena, seeing to Domitia.

But Frey and Lahn were now out in the hall, Lahn looking angry, Frey looking lethal.

He took his gaze from them and turned to Horatia.

"Antonius, arrest this woman for abetting a rape," he ordered.

Her eyes grew enormous, her face went ashen, and she started backing away.

"Wh-what?" she asked.

"I see I was not taken seriously when I heralded my first proclamations as this realm's Prince Regent. Thus, it's necessary I make my peoples understand, when my will is known, it will be obeyed. I do not thank you for giving me a powerful example to prove my determination. But as you have provided it, I will not waste the opportunity," he told her, turned to Antonius and jerked his head her way.

Antonius moved.

"But...you can't. He's king!" Horatia cried.

Cassius put her out of his mind and looked to Frey.

"How long would it take for your dragons to make Airen?" he asked.

There was some racket as a king and his wife were forcibly removed from the area, but Frey gamely ignored it.

"They fly fast, not long."

"I may need to make more examples," Cassius said.

Frey nodded.

"Your wives?" Cassius asked the both of them.

"They were with us when she came out," Frey told him, his mouth tight, making his words the same. "They went with Elena and Cornelia to see to her."

Cass nodded and began to move to follow his men and assist them in dealing with what must be done.

Frey stopped him with a hand on his arm.

"Ruling through fear is risky," he advised low.

"It worked for me," Lahn stated, and Cassius shifted his eyes up to the Korwahkian king.

"And then you shifted to something else," Frey reminded him.

Lahn shrugged. "I would give my son a peaceable kingdom. It is his mother's wish."

Frey sighed and took his hand from Cassius.

Cassius almost smiled, for it was not lost on anyone that anything Circe might wish would be something Lahn would see to her having.

He did not smile.

"I would give my daughters a safe kingdom," he stated, and earned both men's attention. "It is their right."

And after he said that, he strode away.

It was late in the evening when she found him, standing on the ramparts, staring down at Sky Bay.

He felt her approach, and then he felt her hand at his back before she laid her cheek there and her other arm slinked around his stomach.

She held him even as she gave him some of her weight.

"Are you all right?" Elena asked.

"What else have you done?" he queried in return.

"Sorry?"

"To make this nightmare a home."

She pressed closer to him and whispered, "Cass."

"Tell me."

"Well, the royal gardener has said it's actually optimal to plant ivy in the autumn, so he has done so. And, erm...there may be quite a few wisteria vines come spring as well."

Cass stared down at the lights in windows, streetlamps on avenues, dark smoke curling from chimneys in Sky Bay.

And he heard Elena's words.

But he did not say anything.

She slid to his side, forcing herself under his arm. Therefore, he moved it for her as she pressed her front to his side, her hand gliding up to put pressure on his neck to look down at her.

He did so, seeing her peeking up at him from her place, wedged under his arm.

"You're frightening me," she said quietly.

He lifted a hand and smoothed it over her cheek before cupping her jaw, watching his hand's movements, murmuring, "I wonder what your life would have been like, if the fates had allowed you to have True."

She wound both her arms around him, shook him, and ordered, "Stop it."

"You saw that," he replied.

"So did *you*, and that's what I'm worried about."

"You saw my father raping his wife."

She shook him again, harder. "Cass, I need you to focus on me."

"Is she all right?"

A shadow crossed her face.

Domitia was not all right.

But then, how could she be? Without her consent, married to a man more than twice her age, used, abused, debased.

"Cassius," Elena whispered.

"Flowers will not transform it, my beautiful warrior," he whispered back.

At his words, she forced herself to his front and took his head firmly in both her hands.

"Bright always beats the dark," she stated fiercely. "Do you not think one day Domitia will walk down those stairs, see flowers where they had never been before, know her torment is over, and this will not make her heart light?"

"Elena—"

"Do you not think our daughters, the ones we already have, the ones we will make, *and* our sons, will not play amongst the wisteria one day, having no idea that this place was once a nightmare? All they will know is it awash with blooms and *life*. And they will laugh at their father telling them tales of their mother arranging flowers and arguing with the steward over red cushions."

It was a pretty picture, but one that he could not quite bring into focus.

"It is too simple a solution for a magnitude of problems."

"Why does a difficult problem have to have a convoluted solution?" she asked.

He had no answer to that.

"Sometimes, the solution is missed, for those who search for it are looking for something grander, when what they need is right within reach."

"I will make an example with the dragons, Elena," he shared his simple solution. "If I hear aught of this continuing in my realm, I will rain fiery hell on the transgressors and cow them into submission if I have to."

"And I will champion that decision, not because the oppressors should be forced to understand how it feels to be cowed, but because that will be your decision, and I will stand by you."

He stared down upon her.

With his head in her hands, she now gave that a gentle shake.

"We will do what we must, Cass, *together*."

Gods, he loved her.

His shining warrior.

His magnificent princess.

He loved her to his bones.

Precisely where the terror lay.

The terror of losing her.

"Do not leave me abed alone in the mornings," he whispered.

"If that is where you wish me, that is where I will be," she whispered in return.

His head dropped so he could press his forehead to hers.

"I saw my mother like that," he told her.

She slid her hands over his hair and linked them at the back of his head, holding him close. "I know."

"It will be a spectacle, a king tried for rape."

"It will be a message that cannot be missed."

I would not know what to do if I lost you, he thought but did not say.

"Come inside. Come see Domitia." When he visibly balked, she held on and encouraged, "Just share she is in your thoughts, and if she needs anything, you will get it for her. Then you can leave. We will have wine. We will go to bed. We will close our eyes and sleep and this day will be done."

"And more flowers will be arranged in the foyer upon the new."

"And perhaps the Great Hall will be cleared, for I might have commissioned a number of settees in a rather smashing silver brocade that will work wonders in brightening the space, and I hope, make it rather warm and welcoming for visitors."

He could not believe it could happen, but it did.

He smiled.

He then shifted his head so he could touch his lips to hers.

After that, he shifted them both so he could guide her along the rampart to take her out of the cold.

"Cornelia is somewhat worried. She fears her loss of status here and that you will turn her out," Elena announced, but before he could open his mouth to share that would not be so, she went on to say, "I have assured her that you would never do that, this is her home, until she wishes to make that elsewhere."

"Just so," he muttered.

"And there is a maid who I have found alternate employment in the city," she carried on.

Cassius braced.

He then sighed.

"It is good employment and her wages will be higher than in the castle," she continued. "However, if she does not wish it, I will find something else. Though, her choice will not be to remain here."

"A man has a man's needs," he murmured but stopped them both at the door to the turret and looked down at her until she looked up at him. "And I assure you, my lamb, that was consensual."

"Well this man," her arm about his waist gave him a squeeze, "now has someone to meet those needs. And I have no doubt it was consensual with the way she looks at you and at me. But you are prince and she is maid, so consent could be blurry. Therefore, we'll just sort that out as best we can at this juncture, shall we?"

"Simple solutions," he remarked.

She tipped her head to the side and shrugged her shoulders.

"Mm," he hummed then moved to her side and reached to open the door. "We shall visit with Domitia. Then, we have a blue velvet sofa to christen."

He heard her laughter ring in the tower as he guided her into it.

Cassius did not know if laughter had ever rung in that tower.

Bright beats back the dark, she was not wrong.

Transformed.

99

THE QUARREL

King Mars
Bedchamber of the King, Catrame Palace, Fire City
Firenze

Mars took his mouth from between his queen's legs, grinning as he heard the disgruntled noise she made.

He then surged over her and rolled to his back, his hands at her hips bringing her over him.

His Silence wasted no time sitting up, straddling him, claiming his cock and impaling herself on it.

Mars was still grinning when her head, that had fallen back in taking him, righted, and she looked down at him.

"Arrogant," she murmured

He then saw the mercury shift in her eyes and should have known what she'd get up to when he did.

But she was moving atop him, slowly undulating her hips, gliding him out, taking him back, as her hands went to her body, both sliding over her hips to her breasts where she cupped them coyly, her rosy nipples peeking through her fingers.

Her gaze on him was hooded, a small smile was playing at her lips, the movement of her hips, her hands meant more to entice, to tease, than to give.

And she was enticing.

"My queen is a minx," he murmured, sliding his hands up the tops of her thighs.

"I was very close with your mouth to me," she murmured back, shifting her hips forward a bit on an upward stroke, the head of his cock dragging hard inside her as she glided back down.

What she gave him was so fantastic, he grunted and bucked.

The smile continued to play at her lips as she drifted one hand down her belly to between her legs.

Her head again fell back.

The sight of her thus, Mars clamped onto her hips and took over.

Her head again righted.

"Mars," she warned.

"Do not act as if this was not what you wanted," he grunted, slamming her into his shaft.

Her lips parted, and he lost her gaze when her head again dropped back. She then found his rhythm at her hips and rode him, her hand at her breast tracing up her neck, over her jaw, back into her hair, while the finger of her other hand continued to work between her legs.

As such, she was fully, gloriously exposed to him, riding his cock.

Gods.

"Hurry," he growled.

"Mars," she gasped, urging them both to go faster, something Mars gave her.

"*Hurry*," he clipped.

She arched back, pushing her bouncing breasts forward, moaning deeply and gripping both his wrists with her hands.

He reared under her for as long as he could hold his own orgasm back.

This being until she fell forward, planting her hands in his chest on a whimper as her pussy clenched around him in her climax.

Only then did he let go, yanking her hips down, filling her, his vision blanking as he shot his seed inside his queen.

He felt her collapse fully atop him, but he was grunting through his final bursts, enjoying them immensely and not simply because he now felt the silk of his wife's hair all over his chest, shoulders and tangling in his beard along with the sleek clutch of her sex, the smell of her, and the feel of her wee body resting against his.

When he was done, he wrapped his arms around her and murmured, "It's good to be home."

He dipped his chin down when he felt her lift her head up.

And thus, he watched Silence settle her own chin on her hands piled under it at his chest as she looked into his eyes.

"Did you miss it, my darling?" she asked.

"The sun is back on my skin," he muttered, sliding his hands up her spine. "But now it's better than it has ever been with my wife on my cock."

She grinned a grin that was half sultry, half Silence, before she moved her hands and tipped her head in order to kiss the skin of his chest.

He gazed down at her shining ebony hair, marveling at what wonders were at work that the fates had deemed him fit to grant him this beauty.

He was thinking this as his queen lifted her head and blindsided him.

"We must talk of my father."

"Silence, you rest on my cock."

"It has been some time since—"

She ceased speaking on an outcry as he pulled her from his shaft and tossed her to her back on the silks beside them before turning himself to cover her down one side.

"You do not bring him to our bed," he ordered on a growl, and her face screwed up in a manner he found adorable, which was inconvenient, as it should be aggravating.

"I bring him to our bed because I have asked repeatedly, and you do not—"

"Has it occurred to you that I do not because it would upset you?"

"Has it occurred to *you* that you not doing it is upsetting me *more*?"

He growled, for it had not.

"Mars—" she began.

"I will say first that you do not find your way to *getting* your way by playing my cock," he told her.

"And *I* will say first that it is most exasperating when you do not allow me to finish what I intend to say," she retorted.

Another growl came from him.

His wee queen gazed up at him narrowly and continued speaking.

"And I will get my way however I decide to go about getting my way."

He was not going to be cornered into demanding his wife not fuck him blind in order to get what she wanted, because in all truth, he quite liked when his Silence fucked him blind.

Thus, he said nothing.

"And I will say *second*," she went on, "that it was not *me* who woke *you* by playing with your cock, but a scenario quite different, my king."

She was correct about that, thus Mars remained quiet.

She studied him through his silence, and he watched her shift to using another tool she possessed to get whatever she desired from him.

She cupped his jaw in both her hands and said softly, "Mars, I would know about my father, and I would hope you'd understand that I *need* to know."

He did understand this.

And because he did, he drew in a breath through his nostrils before he rolled to his back.

He was staring at the canopy of their bed for naught but a second before he felt her soft breasts pressed to his chest and saw her beautiful face hovering over his.

"My love, now I'm becoming frightened," she whispered, peering closely at him.

She appeared just that.

Fuck.

He had left it too long.

But how did one tell one's beloved wife that her father was not her father, he'd whored her mother out in order to gain an heir, and the man had never loved her?

Mars moved his hand to trail a finger down her cheek, murmuring, "Perhaps you should put on a dressing gown and we can go to the other room."

Mars then saw she had not been frightened.

For *now*, she was definitely frightened.

"Oh, my goodness, Mars, what did he say to you?"

He took her head in both his hands, brought it closer, and held her eyes.

"The man you knew as your father is unable to make a child," he said quietly.

Her eyebrows twitched in bewilderment.

"But that's—" she began.

Cautiously, he went on, "Your real father is a Zee with silver eyes."

He watched another set of silver eyes grow wide.

"And part of why I had not told you this is because I have ordered men to find this man and bring him to me so I could meet him and see if he is worthy of introducing to you," he finished.

"My father is not my...?" Her voice trailed off.

Even if his wife did not finish the question, Mars answered, "No."

"My mother...*had an affair?*"

Fuck.

"Not exactly," he muttered.

Her voice was becoming shrill and her head was fighting his hold when she asked, "How 'not exactly' if I am not of my father and this is known?"

"Silence," he whispered, but said no more.

It took her a moment before she whipped away.

He knifed up and caught her in his arms before she could scurry out of bed.

"*Piccolina,*" he murmured.

"He sent her...he-he *forced her...*" She did not finish that either, and this he knew would be one of the few times of their lives together that he would wish she was not nearly as clever as she was. "Oh my *gods,*" she breathed and focused on him. "I am not Countess of the Arbor."

"No," he agreed firmly. "You are Queen of Firenze."

She grasped onto his neck in a tight hold. "Mars, this is disastrous."

"I cannot imagine how," he replied.

"I am...I am a..." And yet again she could not finish.

"You are royal blood. Your mother is Wilmer's sister. And your father is a Zee. A nomad. His people are like our tribes. They have no use for nobility except when forced to do so. But if the tribes ever learn, which they will not, they will be glad of the fact that you are of people like them."

Her gaze moved over his face a moment before she accused, "You're inventing things to make me feel better."

He was.

The tribes wouldn't care either way for they had no use for nobility except when forced to do so.

"Not at all," he lied.

Something else occurred to her, he saw it before she voiced it.

"My mother was there when this was discussed."

He sighed, pulled her closer, and as gently as he could, said, "She was, *amore.* And I will assure you I told her we would give her a home should she wish hers no longer to be with him. She chose him. This is not an arrangement I understand. Then again, in order to give him what he desired, an heir, she made her choice long ago, something else I do not understand. The only thing I can take from this is that I am glad she did for you are here, you are my wife, my queen, and if she did not, I would not have you. All else fades for me. They have no meaning to me, except that I am glad they made this arrangement so I could have you."

"How could you make something so awful sound so wonderful?" she asked, her voice husky, and he knew her emotion was high.

He did not answer her question.

He made an assertion.

"And for you, it explains why he has not been the father he should have been all these years, no?"

"I suppose," she mumbled.

"Silence," he called when he noted her eyes going vague.

Her attention came back to him.

"It is how it needed to be so we could have what it gave us. Think naught of it but that," he urged.

"You are able to make something so awful sound wonderful because you *are* wonderful," she whispered.

Of course, her doing this meant he was forced to kiss her.

This he did, for quite some time.

He was pressed to her, when he relented.

"What does my queen do today?" he asked softly.

When she answered, her voice was breathy, which he liked.

It was what she said he did not like.

"I thought I would practice with my dagger, and if Kyril has time, I can continue to try to take him to his back, something I have not yet been able to do."

This had been her bent since leaving Birchlire. When they were not astride horses, she worked with her dagger or attempted to fell Kyril, Basil, and once in a sneak attack (that was unsuccessful, though it did lead to something pleasurable), him.

"You do know, my beautiful Silence, you will never need these skills."

"One cannot be too prepared."

Mars sighed again.

Silence regarded him.

Then she changed the subject. "Is that invitation open-ended?"

He was perplexed.

"What invitation, my love?"

"For my mother, should she ever desire to leave him."

He felt his face soften, and he bent to touch his lips to hers before he lifted away and answered, "Yes. If she comes to us, and you wish her here, she will be welcome here."

"I think he loves her, in his way," she said.

Mars did not, for that was not the way of any love he knew.

He thought Johan Mattson of the Arbor was selfish and manipulative and very likely showed his wife love to control her.

But this was not his concern, and as it was not, but more, if he gave them to her, his thoughts on the matter would not make his wife happy, he did not share them.

"I think it is not yours to worry about anymore, *piccolina.*"

"Do you think that you'll...erm, find this Zee?" she asked.

"I think if you wish to meet him, I will have every corner of Triton searched until he is found."

This was when Mars watched *her* face soften before she lifted her head off the pillows to kiss him.

Sadly, they had been away from their home for some time, only arriving at the palace the evening before.

There was much to do and spending the day abed with his wife was not it.

Thus, he had no choice but to stop kissing her.

But he did it giving something to her.

"I would wish to pierce your navel, and soon," he murmured. "We shall plan for that with a ceremony between ourselves."

"I would like that, my love," she said in a tone that underlined her words. "And yours?"

His piercing at her navel was indication she was naught but his in body as well as in her heart and mind. The piercing he had promised her at his cock would mean the same.

He shook his head. "I would need to heal, which would mean I would need to not make love to you and I'd wish a few days in our home, in our bed, before I am forced to abstain from that."

"Agreed," she stated immediately.

Mars exploded with laughter.

He felt her body shake beneath him with her giggles as he did so.

Unfortunately, when they were done, this interlude needed to be the same.

Thus, he kissed the giggles still at her lips, and then he pulled them both from the bed.

She went to her dressing room.

He went to his.

And Mars decided to tear down the wall between these two chambers.

But that would be for another day.

This day needed to be for something else.

~

"THEY'RE UNBREAKABLE," Lorenz said, standing at his side in the musty, torchlit chamber below the earth in the necropolis.

"Hmm," Mars hummed, staring at the prone men chained to the stone floor before him.

"News of the loss of Mercy has traveled wide, Mars," Lorenz carried on. "We have heard word of three Go'Doan temples in our realm that have been overrun. Looted. One burned."

Mars kept his gaze steady on one of the men restrained on the floor, seeing a twitch in his cheek as he heard Lorenz's words.

"The priests are scattered," Lorenz continued. "We know not where. Rumor has it they are using tithes and trading relics to pay tribesmen for safe passage back to the Dome City."

Mars raised his brows but did not shift his gaze. "You tell me this because you wish me to secure their temples?"

"I do not care about their temples. I tell you this because it might be Rising priests who are escaping our borders."

"Hmm," Mars hummed again.

"If we were to question them, I feel certain we'll get useful information from the Go'Ella," Lorenz went on.

Another twitch from the prisoner on the floor.

"Gather them," Mars ordered.

The eyes of the man on the floor closed.

"Pardon?" Lorenz asked.

"Gather them for interrogation. All of them."

"The Go'Ella?" Lorenz inquired.

"Yes."

"*All* of them?"

"Yes. If you can, find the ones that belonged to these men." He swept an arm out to indicate the men on the floor, but he turned his attention to his captain. "Talk to your friend. If he knows, discover who they are, names, descriptions, and seek them. In the meantime, bring the ones that are currently serving priests in Fire City."

"The Go'Doan will not like this," Lorenz warned.

"They worship on my soil at my consent, but this gives them no rights.

They are not Firenz. If they give you trouble, they have a choice. They either forfeit their Go'Ella for questioning, or they leave this land under guard, and they take nothing with them but the amount of coin that it would take to feed them and their mounts on their journey. No negotiation. One, or the other. See to it, my brother."

Lorenz nodded and moved away.

Mars stood for a moment in contemplation of the prisoner of note.

He then walked to him where he rested, not terribly comfortably, chest down, legs bent, with a post behind knees that were spread wide, that post tied to his knees and his wrists, meaning his cheek rested against the stone. He could not move for his neck was collared, and it was there he was chained to the floor.

Basil had shared this was a favored position for him when he played in the Heden District.

Mars could see that, but he had no taste for it.

He would like his Silence in somewhat this same position, but without the posts and chains.

"What will *your* Go'Ella share with us when we find them, priest?" he asked quietly.

The man said nothing.

Mars did not share in the silence.

"I have always been most curious, how these women come to you, doing it when their circumstances are dire, and you offer them succor in return for using them as you see fit," Mars remarked. "Thus, to me, it is not a surprise, this offshoot of the Go'Doan. You all have it in you to feel you have the right to take what you will from people in need. I suspect it will be illuminating, when we have the opportunity to speak with them, what they will share."

Weakly, the man mumbled, "Long live The Rising."

"Hmm," Mars hummed as he straightened and strode away.

THE SERVANT CAME QUICKLY to him as he reined in his mount, Hephaestus, at the steps of the palace.

He threw his leg over his horse's rump, patted the steed's neck, and handed the straps to the servant before he strolled up the steps toward the doors.

The palace overseer came directly to him as he entered.

"I have placed the barons in the throne room, my king," the man said in Firenzii.

These clan barons, five of them, had journeyed to Fire City upon hearing all that was happening, and demanded an audience with their king at his earliest convenience upon his return.

Which Mars had deemed was now.

He nodded, strode through the vestibule, turning left to head to his throne room.

He took but two steps before he stopped short and saw nothing but red.

This was because, at the far end of the hall, at the opened doors to his throne room, stood his wife peering around the doorjamb, a hazy shimmer all about her.

She'd pulled her shadow over her.

And she was spying.

His blood coursing hot through his veins, he stalked down the hall. The sounds of his boots hitting the floor were stifled by the thick rugs, and his queen was so involved in her occupation, she did not sense him until the last minute.

When she did, she turned, looked up at him, began to smile, but halted in offering that to him when she caught a look at his face.

"Go to our chambers, now," he whispered.

"Mars, I—"

"You will go, or I will find a man to escort you, and I will instruct him to lock you in."

Her head jerked in surprise and her expression began to shift again but he did not have the patience to deal with whatever it would become.

"Do not try me, Silence. Go." He drew in a deep breath and finished, "*Now.*"

She took in his face, hers settled to impassive, before she moved around him.

The shimmer remained about her as there were guards stationed down that hall and it might be strange to see their king appearing to be conversing with nothing, but it would be far stranger, watching their queen form out of thin air.

As such, Silence hurried down the hall.

He watched her, still controlling his breathing, before he moved into the room where the barons awaited him.

Mars took his throne. He shared news they needed to hear regarding what had happened in Wodell and what was happening in Firenze. He answered questions, including ones put to him about the state of Farah, for the baron of her clan was there.

The man seemed concerned but was mollified at hearing Mars report she was not only now the Queen of Wodell, but also the Dellish were most enamored of her, though not nearly as much as her new king.

He then cut the meeting short and left the men in the room as he walked out, his strides long but unhurried, his deep inward and outward breaths his main focus.

However, he took the steps of the staircase three at a time and wasted no more of it as he moved down the hall to his and his queen's chambers.

He entered them, their large bath before him, and he looked right to their bedchamber.

He then looked left to their sitting room and saw her standing at the side of his desk on the far end.

He walked into the room, distractedly noting that she and her maid Tril had concocted yet another remarkable gown that was not the bejeweled brassiere and waistband above sheers that fell over her legs that was worn by the female Firenz.

Instead, it was a filmy creation in a shade of apricot that covered only one shoulder in an elegant gathering of material, leaving the other bare, and it had a deep slit up one side of the hem that would expose her leg as she walked.

Her hair was caught up in a graceful bunch of curls at the back, the front adorned with thin braids across her crown.

This was not Firenz.

It was not Dellish.

It was Silence.

And it was stunning.

He had no mind to that. He would pay mind to it later.

Now, he had his mind on one thing.

He stopped five feet from her and asked, "What did you think you were doing?"

She opened her mouth but shut it when he lifted his hand, palm her way and shook his head.

"No," he said. "I do not care. Don't do it again."

"But, Mars—" she began, and at her sweet, quiet voice, one of the myriad things he loved about her, one of the myriad things he would miss unrelentingly if she was taken from him, he lost the control he had been carefully holding when red again covered his vision as his blood scoured through his veins.

Thus, he leaned her way and thundered, *"Do not ever do it again!"*

She stood motionless before him, her eyes locked to his.

"I cannot even *begin* to entertain how fucking, bloody *foolish* that was," he bit. "What if one of them could see through your shadow?"

"They could not," she said quietly.

"And you know this?"

She lifted her chin. "I tested it."

He fisted his hands at these words, not about to entertain thoughts on how she'd done that either.

"Do not do it again," he growled.

His wife did not speak.

"Did you hear me, Silence?" he demanded.

"It would be hard not to, my king, for you shouted it at me," she returned.

"I did indeed, for I had been kind earlier. It wasn't foolish, Silence, it was stupid. And it was stupid because it was dangerous, *and* it was unnecessary. There is naught those men would say to each other in that chamber that I would need to know."

"Not that you know of," she retorted.

"Silence," he gritted between his teeth.

"You told me yourself they are not all allies, and in times such as these, we need allies," she shared. "But more, we need to understand who are *not* allies."

"And it will be I, the fucking *king*, who will establish alliances, Silence. And it will be I, the *fucking king*, who will determine who is not."

"Right," she whispered.

"And if you were found out," he kept at her, "spying on my barons, it would be detrimental to me making such alliances."

"I have been using my shadow for many years, my king."

"And you will not use it again for reasons I do not permit, my queen."

At this, she blinked.

"Right," she again whispered. "Are we finished?"

"Silence—"

"We are finished," she decreed.

She then moved to him only to walk by him, but he was not in accord that they were finished, thus he reached out and caught her arm.

She tugged at it viciously at the same time she snapped, "Take your hand from me."

He instantly yielded, letting her go, a pit forming in his stomach for she had not shirked his touch. Not once since they had learned to communicate, and shortly after, shared their love for one another.

She took three steps from him, placing herself out of his reach.

She then said, "In hearing these barons were in the city, awaiting an audience with you, one you granted them this day, I asked a special meal to be prepared. Thus, I intended to invite them and their wives to dine with us this eve. As you did not know these were my plans, I can only assume you did not extend this invitation."

His mother would extend the same invitation, for even if he and his wife had been back in their home not a full day, and thus might (and did) wish time alone, it was not only the right thing to do, it was the strategic thing to do.

"I did not but I will have my secretary send a messenger to them and share I was remiss in this and rectify that mistake," he replied.

She nodded, before she turned, continuing to move away, saying, "Elpis's secretary shared I have much correspondence to catch up on. Now, I shall see about doing that."

"*Bellezza*," he called.

She stopped at the doorway to their bathing room but spoke no words as she turned and caught his gaze.

"You must understand the strength of my desire to protect you," he stated.

"I do, for I would assume it is much the same as the strength of my desire to offer the same to you," she returned.

And with these parting words, his queen swept from their chambers.

It would seem his Silence was intent on doing what she had shared was her most fervent wish, outside being a good wife, and when that time came, a good mother.

This being a good queen.

For during dinner that eve with his barons and their wives, although she was not effusively chatty, for she was not this naturally, she was attentive to all, including him.

Her lips often curved in smiles that appeared genuine, even aimed toward him. And she allowed him to hold her hand, and she held his in return. Indeed, she did not move away from his touch in the slightest, at her elbow, at the small of her back.

And she launched her brand of charm offensive by calling for their pet monkey after dinner and allowing Piccola to scamper and entertain. But mostly she did this as she openly shared her affection for the animal, which would win over even Mars's most staunch detractor, or at least it would win them over to Silence, for Firenz had a deep affinity for all animals. Indeed, they considered those taken as pets to be as important to a family as children.

No, it was after the men and women separated—the men to take in smoke or *taibac* and consume cognac and whiskey, the women to do the same, but with sherry or brandy in another room—when he escorted the men to their wives to take their leave, that he was told that Silence's maid had called her away on a matter of some import and she had said her farewells earlier.

She had not been called away on a matter of import.

She was escaping him.

Mars detested when she did as such, but he had had some hours to consider his reaction to what she had done earlier. And although he did not think he was wrong in his concerns, he perhaps had not shared them as he should have done.

Thus, he bid his own farewells, and for the second time that day, he wasted none of it going to the chambers he shared with his wife in order to explain he had come to this conclusion in an effort to work through their quarrel.

When he arrived, he saw the lights were dimmed in all but their bedchamber, and thus, he headed there.

Silence was not abed, but hearing him arrive, Piccola scurried out of her dressing room, found a piece of furniture to climb and launched herself at him.

He caught the wee monkey and allowed her to scuttle up his shirt in order to hang onto the side of his neck as he moved to his wife's dressing room.

He pushed aside the sheers that covered the doorway.

His queen was seated with her back to him, wearing a nightgown he had a feeling he would like very much, for he already did only seeing one side of it, and Tril was at work, brushing her gleaming hair.

Tril gave him wide eyes.

Mars shook his head to her and cast his gaze to the back of his wife's head.

"The barons have left," he announced.

"All right," Silence replied tonelessly, not turning to look at him.

Tril kept brushing, now averting her eyes and biting her lip.

Mars fought back a sigh and shared, "I shall meet you in bed."

"Yes," was all Silence said.

He turned, taking Piccola with him to his own dressing room where their pet had to release him so Mars could disrobe and put on his silk sleeping pants.

This he did, and then he entered their bedchamber, fell to his back on their bed, his shoulders and head against the headboard.

He folded his hands behind his head but took one away to stroke Piccola's back when she curled in a ball on his stomach just above his navel.

She was tired out, their baby, from all the activity and attention of the night.

He thought this, aiming his eyes to Silence's dressing room.

No murmur of conversation came from there, but it took a frustrating amount of time for his queen to emerge from behind the sheers with Tril following her.

And at one sight of his wife, Mars's body turned to stone.

This was not because her nightgown wasn't fetching.

It very much was.

It was because her marital chain was gone.

Tril swiftly made her way about the room, blowing out lamps, though she did not approach the bed to blow out the ones glowing at each side.

And when she started to make her way back to the dressing room, through which was a door to her room, she called Piccola, who did not want to leave her papa. But animals had instincts and the mood in the room was far from lost on their wee one.

Thus, the monkey scuttled away.

Through this, Silence had made the journey slowly to her side of the bed. She'd thrown back the silks and had sat her arse on the side in preparation to fully enter it.

"You will not lie down in our bed."

It did not elude Mars's notice, the rumbling quality of his voice.

It did not elude his wife's either, for she turned to look over her shoulder at him.

"Come around to this side," he ordered.

"My king, I am tired."

It struck him then that, even in company, from the moment he'd shouted at her, she had not addressed him as anything but "my king."

"Come around to this side," he repeated.

"Perhaps we can—"

"Do it."

In the now, his tone brooked no argument, and although she appeared for a moment as if she would disagree with that notion, she did not.

She stood and walked to his side of the bed.

As she did, he sat up and twisted so he was seated with his legs splayed wide.

When she was before him, he commanded, "Come here," explaining "here" by pointing at the floor between his feet.

Silence hesitated but moved there.

He did not touch her.

What he did was tilt his head to look at her.

"It was not so long ago, no? Not so long ago when I removed my wedding chain even though we had promised always to remove one another's before sleep," he reminded her.

"It was not so long ago," she replied. "No."

That was all she said.

Mars felt that pit that had developed in his stomach earlier start to burn.

"Therefore, it was not so long ago you felt what I am feeling right now," he continued.

"You're right. It was not so long ago."

And again, that was all she said.

He did not have vast reserves in this situation, but he gathered what patience he could muster. And he did this primarily because of what he said next.

"It was much I shared with you this morning," he told her softly. "It was bad timing. Not *my* timing, I will remind you. But bad, for we had both been away long, and there was much to see to, and due to that, I could not see to you after sharing what had to be confusing and upsetting news."

"I have had time to think on it during the day, my king."

My king.

Mars clenched his teeth.

"And I will admit to a bevy of emotion felt throughout this day," she carried on. "Including upset and concern, that mostly for my mother, and anger, that mostly for my father. But in the end, I found you were right. It explains a great many things in my life as pertains to my place in the house where I was raised. So, although I am not unaware that these emotions will likely careen for some time, I feel strong in saying that I will settle on simply being relieved that I was unloved not because I was unlovable, but my father is the man he is."

Her words made the burn in his stomach dim and a tightness form in his chest.

"You are definitely not unlovable, my Silence," he murmured.

"No, I am not. For Tril loves me and always has. Nearly from the moment we met, we have been friends. And True loves me and has shown that to me for as far back as I can remember. And even though you were also right, not only about the ugly nature of my father, but the weak one of my mother, she loved me as well, as much as he would let her."

She missed somebody.

"And I love you too," he reminded her.

"Yes," she replied without conviction.

He clenched his teeth, reached out and took her hands in his.

She tugged slightly, but he held strong, feeling a vein pulse in his temple at her attempted retreat.

"Much has happened in the time we have been together, but we are still new, *amore*," he stated as patiently as he could. "We must not lose sight of that as we navigate these early times in our marriage."

"Agreed."

At least she granted that.

Mars endeavored to take heart in it and carried on.

"Thus, I will admit to perhaps not communicating my concerns earlier as I should have done."

"Perhaps," she replied, a bite to that word not sharing she concurred with what he'd said, instead disliking he'd used that word.

"Silence—"

"You treated me like him," she accused, and Mars again went stone still. "You called me stupid. You have no use for me, my king, except one. His was to marry me to the husband that best suited his stature. Yours is in this bed."

He could not believe his ears.

No.

He did not *want* to believe she had said what he had heard.

"You cannot possibly believe that," he ground out.

She lifted her brows. "Is this not what you said to me earlier today?"

"It is not."

"I have used my shadow many times in my life, my king, *many*." She put great stress on her last word. "No one can see it, save you. It is a gift. A gift from the gods to me. There is a reason I have it. There is a reason you can see through it, and *only you*. But I will repeat, there is a reason *I have it*. And although I will admit that you were right, the barons said naught that you might need to hear while I was there, it was not foolish *or* stupid that I did what I did."

She took a breath, but he had no chance to get words in, for she quickly recommenced in returning to hers.

"I know this, for I did it because I love you. I did it because I believe in you and your vision for your realm. I did it because I would have you face no adversity or even uncertainty as you carry it forward, but since I cannot make that happen, I would do what I could. I did it safe in doing it because I have long since learned how to be unseen not only using my shadow.

But in this instance, I was using my shadow."

"You must understand how I would worry for you and *our* realm should you have been discovered," he retorted.

"What I understand is that you look upon my practice with my daggers and my scrapping with Kyril and Basil with amused condescension. I understand that you shouted at me like a misbehaving child earlier and shared with me what you would permit, no...what you would *not*, again, as if you were speaking to a misbehaving child."

"And you also must understand, for I spoke the words not minutes ago, that I realize I did not communicate well with you earlier."

"You said *perhaps*," she returned.

His hands held hers tighter.

"Silence, I cannot believe *you* do not understand the insult you leveled upon me by comparing me to your father."

"Then perhaps you should cease behaving like I am a belonging and instead behave like I am a being, I am your wife, and I have your regard."

Mars released his hold on her hands, his chest no longer tight, his gut on fire with his fury.

"Truly, my king," she said in an even voice, clearly not noticing the change in him, "it was also *you* who decided when I would have the knowledge the father I had always known was not my own. It was also *you* who decided to seek my true father and shared with me you would let me know him if *you* decided he was worthy of me."

She took a startled step back as he stood.

He took an unhurried step away from her and their bed.

She turned to continue facing him as he did.

"You sleep alone tonight, my queen."

Pink hit her cheeks, and it was the first time he did not like it.

"Mars—"

Now he was Mars.

But now it was too late.

"And I bid you to do it well," he said before he turned his back to his wife and strode directly from the room.

100

THE MESSAGE

Queen Ophelia
On Approach to Kilcree Break, at the Fork of the Dunleth Abhainn and the West-fork River
AIREN

Ophelia did not like the mood of the moors as she, with her warriors at her back, slowly made their way toward Kilcree Break, where they had been told Fern was being held in the stronghold there.

And it was not only the gray and dreary skies that shrouded their approach that affected the mood.

Throughout their journey, she had had spies move ahead to ascertain the lay of the land.

But until they approached the Break, she had not credited their reports, which had been that the place was deserted.

However, it appeared just this.

Eerily so.

The pennants of the Lord of Kilcree slapped above the keep that rose high from the center of the fortified town.

And as they approached, her archers with arrows set to pulled bows fanning out, Ophelia saw the gate to the walls around the town was open.

"Halt," she called, and they halted.

She then opened her senses, feeling the tingle at her back, casting out.

Nothing.

She turned her head right, toward Lucinda.

"Take a team, go," she murmured.

Lucinda nodded and rounded her steed, gathering her team.

She turned her head left, toward Agnes.

"Ride the perimeter."

Agnes lifted her chin and turned her mount, calling quietly to her squadron.

With her eyes, her senses still opened, Ophelia scanned the ramparts of the wall surrounding the city, and then the pinnacle of the keep.

She had not felt the tremor of the veil. She had not felt Fern's loss.

She must be alive, somewhere.

But they had to have moved her from this barren place for she was not here.

She watched Lucinda ride cautiously forward with her team as Agnes's warriors struck out, side to side.

There was something not right here.

She did not sense it as wrong.

But it was not right.

She felt worry dog her mind as her lieutenant, her friend, Lucinda, and the twenty-five Nadirii who went with her disappeared behind the open gate, and she did as she'd trained herself to do over the years.

She set aside that worry.

And she waited.

But as she did, something else that she had trained herself to keep close about her over the years escaped her.

Patience.

"Keep bows up and stay alert," she called and clicked her teeth for her mount, Midsummer, to move forward.

"My queen," a warrior said in warning behind her.

She put her heels to her steed and the mare went from a walk to a canter.

"Remain behind," she ordered as she trotted toward the gate.

She'd barely cleared it before the pall settled on her.

This was a place of death.

She swallowed the saliva that filled her mouth and met the eyes of two warriors who exited a dwelling to her right that they were working as a team to clear.

"Aught?" she asked.

Both shook their heads and moved swiftly to the next dwelling, easily breaching it, for its door was ajar.

She turned her head left and watched another crew of Nadirii creep down an alley.

Slowly, she walked Midsummer forward toward the small castle in the middle of the town.

She stopped when she saw two of her women come out of an abode.

One nodded to the other, the other remained where she was as the first strode toward Ophelia.

The Nadirii queen looked down at her warrior when she stopped beside Midsummer.

"There is blood, my queen, everywhere. A good amount of it," she reported.

Ophelia felt her lips tighten.

And the nagging fatigue that the draughts she had been taking had held at bay, as it had these last few days they had rode through Airen, threatened to overwhelm her.

She set that aside as well.

"Bodies?" she asked.

"None so far," the Nadirii answered.

Ophelia nodded. "Keep clearing."

After issuing her order, she turned her mount and trotted back to the gate, where she stopped and whistled, lifting a hand with one finger extended.

Another team of twenty-five broke ranks and rode forward, leaving the remaining three hundred Nadirii fanned out on the moor.

The rest of their contingent, numbering one hundred and twenty-five, had earlier taken posts through the Argyll Forest to their back and along the Westfork and Dunleth, to the south, north and east, in order to act as scouts for danger that might threaten the whole regiment approaching Kilcree.

Ophelia again whirled Midsummer and made her cautious way through the town toward the castle.

She had reined in at the end of the footbridge over the moat when she saw Lucinda on horseback enter the drawbridge riding at some speed toward the barbican.

Lucinda pulled back so quickly, her steed reeled, but her lieutenant only jerked up her chin toward her queen.

Thus, Ophelia rode on, over the footbridge, through the arch at the barbican, over the lowered drawbridge and through the opening under the guardhouse, following Lucinda and rounding the guardhouse once she cleared it, walking Midsummer across the bailey toward the opened door to the keep.

But Ophelia smelled it before she stopped where Lucinda was still astride her horse at the door to the tall building.

"What has happened here?" Ophelia asked.

"I would have to examine the bodies," Lucinda answered in her taciturn lieutenant's usual manner, that being emotionlessly, but with these opening words, Ophelia braced. "And there are two sets. One of men, shrouded carefully, respectfully, though from the little I saw under the dressings of the one I examined, their corpses were not always treated with such deference. They are laid out in an upper room in the keep and they have been dead for some time. The others, many of them, tossed unceremoniously in a large room below the earth. This closed off in order not to be ravaged as carrion, as it is clear they were meant to be found as they are. They have been dead for a while, but not nearly as long as the others."

Ophelia did not understand what she was hearing.

"Does Cassius have allies he does not know?" she inquired.

"You would need to ask him, though I will say it is not known widely the Zees are his friends."

Ophelia, not often taken aback, was just thus.

"Zees?" she queried.

"Zees gather weapons where they can steal them, but in hand-to-hand combat, they utilize them in a rather distinct way."

"By the goddess," Ophelia murmured.

"The decay has long set in." Lucinda's voice now held a slight tone of regard. "But I would hazard to guess the shrouded men are Otho and his squad. And I will note, Ophelia, that I mentioned the others piled below, and we have not sorted through them, but I did not see a single woman amongst them."

"Dear goddess," Ophelia breathed before she gathered her wits and proclaimed, "It would not be good for peace in this land if the women rise up peremptorily. And I cannot credit it, for they never get involved in politics. Zees?"

Lucinda did not have a chance to reply, one of her team moved out of the keep.

She nodded to Lucinda as she halted by their horses.

But she looked to her queen.

"Fern was held here. And she is here no longer. But we were left a message," the warrior reported.

"And that is?" Ophelia asked.

"I would magic a mask for the smell, and then it's best you are shown," the Nadirii replied.

Ophelia dismounted immediately, saying words to Midsummer that would keep her horse where she was, and she, with Lucinda coming off her steed to follow, moved into the keep.

The smell was such she had to cover her mouth with her hand while casting a quick spell so she would scent lilies, not the ugly stench of death, as the warrior guided them to the stairs.

They went nearly to the top before Ophelia and Lucinda followed her through a door.

All of the women stopped.

The room was part circle, and dead center from its ceiling hung the rotting corpse of a man of means. His rich clothing was in tatters, however, not due to use but abuse. And his pants were about his knees, hanging from his decomposing limbs precariously. Fortunately, his genitals had not been mutilated, but there were drawings in charcoal with arrows pointing to them on the flesh of his thighs and stomach that Ophelia could not decipher due to the level of decay.

The Lord of Kilcree, humiliated, then hung where he had imprisoned a witch.

And along the rounded wall, in large words, also scrawled in charcoal, it said...

We will bear no more your burden.

And it was signed...

Fern's Army.

And off from that, in smaller words...

What they said.

And that was signed...

The Patra.

And just beyond that...

Extend our greetings to Cass and Ellie.

"Bloody hell," Ophelia muttered.

Then she closed her eyes.

And heaved a mighty sigh.

IOI

THE READINGS

Princess Elena
Bedchamber of the Prince Regent, Sky Citadel, Sky Bay
AIREN

Wearing naught but one of Cass's undershirts that was fashioned in a thin knit of cotton and had four buttons at the collar that I assumed were there so he could loosen them and get his head through, after procuring my cards, I approached the bed where my prince slept.

Once there, I studied his face in repose and wondered first, if he knew how handsome he was. Second, I wondered what all his beautiful markings meant. And last, if I would ever get him to the point where he did not appear somehow anguished, even in sleep.

On this final thought, I carefully braced a foot on the side slat of the bed, swung my leg around, and landed quite firmly astride his gut.

His eyes shot open, his lips emitted a strained *"oof,"* and his hands clamped on my hips as his stomach muscles tensed in a divine way in preparation for him to knife up.

"Good morning, my warrior," I greeted on a huge smile.

"Woman." He settled back into bed, the deep definition of the boxes at his stomach going away, but some definition remained as it always did, so I did not complain. "What the hell?"

I lifted my hand in which I held my cards and shook it side to side.

And when his beautiful blue eyes slid to them, I announced, "Time for a reading."

His gaze returned to mine.

"I don't want a reading."

"You're going to get a reading."

"Elena, I don't *want* a reading."

I scanned the heavily curtained canopy over his bed and told it, "He repeatedly asks me for a reading, but when I *want* to give him a reading? *Nooooo*. He suddenly doesn't *want* a reading."

"Stop being endearing."

The despondent tone to his deep voice had my eyes jumping back to his.

"I don't want a reading for I don't need a reading, my darling. I know what today will bring," he informed me.

I leaned to him, reaching out a hand to tug the beard at his chin affectionately, and suggested softly, "How about we let the cards tell us?"

"Elena—"

"Five," I whispered. "Just five. Not a full reading." I pressed the cards to his chest. "Just five."

"Have you turned your card today?" he whispered back, knowing I did just this every day if I had even the slightest amount of time.

"Yes," I shared.

"And will you tell me what it was?"

"It was the Lovers," I told him unreservedly. "Union. Balance. Harmony."

He stared into my eyes, and I could see the flash of hope in his as given to him by my card.

And I seized on that.

"Please, Cass?" I cajoled.

He let out a heavy breath before he pushed up. I then allowed him to manhandle me until I was arse to his lap with his arms around me.

"What do you wear?" he asked, noticing his shirt of a sudden.

"Your shirt."

"Why?" he pressed.

"Because it smells of you."

His head was turned to me, and at my words, his eyes veritably *drank* in my features.

All right.

Er...

It had to be said (though not out loud), I loved, adored, and maybe even *worshipped* this man.

And not simply because he could look at me in that manner.

"You can smell me, my princess, for I am right here," he noted quietly, but his words nor tone did aught to hide how much it meant to him the reason I wore his shirt.

"Well, I wanted to smell you everywhere I went this morning, which was not all *right here*, so I made it so I could do that," I stated, trying to hide my fluster.

I then jerked the cards to him.

"Shuffle and cut, set aside the bottom cut, shuffle again, then cut, set aside the bottom, shuffle again and hand me the top five cards," I commanded.

"As you wish," he murmured and took the deck from me.

He did this decisively, handed me five cards without looking at them, and all this lasted perhaps twenty seconds.

"Most people spend time with the cards," I educated him.

"I do not need to spend time with the cards for I know what they'll say," he retorted. "Now turn my first, Ellie."

"Are you certain you don't wish to reshuffle?" I offered.

"Yes."

"Positive?"

It was then I received what I was working for.

His full lips framed by that dense, dark beard I liked so much hitched into a grin.

"Just turn the first card, woman."

"Happy to oblige," I stated, nestling my ass more firmly in his lap, feeling his body tense about mine, which I was also working for, and I turned the first card, letting it fall to the velvet-covered duvet in front of us.

Drat.

It was the Earth

A high card.

Sometimes not bad.

This time, maybe not good.

"And that is?" Cass prompted.

"Earth," I told him. "Training. Study."

"Mm?"

He knew I was holding back mostly because neither he nor I in this time of our lives needed either training or study.

"Work," I pushed out. "Toil."

"Ah," he murmured.

I quickly tossed down the next one.

Shite.

The Crow.

"That does not look like it bodes well," he noted, staring at the inauspicious black bird sitting on its black perch, the background a foreboding mix of blues, purples and grays.

"The Crow." And before he could ask, I quickly shared, "It is not bad. It is a middling card. It means second sight. Reflection. Magic. Mystery."

"And you read that as...?"

I turned my head to look at him. "Perhaps, after the toil we both know today will bring, you need to take some time to center yourself."

"Center myself?"

"Think. Meditate. Recognize you're on the right path but ascertain if the way you intend to move down it is correct."

He cast his gaze to the cards and again hummed, "Mm."

I threw down the next, and seeing it, I was surprised he had two high cards come so swiftly, at the same time I was thinking what that card said was not all that card meant.

"The Moon," he said.

"The Moon," I confirmed. "Intuition. Magic. Womanhood. Power."

His arms about me tightened as he remarked, "That one is not difficult to read."

I would let him think that, for the now, even if I had a feeling it meant far more.

I threw down the next.

Goddess damn it.

"The Manticore," he stated tonelessly.

He knew that one. He'd seen it before.

"War. Battle," he went on.

He had a blasted good memory.

I turned and reminded his profile, "Also power. Victory."

He too turned and looked into my eyes.

"The last one, Ellie."

I was so certain this would go well. I felt it in my bones that morning after turning my own card.

It had to go well.

For things as they were in his realm could not get worse.

I turned the card.

And felt my heart leap.

"The Phoenix," I whispered. I then aimed a big smile at him before I went on, "Renewal. Transformation. Rebirth."

He looked from the cards to me and pointed out, "We do not know what that rebirth will be."

"Yes, we do."

"No, darling, we don't."

"We absolutely do."

"Elena—"

I shifted in his lap, took hold of his head in both hands and pressed my lips hard to his.

When I felt his hands glide up my back to keep me close, and perhaps carry on with activities that could lead from a kiss, I disengaged and declared, "We will work. We will toil. We will reflect. We will fight. We will meet victory and be renewed."

"Your unrelenting optimism is exhausting," he muttered.

"Well then," I began, twisting even farther in his lap and pressing my hands to his shoulders to take him down to his back, "if my prince is so fatigued, I shall be forced to do all the work."

That earned me another grin along with an outright lie.

"It's devastating to admit, but even just awake, I am remarkably weary."

As he settled onto the pillows, and I straightened my frame atop him, I felt something not weary at all prodding my stomach.

"Perhaps I can energize you," I whispered into his neck.

And then I trailed my mouth down, taking my time at his swelling chest, and his delicious stomach, until I found something more delectable between his legs.

I took my time with that too, and my efforts were rewarded.

I energized my prince.

So much, he did not take his time while taking me on my knees from behind, his hand over mine curled on the headboard.

His bed was most sturdy.

But it banged so mightily against the black stone wall, I feared it would crash right through it.

Energized, indeed.

To say the battle that opened the harbor and the subsequent one that ended the siege did not much affect the citizens of Sky Bay was an understatement.

However, the arrest of their king and one of his wives for crimes pertaining to violating a woman did.

I had learned since we arrived in the capital city of Airen why Cassius's soldiers were lined along the avenue to the Citadel and not off fighting the besiegers.

They were posted thus to be poised to fight any disorder that might occur *in* the Bay. And as the city was well supplied as a matter of course, and it would take some months for a siege to have significant negative effects on its citizens, they'd been ordered to ignore what happened beyond it until Cassius arrived home.

He needed to hold his capital at all costs, he'd shared. Not only because its harbor was crucial, but also the message it would relay to his people if he could not even secure his home.

And his soldiers had been very busy doing this the four days since Gallienus and Horatia had been incarcerated in Slán Bailey, Airen's largest prison which was situated on a small island just off the harbor.

In this time, I took great heart in noting the disorder that occurred was not only men acting out who were angered that their until-now steadfast position of power was being threatened (and there were many men who acted out as such, Slán Bailey was getting most crowded).

There were also men making clear they stood by their Prince Regent and celebrated the changes he was making. They demonstrated somewhat peaceably (these demonstrations being "somewhat," for liquor on occasion turned the tide of these celebrations, and the men who disagreed with them did not mind doing it using the tactic of engaging in fisticuffs in the streets).

Indeed, Jasmine, Hera, Finnie, Circe and myself had watched from the ramparts just such a parade march up to the gate at the end of the avenue to the Citadel and it was a glad sight to see.

What was not glad was that there were very few women amongst them.

I told myself, it had not been a long time.

They would learn.

After toil, the Phoenix would rise.

And when she did, she would be free.

And as I rode at Cassius's side that day, surprisingly where I was without having an argument with him to allow me to be there (indeed, he'd actually *asked* me to do so), I thought of the Phoenix and rebirth for this land and reminded myself staunchly (and unrelentingly optimistically) the cards foretold it so.

I knew my man was unnerved with me beside him, even if my warriors and his surrounded us closely, there were many of us, and all were heavily armed, including Cassius and myself.

I also knew my betrothed could not make the statement he wished to make by hiding me in his Citadel.

He needed me seen.

He needed me strong.

He needed my head held high.

And that was how I rode beside him, wearing full Nadirii regalia, including my royal headband.

There did not appear to be more women in the streets during this journey than there were the day I had arrived, and again no children, but if I caught any gazes, if they were not staring at me with hate, I smiled.

I counted, and by the time we made the wharf, seven men had smiled back.

All tentatively.

But it was something.

I could not think long on that, for ahead was Slán Bailey, and in the now, we needed to dismount and board an odd boat with a strange paddlewheel at the back. It was somewhat square and had a canopy in the middle to make an interior portion to keep rain or mist from your clothing.

And I did not want to enter it.

On my feet or on Diana's back, I could do anything.

In a boat?

I hid my discomfiture at this and followed Cass's lead.

When he walked directly to the uncovered bow of the boat, I went there with him.

Two other such boats filled with our guard would go with us, the rest of our guard remaining ashore.

But in our boat was Cass, me, Jazz, Hera, Mac, Ian and Nero.

I kept silent and stood next to Cassius as we broke away from the dock.

And I watched the daunting Bailey get closer as the men who labored at paddles that somehow rounded the wheel at the back propelled us.

Slán Bailey was close enough to reach by boat in a short period of time, but it was far enough away, in the unlikelihood a prisoner should escape, unless they were in the best of health, they would find it impossible to swim the distance to shore.

However, through the cold, choppy waters, even for the healthiest of prisoners, it would be a self-imposed death sentence.

It was, I could see, a pentagram of five towers connected by curtain walls. The entirety was built to the very edge of the ragged cliffs that made up the boundaries of the island. There was one ingress, thus, one egress, the front gate with its dock below. One tower, the one at the back, was rather low, perhaps four stories. The one facing Sky Bay was very high, at least nine. The other three were six.

Long, thin, black pennants flew atop all of them.

Fortunately, we made the dock of Slán Bailey without incident.

Cass did not wait for all three boats to arrive.

He took my hand in his, lifted it to press to the side of his chest, and immediately led us up the pier, to the gate and through it.

A man not in the black leathers of the Airenzian army, but instead wearing black wool trousers tucked into black boots with a thick black wool sweater with a rolltop neck and epaulettes sewn at his shoulders greeted us.

As he got close, I saw he also had stitched over his left chest in black thread an insignia that looked like a window covered in crossed bars.

He bowed smartly and said, "Your Grace." I watched him carefully and continued to do so as he straightened only to shift my way, bow again and repeat, "Your Grace."

"My betrothed is not fond of bowing, Reginald," Cass drawled.

The man lifted and grinned at Cassius.

I was surprised at this response, but I just kept watching.

"Of course," he said and turned his grin to me. "A Nadirii at the Bailey, here to assist in questioning prisoners," he stated openly gleeful. "My wife is currently at her window on the shore with a telescope, hoping to catch sight of this historical event across the water."

"You should have allowed her to come to be a party to it," I replied.

"Hells no," he said on a whoosh of air, and I stiffened. "She'd be right in *all my* business. 'Reginald, you *must* trim the fat on the meat you give your inmates. Fat is not healthy. They need lean meats.' And 'Reginald, just *look* at the state of these blankets. Bring them home in batches. I'll gather my women and mend them.'" He looked to Cassius. "As if prisoners deserve decent blankets. Crikey."

I turned astonished eyes over my shoulder to look at both Jazz and Hera.

Jazz was staring at Reginald with her lips parted in surprise.

Hera looked like she was about ready to laugh.

"Righty ho!" Reginald cried with more excitement than was healthy in this dismal place with its thick black walls that veritably wept moisture. "Let us get you about your business so you can get away from here and home. Which do you want first? Her honorable Horatia or the man who once was king."

The man who once was king?

Well then, didn't *that* have a lovely ring to it?

"Horatia," Cassius told him.

"To the palace we go," he stated cheerfully, faking a doffing of a hat he did not wear with a maneuver of his hand.

He then moved us into the dank confines beyond, tipping his head jauntily to guards along the way, all of whom bowed to Cassius and me, none of whom looked spiteful, though many looked speculative as they regarded me.

Reginald entered a doorway that was opened by a guard at the tallest tower (apparently, the "palace") and up we went.

Up, up, up, past eight doors, before he called out on the final flight, "Oy, there! Open up. The Regent is here."

Thus, at the top, we were able to move right through the door there that was manned by another guard wearing Reginald's uniform.

"Best room of the lot, coziest," Reginald declared on a tip of the chin at the guard tending the first door we came to, one I knew would have an unadulterated, and perhaps even stunning view of Sky Bay.

The door was opened to us, and as we entered (only Cass and I, due to the limited space), I was thrown by how tidy and well-appointed it was.

Everything was in blacks, grays and browns (as per usual in this land).

But there was a rather large bed with a fluffy mattress, puffy pillows and thick duvet over it, as well as several woolen throws and even a fur. An armchair with ottoman. A table with four chairs, as if awaiting a small dinner party or a game of chance. Thick rugs overlapping each other on the floors to keep draughts at bay. Lanterns all around to fight the gloom. And a roaring fire in a small fireplace, but one that heated the space relatively thoroughly.

And I was correct.

Upon turning my head from Horatia, who rose from the armchair after setting aside a book (setting it on top of a stack of others), I saw from one of the three albeit narrow windows (so narrow, it would be impossible for but the smallest of children to push through) the view was astounding.

"You are keeping well?" Cassius asked.

"I have nothing to say to you," she spat.

"No need to answer that, I see you are," he muttered.

And she was.

She did not look sallow or unwashed.

In fact, her hairstyle was lovely, her clothing clean, and although she did not have the yards of chains at her neck and wrists she normally wore, and no paint on her face (which I thought made her far more attractive), she looked positively robust.

It had not been long she had been there, but still.

"I come to make you an offer," Cassius told her.

"You have nothing I desire," she returned.

"Not even your freedom?" he queried.

She glared at him.

"It would help greatly if all three of my father's wives were to share openly about their treatment at his hands—" Cassius began.

"That is not happening," she snapped.

"Is it simply that you feel you did not suffer at his hands? Or that you would not be willing to attest to what you knew about what the others endured?" Cassius asked.

"Your father, my husband, my *king* was always most kind to me. To all of us," she declared.

And at that, I jumped, for Cassius let out a bark of genuinely amused laughter.

I studied him closely, wondering if strain was perhaps having an effect, but as his laughter waned, he said to Horatia, "That was most amusing."

"I wasn't being funny."

"You do know I saw with my own eyes Gallienus *not* being most kind *at all*," he reminded her.

"What happens in a man's bedchamber—" she started.

"Enough," he interrupted, then regarded her before musing, "I don't understand it. Do you have some sort of madness?"

"No," I answered for her. "She had status, she had power, and she used it, did you not?"

"I am a woman, and I—"

"Saved yourself by offering them up," I surmised. "You cowed them so that he could truly cow them, and at their expense, you thrived. Not queen of a land. Not partner to a king. But queen of your little dominion. In order that you would not face it, you made it so he turned to them."

"It is their duty to their lord and king," she retorted, finishing snidely, "And *husband.*"

"And it was yours as well, was it not?" I asked.

She sniffed. "He would use me."

"Would he?"

"Of course, I am his wife."

"We have kindly not discussed this with Domitia. She needs some time to heal," I shared. "Cornelia is quite closed off. She needs some time to learn to trust. But when the time comes that they feel safe to chat, what will they tell us?"

"I couldn't begin to imagine," she replied.

I took a step toward her. "You do know, it is understandable...not acceptable, but in your world and how you had no choice but to exist in it, it is understandable that you would seek to protect yourself. However, now you have other protections, and I encourage you to use them."

"You think the Regent will prevail," she said with no small amount of disgust.

"I know he will," I told her.

"Then it is *you* who will see *precisely* what it is like to exist in this world if he does not spirit you from it when he fails," she spat. "Until then, you cannot stand there and judge *me*. You have no idea."

"I have more idea than you can imagine," I retorted.

I immediately pulled back when her face twisted in wrath.

And pain.

"I had a love," she bit out. "A gentle man who was gentle to me and he loved me." She leaned my way so threateningly, Cassius moved partially in front of me. "*Loved me,*" she hissed. "But then, I caught the eye of *the king.*"

Oh no.

"He petitioned, my Coram did," she went on angrily. "He petitioned the king to release me so he could have my hand. There is one thing I'm sure you know, my Princess *Regent*. You know what the king's answer was to that."

"Horatia," I whispered, stunned at hearing this news and hating the hearing of it.

"And my king," she threw her hands to the sides and continued to glare at me, "oh, how delighted he was with his new acquisition. Yes, he was." Her expression became a sneer. "He simply *could not* get *enough* of me."

I felt cold overtake me.

"So yes, absolutely, when Cornelia came along, I saw an opportunity," she shared. "And yes, when she was there, I knew I would finally have some relief. So *yes*, absolutely *yes*, my Princess Regent, I contrived to offer her up. I contrived so he would turn to her and not to me. I schemed to keep her his favorite and bow her to my whim, for I had few whims available to me. And when Domitia arrived, I did the same. And I'd do it again. Make no mistake, I feel no remorse. I'd do it again and again and again."

"You were correct," I said carefully. "I do not understand your world."

"You still judge," she retorted snidely.

"I don't," I said softly.

It was as if she didn't hear me when she carried on, "Living in your homes in the trees, free from tyranny. You have no idea how it feels to wake in the morning every morning and know there is no goodness to be had that day, as there was none the day before, and there will be none the day after, and yet you wake, but you wish you did *not*."

I decided, belatedly, to stop speaking.

Though I did it knowing my heart was bleeding.

"Will you speak to his treatment of you and the others?" Cassius asked, his voice reserved.

"No, I will not," she returned.

"It is not on deaf ears your words have fallen," Cassius told her. "But you will face tribunal yourself, Horatia, if you do not agree. In what you have shared, I hope you understand that all who aid this kind of behavior must learn not to do as such." Cassius warned. "I lament that was the life you led. But I can do naught about the past. Only your future. And your future includes a long time in this room, Horatia, if you do not agree to speak to his treatment of his wives."

She looked side to side and declared, "It is not so very terrible here." Her attention returned to Cassius. "Indeed, sire, a fire, a book, naught but my own company, this is *paradise*."

I could imagine it was.

I was then surprised when Cassius did not relent.

"Horatia, before, you had limited choices on the actions you took to end your own suffering. But now, you have the opportunity to make the right ones. With that, and the many who will benefit, the many who will not be forced to live the existence you did, will you not make the right ones?" Cassius pressed.

"I have already told you, Your Grace," she stated, "I feel I *have* been making the right ones."

All in the room and out of it remained silent until Cass broke it.

"I am sorry all that befell you," he said quietly.

"I am sorry, for I do not believe you, as you lived in the very same home as me, and you did naught to help me."

I got closer to Cassius after he flinched at her words.

"I am sorry for that as well," he shared, but he offered no excuses about the fact he was near as powerless as she.

"Your apology means nothing to me," she spat.

Cassius took that.

But I would not allow him to absorb it.

"Did you share with him what you were enduring?" I asked.

"He knew," she returned.

Maybe he did.

But at his response to what he saw happening to Domitia, I had a sense he did not.

"It is my understanding he had as little to do with his father as he could," I noted, not entirely pleased with myself she conceded that with her expression, though I hoped Cassius caught it. "It is also my understanding he was but a boy when you came to the Citadel."

She looked away.

I decided that would be enough, thus I said no more.

"As you said, you can do naught about the past, but you can about the future, so please," she stepped back in a mock curtsy, before righting herself, looking to Cassius and finishing, "use me as your example. I shiver in excitement at the opportunity to be exposed and humiliated in order to liberate the females of my realm."

Cassius studied her a moment before he returned a quick bow and turned, his mantle flashing out behind him as he strode to the door.

Hera and Jasmine leaped out of his way as he exited the room

"Take me to my father," I heard him order Reginald. "Swiftly."

I looked to Horatia. "You have my apologies as well."

"I don't very much care."

I drew in breath.

So be it.

I then exited the room, doing it quickly in order to catch up with Cassius.

When I did, I called, "Cass."

"I need her testimony," he decreed, not breaking stride on his descent of the stairs. "I need it on record. I need those who support me to understand I do not do this on a whim. This is no power play. I need it as evidence of the righteousness of our cause, for now and for history."

"I will speak to Domitia. Cornelia. They will bear witness to this," I replied.

He stopped in the stairwell and looked up at me.

"She is right. I did not help her."

"My prince," I murmured. "Think. As things were, even if you knew what she endured, how would you have done that? You were but a crown prince. You could not spirit a king's wife away, for what would befall you if you were caught? Where would this realm be if you were not as you are now?"

He listened to my words before he turned abruptly and resumed his descent of the stairs, stating, "We will speak of it later."

I followed him quickly, my hand on the rope rail to guide my way as I looked behind me to Hera and Jasmine.

They appeared unhappy.

Mac, Ian and Nero, following them, looked much the same.

The march to his father's cell was long. With Reginald at the lead, we walked along the clammy halls inside the curtain wall through one tower to the one at the opposite end of the island.

The short one.

And we did not ascend when we got there.

We descended.

The king's chamber, however, was much the same as Horatia's. Perhaps smaller, and there were no windows, but there was a fire and furnishings that made it comfortable.

As we entered, though, and I caught sight of Gallienus, I saw the differences were striking.

Instantly, I wanted Horatia to see him.

Four days in a prison, she was vigorous, and her spirit had not been broken.

She was bitter, the woman who was once her long ago was gone.

But in the now, she had not been broken.

Four days, and Gallienus was wasting away.

I noted Cassius was just as surprised as I was.

"You must release me from this hell," Gallienus demanded.

Cass turned, looking over my shoulder, presumably to Reginald.

"He does not leave this cell even when he can," I heard Reginald respond to Cass's unasked question as I continued to examine Cass's father. "He is offered exercise, he does not take it. His food is plentiful, he does not eat it. Though he drinks much wine."

"I have no appetite. Would *you* have an appetite if you were forced to live this nightmare?" Gallienus asked his son.

"This is hardly a nightmare, Father," Cassius said slowly.

"Not to see the sky? I am the Sky King, and I am not allowed to see the sky?"

"You have the rights of an issue one prisoner," Cassius told him, peaking my attention.

An issue one prisoner?

"When you actually are an issue five," he carried on. "This means three opportunities each day for exercise out of doors. After breakfast, after luncheon and after supper."

"I have no energy. My life is being sucked away by these four walls," Gallienus retorted. "And I go nowhere without *a guard*."

"All your life you've gone everywhere with a guard," Cass reminded him.

"Not one meant to fence me *in*."

It took a moment for Cassius to reply with unhidden astonishment, "By the gods, you're being a child."

"My son had me arrested," Gallienus sniped.

"You were raping your wife," Cassis returned.

"She was denying me her body, which is my right to take."

"You are mistaken for you said it yourself. It's *her* body."

At this juncture, Gallienus took a moment before he replied, also with unhidden astonishment, "How did I go so wrong with you?"

"I do not know, but I thank the gods you did."

Gallienus glared at him, at me, then back to his son.

"Did you come solely for this affectionate father-son chat?" he asked sarcastically.

"No. I came to share that, if you proclaim your guilt, and your remorse, and assert that you've come to understand what you did was wrong as well as your belief this should be abolished throughout our realm and any who perpetrate it punished. Not to mention, you offer public support of the new laws heralded throughout the land, when you are sentenced, you will be sentenced to exile at Bishop Cross."

Cass had told me this would be his proposition.

I, personally, felt it was too kind. I had heard of Bishop Cross, a small, isolated island off the southeast coast of Airen, very close to Firenze. But it had an old castle there that tales told was quite lovely and the weather was most temperate, sunny skies and warm climes.

It was far from any civilization, both in Airen and Firenze.

But it would be better than this cell.

"I will not do anything that preposterous," Gallienus spat.

"Then when you are found guilty, facing tribunal in front of courtiers and laymen alike, Father, you will receive an issue five sentence," Cass warned.

My prince had not shared about these "issues."

Though, I'd ask about them later.

"As if that will be worse than this," Gallienus retorted.

"You will not be in this cell. You will have a cell elsewhere and it will be shared. You will sup in the canteen with the other issue five prisoners, who have all demonstrated an extreme propensity for violence. And you will have but one hour out of doors each day." Cass paused before he concluded, "Though your cell will have a window."

"This only if my army does not vanquish yours."

"Your army will not vanquish mine."

"You do not know how happily the lords of this land jumped at the opportunity to rise up against you and your," Gallienus jerked his head my way, "Nadirii."

"So it *was* you who conspired to break the treaty we signed with all the realms of Triton *and* your promise to relinquish reign."

Gallienus looked foiled for a moment before he rallied.

"That's hardly a surprise."

"No, it isn't. Though, when I share with my fellow monarchs how you so swiftly reneged on your promises, I wonder how they will feel, should the impossible happen and your army vanquish mine. You do realize, with the seas freed for use, how very small Triton has become and how very lonely, and trapped, Airen would be if we were the only one suffering under sanctions. I assure you the other realms could do without our olives and wine, our golden salt, even our leather and steel. But no Dellish wool or wheat? No Firenz silk and spices? We could do without, but we cannot do without the coin we earn in return trade."

Gallienus had no reply to that.

Cassius waited.

Gallienus remained silent.

"So be it," Cass said on a sigh. "You face tribunal in two weeks."

"I demand to be held in Carleigh Manor during my confinement," Gallienus declared.

"Father, I feel I have failed to impress upon you that you are in no position to make demands," Cassius said.

"This," he moved to the table in the room and slapped his hand on it, "is not to be *borne*."

"This is not for you to decide."

Hate filled Gallienus's face as he stared at his son.

"When I am victorious—" he began.

"You will never be victorious," Cassius said quietly. "You will never again be free. And the only thing I find troubling about that is that I have no feelings on the matter. Not desolation my father will live out the rest of his life as such, not jubilation that you will be treated to something akin, but nowhere near as monstrous, as how you treated your wives and the women who are your citizens who were also yours to protect. Including and especially my mother."

And with that, Cassius said no more.

He left the room.

I, and the rest of our party, followed.

"Issue one?" I asked, laying nude atop an equally nude Cassius in our bed much later that night, asking questions at the same time tracing the ink on his face with my eyes.

"Minor offenses or the first of some less minor ones. Such as disturbing the peace. Brawling."

"And issue two?" I prompted.

"Destruction of property. Unpaid debts. Petty theft. Issuing threats.

Forgery. Minor assaults." He aimed a small grin up at me. "And before you ask, issue three is kidnapping, assault, robbery, arson, embezzling. Four is battery or repeat offenders of any of issues two and three. And five is murder."

"Ah," I murmured.

"Violence against women will start at four. Rape will start at five," he declared, and I felt my eyes round.

"Five? Really?"

He nodded before he explained.

"I have thought on this. And what I have thought is that many years ago, when Mars was in training here in Airen, Trajan targeted him. The scars on Mars's face were delivered by Trajan and his mates. They would have done worse to him if Mac had not seen them attack, and he, I and my mates intervened. And the worse they would do was their intent to rape him."

"Oh, my goddess," I whispered, shocked to know Mars's scars were delivered by Trajan, and even more shocked at all the rest.

"I shudder to think of the man he might have become if that had not been stopped. He might have had the strength of will to persevere and be who he is now. Or the man we know might be as good as dead. Which is a form of murder. The killing of the life someone could have had if they had not been forced to endure such. And so, I have decided, as this is the way, any rape will be treated as such."

"This makes sense, though, sweetheart, there are other instances of a crime committed against a person that have much the same effect."

"I have been beaten up, Ellie. I have even been jumped by surprise and assaulted. It is the way of training a soldier in Airen, and also in Firenze. Especially if you are a prince who others wish to take down a peg. But I have not had my body invaded. The very thought threatens to suffocate something inside me. And thus, I think this is the way forward."

It also had to do with his mother suffering that same fate.

Repeatedly.

However, I did not mention this.

"Horatia will not face tribunal," he decreed. "I will quietly pass her sentence, though I think she has served enough, as it were. Thus, I will find somewhere safe and pleasing where she can spend the rest of her days."

"I think this is the best way," I murmured.

I rose and fell with the mighty rise and fall of his chest.

Then I lifted my hand and touched the markings under his eye. They were a sort of brackets, but the top of the one to the right had a short slash going in, but none at the bottom, the opposite on the bracket to the left side, and a miniscule four-sided star was in the middle.

"What does this mean?" I asked.

"Completion," he told me.

I looked into his eyes.

"Of training," he went on. "When I became an officer."

"Oh," I whispered, not surprised at this for all his men had the same under their eyes. I moved my finger to his temple. "And these?"

I touched my finger to two swooshes, both truncated at one end. And under them, the same swooshes, but they emitted from two four-sided stars.

"Conception and birth."

My gaze jumped to his.

"The top I had inked when we found Aelia was growing in Liviana's belly," he shared. "The bottom I had inked after she'd safely arrived."

I decided, for that day, not to ask more.

"Oh no, my princess," he whispered, turning us, me to my back, him looming over me. "You did your reading, now you shall have mine."

I wanted his.

But I did not wish to take him to places that would open old wounds in getting it.

"Cass, you don't have to do this."

"I do," he stated, these two words seeming to be torn from somewhere deep in his soul. "For you must know, she is here."

He took my hand, pressing my fingers to a larger bracket that was over his heart, the top end bent inward more, shielding to its right a small swoop that was inked over another four-sided star.

"Protection. Liviana," he grunted, dragging my hand up and pressing the tips of my fingers to a symbol at the pulse of his neck that I did not look at, for I was gazing into his eyes.

But I did not need to look, for I had it memorized.

Two downward sweeping swooshes, one smaller and tucked into the other.

"Pulse," he said. "This symbol depicts a heart that beats for another. Also, Liviana."

I was finding it hard to breathe, hearing his words, having this further demonstration of his love for her, as he pushed his body farther away.

Arching, he pressed my hand to the skin of his stomach and slid it down toward his groin.

He flattened my hand under his, my fingers separated by his shaft, my palm teased by the hair above it. "But you will be here. And I will keep it shaved so I will see you there as I take you and you take me. And when you are inked there forever, it will be the symbol of ownership."

Oh my goddess.

"Cass," I breathed.

"I will not be the first Airenzian man who is owned by his woman," he said thickly.

"I do not own you."

"You do."

"Cass."

He shifted our hands, closing mine around his rock-hard cock.

I trembled.

All right, maybe I *did* own him.

"I will ink you elsewhere, Elena," he vowed, his voice now throaty as his hand over mine stroked his shaft. "I will cover all that is blank with symbols of you, our girls, the children we will make, the life we will lead."

Optimism.

Thank the goddess, he was sharing *hope*. Hope for us. Our girls. Our family.

The future.

"Yes," I agreed readily, my body shifting greedily, pressing as best as I could to him. "Let me take you inside," I murmured, needing that, and not caring where he wanted to be inside.

I would take it, adore it, *worship* it.

"No," he grunted, and his eyes held mine captive. "Own it."

"Yes," I whispered, stretching to him to take his mouth in a deep, wet kiss before I moved slightly away and took what was mine.

I dropped my head.

Watching.

Cass's hand tightening over mine deliciously.

I saw his movements, heard his noises, sensed his strain.

I reached in, he spread his legs for me, and I gently squeezed his sac.

He groaned, surged into our hands, and we both stroked his cock as he jetted his seed all over his stomach.

His hand fell away from mine, and I milked him as I massaged his sac until he made a noise in the back of his throat. I then released my hold only for Cass to pull me over him, my belly sliding over the wet at his.

When our faces were close, he sifted his fingers in the side of my hair and with his other hand clamped on the cheek of my arse, and he murmured, "You own me."

Would I say it?

I would.

"You own me too," I admitted.

He grinned arrogantly.

"Oh, I know."

I frowned and narrowed my eyes at him.

He kept grinning as he stated, "You were surprised meeting Reginald. I have met his wife. He is lost in his love for her, and she rules their home. It works for them for he administers a prison, which is a great responsibility that is often a great burden, and it is a relief for him to come home and let his wife have the running of their lives, something she in turn enjoys."

"All right," I said when he stopped speaking.

"As you know, this is not the way with all Airenzian men, but it is the way with a fair few."

"Including you."

His body settled more fully under mine. "Yes, I've found of late it's best to let my woman have the running of my home."

I started laughing.

"You were right, the silver settees are rather bright and welcoming in the Great Hall," he teased.

"I'm glad you concur."

"Though I cannot approve your destruction of part of a barracks to enlarge the greenhouse."

"Hmm," I mumbled.

He smiled at me.

I stared at him.

My Cassius was smiling, after that day, after all his days in this dreary place. He was abed with me, his stomach awash with his seed, he was going to ink me into his skin, he had hope for our future, and he was smiling.

"Can we carry on with my reading?" I requested.

"Of course, though my answers might be muffled as you'll be sitting on my face while you trace my skin."

I shivered.

His smile turned wolfish.

Then his hands took control of me.

I would soon discover he did not tell the truth, for he didn't even attempt to answer while his mouth worked between my legs as I sat astride his face and traced his skin.

But then, with all he gave me, if he had tried, I wouldn't have heard him anyway.

IO2
THE OATH

Jellan
Underground Lair of the Beast
WODELL

When he came to Jellan in his dark hole, Jellan braced.

He had been making an effort with the Beast, and although there were occasions when the creature seemed perplexed by its thoughts or feelings, or its ministrations were gentler than they had been, the Beast was still solely ruled by the witch Marian.

There was nothing Jellan could do, for she was always there, watching.

Though, not now.

She had gone to the surface with her females to gather food and other necessities.

Leaving Jellan alone with the creature.

Cowering while trying not to appear like he was cowering atop the thin blanket she had allowed him, Jellan watched the handsome being toss itself despondently on the ground opposite him, its thick, waving golden hair shining in the torchlight, its finely honed features a beguiling mixture of swells and shadows.

It lifted its knees, rested its wrists against them, and dropped its head.

Jellan waited, but the Beast said nothing, nor did it move.

"Do you intend...?" He did not finish that as he pushed up and back, pressing to the stone behind him, and he changed his question, "Are you all right?"

"She does not take me to the surface any longer," the Beast replied.

"Well, I—"

"And I have been down here *forever*," the thing whined.

Jellan did not speak.

The Beast lifted its head. "She does not care about me. All she wishes is to use me. She has not even given me a name."

Jellan's head grew light with elation.

"Oh, that is—" he began, but did not finish.

"She calls you our pet, but I am as well. I am *her pet*."

Could this be his opportunity?

If it was, he could not waste it.

Jellan gathered the blanket and pressed it to his chest as he rose up even farther to sit on his thigh.

The Beast's eyes dropped to his body before they lifted to his face.

"I will not use you," it asserted.

"Do you not...do you not...like me?" Jellan stammered.

"Of course, I like you. You are very hot and tight. She is very *moist* and *loose*."

Jellan bit the insides of his cheeks not to leap too quickly on that.

"And *bossy*," the creature continued.

"What would you like to be called?" Jellan asked.

The thing's head tipped to the side as if it was considering this.

It didn't come up with any ideas so Jellan queried, "What were you called before?"

"Daemon."

Daemon?

"Daemon as in, *demon*?" he inquired.

The creature studied him in open befuddlement. "Maybe. Dee-mon was said much. Though I liked Day-mon."

By Vicee.

He had been correct when he'd first seen this creature.

It *was* a demon.

Jellan tried to remember what he had read in the Go'Doan tomes of the creatures long ago known as demons who were banished by the gods.

What was known about them?

Why had they been created?

What was their power?

Why had they been banished?

And how did this one get loose when they were cast away by the very gods?

He did not remember. He knew there were a number of them. And he knew they had power, though not what it was, but they also wielded might.

It was a long time ago. Before recorded history.

But tales that remained had been recorded in the Dome City.

Jellan just did not study them acutely.

He needed to get to those tomes.

"Did you have brothers and sisters?" Jellan asked.

The gaze of the creature went vague as it drifted away, and it murmured, "I think. A long time ago. Though, they are lost to me."

Banished deeper in the under-realm?

If so, how did this one rise?

"You know, Daemon, I have magic," he told him.

Daemon looked to Jellan.

"If you like, I could try to get us to the surface," he suggested.

"Do I please you?" Daemon inquired.

"I'm sorry, in what way?" Jellan asked.

The being indicated his face and body with a swoosh of his hand.

"You are very handsome," Jellan muttered.

"Do I please you in other ways?" Daemon asked.

Jellan did not know how to answer that.

"You do not...*emit* like I do when you please me," Daemon explained.

Jellan had tried to do this, but he found he could not with Marian watching.

"I do not like an audience," he said quietly.

"Ah," Daemon replied.

"And it would be good if you found some oil," Jellan mumbled.

"Oil?"

"For ease, and um...friction."

The Beast's lips split in a beatific smile.

"We will try to rise, and when we do, we will find some," Daemon decreed.

Yes!

"I will...gather my magicks. I will...conserve my strength," Jellan promised.

"I will make sure you have more food, and in the meantime, I will tell her I want oil so I can have friction when I use you."

Jellan nodded, trying not to do it enthusiastically, about the food, or cringingly, about the other.

"It will also be better for you," he shared.

Daemon grinned at him. "It is already good."

Jellan gave him a tentative return smile.

"And I will share I do not want her watching."

"No," Jellan said, too swiftly, for as he spoke, the creature's brows drew together. "It might make her angry."

"Why do I care if I make her angry?" Daemon asked. "I could crush her head against the stone." It lifted its hands and clapped them together, making a loud noise that caused Jellan to jump. "But I cannot, for she is the only way I have to make me rise." He shook his head. "When she took me up, I should not have let her bring me back down."

"Well, you might have me."

The creature brightened.

"However, we do need to keep her around. If I cannot access my magic down here, we may need her to get to the surface."

"Oh," Daemon mumbled. "Right."

"I will..." He swallowed his excitement and carried on. "I will try to do what I will. More food will be good. Clothes."

The thing grinned again. "I like you as you are. Though you are now too skinny."

"I will need clothes on the surface."

Daemon nodded. "I will have her females mend your robes."

Excellent.

"Be careful, uh, showing your mistress any concern for me."

"It will be difficult for you to be of use to me if you waste to nothing or catch a chill that also," it grinned again, "wastes you to nothing."

"Yes," Jellan agreed. "And if I find my magicks are bound down here, like yours, I will find a way to tell you, and then we will plan what we will do next in order to get you to the surface."

Daemon nodded.

"But we will get you free," Jellan whispered.

The Beast stared hard at him and replied, "I want to be free."

"It is my calling to make you thus, and I will do it. That is my oath to you, Daemon. Believe in me and understand my resolve. That is *my oath*."

The Beast continued to stare hard at him.

And he did not smile when he ordered, "Make me free."

Jellan nodded.

The Beast came at him.

And, with no audience, Jellan made certain his oath was sealed with an offering.

The Beast approved.

103
THE COUNSELLOR

King True

Outside the Bedchamber of Sir Alfie, Birchlire Castle, Notting Thicket
WODELL

"Are you ready?" True asked Bronagh.

She did not look as such, entirely, but she nodded.

He turned and looked to Bram and Florian, Wallace and Luther.

"And you?"

They nodded as well.

He turned to his wife at his side

"Here goes," he whispered.

Her eyes shining bright with hope and happiness, she leaned into him, coming up on her toes, and touched her mouth to his.

"You are perfect," she whispered back when she pulled away.

"I'm afraid you are wrong, my sweet, for you are."

"For the gods sakes," Florian complained. "You both can be perfect. And what's more annoying than you being ridiculously in love, is that as far as I can tell, you both actually *are*. Now, can we do this?"

True chuckled as he gave his queen's waist a squeeze, caught her smile before she aimed it at Florian, and then he turned and walked down the hall to Alfie's door.

He knocked, and when his friend called out, he entered.

These past days, Alfie was sitting far more up in the bed than he'd been in the beginning.

Then again, although Bronagh had taught the other nurses how to exercise his captain's legs, for she did this no longer (and now Alfie was complaining about the fact she barely came into his room, stating she was shirking her duties, instead of the other way around), she had also set up what was right then in the corner.

A folding screen beyond which was a commode with handles at the sides.

She, nor the nurses, said a word.

It was Alfie who dragged himself from the bed to beyond that screen and back.

And now it had been reported he was dragging himself out of bed for other purposes, to heft himself about the room just to do so or in order perform his own exercises to strengthen his chest, shoulders and arms.

This was all very hopeful.

And as it was, the ones who loved him felt that hope.

True just worried they might not be right in these feelings and that their hope would be dashed.

"What are those?" Alfie asked.

"Greetings to you too, my friend," True teased, leaning the sticks he was carrying against the side his bed.

They were not like any either man had ever seen, for Cora and Maddie had asked after Alfie, and then shared in their world medicine was more advanced. Therefore, when they'd explained a variety of things to True and Farah, and then directly to Bronagh, the nurse had ordered some adjustments.

"Sorry, True, I'm in a foul mood," Alfie muttered.

"Would this foul mood have anything to do with a pretty nurse no longer exercising your legs?"

Alfie shot him a killing look.

True grinned at him.

He then answered belatedly, "Your sticks."

He watched his friend's brow knit in confusion as he stared down at the sticks.

He understood the confusion because the others they had seen did not have the forearm guards curving about the top, and at the bottom, instead of coming to a point, they came out to three with resin pads on them for better sticking to whatever they touched. All of which, as Bronagh explained delightedly, would make them more stable.

True carried on, "Bronagh reports you're getting yourself around. She says you have remarkable upper body strength—"

"She said I have remarkable upper body strength?" Alfie interrupted him to inquire.

True beat back the laugh, but not his smile.

"Yes. She was also quite breathy when she reported that."

Alfie took in True's smile and grunted.

"Thus, she says it's time you practice with your sticks," True finished.

"It will be good to have something to do," Alfie muttered.

"Indeed, and this is another reason why I'm—"

Alfie interrupted him again to declare, "She won't let me apologize."

"Pardon?"

"Bronagh. It's been days since I acted like such an arse. And she scurries in," he lifted his hand, motioning with his fore and middle fingers to demonstrate scurrying, "and she scurries out. 'Are you hungry, Sir Alfie?' she asks. I have enough time to say yes, or no, and she's gone. 'Are you in pain, Sir Alfie?' A yes or a no, and she leaves. 'Do you need another book, Sir Alfie?'"

He did not continue after that, just scowled at the door as if his scowl could make Bronagh appear, stay still and listen to his apology.

Abruptly, Alfie turned his head as well as his scowl to True.

"You're king. You can make her stand still for five minutes so I can tell her I acted like an arse and I'm sorry."

"I am king, indeed," True replied. "But I am not ordering that woman to stand here and listen to your apology."

"True—"

"It is your mess, Alfie, yours also to clean up."

"I cannot do that if she keeps *scurrying*."

"You have remarkable upper body strength, my brother. Find a way to get her close and use it."

Alfie stared at him with a face full of shock.

True ignored it.

"Now if we can talk about affairs of the realm, the Go'Doan emissaries have shared at long last they're ready to discuss things, and I need you at the table. And as it will take some doing to get you there, we need to get that started."

"Sorry?" Alfie asked quietly, now regarding him closely.

"Oh yes, right," True replied. "I hereby appoint you my counsellor."

Alfie again had an expression of shock.

"I will warn you," True carried on, "although for now, you will be my only one, I will add more as I make decisions about who they will be. This, until we can elect a parliament. I will have a gnome, a fairy, a pixie, a sprite and of course I will have men, or women, if that's my decision, from different counties—"

"You want me to be your counsellor?"

True nodded. "I should ask, but I don't have the time. I need you. Ophelia's gone. Cass has called Rus back. Mars asked his mother to return home. Tint left this morning. Serena is working clandestinely in the Shanty. Tor is also working our operatives there. And Apollo is brilliant, but he not only does not know this realm, he is not you. But regardless, at this juncture, I'd have no other but you. When I make further appointments, you will remain as the representative counsel of the Dellish military. And I would urge you to continue being so when we have a parliament."

When he ceased speaking, Alfie said low, "You do not have to do this, True."

"No. I don't," True replied.

They held each other's gazes.

This went on some time.

So long, True had to break it.

"We need you in clothes and we need you seated at that table, Alfie. And we have half an hour. The men are outside to assist. Though I think you can get yourself sorted, if you need aid, we are here. Bronagh says it takes some practice and requires a good deal of stamina to use the sticks. If you wish to try, we will try. But we can get you there more expediently on a stretcher and the halls will be cleared when we do so."

Alfie said nothing.

Time was wasting.

"Shall I ask Wallace to bring in your clothes now?" True prompted.

Alfie looked down to his legs.

True gave him a moment.

However, he did not have many moments. He'd timed this precisely, making it a matter of urgency for the purpose of *not* giving his friend too long to think about it.

Therefore, he repeated, much quieter, "Alfie, shall Wallace bring in your clothes?"

"Have Bronagh bring them."

"Pardon?"

Alfie turned to him, and there was a curious, but not at all bad, light shining from his gaze.

"If I need help, and I shall need help, she's my nurse. She can help me."

Slowly, True smiled.

Then he murmured, "As you wish," rose and left the room.

He had six pairs of eyes aimed his way as he walked down the hall to where they were huddled.

He tore his from Farah to look at Bronagh.

"He wishes you to bring his clothes and assist him if he needs help."

"*Me?*" Her voice was a squeak.

He heard a truncated guffaw, a couple of amused grunts and an odd high noise he knew was Farah's, though it also was amused.

"Yes, you," True confirmed.

Slowly, her gaze moved to True's wife.

Not missing a beat, Farah pulled the folded clothing from Wallace's hands and shoved it Bronagh's way.

Tentatively, the nurse took it and trudged down the hallway to Alfie's door as if she was heading to the gallows.

"Do you have a royal counsellor, *amore*?" Farah asked.

He looked to his side and down into her beautiful eyes.

And he smiled.

"THIS WILL NOT BE TOLERATED!" G'Aron fairly shouted, slamming the side of his fist to the table.

"You need to calm yourself," Apollo warned.

"You are not from this place. You don't understand," Aron snapped.

"I understand you need to calm yourself," Apollo retorted.

"These are our *acolytes*," Aron hissed. "They have our *protection*."

Needless to say, when the Go'Doan shared they were again ready to sit the table, they did not share this with the intention to discuss matters of import to anyone but them.

Apollo looked to True. "I'm sorry, did I miss something? It was my understanding that Mars brought these Go'Ella in solely for questioning."

They had heard word of the bent Mars had taken in his realm in an attempt to gather information.

And the Go'Doan had heard it too.

"This was my understanding as well," True confirmed.

"That is not to be abided," Aron decreed.

"Explain why," Apollo ordered.

"It is not to be *abided*," Aron repeated.

"Bloody explain *why*," Apollo shot back.

"I would like to know this as well," Alfie remarked calmly.

"If you need to speak to an acolyte, you talk through her priest," Aron declared.

"Why?" Apollo asked.

"It is the way," Aron answered.

"That's all you have?" Apollo inquired when Aron said no more.

"They're terrified one, or more, of the Go'Ella speaking with King Mars will share they're being, or have been, mistreated," G'Ry stated, and all eyes turned to him.

Only when he had everyone's attention did he finish.

"That being mistreated by Go'Doan not only of this Rising."

"Ry," Aron spat. "You'd do well to be quiet."

Ry slowly shifted his attention to Aron.

"I have not known a time like this. A time of trouble and sorrow. A time of danger and aggression. A time like this at all when it is the least good to be quiet," Ry returned. "There are things we can share, Aron. There are ways we can help. I have been adamant that this should be our stance, as you know. And right now, I find I can no longer carry on being a part of a strategy I find fundamentally flawed when the stakes are this high."

"You will be sanctioned," Aron warned.

"I have no doubt," Ry said.

"You will be cast *out*," Aron threatened.

An expression of deep concern moved over the older man's face before he controlled it, and on a release of breath, said, "With what is at stake, I cannot allow myself to care."

Aron rose from his seat. "I will not be a party to this."

"Luther, Florian," True called to his men standing flanking the door. "Escort Aron to his chambers and then arrange for a military escort for him and his Go'Ella direct to the Dome City."

"You will regret this when you need our healers, when you wish your citizens to enter the Go'Da," Aron cautioned True.

"We have very good universities here," True replied.

Aron looked to Ry. "You do this, you are a sacrilege."

"I do not think Go'Bedi, Go'Vicee and especially Go'Chas would agree."

"It is not yours to think for the gods," Aron rejoined.

"It is not yours either, my brother. And yet it is. As it is mine. We have no choice but to follow our hearts to where we feel our gods are guiding us," Ry said quietly.

Aron apparently had no retort for he stormed from the room, slamming the door behind him.

"You make the right choice," True told Ry.

"You do," Alfie added, his two words far outweighing True's.

Ry took in Alfie.

"I find you astonishing. If you were not here, so soon after what befell you..." Ry trailed off but shortly again picked up that trail. "I do not know if I'd have had the courage."

Alfie looked to True.

True did not make his friend communicate it, even through an expression.

That "it" being that True had been correct.

There was much to live for, much he could contribute, even in ways he could not imagine until they happened.

He gave his attention to Ry.

"What do you have to tell us?" he asked.

"I can give you names. However, I hasten to note that these names I will give are only those I have heard in whispers of priests that are in Wodell, Airen and Firenze who might, *might* have ties to this Rising," Ry said.

"We will proceed with that caution in mind," True replied.

Ry nodded.

"I will tell you, though, I did know of the three you already...er, dispatched," Ry shared and when True made no comment, he carried on, "And that there were murmurings of their ties to these agitators. And the ones that have been reported since, some of them, not all, I had heard their names too," Ry shared.

True nodded, pleased to know they were on the right track.

Ry continued, "With this Rising, it will not negate the mistakes we have made, but I will share also there is a good deal of discord amongst priests in the Dome City in how to deal with it. Including many who wish to take a much more aggressive route to banish these followers from our ranks. And alongside this, there is a swell of support for an initiative to change the status of the Go'Ella. It is important you know all of that."

"This is noted," True said. "Have you heard aught of a treasury?"

Ry shook his head.

True drew breath into his nostrils and sat back.

"I do not share what I shared with you for this reason," Ry went on. "However, it is important enough to me to bring it to this table at this time. A small number of Go'Ella have gone missing."

True's gaze moved to Alfie before hitting Apollo and then he turned it to Farah.

She was leaned forward into her elbows on the table, intent on Ry.

True looked back to Ry.

"It began with Marian. A very bright woman. I am old, but I could still see she was attractive. She is from here," Ry told them. "Wodell, that is. Originally. She did not share, but I suspect she had some ...troubles with an earlier priest to whom she was assigned. But she seemed content in our little family."

"Family?" Farah asked softly.

Ry shrugged. "It is better than what they had before they came to us, and I would hope, at least with mine, they found peace after lives lived that did not offer such."

"You allude to not a small amount of issues that might be disturbing as pertains to the Go'Ella," Alfie remarked.

"Indeed," Ry replied on a sigh. "And after this Rising is quelled, regardless of what befalls me, in dealings with the Dome City, I would make it one of your priorities to research a new ideology that is quite sweeping our own that our handling of Go'Ella change rather drastically and that priests can marry and take only one spouse. And I would hope, once you research this, that you would throw your strong support behind it."

This was news, and not his business, but he would most definitely be looking into it.

Eventually.

"I will have this researched," True promised him.

"You have much to concern yourself with," Ry stated the obvious. "However, I fear the coincidence of Marian's disappearance, some others of my Go'Ella after her, and a small amount more vanishing as well, this happening during these times..." He drew in a deep breath. "Well, Your Grace, it makes me uneasy."

"And you wish to find her," Farah said.

Ry nodded. "I worry for her. Her mother was ill. She would go often to care for her. But once, she left and did not come back. Aron was not wrong. In the purest sense of our religion, it is the priests' responsibility to protect our Go'Ella. I can assure you that many take this much to heart. I am one of those many. But as happens, this concept has become bastardized over time. I am just gladdened to understand there are hearty discussions about it. For the time is nigh."

When all at the table simply regarded him, Ry took his cue and stood.

"I will find parchment and pen. And then I must be away home, if they will take me."

"Your accent, you were Airenzian before you pledged to the Go'Doan?" True asked.

Ry nodded.

"Regardless, you can make your home here if aught befalls you on your return," True offered and felt Farah's gaze warming his profile with her approval.

"Thank you, Your Grace," Ry said on a bow of his head. He lifted it and murmured, "I'm to a parchment."

And with that, he left the room.

When the doors closed behind him, Alfie inquired, "Has Mars learned aught yet from the Go'Ella?"

"Not that I've heard. But if he does, he will share," True answered.

"Serena? Tor?" Alfie asked.

"We have, as of two days ago, one man planted in The Rising. I would wish more, and any information he might procure will take time, and I fear the quest for it is most dangerous. But they carry on."

"News from Mar-el?" Alfie continued.

"There is some issue with the pirates," True shared. "Aramus is calling a summit."

Alfie nodded and pressed on. "Airen?"

Yes, his counsellor had accepted his new role.

Wholeheartedly.

True did not shout his gladness at this.

He looked to Farah, who he'd already told the news he was about to share, before he returned to Alfie.

"Gallienus has been arrested for the rape of one of his wives. He awaits tribunal."

"By the gods," Alfie muttered, this before he started chuckling.

True felt Farah's fingers curl around his knee and squeeze deeply, such was her joy at seeing Alfie chuckle.

"They very much wish Farah and I, Silence and Mars and Aramus and Ha-Lah at their nuptials and are keen to press forward with them, something they intend to do quickly after the trial. Farah and I might be able to get away, it is but days on a ship, Ha-Lah as well. But I fear they will not have..." He trailed off, not wishing to bring up something that might dampen the goodness of this day.

But Alfie steadfastly picked up the thread. "The pomp of your own."

"Alfie," True murmured.

"They should elope," Alfie suggested, taking them right around the subject.

And the day was not dampened.

"It would be wise," True replied. "And at least that will be done, the alliances made official that will defeat the Beast."

At this, Apollo cleared his throat and stood, saying, "I will seek Ry and get those names."

True nodded to him.

After Apollo left, Farah again squeezed his knee.

"Progress," she said.

He smiled at her. "Progress."

"I have concerns about this Go'Ella business," she shared.

"As do I, my sweet, but it will have to wait."

She looked contemplative before she said, "I also have concerns about this Marian."

It was peculiar she would focus on that one Go'Ella, and True wished to quiz her on that, but he did not when Alfie spoke.

"As happy as I am to be out of that bloody room, True, I must ask to get back to it. I have sticks to practice with."

Ah, yes.

Progress.

And hope.

"Then let us see to that, shall we?" True replied.

Alfie looked to Wally and Bram who were already moving his way.

True did not watch this.

He looked to his love.

"A good day," he said and watched her eyes again shine with happiness.

"Finally," she agreed.

IO4
THE REALIZATION

Queen Silence

Parlor of Guard of the Trusted, Fire City

Firenze

T drew deeply at the scent of the dark fluff on the baby's head, a baby I held tight to me.

And I closed my eyes.

"They smell beautiful, do they not?" Nyx asked.

I opened my eyes, looked to my friend and smiled.

"No other scent is as beautiful," I replied.

Though that was not true.

One was.

The spice of my husband's cologne.

However, I had not smelled much of that lately.

Indeed, none a'tall.

"Is everything all right, my queen?" Zosime asked from where she was lounging back on the bright cushions of a daybed, appearing to glow more than she did when she was expecting.

However, she glowed though also appearing worried, her gaze kind on me.

I drew in the smell of dark baby fluff again to give me fortification in order to lie, "All is quite well. And please, do not address me as your queen. We are friends."

"I quite like addressing you as my queen," Zosime returned on a jaunty grin. "Though my husband is most cross with you."

I blinked in concern. "For goodness sakes, why?"

"I have told him I need an entire new wardrobe," she answered, dipping her chin to my gown.

"I dare to say husbands and fathers all over Fire City, indeed all of Firenze are cursing you, Silence," Nyx put in. "But the merchants are not. There has been rather a run on silks since your wedding, not to mention all the finery you've been displaying since your return."

That would be my contribution to the state of Firenze.

Women wanting new frocks and the men in their lives cursing me because they did.

"Perhaps I should try a jeweled brassiere," I mumbled, wondering if I could manage to pull one off without expiring of mortification.

"No, just be as you are because you are *lovely*," Zosime said.

No, she was for saying as such.

"I hear Elpis returns," Nyx changed the subject as I suspected she sensed the other was not entirely comfortable for me.

Which made her lovely.

Or lovelier than she already was.

"She does," I confirmed. "Mars sent for her."

This I had learned from Elpis's secretary, not my husband.

"But I received a letter from her just yesterday," I told them. "And in it was lovely news. For she shared that she and Farah had a reconciliation."

Zosime murmured *marvelous* in Firenzii while Nyx smiled happily at me.

As for me, I was as delighted about this as I was that Elpis would return, even if I did not allow my mind to consider why Mars had sent for her.

They were close. There was great affection there.

This was all I told myself it was.

It felt selfish, being glad she was returning. Farah needed a motherly presence much more than I (and True did too).

But I was drowning in clans and tribes and invitations and there was some Firenz celebration upcoming that I knew naught about, but Elpis's secretary repeatedly shared I should be planning something in regards to it at the palace.

And I could not ask my husband.

I also could not ask Nyx and Zosime, as they might wonder why I did not inquire after this from my husband.

So I had no idea what to do.

What I should not do was go yet again to Zosime to smell her daughter's head and waste time I did not have for I should be at my desk or ordering flowers to be arranged (or some such).

But here I was, yet again, at Zosime's, smelling her daughter's head and being with my friends even if it did not make me feel better as I'd hoped it would.

One could say I needed a mother's presence too, as, for all intents and purposes, I had lost mine as well.

I pushed that to the back of my mind, but when I did, all the rest I should be thinking came forward.

"I hate to say this, but I must go," I announced. "There are things to do with *Miet*. Would you like to hold her?" I asked Nyx, bouncing the baby in my arms. "Or shall I give her back to her mama?"

"Me." Nyx reached both hands out my way.

I rose and moved to her, feeling bereft as I transferred the precious bundle to Nyx, and watching Nyx coddle the baby, hoping my friend and her husband would start their family soon too.

After I did this, I turned to Zosime and queried, "Have you named her?"

Zosime smiled a secret smile and said, "We have decided to perform her naming ceremony the day before *Miet*."

Naming ceremony?

"This means yes, she just isn't going to tell us," Nyx put in.

Zosime's gaze dropped to her daughter and gentled. "She is for Guard and myself, for now."

There was something beautiful to that, as Zosime entertained a variety of company, all falling in love with her daughter, so she and Guard had to share.

But they were able to hold that, something so vital as a child's name, to themselves until they deemed fit to offer it to others.

I would wish to do that with Mars, if I ever spoke to him again.

Or if he spoke to me.

I lingered over my farewells (foolishly), then met Kyril at the door and allowed him to help me astride my horse.

We were on our way back to the palace with my extravagant guard of four in formation in front of us and ten behind us when he began, "My queen—"

"I don't want to talk about it," I interrupted him to say, doing it smiling at a little girl on the red cobbles waving at me while her mother curtsied.

"Did you talk to your friends about it?" Kyril pushed.

"I do not want to talk about that either," I answered, dipping my chin to a man whose eyes I caught before he bent at the waist my way.

I did more smiling, dipping, head inclining, and gave a few children waves before Kyril educated, "Mars ignores them."

"Well, I am not Mars, am I?" I retorted.

"I shall remain quiet from now on," Kyril grumbled.

Balls.

I felt badly I took my foul mood out on him. It was not right.

And making matters worse, him being quiet meant things could plague my mind I did not wish to think of.

"Can you explain *Miet* to me?" I asked Kyril.

"Your husband could explain," he said by way of answer.

It was me who was silent the rest of the way to the palace after that.

However, when he helped me to dismount, he began, "Silence—"

I looked into his eyes. "When you are first married, I will thank you to tell me how easy it is. Until then..."

I said no more and swept by him, up the steps, and did this bracing, for I knew either Francesco, the palace overseer, or Angelo, Elpis's secretary, would beset me the moment my foot was over the threshold.

This would include a variety of questions and demands for answers, ranging from what guests we may have that night and into the coming weeks, what I wished to feed them if they were dining with us, to if Mars and I deigned to climb the Sheeonee to attend some clansman's cousin's wedding.

I was not wrong.

It was Francesco (with Angelo hanging back, looking anxious), who practically fell upon me.

"Your Majesty," he said in Firenzii, for he spoke very little of my language. "The king requires your attendance with him in his study."

My heart took flight.

Mars wanted to see me.

Wanted this so much, Francesco won out on who would get to demand something of me first.

This meant, I was certain, that Mars meant to apologize.

I knew he would, and I was so very happy this dissension would finally be over, that he would come back to our bed, our marriage, *me*, I smiled brightly at Francesco.

"I will attend him straight away," I said. "Thank you."

He looked confused at my bright smile (and I did not blame him, I had not been very bright of late), bowed again, and I dashed past Angelo with another brilliant smile that had him blinking.

"And I will be with you shortly," I told him while on the move, now being able to ask Mars questions, I'd actually be able to give Angelo answers. "Or as soon as I can."

And I hoped that was not too soon, for after he apologized to me, I would allow him to ravish me on the carpets of his study.

I then darted down the hall, suppressing my smile (for the now), and it felt like my sandals were skimming air when I saw his study door open.

I was in such a rush, I was not able to slow (or halt) when I heard the thunder of his laughter but steps before I turned into his doorway.

Thus, it was there I stopped, only to see him leaning against the front of his desk, his head thrown back, the rich sound of his humor filling the room.

And an absolutely stunning Firenz woman sat before him in a chair.

She had clouds of thick, dark hair and was wearing not a brassiere but a top (that still cut off below her breasts) with cap sleeves and skirts of orange satin with deep purple falls of chiffon.

All of this was bespangled with tassels and beading and sequins. But there were triangular panels at her hips adorned with purple jeweled chevrons that were absolutely *sheer*.

She was lush. She was *sumptuous*.

And she was smiling white, blinding and *ravenous* at my husband.

I was about to step away when her head turned to look over her shoulder and her winged brows rose.

"Well, is this our little queen?" she asked.

Our *little* queen?

Mars ceased laughing and looked to me.

"Indeed," he said, lifting his chin my way. "Silence, come meet Ines. Farah's cousin."

I moved into the room slowly.

Ines stood just as slowly, and I noted, with all the bowing and curtsying I received, she did neither.

Her eyes moved up and down the length of me.

"And all the talk is true," she purred. "For our queen has quite a way with a garment."

I really did wish people did not speak so much about what I wore.

That said, it was with receiving a knowing look that I had asked Tril to bring the pale pink silk that morning.

It had two very thin straps over each shoulder from which drapes of material hung, covering my breasts, with a very deep plunge in between. The drapes were held to my body by a belt of the same material.

There was no back. The silk that covered my behind held in place by the four thin straps that held the front.

And as you pulled it on like a dressing gown, the two sides came together at the front, meaning when I walked, quite a bit of leg was exposed.

I wore my hair in a bundle of curls at the top and it was threaded with gold chains on which were affixed tiny seed pearls.

The silk was clingy, the gown revealing, it was meant to garner attention.

And my husband was entertaining a beautiful woman in his study.

I moved to standing between the two chairs in front of Mars's desk and looked up at her, lamenting my lack of height for perhaps the millionth time since I gained conscious thought.

"Ines," I said. "Lovely to meet any family of Farah."

"Your queen," she replied oddly.

I did not understand her words.

But I did feel Mars's reaction to this.

As did Ines.

Thus, she smiled enchantingly at him. "I'm sorry, Mars. Of course, she is *my* queen, but she is Dellish, so in a sense, our Farah is hers."

"A queen has no queen, Ines," Mars stated in a flinty voice, and it was at that I fully understood her words.

Thus, I fought seething.

She dipped her chin in a way that seemed an invitation and murmured, "Of course."

"You're in the city for how long?" I broke into their discourse.

Ines looked to me. "Oh, I don't know. At least through *Miet*."

"You'll of course dine with us this evening," I invited.

"Yes, of course, for Mars has already asked me."

I tipped my head back and to the side to look at him, finding him peering down his nose at me.

Blankly.

It was not my favorite expression of his, but it was all I had been treated to since our quarrel (if I saw him at all).

"Well," I stated, again shifting my attention to Ines. "I shall tell Francesco you'll grace our table tonight. But I'm afraid I will have to get to know you then, Ines. I've been away, visiting a friend, and not seeing to my duties. I'm sure my secretary is keen to get me to my desk."

"How extraordinary," she murmured. "You've already made friends in Firenze?"

I stiffened, wondering why she would say such, and forced through tight lips. "Yes."

"Hmm, I would be about much different endeavors as a new bride," she remarked.

"Yes, well, when you are one, you will not also be a new queen," I retorted.

Her eyes flashed with ire.

"Until dinner," I murmured, sliced my gaze across Mars's chest and kept murmuring, "My king."

And then I turned and walked out of the room.

With determined steps, I strode down the hall, catching Angelo's eyes, wondering why the man didn't come to me for if he wanted me at my study, it was right across the hall from Mars's.

Nevertheless, upon seeing me, he looked relieved.

This being, he did so until Tril veritably stumbled down the stairs into the entryway.

"Silence!" she cried. "There you are. I need a moment."

Angelo's expression turned beleaguered.

I stopped at the foot of the stairs amongst them both.

"I need to get to my study, Tril."

Although, what I'd do there, I had no idea, for I had very little idea what I was doing a'tall.

"You didn't…" She gazed down the hall, then at me, down the hall, and back to me. "Did I not catch you before you saw King Mars?"

"No, you didn't," I told her.

She examined me.

She then turned to Angelo and asked for, "A moment."

His gaze came to me. "My queen, we really must—"

He did not finish for Tril took my hand and was dragging me up the stairs.

"A moment," I said to Angelo, following her.

She only went as far as the landing before she stopped us, facing me, and took my other hand.

She then began babbling.

"They wanted you to know, the staff that is, that it was nothing. It happened. It was over. It meant nothing. In fact, from what they could tell, he didn't even like her."

I shook my head in confusion.

"What are you talking about?"

"That chit in with King Mars."

My stomach dropped.

"She causes troubles," Tril went on. "This why they warned me to be sure to warn you. She's the opposite of Farah. There was even talk about how some witch somewhere broke the dawn to separate the dark and the light, for they were born on the same day, nearly at the same time, this being at the dawn. That one down there first, then Farah. That one down there the dark. Farah the light."

I barely heard a word she said.

It happened. It was over. It meant nothing. In fact, from what they could tell, he didn't even like her.

"Silence," she shook my hands, "are you listening to me?"

I focused on her.

"I really need to know what *Miet* is."

She stared at me.

"It's crucial, Tril," I continued. "What it is. How it's celebrated. What has happened in the palace at *Miets* past. Can you ask the staff?"

This had not yet occurred to me.

Then again, I did not think they would share such things openly with Tril, not to mention, I was drowning in all things *queen*.

"Yes, Silence, but..." Her head tipped to the side. "You are all right with that woman down there?"

I.

Was.

Not.

My husband was entertaining an old lover *in his study*.

And he'd "required" my presence in order to introduce me to her.

"I can trust Mars," I said.

"Of course you can," Tril agreed. "But, she's trouble, my lovely. And I do not know if you know what that means. More, you are not getting on with King Mars very well in the now."

I did not need that reminder...

In the now.

Or at all.

"I know I can trust Mars," I returned.

And I felt I did know that.

There was the fact that he was not happy she insinuated Farah was above me.

However, other than that...

"You can, of course you can," Tril said, squeezing my hands.

"So Tril, the *Miet.* And also, anything you can learn of the clans and tribes. Who are allies, who are not. Favorites of Mars. Those of Elpis. Anything. Everything."

"Right, of course." She regarded me closely. "But, my love, you can ask Mars these things."

"It is good to know all, especially servant chatter."

"Which means you do not intend to ask Mars these things, when it is he who knows them best, also when it is high time you two worked out whatever is coming between the both of you."

"We will talk, I am certain," I assured her.

"When?" she asked. "He has not slept in your bed in six days."

I did not need that reminder either.

"Tril, I have things to do," I replied.

Her hands held mine fast. "Silence, you have not been yourself these past—"

"Tril!" I snapped. "I have things," I tore my hands from hers, "to *do.*"

She took a step back.

I was instantly contrite.

"Tril," I whispered.

"Yes, you do. You are queen, after all," she declared before she turned, lifted her skirts and raced up the stairs.

I closed my eyes tight.

A lyrical peel of feminine laughter drifted down the hall from the direction of my husband's study.

I turned on my sandal and walked down the stairs.

"To my study," I said to Angelo.

And as I led the way, sadly going in the direction of Mars's, I thought, really.

Angelo was Elpis's secretary.

There was no reason not to ask *him* what I should do.

I was Dellish. I was a new wife. A new queen. I would not magically know what to do when thrown into my role with utterly no guidance whatsoever.

And although I did not fancy becoming dependent on someone who was not close to me or a member of family, as my uncle did with Carrington with disastrous effects, it would have to do.

For now.

When we arrived, I did not look into my husband's study.

I turned into mine and ordered, "Close the door."

Angelo obliged.

And then he explained in a roundabout way why he had waited down the hall for me to come to him.

For in whispers, as if the woman had supernatural hearing (or Mars did), he told me about Ines, and indicated in a diplomatic way that I should proceed with her with great caution.

Well, there was one good thing about that.

At least I had learned the staff was willing to educate me.

~

"AND DO YOU REMEMBER WHEN...?"

Balls and *begorrah*.

This woman had the best memory in the history of Triton.

I studied the stem of my wineglass which I was twisting with my fingers to and fro.

Piccola hung from a lock of my hair.

I heard Mars's deep voice murmur something in response to whatever Ines was remembering now, for she had a great deal of memories that involved Mars.

Scores.

Scads.

I decided ten more minutes I would endure the torture of their reminiscences (or hers, for Mars had not said much), before sharing I had a busy day the next day, offering my goodnight and heading to my chambers.

"So, will you? Silence?"

Her voice coming at me for the first time of our long-finished dinner caught me by surprise, and I looked to her.

"I'm sorry?" I asked.

"Will you go to the orgies for *Miet*?"

I blinked at her.

"No," Mars decreed.

Orgies?

Angelo had said nothing about orgies.

He had turned an alarming shade of red when I asked about the *Miet*, something which confused me for he then shared it was the celebration of the yield, that meaning of the crops, and went on to explain there was a good deal of food consumed and liquor imbibed.

But he'd breathed no word about orgies.

"Oh, that's too bad. I'd hoped the two of you would be there," she mumbled, looking as if she was pouting. She quickly brightened, but did it in a catty way, and then asked Mars, "Do you remember when—?"

"Ines," Mars growled.

"What?" she queried with sham innocence.

"If you intend to speak of what I think you intend to speak of in front of my wife, I would reconsider," he advised.

She shot him a dazzling smile.

I felt bile rise in my throat.

They had...

At an orgy...

Piccola chirruped.

I stood.

"Please, do not allow me to further interrupt this reunion," I said, right to *her*. "It is clear you've spent some time apart, but were once *very close*, and you wish to bond over shared memories. I would simply *love* to know all about these, *in detail*, but I'm afraid I have a number of letters to write before I can be to bed. Though it was *such a delight* to meet you, Ines. I will be certain to mention you to Farah, one of the letters I shall be writing, you know, *queen* to *queen*. Now, please enjoy your visit to the city and the celebrations of *Miet*."

I then turned to Mars, bent to him, Piccola swinging from the lock of my hair, and I caught the point of his beard in my grip.

His brows shot up.

I bent, pressed my mouth hard to his, straightened inelegantly the second I felt his hand touch my waist, and mumbled, "My king."

"My queen," he mumbled back, eyes dancing.

Eyes bloody dancing!

Of all the cheek!

I glared at him, twirled, Piccola chirping gleefully as she went swinging, and I smiled as sweetly as I could at Ines.

"Goodnight," I bid.

"And a goodnight to you too," she replied on a nasty grin.

"My queen," Mars rumbled.

I turned to him.

But he was not addressing me.

He was looking at Ines.

"*Scusa?*" she asked.

"As you're aware, you could also address Silence as 'Your Grace' or 'Your Majesty,'" Mars declared. "But it is one of those three until she gives you leave to address her elsewise. You have slipped in this during our discourse, and Silence is too kind to correct you. That left doing so to me."

Ines's face hardened before she said dutifully to me, "And a goodnight to you too, my queen."

"Mm," I hummed before I began to make my escape from the room on a billow of the pale pink silk of my frock.

I did not make the doors before Mars called, "Do not remove that gown."

"I'm sorry?" I asked, turning his way.

"Do not remove that gown," my husband repeated. "I'll be doing it."

I felt heat hit my cheeks, my eyes becoming slits, and then I turned again and swanned (I hoped) out of the room.

After the attack on the palace, Mars was taking no chances, so the hall was rife with guards, and thus I could not run to my chambers.

However, try as I might, I did not exactly walk sedately.

Upon arriving behind the doors to my chambers, I did run.

Directly to my dressing room, through it, and I knocked on the door to Tril's room.

All right, I banged on it.

She took her time but opened it.

"Are you ready to prepare for bed, my queen?" she asked flatly.

"I was horrible because I'm quarreling with Mars, I do not know what *Miet* is, Elpis is at least a week away from arriving and...and...so much more I have not told you, my head is swimming in it."

Her deserved pique instantly melted away as she moved into the room, saying, "Let's prepare you for bed and you can tell me all about it,"

There was too much to tell for I hadn't even told her about my father and my mother and...

With these thoughts, something unpleasant slithered through me.

I pushed them to the back of my mind and shook my head jerkily.

"No, I think Mars will be here shortly," I told her. "And I think...I think that is good, for we need to get a few things straight."

"Can I suggest you loosen a few things before you get them straight?"

I pushed thoughts of loosening things to the back of my mind as well, for I very much missed getting loose with Mars.

And to accomplish burying these thoughts, I wrapped my hand around Piccola, pulled her from my hair, cuddled her to my cheek and then held her out to Tril.

"You could take care of my darling for me."

"I will," Tril said, taking hold of Piccola. "And Silence."

When she spoke no more, I asked, "What?"

"He adores you," she said quietly. "Whatever you're quarreling about, remember that."

I drew in breath and wondered what manner of adoring man made his wife sit opposite his former lover at dinner.

I then nodded.

She nodded back, lifted a hand, cupped my jaw briefly and then walked to the door of her room.

She stopped there and turned back.

"And I am always and forever here to listen to you, to help you, to do anything for you," she reminded me.

I bit my lip to stop the sting in my eyes.

"You know that?" she asked.

"I do," I answered. "And I am the same for you."

"I do not have to figure out how to host an orgy in my garden," she mumbled.

Eep!

"What?" I asked.

"For later, my love. I wish you luck."

She blew me a kiss and disappeared behind her door.

I stared at it after she closed it, and then I realized I had no idea how much time I had, and thus I had no time to waste.

Therefore, I needed to decide, when my husband came to me, where the conversation we would need to have should occur.

And I knew instantly it should not be in the bedchamber.

I did not hurry (in case he came in), but I also did not dawdle on my way to the sitting room.

However, I found myself having to stop pacing because he did not come quickly.

Instead I had to find parchment in his desk, inks and pens, and I took these to the settee to write the missives I had lied to Ines that I needed to write (though it would be good to have them done for a clearer day the next day).

And I did this beginning to feel less flustered and starting to fume.

For apparently my husband took my insincere invitation to reminisce with his old lover as sincere.

And equally apparently, they had much to reminisce about.

Not long after, I found I was beginning not to fume, but instead feel as if I would weep as the minutes ticked by and he did not come to me.

Finally, I realized he did not intend to come to me, and perhaps he thought I would go to him (even if I did not know where he slept at night as I had not asked).

But that would not be happening.

I had nothing to apologize for.

He did.

And this list was ever growing.

He had been dictatorial.

He had treated me like a mischievous child.

He was withholding from me.

He had retreated from me.

And *he* had introduced me to and made me sit at dinner with *that woman.*

It struck me that perhaps he had no intention of settling matters a'tall.

I could not finish my letter to Ha-Lah and would probably find on the morrow that it made little sense.

I decided to set it aside, and was about to do this, when the door to our chambers opened.

I looked that way and watched Mars at first walk to our bedchamber.

I did not have time to call out before he turned on his foot and headed my way.

I sat on the settee and watched his approach, hearing the strong cadence of his sandaled feet hitting the tile in a manner that was remarkably but oddly, in that moment, soothing.

He cleared the entryway, saying, "Excellent. You did not disrobe."

I felt my head twitch and was no longer soothed.

Had he lost his mind?

"My king—"

He arrived at me and wasted not a moment pulling the pen from my fingers.

He tossed it to the table in front of me.

"Excuse me!" I snapped.

He pulled the book upon which was the letter I was writing out of my hands and the book landed with a thud on the table while the parchment floated there.

"Well!" I cried.

And then I went stone still as he planted a fist in the cushion on either side of my hips and he was all I could see.

"If you address me as 'my king' one more time, I will redden your arse to the point you will not be able to sit for a week," he warned low.

Of all the...

"You *are* my king," I retorted heatedly.

"Do not try me, Silence. My wife has denied herself to me for a week, and I am in no mood."

He...

He...

He was in no mood?

And *he* was accusing *me* of denying *myself* to *him*?

He'd walked away from me!

"Well, by all means," I hissed. "Take what is yours, *husband*."

His anger wafted over me like a wave of heat.

"This is trying me," he cautioned.

"Well, perhaps I should force you to have dinner with one of my old lovers so you will know the definition of *trying*," I retorted. "No, wait. Strike that. There are none *I* could try *you* with."

"Her clan is the most powerful of my realm, outside my own, and she has the eye of the eldest son of the baron, that being the man who will inherit the title. So, although she is venomous as sport, she is not someone I care to bother with right now."

"But you did care to invite her to dinner," I returned.

"It would be impolitic not to."

"Regardless of the fact this meant your wife would have to sit opposite a woman who knows you as intimately as she does."

"Ines is nowhere near knowing me as intimately as you do," he growled.

"Truly, *Mars*," I bit. "Although there is no possibility of this happening, I suggest you consider how it would feel with the shoe on the other foot. I mean, can you not understand how insulting it was for you to expect me to dine with *that woman*?"

"It is good we are talking about insults now for there is another one I prefer to discuss," he shot back.

I felt my skin start to burn.

"I'm seeing you did not come up here to share your regret at your behavior toward me that set this off between us," I noted.

"*My* behavior?" he demanded.

"Did you hear a word I said during our quarrel?" I asked.

"Oh yes, Silence," he whispered sinisterly. "Some are still ringing in my ears."

I stared at him.

And then I whispered in return (though, not sinisterly, disbelievingly), "You are angry with me."

"What gave you that impression?" he asked sarcastically.

"There was not a hint of love...in that house...from him, to me," I said deliberately slowly.

"And yet you compared him to me," he clipped.

"There was not...a hint of love...in that house...from him...*to me*."

Everything that was Mars went completely inert.

I sensed this.

I even saw it.

But I did not register it.

"And she only gave me what she could get away with giving."

"Silence."

"I am wrong."

"What are you wrong about?" he asked quietly.

His question drifted right through me as if it had not been asked.

"I am wrong. I am not right. I am a bluestocking."

"*Bellezza*—"

"The Mouse. Incidental. Useless."

One of his fists went out of the settee so he could curve his hand under my jaw.

"My love, focus on me."

"Back there, I would have lived in my shadow if I could. Not to be seen.

Not to be known. Nothing expected of me. No one to disappoint. My shadow was everything to me. It was my saving grace. If I had not had it, I would have gone quite mad."

"Gods damn it," he murmured, shifting as if he would take me into his arms.

But I shoved against him and scuttled away, shouting, "No!"

I nearly tripped over my skirt as I made my feet.

I then whirled to him, backing away.

He had straightened and was facing me.

"I would wish you to come to me, my Silence," he urged softly.

"And all this time I was not even *his*?" I asked.

His voice had changed to one I had never heard when he repeated, "Silence, I wish you to come to me."

"I know why I have my shadow now, Mars," I informed him. "I have come to understand it. I understand why I can disappear into nothing. This is because I was never even meant to be."

"You were."

"I wasn't."

"You were, *mia bellezza*."

I leaned toward him, emotion bubbling up in me, boiling me from the inside, and I screeched, "*I wasn't!*"

He came at me then, and I struggled, I fought.

I did this because I had to flee, I did not know to where.

All I knew was I had to *flee*.

"I will not fight you, *amore*, but I will subdue you," Mars said, doing just that. "But I do not wish to hurt you as I do, so please, calm for me."

Abruptly, I did as he asked, finding myself caught tight in his arms.

I looked up to see his face, awash with concern, staring down at me.

"I believed," I told him.

"What is it you believed?" he asked.

"That he...that he...that there was something there for him with me."

"It is not your burden he is a revolting man."

Again, I spoke like Mars hadn't.

"All this time, all these years, I wanted there to be."

"Of course you did, you were a daughter and you thought he was your father."

"All these years, he made me feel like nothing, when he was."

"Yes," Mars said firmly. "Yes, Silence, it was he who is nothing."

"But he made me feel like nothing."

"Fuck," he bit. "I did not mean to make you feel that way, my love."

"He made me feel like nothing."

"Silence."

"Nothing."

"*Piccolina.*"

"A shadow," I whispered, right before I dissolved into tears.

I would have collapsed in his arms, but he lifted me up in them instead, and he carried me to our bed.

There, he entered it, holding me close, and he continued to do so as I wept into his skin.

I did not want to feel this.

I did not want to give my father this.

But I could not seem to stop.

Mars tutted and stroked my hair and back and held me tight, altering this with rocking me like a baby.

And moments before I cried myself to sleep, I heard my husband say, "Your shadow is not nothing, my queen. You were right. It *is* a gift. And the gods do not grant something this important, this beautiful to someone who is nothing."

King Mars

The King's Study, East Wing, Catrame Palace, Fire City
FIRENZE

LORENZ ARRIVED in Mars's study looking alert even if it was late and Mars was certain his call took his captain from his bed.

And it was a bed Lorenz was also late to, Mars knew, for they had had a very long discussion about things they were learning from the Go'Ella. None of it about The Rising, but none of it was good. This happening after he had scraped off Ines which was soon after Silence had left them.

He did not see Lorenz directly.

Mars was standing behind his desk, looking out the window.

And he was doing this keeping his body very still.

It was Lorenz's reflection in the window that he saw.

"Mars?" Lorenz called.

"Select men, the best you know for this sort of operation, and deploy them immediately."

"What operation?"

"I want Johan Mattson, Lord of the Arbor, ruined."

"The queen's father?" Lorenz asked with verbal shock.

Mars turned from the window.

Upon one glace at his king, Lorenz stood straighter.

"Ruined, Lorenz. Fucking *destroyed*. All that he cares about, all that is important to him, I want it *gone*. And once that is done, I want him to know it was me who took it from him."

"What did he do to her?" Lorenz whispered, his face now carved from stone.

"He made her feel like nothing."

A muscle ticked in Lorenz's jaw.

He then dipped his chin and stated, "It will be done."

And without another word, Mars's captain pivoted and walked out the door.

Mars turned to the window.

He did not see anything out of doors, but not because it was dark.

All he could see were the twin flames that burned as a reflection in the glass.

MARS DID NOT SLEEP a moment of that night after he returned to his Silence and again pulled her into his arms.

And thus, he was awake in the morning when she stirred.

He tipped his chin down and watched her rub her face against his chest before she pulled slightly away, blinked sleepily at it, and then tilted her head back to catch his eyes.

The silver in hers went liquid with affection before it shifted, and remorse filled her face.

She opened her mouth to speak, but Mars moved swiftly.

He pressed the pads of his middle three fingers tenderly against her lips and murmured, "You need not speak of it."

Silence moved in order to wrap her fingers around his wrist and pull his hand to her throat.

"I compared you to him," she whispered.

"You need not speak of it," he repeated.

"My love—" she began but ceased speaking when he crushed her to him.

Curling into her, falling into her, forming a shield around her wee body, he pressed his face into the fragrant hair at the top of her head.

There, he declared fiercely, "I wish my father was alive. He would dote on you, Silence. You would walk into a room, and he would smile, and the world would fall away until he had asked how you were and knew you were well and happy. He would boast greatly of your hair and your wit and your silver eyes and your intelligence. He would live for the sound of your laughter. He would memorize every single smile. He would slay dragons for you. He would move mountains for you."

Her, "Mars," was muffled.

But he was not finished.

"He would love you, *amore*, to the marrow of his bones."

It took effort Mars forced her to make in order to push her head back to try to catch his eyes.

He, however, did not force her to make the effort of gaining his gaze.

He gave it to her.

"This is what you had from him," she whispered.

"Yes," he confirmed.

"And this is what you give to me."

"Yes," he stated.

She closed that silver from him.

Thus, he demanded, "Give me your eyes."

She opened them for him.

"I love that you had that, Mars."

"I do as well."

"And I owe him much for he gave you that and now you can give it to me."

He loosened his hold on her enough that he could bend his neck to rest his forehead to hers.

"I am so very sorry I said what I—" she began.

"Do not speak of it, my love."

"I *was* angry that you spoke to me the way you did, but I should never have said those words to you. We had become heated, you were trying to open a discussion to cool things, and I lashed out, and I cannot tell you how much I regret it."

He let her have that before he pointed out, "You are speaking of it, Silence."

She wrinkled her lips into her nose, and this was so adorable, Mars grinned at her.

Her face relaxed at seeing the smile on his lips, and then she pulled her head away and forced her hand between them to touch the chain that ran from his nostril to his lip.

"You did not take off your chain," she said softly.

"You slept in yours as well."

"I missed taking off your chain, Mars," she whispered.

"As did I, my Silence."

He felt her body expand with a big breath and then he felt her let it go.

"I think I may not be handling things as well as I would like," she admitted.

"You have much to wrap your mind around. We will spend the coming days in each other's company so I can take better care of my queen."

"It's not just that, it's that I...well, it will be good when your mother returns."

Ah.

"And we will spend the coming days in each other's company not only so I can keep an eye on you, but also so I can help you navigate things until Mama arrives."

"I think that would be good," she murmured, then began to look uncertain. "Do we, erm, need to host an orgy in the garden?"

Mars started to chuckle as he pulled her up so they were face to face, doing this still holding her closely.

"For *Miet*, there will be a number of them throughout the city, the largest in the Heden District, and yes. It is tradition that Catrame Palace has one in the royal garden."

"Oh faith," she muttered.

"If you do not wish to do this, you are queen, Silence. This can be your decision. We can offer food and drink, and if they must, people can fuck behind the hedges."

A giggle burst from her.

Mars stroked her back and smiled through her amusement, and only when it had waned, did he suggest, "How about we proceed with that plan, and if you change your mind, so be it."

"That would be fine."

"Mm," he murmured.

"Mars?" she called.

"I am right here, *piccolina*," he stated, again smiling at her.

"I love you very much."
He was, indeed, right there.
But at her words, he was *right there*.
He could, of course, return her words.
However, Mars preferred to show it.

105

THE FRIENDS

Princess Serena
The Shanty, Notting Thicket
Wodell

She heard the noises outside the door, and thus had awakened on the pallet and was reaching for her steel star when the knock came.

There were seven knocks Brix and Gal had made her memorize, for they did not know who might be watching and did not want it to appear as if they had a secret code.

Thus, instead, they had seven secret codes.

They were most cautious, Brix and Gal, and she had to admit, good teachers.

Perhaps Chu would have gotten into such if they had taken on this task together.

But she would never know.

She took no chances regardless she knew it was the gnomes outside and had pushed off the blankets to sit up on her arse, had her star in her throwing hand, her dagger in her other for a quick switch if it was needed, when the door opened.

A human came in.

She tensed, until Brix called out, "It is fine. It is us."

Only when she saw Brix and Gal both walk in around the tall man's boots did she set aside her star in order to strike a match to put to the candle on the floor by her pallet.

Once she did that, the door closed.

The candle did not do much to dispel the murk in the room, but fortunately Brix and Gal wasted no time lighting those at the mantle and on the table.

And thus, Serena saw King Noctorno of Hawkvale standing there, now with the hood of his long, tatty cloak pushed back.

She had only been around him a few times.

However, even if he was dressed much like her (though he was cleaner, then again, she had now not bathed in weeks), his raw magnetism, his big body, the fierce expression on his handsome face made the dingy room they were in seem small.

Cassius Laird had that magnetism, that frame, that fierceness.

And he was Elena's.

Chu had all the same, except his demeanor was cool and haughty and tremendously attractive.

She would never have said she was a female who had use for a male outside his cock.

In fact, she would laugh in the face of anyone who would suggest it.

She had been wrong.

She had been wrong before she even met Chu and learned how it felt to sleep in the arms of a man you felt affection for. Learned how it was to go about your business with the skills ingrained in you and the intelligence granted to you by the goddess and have a man look upon you with respect.

Learned how it was to have a partner and not be alone.

She now knew in some part of her, although she denied it, even fought it, she had always desired this.

But a man like King Noctorno would not be for her.

A man like Cassius Laird.

A man like Chu.

She shoved up to her feet, wishing she did not have a mind to her state, her smell, but she did.

"You need to eat," Tor's deep voice came her way.

"I am in disguise."

"You still need to eat."

"I need to embody my disguise."

"No longer, True wants that building taken."

She looked to Gal standing on the mantel, then to Brix on the table.

Both nodded.

She then returned her attention to Tor.

"It's my understanding True has only one man covert in The Rising, and he is but a newly recruited soldier," she said.

"We now have three, but they may not be needed. Because we also have names."

They had names.

Bloody *brilliant.*

"True is positioning throughout his land and has sent word to Mars and Cassius for them to do the same," Tor continued. "The best scenario would be that all strike at around the same time. As that would take some weeks to arrange, and we do not know what they are up to, True and Alfie have decided that we will move now. You need to eat and garner strength, for True wants you to command the taking of that building."

True wanted her to do it.

Serena, the harridan of the Nadirii.

She did not want that to feel good.

But she could not deny it felt good.

"How many names?" Serena asked.

"We think enough that taking them, along with seizing that building and what we hope lies within, will be a blow from which it will be difficult for them to recover. Especially if Mars and Cassius move just as swiftly to disable other agents of this organization."

"It could also serve to press them into action peremptorily," she pointed out.

"Perhaps, but it is difficult for an army to act without its generals."

This made sense.

Serena looked between Gal and Brix.

"Are you both in accordance with this strategy?" she asked.

They shot each other glances, seemingly surprised she asked, before Brix said to her, "It is the will of our king."

Serena nodded and turned her eyes to Tor.

"When?" she queried.

"Three days hence," Tor told her. "These priests are located throughout this realm. True has sent word, and now awaits birds and riders. But True needs to hold for confirmation all are in place to make arrests before we seize that building. Therefore, be advised, it might be longer."

Serena nodded.

"In the meantime, keep watch and *eat*," Tor ordered.

It was odd it did not chafe when, at his order, she nodded again.

"You'll get the go ahead from Gal or Brix," he said.

"Right," she replied.

"Not long, Serena, and you can be away home."

Home.

Why did the sun and green no longer appeal to her?

"Right," she repeated.

"Until it's over, be careful," Tor warned.

"You as well," she said.

He tipped up his chin her way then dipped it to Gal and Brix.

Pulling the hood over his handsome visage, he then moved to and through the door.

When it closed behind him, Gal asked, "What do you wish to break your fast?"

She had no appetite whatsoever.

"Whatever you can lay your hands on," she mumbled, falling to her arse on the pallet and wondering, even on the somewhat thick mattress and under the definitely warm blankets Gal and Brix had provided, thus getting a sound sleep, why she still felt exhausted.

Brix dropped down from the table and walked to stand by where she sat, putting his fists to his hips.

"If all happens as True wishes, you will have time to make Airen for your sister's wedding," he informed her.

Elena wanted her nowhere near at all, much less attending her wedding.

"That'd be good," she said.

Gal had swung down from the mantel, and now he stood on the floor opposite Brix, her feet separating the two gnomes.

"She needs food," Gal told Brix. "She's been existing on grog for weeks."

"She needs a kick in the arse and to open her mouth to share what is bothering her," Brix returned.

"Nothing bothers me," she lied.

"You lie," Brix accused.

She fell fully to the pallet on a sigh, turning her back to them and muttering, "I just need more sleep. Then I will go back to my post."

"Her arse is right there for me to kick," Brix noted.

"You kick my arse, I'll wring your gnome neck," she told the wall.

"At least there's some rise in her," Brix said, not to her.

"Leave her be," Gal retorted.

She closed her eyes.

"I will not. She is in pain. A pain that can be muted with words spoken, releasing some of it."

She opened her eyes, partly in surprise he sensed this about her, partly in surprise he wished to do something about it, but mostly in disbelief that his assertion was correct.

"It can also be muted with time, my brother, give her more," Gal said quietly.

"A friend does not let another friend wallow in pain, Galbdor."

A friend?

"A friend does not push a friend further than they are willing to go either, Welbrix," Gal retorted.

They thought they were…

Her *friends*?

She allowed herself to feel the warmth in her belly that brought.

And then she ignored it.

"I will note, you two here, arguing about me like I am not, no one guards that building," she shared.

"Oh, right," Brix muttered.

"You go, I'll get Serena some food," Gal said.

"A juicy steak," Brix ordered for her.

"Nadirii do not eat meat," Gal reminded him.

"Shite. I forgot."

Serena ate meat.

And for the first time in days, her stomach rumbled.

She rolled toward them.

"Rare, with biscuits and butter," she demanded.

"That's more like it," Brix stated tetchily, arms crossed on his little, but for his frame, wide chest.

"Don't you have a troll to watch?" she asked.

He sent a glower her way before he turned on his boot and marched to the door. He swung up a rope attached to the wall beside the door for the purpose of allowing the gnomes to turn the handle, something he did.

And then he was gone.
"Steak, biscuits and butter," Gal said, and she looked to him.
He was grinning.
"Coming right up," he declared.
And then he was gone too.

106
THE MISSIVES

Queen Farah

Outside the Bedchamber of Sir Alfie, Birchlire Castle, Notting Thicket
WODELL

"I do not wish to speak of it."

"Well, I wish to speak of it."

"You need to be at your sticks, sir. And if you are too weary, then you need to be abed."

"I am abed. I've been bloody abed for weeks."

"You are not abed. You are sitting on the side of it."

"For I am about to take up my sticks and move to that chair and sit in *that* and you will be here to make certain I manage this feat. But before the attempt, you'll answer my question."

"I am your nurse. My duties are seeing to your health, not enduring an interrogation."

"It's hardly an interrogation, asking you why you have not given up on me when I have been so unkind to you."

"Again, I am a nurse."

"That is not all it is."

"Yes, it is."

"No, it isn't."

"It is."

"It is not."

"It *is*."

"Bronagh, answer me."

"Fine! I do not give up because you are a *hero*!"

I listened very hard.

But there was only silence from Alfie.

Not from Bronagh.

"You gave so much in order to save the queen and you did it without thinking all that you'd give," Bronagh stated. "And it could have been much worse. All over Wodell, people talk about the former king diving behind the pew. But not you. Not *you*. And they all talk about you too and what they say is that you are a hero. And they say it because it is true."

More silence from Alfie.

"And...and...you're annoyingly handsome," Bronagh went on.

I smiled at the door I had my ear to.

"And I like your eyes and you have the most attractive hands I have ever seen," she finished. "So there. You know why I have not given up on you. Now will you either lie abed or get on your sticks?"

Alfie finally spoke.

"Come here, Bronagh."

My smile got bigger.

"I don't...don't think it would be proper if I did so, considering that look upon your face."

I almost didn't hear it when Alfie said quietly, "Please, Bronagh, come here."

"My queen."

I jumped in shock, my hand going to my leaping heart, and whirled at those two whispered words said behind me.

Helga stood there.

She looked to the door, then to me, the door and then she asked me, "My queen, are you...*eavesdropping?*"

Swiftly, I moved to her, hooked my elbow in hers and drew her down the hall.

"I just..." I searched for a lie. "Was making certain Sir Alfie was all right."

Helga glanced over her shoulder worriedly. "Has he taken a turn?"

I hoped he was taking a turn.

"Not for the worse, no."

"Good," she murmured.

"Now, did you need me?" I asked.

"I do not know. I was…"

She stopped at the end of the hall and turned to me, thus I unhooked our arms.

"Well, I was clearing some things away of…of…Queen Mercy's," she shared.

I reached a hand to her arm and gave it a squeeze. "I'm sorry, Helga. It needn't be you who does that. Would you like me—?"

"No, you see, I found these." She reached into the pocket of her skirts and pulled out a set of folded missives tied in a green satin ribbon. "I have not read them." She proffered them to me. "And it likely matters not now, as he is gone and good riddance. But they are letters she had intercepted. As I have not read them, I know not what they say. But she kept them, so I thought it best to give them to you and you can decide."

I nodded again and took them from her. "Thank you, Helga. I'll get them to True. If Queen Mercy did nothing with them, they probably are not of import. But we'll let True decide, no?"

She nodded in return and bobbed a slight curtsy, gave me a smile, and started to move away.

I was going to make my trek to my study, which would take half the day in this big castle, but I did not move when Helga turned back.

"I am glad you and our king did not give up on him, Your Grace," she said, jerking her chin down the hall toward Alfie's room. "This world needs men like Sir Alfie."

Wodell's hero, indeed.

I smiled at her and agreed, "It absolutely does."

Another bobbed curtsy and she scurried away.

I then decided to give Bronagh and Alfie some privacy considering what I hoped was happening in that room, and thus began the journey to my study.

In order to have something to do as I did this, I untied the ribbon on the letters and folded open the first parchment.

I skimmed it, and then opened the next.

I skimmed that, and on to the next.

It was on the fifth that I stopped dead in the hall.

But only for a moment.

Then I raced to find True.

107
THE HEALING

The People of Airen
Highgate (Eastern Gate into Sky Bay)
AIREN

Their arrival caused a stir.

No one in Sky Bay, indeed Airen, had seen such things.

And as such, and what it might mean, a soldier had been sent to the Sky Citadel with haste to share the news with the Prince Regent.

They did not get very far into the city, what with the crowds that gathered, and how very hostile the female was.

Although at first some tried to get close, eventually her aggression was such they had no choice but to give them a wide berth and wait for word from the Regent as to what to do with things so fantastical wandering into the Bay.

They had to have something to do with the Nadirii being amongst them.

Nothing that magical ever touched the soil of Airen before the Nadirii came.

It was with great surprise that anyone along the route to Highgate watched the Regent himself riding his steed Caelus like an angry troll dogged his heels, the prince's black mantle billowing at his back.

His intended, the golden-haired Princess of Nadirii chased behind him, her cloak of purple floating out behind her, its brilliant color stark against the drab colors all around her.

Seeing it, some decided to paint the doors to their homes purple.

And others decided to buy their wives purple cloaks much like that.

Still others desired to rip it from the Nadirii's neck and burn it.

And behind the Nadirii princess, Cassius's lieutenants, and hers, and a cadre of others, all went clattering over the cobbles at breakneck speed.

The crowd that had gathered around the volatile female and the timid male was great.

But it parted instantly when the Regent, his intended and their band approached

But all of them reined in abruptly at what they saw in the opening of the center of the crowd.

The female unicorn brayed her warning at their approach and went up on her hind legs, flashing out with her front hooves threateningly.

The male sniggered and dipped its once proud head, sidestepping away from the wheeling horses.

It was then, it happened.

It was then, the entirety of the realm of Airen changed.

It was then, perhaps, the entirety of the continent of Triton changed.

Maybe even the whole of the earth.

For at one look at those two unicorns, Prince Cassius swung off his horse, walked two steps into the clearing, and stood immobile.

And those close enough to him saw with some shock fierce thunderstorms erupting in his gaze.

Elena of the Nadirii quickly followed him.

Those close heard the faltering, "Cass," as murmured by the woman who would be their queen, but all who had a sightline saw her touch his arm.

But they would all soon learn there would be no pacifying the Prince Regent of Airen as his gaze stayed locked on the male unicorn with his shorn horn.

And then it happened.

Their prince threw back his head and roared to the sky, the raw fury in the sound moving up and out, blanketing the entire city.

Fearful murmurings and panicked shifting happened amongst the crowd.

For as he did, the sun disappeared.

Day turned to night.

And darkness descended all around.

Queen Ophelia

At the Foot of the Night Heights Mountain Range, Two Hundred Miles East of Sky Bay

AIREN

OPHELIA REINED to a stop as she felt it, then wheeled Midsummer around and threw up her hand.

The Nadirii behind her halted.

"Good goddess, Ophelia, what could possibly be causing—?"

Agnes did not finish.

The sun left the sky and night fell all around.

"Ophelia!" Lucinda snapped with some alarm.

Ophelia said nothing at first.

This because she did not know whether to laugh or change their direction from tracking Fern to going directly to Sky Bay.

She looked to her lieutenant.

"Someone has made Cassius Laird very angry."

Lucinda's head twitched.

Ophelia made her decision and circled her horse back around.

And even if she did not have the energy for it, for hers left her earlier and earlier in the day as each one passed, she called up what she had, and shouted, "We ride!"

The Nadirii rode, through day turned to night, tracking Fern in the Heights.

The People of Airen
Highgate (Eastern Gate into Sky Bay)
AIREN

"CASSIUS!" the Nadirii princess called urgently.

The crowd watched through the stars twinkling all around, hanging low in the very air, as their Prince Regent strode boldly into the clearing, directly to the female.

"Cass!" Princess Elena hissed, looking as if she would follow him.

She did not.

She stopped when the mare butted Prince Cassius's outstretched hand and whinnied.

She then moved her beautiful head with clear intent to invite the prince to stroke her nose.

This, Cassius did.

Those of the crowd were stunned.

What was this marvel?

A male of the royal house of Airen at one with a unicorn?

Was all of this indication that magic would be back in their bleak realm?

"Bring him to me," Cassius demanded, to who, the people didn't know.

Until the mare lifted and shook her head, braying.

"Bring him to me," Cassius repeated.

Another shake of her noble head before she blew out of her nostrils, jerked from him and trotted, rounding and herding the reluctant stallion toward the prince.

"Tch, tch, tch," Cassius fussed. "Here now. Come here, boy."

The stallion swung his head side to side and danced this way and that, trying to evade getting close to the prince, not as if he feared the man, as if he was ashamed, but his mare was always there to foil escape.

And finally, as the crowd looked on in amazement, Cassius caught the stallion's velvet jaw in two hands.

"You came to Ellie and me to be safe, eh?" he asked the creature, moving his head side to side to catch the unicorn's evasive gaze.

It was not lost on many that their prince referred to his intended as "Ellie."

Many thought that was very sweet.

Some thought it nauseating.

"And now you are with us and you will be safe," the prince promised. "For you are my Sky, and she is my Star, and the Sky King cannot do without either. Hmm?"

The stallion nickered.

"Yes, that's right," Cassius murmured.

The stallion nickered again, dipped his head and pawed at the cobbles with his hoof.

Cassius moved his hands from the unicorn's jaw, toward the truncated horn at his head.

And when he did, Princess Elena sprang forward with great alarm, crying, "Cassius, don't touch his—!"

But the Prince Regent touched the horn.

And the darkness went from the day, the air went stark white and the ground shook.

~

Triton

At the movement of the earth, Mars raced for his Silence.

And when he found her, she turned her silver gaze to him, and she was smiling.

Marian put her hand to the wall of their underground lair, looking up.

And she frowned.

The pirates ceased shouting at him at the summit table, and Aramus turned his head to look at his wife.

And he caught Ha-Lah grinning.

Serena lifted her head from the crumbling stoop as she felt it, her eyes watching the troll across from her blinking stupidly as he did.

"Sister," she whispered.

And her heart grew light.

Even as her eyes filled with tears.

Jellan pressed his hands to his throat, closed his eyes, sensed the seismic shift of the veil.

And decided it was time.

True broke his embrace with Farah.

And when he gazed down at her, he saw she was gazing up at him, laughing.

Nandra of Firenze appeared at the henge first.

Rebecca of Wodell flashed in second.

Lena of Mar-el arrived third.

They all went directly to the slab.

But it was Nandra who spoke.

"It is beginning."

A god moved from the shadows and smiled into the dark.

"Finally, my love, our wait is almost over," he murmured to nothing.

The Nadirii galloping up the side of the mountain stopped abruptly, for their queen had suddenly tumbled from her horse.

Her lieutenants dismounted instantly and raced to their friend.

And Ophelia lay on her back, gazing up at them...

Dying.

~

Princess Elena
Highgate (Eastern Gate into Sky Bay)
AIREN

THE WHITE LEFT NEARLY AS QUICKLY as it came, but it was as if it was still there, for I could not believe what I was seeing.

Cassius's hands had not been charred to dust at touching the shorn horn of a living unicorn.

The unicorn was up on two feet, scraping the air with his hooves as his mare pranced around him and Cass slowly stepped back from him, its horn renewed.

Renewed.

"The Phoenix," I whispered.

And as sheer joy soared through me, I sprinted to my man who turned just in time to catch me up in his arms.

"What did you do?" I asked, framing his face in my hands and looking down upon him as he held me high.

"I'm seeing you aren't the only one in the family who has magic," he replied arrogantly.

I gazed at his handsome face before I threw my head back and laughed.

While doing it, Cassius lowered me, my body gliding along his as he did.

And I did not mind our audience, and further paid no mind to the miracle that had just occurred.

For my prince was kissing me.

The People of Airen
Highgate (Eastern Entrance into Sky Bay)
AIREN

ALMOST ALL THE population of Sky Bay were most startled to see their prince openly embracing the Nadirii.

He was known to have very much loved his wife.

He was known to very much grieve her death.

But now, seeing him vital and happy, it appeared he was healed.

Reborn.

A goodly amount of the population of Sky Bay fell in love with Princess Elena in that very moment.

Another number continued to detest her.

But those last realized they had a very serious problem.

Especially in the now, with their plans so close to being put into action.

For their prince could heal a unicorn.

And that begged a very important question.

For if he could do that...

What other powers did he have?

108

THE TAKING

Tedrey
Heden District, Fire City
FIRENZE

Fortunately, it was not unusual for a man to move through the narrow alleyways of the Heden District wearing a short, belted sarong at his hips, crossed straps on his chest, and a short cloak with the hood pulled over his head.

For this was how Tedrey had left the home of Nyx and Lorenz after receiving the message from Faunus.

Taking the alleys as instructed, he was deep within the District when he saw the purple lotus flower painted on the shingle above the purple door.

He moved through that door, turned to the burly Firenz man sitting directly inside, and handed over his coin, not lifting his gaze, thus his visage, as he gave this token.

He then grunted, "Faunus."

"Up the stairs, second door on the right," the man said in Firenzii.

Tedrey did not waste time below stairs.

He wound his way around the couches, cushions, thus the lounging bodies embracing or smoking *ashesh* or sipping spirits.

The air was cloying.

The noises he heard and gazes he felt were discomfiting.

He rushed up the wide steps with their thick purple carpet and down the hall.

Second room on the right, he knocked twice, then a pause, and once, as the missive had instructed.

The door opened, he was caught at a strap at his chest and pulled inside.

The door was then closed behind him.

"Faunus!" he snapped.

But he stopped speaking when his warrior shoved him to the door and pressed up against him.

Faunus said nothing.

Tedrey said nothing.

Faunus *did* nothing.

Finally, Tedrey whispered, "Fau—"

"Shh," Faunus shushed him harshly.

"This is so unwise, it is downright reckless," Tedrey hissed.

And it was. So much so, he did not know why he was there.

Except he now had Faunus's handsome face filling his vision and pressed to him was Faunus's powerful body.

Tedrey was weak.

But his warrior was so beautiful.

And he missed him.

Faunus dipped that handsome face to Tedrey's.

"I...said...*shh.*"

Tedrey scowled at him.

Faunus grinned at his scowl.

A knock came at the door and Tedrey tensed.

One, a pause, then two.

He felt Faunus relax.

He then felt his eyes narrow.

"You had me followed?" he demanded.

"How else would I be certain you weren't trailed by someone I did not wish to track you?" Faunus asked in return.

"You could have mentioned that in the missive," Tedrey pointed out.

"How would that be exciting?"

Tedrey pushed at his chest.

And found himself flung across the room, landing on his back on a pile of cushions.

He came up on his elbows as Faunus stalked toward him.

"Your sarong is very nice," his warrior drawled.

"I should not be here. I should be *anywhere* but here," Tedrey returned as Faunus crouched at his feet.

"It will be good when all of this is done, and you can wear the garments of your land at all times."

"Trousers, boots and a frock coat?" Tedrey asked. "Wearing all that, I would melt in this heat."

"Wodell is not your land. *This* is your land, Teddy."

Tedrey felt a pinch at his heart.

He did not carry on this particular discussion.

"This is not smart," he whispered.

"I have missed you," Faunus whispered in return.

Tedrey closed his eyes.

This was a mistake, for when he did, Faunus caught his ankles and yanked him across the cushions, so when Tedrey again opened his eyes, Faunus was all he could see.

Faunus's voice had dipped lower when he asked, "How often has he fucked you?"

Oh no.

He should not be there.

But now it was more, for they should not be speaking of this.

"We have this time, let us not do this," Tedrey suggested.

"How often?"

"Faunus."

Faunus caught him in a light hold at the front of his throat.

"How often, Teddy?"

"He now finds me...lacking," Tedrey admitted, and watched his warrior's eyes flash. "So, none at all. But you should not ask such, Faunus. It will only serve to upset you."

"None at all?"

Of course, Tedrey could not find attractive, say, a fellow teacher.

Or perhaps a quiet purveyor of rugs.

No, he had to find attractive a possessive warrior.

"None at all," Tedrey confirmed.

"And he trusts that you are still on his lead?"

Tedrey pressed his lips together.

"He makes you suckle him," Faunus growled.

"Can we not talk about this?" Tedrey asked.

"Yes, we can not talk about this," Faunus murmured. "For I've got something better to do with my mouth."

Tedrey's sarong was then flipped up, Faunus's head dipped down, and Tedrey's head fell back.

Yes.

This was much better.

~

"I want you to stop what you are doing with this Rising and allow Lorenz to find you a safe place until this is over," Faunus declared.

Tedrey lay with the back of his head resting against his warrior's thigh. Faunus was sitting up, his back against some cushions that were set to the wall, his long legs stretched out. Tedrey was reclining perpendicular to him with Faunus as his cushion.

"I cannot stop now," Tedrey denied.

Faunus didn't reply.

Tedrey turned to his side and lifted up, propping himself on his elbow.

"My friend, please understand, this is something I must do," he said.

"I am not your friend, I am your lover," Faunus retorted.

He was definitely that.

"Yes, you are," Tedrey agreed, and rested his hand on Faunus's bare thigh. "And as such, I am asking you to understand and do not push about this."

"A Go'Ella had something to share."

Tedrey stared up at Faunus, his hand dropping away.

"I'm...really?"

"One of the ones you said belonged to one of the priests in the necropolis." A look transformed Faunus's face that, if Tedrey didn't know him, would have him moving away. "He would make her darken her hair and then he would debase her as the 'Firenz whore' who would be slave to him when the Rising took control of all lands. This, although she was fair. And Airenzian."

"This is evidence of his guilt, but naught else," Tedrey noted.

"She also has a good memory, as well as good hearing, thus she knows which priests visited him for business of this Rising. And she knows which ones did not. And last, she heard him mention a Society, and several names in regards to it, including a G'Jell and a G'Thom."

Tedrey sat up.

"G'Thom?"

"Yes."

"He is known wide, for he is a legacy. Quite a famous one."

Faunus's brows shot up. "Born of a priest?"

Tedrey nodded. "It is not that it is unusual for such to happen. It is just unusual for them to stay within the Go'Doan when they come of age. But he is different. He is…" By the gods, how did he not see this before? "He is known as exceptionally devout."

Faunus held his eyes before he said quietly, "King True came into the possession of some letters as written and to have been received by the traitor they executed. In one, a Golden Thomas was mentioned."

"That is he. His mother named him Thomas, and he is known as such, for he is said to be as golden to the faith as our domes. Does King True know who this refers to?"

"I do not know if he did, but Queen Farah had heard her father mention him, so he knows now."

"This is fantastic, Faunus."

"This is indication you can cease with your spying and stay safe, for it may be over soon," Faunus retorted.

Tedrey grew quiet.

Faunus leaned to him and again caught him at the back of his neck.

"You do not need to suck his cock to gather information any longer, Teddy. What you have provided has yielded rewards. Now, be safe and let kings take care of the business of protecting their realms."

"There are many of them, Faunus, and even if he is the leader, there are others to take up the banner. Not to mention, I do not know what this Society is. I have never heard of it."

"Mars is going to close down all the temples and demand the priests return to the Dome City until The Rising is quelled, and it is doubtful he will ever allow them to return. He has wished an excuse to do this for some time. Now he has one. It is done for you here, in Firenze. Once the priests have been gathered that are known to be of this Rising, King Mars will make the proclamations and the whole of Go'Doan will be gone from this land."

"I don't know—" Tedrey muttered.

"Nyx told me if you vacillated, that I should share that she will refuse to get with child until you cease your activities."

Tedrey's gaze sharpened on Faunus. "That is unfair."

Faunus shrugged. "She is most intelligent. She feels things are coming to a head. And she, as do I, and I will say, as does Lorenz, and not simply because he wishes to plant his seed in his wife, wants you nowhere around when they do."

Tedrey again grew quiet as he considered all of this.

"You have made your amends and you have proved your worth," Faunus said softly, giving Tedrey's neck a squeeze. "Now, let it be done and enjoy the life you built with the friends you earned."

The life he built with the friends he earned.

"Teddy," Faunus prompted.

The life *he built* with the friends *he earned*.

"Teddy," Faunus whispered, again squeezing his neck.

"I will get safe," Tedrey promised.

Faunus let out a long breath.

And Tedrey felt a funny feeling in his throat at the emotion his warrior so easily showed in his relief.

"How should we celebrate this exceptionally wise decision?" Faunus murmured.

Tedrey grinned and caught himself from rolling his eyes.

But that eve, he had had his cock sucked and his arse taken by someone who did not find him lacking.

By someone who cared about him deeply.

Someone whose affection Tedrey had *earned*.

And he had been sucking cock he did not want in his mouth for some time.

It was time to have a new taste.

On this decision he was still grinning as he shifted on the cushions.

Faunus slouched back brazenly.

Once in position, Tedrey drew him deep, watching his warrior's face.

As Faunus felt the draw, his beautiful eyes in his handsome face grew hooded.

Yes.

Much better.

～

Necessarily, after a lingering farewell and promises from Faunus that he would visit Tedrey wherever Lorenz took him to keep him safe until the Go'Doan were gone, Tedrey left the Lotus Den by himself.

And he walked the long journey home by himself.

But he knew that he was followed by Faunus's man.

And he hoped he was not followed by anyone else.

But it would not matter.

He did not have to worry about this any longer.

It was over for him.

And he sensed the burden of it lift, knowing that, too, was a precious gift received from his friends.

Not to mention, he was keen to share this decision with Nyx. She also would be most relieved, and because of this, Tedrey was anxious to give that to her.

He felt the presence of Faunus's guard leave him when he smelled the honeysuckle at the side of Nyx and Lorenz's home.

Faunus was correct. It was not only Nyx who would be most pleased at his decision.

Lorenz would as well.

He did not know if The Rising was soon to be done. It had seemed so much grander, so sweeping, those in it so determined, for it to be so easily defeated.

But Faunus was right. He'd done what he could, but his hand had been played.

And now, Nyx and Lorenz could reconcile, and soon there would be a baby in the house.

He would not be there, however (though he would come often to visit).

Once it was safe, he would find his own abode.

He quite liked the idea, once he found it, of decorating it in a colorful Firenz way.

And with the Go'Doan exiled from Firenz, he would be able to teach the children and maybe even take over the schoolhouse and implement the changes that he thought would benefit his pupils.

It was a curiously strong and pleasant sensation to have things in life to look forward to. Seeing the beauty of a child that Nyx and Lorenz would create. Finding his own dwelling and making it his. Learning more about his warrior and enjoying that endeavor. Spending time with his friends without weighty matters on their minds.

These were his thoughts as he turned toward the back entrance.

He stopped dead at seeing the trail of blood that flowed under the door and down the steps.

Then he burst forward, opened the door, and what filled his vision made him take a quick step back.

"Now, now, now," Fenn called. "Do not beat a hasty retreat, my lover."

One of Nyx and Lorenz's servants, her name was Isabo, a quiet girl with a toothy smile, lay inert on her side on the tiles, her lifeblood having flowed from the gore that was now her neck.

And on her knees some feet away in the back hall, her face a hard mask of wrath, was Nyx.

Fenn was on his feet behind her.

Her eye was swelling and there was blood dribbling from her nose, over her lips and down her chin.

Fenn held her hair in one fist.

And in the other hand, a dagger to her throat.

"You could, of course, flee," Fenn shared. "Though if you do, I will slice her throat and your beloved captain will find his wife just like that one."

He jerked his head to Isabo.

Saliva filled Tedrey's mouth as he stared directly into Fenn's eyes, waiting to hear his next option.

Fenn did not make him wait long.

"Or you could come with me," he continued. "For even if your heart is the black of treason, I have an important use for you."

"Teddy, do not," Nyx said angrily.

They had found him out, he did not know how.

But it didn't matter now.

Tedrey did not look at Nyx.

He could not.

His Nyx.

The first person he had met in his life that he had ever loved.

Because she was the first person he had met in his life who had ever loved him.

"If you harm her, Lorenz will fire a swath of vengeance through Triton to find you," Tedrey warned.

And I, he thought. *I will burn down all of Triton until I find a way to make you pay.*

"These Firenz warriors are not as frightening as everyone thinks," Fenn retorted.

"Tell that to the dead men who stormed the palace," Tedrey returned.

Fenn had no reply to that.

"Let her go unharmed, and I will go with you," Tedrey said.

"Teddy! No!" Nyx shouted, but then cried out in pain as Fenn yanked at her hair.

Tedrey took a step forward but halted when Fenn pressed the point of the dagger deeper to her skin and he saw the rivulet of blood trickle down.

"They took our acolytes, because you told them to," Fenn spat.

This was not true.

He'd done other things.

But not that.

Tedrey did not correct him.

"I go with you and let us go, and swiftly," Tedrey urged. "They know much, Fenn. You and the others need to flee."

He heard Nyx hiss as Fenn pulled her hair farther back, arching her neck.

"They know much *because of you*," Fenn bit.

Well, *that* was true.

"And I am yours if you leave her be," Tedrey replied as calmly as he could.

"And what would you do if I drew this dagger across her throat?" Fenn asked.

"I would stop at nothing until I killed you."

Fenn laughed before he queried, "Do you think I came here alone?"

"I would die, happily, if she is gone. This life would not matter to me, if she is not in it. But I would meet my death with grace, only once you are dead too."

Fenn bent and pressed his jaw to Nyx's hair, a sacrilege of her person that made Tedrey bare his teeth.

"Do you love her so, this wet cunt?" Fenn's voice was snide.

That was not that part of her he loved.

However...

"Yes," Tedrey gritted through his teeth.

"Teddy," Nyx whispered.

"Let her go, and I will come with you," Tedrey pushed.

"I will have you and still kill her," Fenn returned, making all of Tedrey's innards seize, his hands itch, his brain hurt.

"You do not know the love she has from her husband," Tedrey said low. "I know I have given you no reason to trust me, but you can trust that. You will not walk into pits, Fenn. What he will do to you when he finds you, you will pray to the gods for the simplicity of pitch filling your lungs."

He saw something shift in Fenn's eyes at this, before the man said, "If he finds me."

Tedrey had to capitalize on that shift.

"He is King Mars's captain, he is also Mars's friend. Because of this, it will not be a man who seeks you. It will be an army."

Fenn and Tedrey stared at each other for moments that felt like an eternity.

Then Fenn straightened, took the dagger from Nyx's neck, flipped it so he held the blade, and brought it down violently at Nyx's temple.

Tedrey swallowed a cry and fought the driving need to burst forward when she collapsed to her side.

Fenn strode over her, pulling something out of his robes.

He held Tedrey's journal in front of him.

"On our journey, I will have some informative reading, don't you think?" Fenn inquired.

Tedrey opened his mouth but did not have the opportunity to respond.

He felt a burst of pain in the back of his head.

And then he saw nothing but black.

IO9

THE TRIBUNAL

Prince Cassius
Bedchamber of the Prince Regent, Sky Citadel, Sky Bay
Airen

His arse in the bed, sitting up, his princess astride his lap, Elena moved on his cock, her head tipped down, one hand claiming his jaw from below, her lips so close to his, he could feel each gust of breath, her eyes locked to his, her other hand tight at the back of his neck.

But she did not kiss him.

She gazed at him with amethyst eyes filled with passion and something else.

Something Cassius knew.

Something precious.

Far more precious than the slick, sweet clutch of her sex around his.

Far more precious than anything on this earth.

Something precious that Cassius would allow having it, *owning* it, to settle in his gut, in his balls, even in his heart.

But not in his mind, as understanding it was his would mean understanding it was his to lose.

"You need to hurry, my darling," he urged, even if he did not want to, for he liked very much the pace she was using. "We have things to do today."

"You rule the realm. You heal unicorns," she teased. "These things can wait for you."

He did not want her to tease. He did not want this to be playful.

He enjoyed the light in her eyes when she was thus, but now he needed the other back.

That day, he needed that *something*.

"From the moment I laid eyes on you, I could not quite fathom the beauty of you," he murmured, and took note.

His words made her move faster.

He growled his approval, dipping his head and taking a hand from her hip to lift her breast and feed her nipple in his mouth.

As he drew her in deeply, she arched into him and moved even faster.

He released her nipple and tipped his head back again.

"Elena, your eyes."

She stayed as she was, arched to him, head fallen back, riding him.

"Elena, I'll have your eyes as you take me," he grunted.

She tilted her head forward.

And there it was, he had it back.

"I fell in love with you the moment I laid eyes on you," she whispered.

The noise Cassius made at her words was animal as he flipped her, jerked up her legs at her knees, and thrust into her.

Her hands roamed the skin of his back feverishly as she breathed, "Cass."

"You are my light," he rumbled.

Her fingers came to his face, and as she was wont to do, she claimed his beard.

"You are the sun streaming through clouds," he continued.

"My warrior," she whispered.

He dropped his lips to hers. "If I had not met you, I would have lived in the night and I would have died in the night, never again feeling the light."

She wound her arms around his head and bowed up into him as her thighs squeezed his hips and her sex rippled around his cock in her climax.

He listened to that. He felt it.

And then he let go and took his own.

When it had released him, Cassius rolled so that she was atop him, still planted on his cock.

And as he watched the velvet darkness with its blinking stars fade from around them, and the light of day again come through, he gathered her hair in a hand and used it at the back of her head to press her face into his neck.

"Cass," she whispered.

"I meant what I said."

"As did I."

"My world comes in three parts, you, Aelia and Dora."

She pushed her face deeper into his neck.

"I cannot speak the words," he admitted on a whisper.

"You do not need to, my prince. I know."

His relief was so great, it felt beyond physical, right to spiritual.

Indeed, he wondered if there were gods.

Or if there was this.

"Do you know?" she asked tentatively.

Gently, he used her hair to pull her head back and find her gaze.

"I think I knew the moment you laid eyes on me," he murmured. "And it terrified me."

She stroked his beard and smiled with her eyes.

He would not object to lying in that bed with her forever.

Especially not in that moment.

Sadly, that was not an option, not that day.

"We have things to do, my princess," he remined her.

Her "Yes," seemed forced from her throat, very unwillingly.

"It will happen and then it will be done," he soothed.

"It is I who should be reassuring you," she replied.

"You do that often, I quite like having a turn."

He received a smile at that, and he let himself enjoy it before his hands on her became a grip so he could take them from the bed.

But in return, she gripped him.

Cassius stilled and gave her his attention.

"There might be...a few changes..." she started haltingly. "In the throne room."

He could not believe it was about to happen, as he could never believe it was about to happen, and he wondered if there would be a time in his life when this was so commonplace, his disbelief would be extinguished.

But he felt laughter bubbling inside him.

"What did you do?"

"Well…" When he gave her hips a squeeze with his fingers, she stopped dawdling. "I might be subtly changing some of Airen's banners from black to midnight blue," she admitted.

This was not barracks torn down to enhance greenhouses, so he had no quarrel with this.

"That is not a big change."

"And silver," she added.

That was when the chuckles started.

"There might also be some purples," she went on.

"How very Nadirii of you," he muttered.

"It's a darker purple," she informed him.

"Right," he said, his voice shaking.

"Though there might be some that is much like the heather and thistle flower that grows so in Airen," she mumbled.

It was that which made him shake with laughter.

When he was finished, she was smiling at him.

He gave her a squeeze for he knew her ploy.

And this was why he said, "Job well done, my lamb."

Her eyes twinkled.

Cassius allowed himself to enjoy that too.

Before he pulled them from the bed.

"I…WELL, bloody hell, I'm speechless," Mac said, wandering into the vast space of the throne room, eyes big, body drifting and shifting as he moved into the room and took it all in.

"Then we should ask Ellie to be certain to make changes in every room of the Citadel, if that's your reaction," Ian replied.

"I vote for that," Rus said.

"And I," Tone agreed.

Cassius just stood at the back, arms crossed on his chest, feet planted on the midnight blue carpet over the black stone floor, and he moved his gaze about the space.

Before, there were no carpets on the floor.

And before, the rest had all been black.

Now, between the windows there were long pennants hanging, each a different color, all the colors of a night sky, ranging from the deepest blues and purples, to what Ellie had said. A purple the color of a thistle flower.

But the backdrop of the dais behind his throne included two thin pennants that flanked a wider one which was directly behind the throne. The thin ones were ombre from sky blue at the top, to midnight blue at the bottom, with all the colors depicted around the room in between.

The standard behind the throne simply looked like a night sky, silver stars twinkling in it.

The throne itself was not the one in which his father sat.

Less ornate, also less intimidating, it was nevertheless elaborate, the carved wood painted a shining silver, the velvet cushions in sky blue.

The floors were covered in carpets of a variety of hues that mimicked the pennants.

There were two curving settees upholstered in a thistle-colored damask that sat at slight angles to the front of the dais.

Cassius moved deeper into the room when he saw, off to the side, looking as if it was not a permanent fixture, a tall box set on a platform draped with black bunting.

He could see the top of a chair over the railings perched high inside the box.

Apparently, his father, the accused, would look down from it.

Or, as Cassius had no doubt Elena intended, he would be separate from all the others.

And on display.

Ah, but he had a clever future wife.

As if in his mind, Nero, standing by the box, called out, "I'm liking this idea."

"This is good, for I would like you to stand guard at it."

Elena's voice coming from behind him made him turn.

And he instantly arrested.

His princess was moving gracefully into the room wearing a gown the color of heather. The skirt fell to cover her feet and it looked made of delicate netting. The same drifted from her shoulders in short sleeves that were reminiscent of pixie wings. The bodice exposed a demure vee at the chest that was not so demure it did not expose a hint of cleavage and was covered in a delicate applique that also rounded the waist and streamed partially into the top of the skirt.

Her hair was arranged in soft curls pinned to the back of her neck.

But threaded through it at her forehead was her Nadirii band.

At her side, and holding her hand, was Domitia.

And trailing her was Cornelia.

They, too, had donned gowns much different than the garments they normally wore. More Dellish, but not quite. Although diaphanous, they were not flimsy.

Instead of artlessness, for Cornelia, there was a sophistication.

Though, Domitia's had an air of innocence.

Neither of them wore the harsh paint of Airenzian upperclass women.

Though they were painted, just far more subtly.

As, he saw, was his warrior.

And yes.

His future wife was most clever.

Jazz and Hera followed, as did Hera's lover, Rosehana.

They wore their Nadirii tunics, battle-ready.

Also battle-ready were Mac, Ian, Rus, Tone and Nero.

"Mac, you'll be on the dais on Cass's left side. I will be on his right. Jazz and Hera will be beside and behind me," she went on to command. "Nero guarding Gallienus. Ian and Antonius, I want you behind the settee where Domitia and Cornelia will sit. Rose and Severus will be at the back, keeping an eye from there. I will also ask you both to patrol but not *appear* as if you're patrolling. Just keep your eye on things."

She (and Domitia) had come to stand beside Cassius.

"What are you wearing?" he asked.

She tipped her head to look up at him.

"A gown," she answered.

"Why are you not in your Nadirii gear?" he inquired.

"Because I am the future queen of this realm and the people of this realm need to look upon me as conventional and approachable, something they will not consider me if I have a sword at my back, a dagger at my belt, and my quiver at the ready. If I appear like that, I will seem to be hostile, which I am not. Except to your father." She pressed her arse back a bit as she lifted a filmy layer of her skirts out to the side, gazing down at it, and finished, "And I quite like this gown."

He quite liked it too.

Quite.

Even so...

"Elena," he called.

She righted herself and again gave him her gaze.

"I think, my princess, you should be you," he advised.

"I *am* me," she returned. "Just wearing a gown."

"Elena—"

"There has been much change expected of all citizens of Airen since your return, Cassius. And many may think this is because of me. Therefore, it would be wise if they see a change in me as well. They need to understand the balance we will have, something they too will enjoy."

He could say no more for she was not wrong.

His attention turned to Domitia, who was still standing at Elena's side, holding her hand.

"You are ready for this, Domitia?" he asked quietly.

She started when her name was said, and she looked at him.

She then nodded unconvincingly.

"I will ask you to say your words and then Ian will escort you from the room." He included Cornelia in his gaze. "The both of you."

"I-I can stay," Domitia said, casting a quick glance to Elena.

Elena nodded encouragingly.

"That would be most brave," Cassius told her gently. "However, I wish you to know you don't have to if you don't wish. Ian will be ready to escort you out."

"I will stay," Domitia replied, struggling to lift her chin and square her shoulders.

But in the end, she did it.

"I will wait to see him sentenced," Cornelia stated.

The fact she spoke at all caused Cassius some surprise, for he had never known any of his father's wives to be communicative, outside Horatia speaking for them all when the occasion arose, and thus he regarded Cornelia a moment before he looked to Elena.

She gave him a slight nod.

He again turned to Cornelia. "I am sorry you must endure this, for I am certain this will be difficult for you."

"This will be the easiest thing I'll have endured in my marriage," she replied.

He hated to hear it, but he had little doubt.

He had not protected these women. He had lived amongst them and been so deep in his own grief, wallowing in self-pity, he had done naught to help them.

"I am sorry that I did not—" he began, his eyes moving between them both.

"He hates you," Cornelia declared.

Cassius fell silent at hearing words said out loud he knew to the depths of his soul.

"When Trajan was alive, and he had an heir, he would have used any excuse to be done with you," she informed him. "It is not kind, but it is true, that your grief for your wife saved you. He thought you weak, the love you had for her. And he despised that weakness. He wished you, and her, cast out. Connived to find some way to make that so. When she was gone and you became alternately detached and combative, only then was he able to stomach you, for these were traits for which he held some respect."

This did not surprise him, the things he liked least about himself, his father liked the most.

"But even if you knew what befell us," Cornelia continued, "you could not have come to our aid. If you had tried, the way he feels about you, it would have been worse for you."

Elena moved closer to him as Cassius remained quiet and listened to her words.

"When he had power, he was a danger to us all," she concluded.

"Even so, I still wish there was some way that I—"

He did not finish that either.

Cornelia talked over him.

"I do as well, but you are doing it now. And that is all."

That was definitely all, for as he could glean from her expression, she intended to speak no more of it.

At that point, he noted Mac on the move, and Cassius looked to the door.

A soldier stood there.

"I would wish to return to my mother after this," Cornelia declared, and regained Cassius's attention.

He nodded. "I will settle a sum on you and—"

"No," she interrupted him. "I will have nothing from this house. I have already sent her a letter, and she has replied. It is arranged. When this is done, we move to Wodell. I have an uncle there who will take us in. As I am finally free to leave, I will leave immediately. And I will not live in this land again. I will not even speak its name."

The vigorous way she shared this, the bitterness surfacing in her eyes, he did not doubt she would see this assertion true.

"This is understandable," he murmured.

She turned her eyes away.

Mac approached.

"Your father's carriage draws near. They say he is fifteen minutes away. We should bring in the courtiers, laymen and the gentry."

"They have all been searched for weapons?" Cassius asked.

Mac nodded. "Thoroughly."

"Right, everyone to their place," Elena ordered. "Nero, can you wait outside the door and escort Gallienus to the box?"

Nero nodded.

Elena guided Domitia to a settee, Cornelia followed, and then she bent at the waist and stood with them, talking to them quietly.

This was where she was when the first courtiers entered the room.

Cass was on a throne that was new in two ways.

From there, he alternated between watching them enter and watching his princess.

Thus, he saw her take up Domitia's hand in both of hers, shake it firmly, and he also watched her touch an immobile Cornelia's shoulder, but at least the woman did not withdraw.

Elena then made her slow way to the podium, the better to see her gown at work, wafting about her hips and legs and shoulders, as she ascended the dais and took her place at his back, right side.

"I would have you in a chair beside me," he muttered.

"I would have this better vantage," she muttered in return.

And there was his warrior.

He chuckled.

And then he got down to the business of what he needed to do that day, something he knew his men were doing as Cassius, not their Princess Regent, had ordered.

That was observing every person who entered the room, the language of their bodies, the expressions on their faces, the cast of their glance, on him, on Elena, on her lieutenants, and to each other.

It was a room filled with enemies, and a hand gesture or a quickly averted gaze could mean everything.

He very much liked the space as Elena had altered it. It had majesty. It was true to Airen, but a different Airen. One of color, one that had life.

But this change about them meant most who entered were so intent on taking it in, they gave nothing away.

They were not offered seats, thus they milled about and found spaces to stand, but a line of the Citadel guard kept an aisle open at the side so his father could come in and get direct to his box by walking along the wall, thus not get near his wives when he did.

Something else Elena undoubtedly maneuvered.

He noted Lahn and Circe, Finnie and Frey arriving. After the men led Circe and Finnie to the settee opposite where Domitia and Cornelia sat, Lahn stood behind them while Frey moved to stand at the far side of the dais, where the recorder's desk was stationed and where he could see the full room.

And it was then, Lahn and Frey (and it must be said, mostly Lahn) took the bulk of the attention of the males in the room (and the females, but for a different reason).

As they waited, Cassius lounged in his chair and noted that the most reaction in general was from the few women in the assembly, women who seemed taken with studying Elena and her gown.

The men gave very little away, except in some cases, they did not hide their antagonism toward Cass.

It seemed to take too long before a herald stood in black regalia (Elena clearly had not had time to affect a change in the Citadel uniform), and he called, "King Gallienus arrives!"

And with that, his father walked in between two Bailey guards, as well as Reginald of the Bailey trailing him, Nero leading.

There was a hush before a rush of murmurings from the gathering as he strode in, thin, ill-kempt, straggly, his clothing clean and fine, but hanging on him.

Elena, it seemed, was not the only one with the skill to create import out of appearances.

"This is a disgrace!" he shouted, being led across the back wall. "A bloody farce!"

Although ill-kempt and straggly, his voice was strong and carried far.

Cassius cast his gaze down to Domitia and Cornelia.

Cornelia could easily be mistaken for a statue.

Domitia was visibly fretting.

"What has become of my throne room? This is *obscene!*" Gallienus yelled.

Cassius sighed.

Gallienus was led up to his box and immediately reached to the pennant hanging beside it, his mouth opened, Cass was certain, to continue to bellow his kingly lament.

"If you tear that banner down," Cassius said in a voice that carried. "I'll hang you with it."

Gallienus turned stiltedly toward his son.

"Now sit. For your wives, this will be done quickly," Cassius ordered.

"I want it on the record, I do not recognize this tribunal," Gallienus announced.

"And I'll go on the record to assert I do not care," Cassius returned. "Now be quiet until you're asked to speak."

"I am king. I will—"

"You are a flailing, useless old man who did not recognize that time had come for change. Who bowed to tradition instead of worked for progress. Who was so weak, he could not secure his own realm, even from his own citizens, and continued to allow them to hold power over him. And who, if you did not show some sense in relinquishing your authority, would have led this realm to ruin as the other lands united as military and economic allies," Cassius declared. "Now, be silent and demonstrate a little dignity during your final public appearance, for the gods' sakes."

Gallienus glared at him.

Cassius dismissed his father and turned to the recorder.

"Read the charges, if you will," he bid.

The charges were read.

"Preposterous!" Gallienus shouted.

The new law was read.

"Ludicrous!" Gallienus yelled.

Cassius had never really paid much mind to his father.

His casual cruelties, yes.

His flagrant sadism, yes.

His childish tantrums.

Alas, no.

He noted them now, but he did so nonverbally.

Verbally, he commenced proceedings as they had planned.

Hadrian shared shortly and without detail what he had witnessed in the king's bedchamber. Antonius did the same.

And when asked, Domitia declared that this was so.

And when asked, both women attested in brief to the physical and sexual abuse that had occurred throughout their marriages.

That done swiftly, Cassius turned to his father.

"It was not law before, but your violation of her Honorable Domitia was an offense after. Do you deny this version of events as presented here today?" he asked.

"It is not a crime to handle my wife as I see fit," Gallienus sniffed.

"This is incorrect. As the law was read, it is a crime now. So with your words, for the record, you do not deny this version of events as presented here today," Cassius repeated on a sigh.

"Of course I don't," Gallienus snapped.

"So be it," Cassius said. "I therefore find you guilty of one charge of assault and battery of a person and one charge of sexual violation of a person. Thus, you are hereby sentenced to ten years as an issue four prisoner in Slán Bailey for the first charge. This you will serve after you serve the sentence of fifteen years as an issue five prisoner for the charge of sexual violation of a person. This sentence will begin immediately. And with that, this tribunal has ended."

There were more murmurings about the room, but Cassius ignored them.

And even as he straightened from his throne, he nodded to Reginald and his prison guard that stood with Nero at the foot of the box, an indication to take Gallienus away.

"I'll be in that Bailey maybe a week," his father asserted.

He would be there for twenty-five years, if he lived that long.

But Cass did not share that.

He noted his father saying "a week."

So, his father's allies intended to move in some manner in that week.

That did not matter for the now.

For the now, at least, this was over.

For Horatia. For Cornelia. For Domitia. For Aelia.

And for himself.

He turned and reached his hand to Elena.

She took it.

"Enjoy this frippery!" Gallienus shouted. "I will have it all torn down and it will burn while your Nadirii watches your head leave your body as you kneel on the gallows and the blade falls. This before she is enjoyed by every lord of this realm."

His body tightened, but her hand squeezed his and his gaze caught hers.

When it did, his grip relaxed.

"Felix has called first go!" Gallienus bellowed, sounding like he was hollering at the same time struggling.

"Ignore it," Elena whispered.

Ignore *that*?

Not on her life.

He turned to a Citadel guard. "Arrest Lord Felix Edgar of the Gairn Plain on suspicion of treason and making a threat against the person of the Princess Regent."

"Do not!" Edgar shouted. "For you cannot! You have no evidence of this!"

"You were accused in my own throne room," Cassius told him then looked to the back toward where his father was being led out. "Would you like to carry on? It would be most helpful."

"To hell with you, Cassius Laird!" his father called from where he was nearly out the door. "I disown you!"

"Thank the gods, I am finally fatherless," Cassius said loudly, and heard a few manly chuckles and nervous feminine twitters.

"Cass," Elena said, standing steadfast and not allowing him to guide her to the end of the dais.

"Let us go," he murmured.

"Cass!" she said his name more urgently.

He looked to her.

Then he aimed his attention where hers was and saw a Nadirii fighting to get through the crowd.

Elena had a number of Nadirii warriors with her.

This one he did not recognize.

In the end, it was his princess who led him from the dais in order to meet her Nadirii sister.

Jasmine and Hera stayed at her back, his men at their posts, which meant Mac was at his.

"What is it, Peg?" she asked when they made the Nadirii who Cassius noted looked travel worn.

"I..." the woman began, glanced at Cassius, then at Elena, "Well, my sister, I am here for your return message to our queen should your bird not make it."

"My return message about what?" Elena asked, her voice reedy, her regard fixed on the female warrior. "I have not had a bird from mother in some time."

The Nadirii appeared surprised.

Then concerned.

"We made Kilcree Break. We..." she trailed off to look about her before she said, "We should have privacy."

Gods damn it.

Cassius communicated with his gaze to a variety of people before he started to lead his princess from the room.

"I demand to be released, Prince Cassius," a male voice called angrily.

Cassius halted abruptly and looked to Lord Felix. "When your militia surrenders themselves to my army, and you, and they kneel allegiance to me and my regency, that will happen. Before then, you will enjoy the views from the Bailey."

And with that, he pulled Ellie out of the room.

THEY WERE in the sitting room with the red cushions.

And Cassius had long since decided Elena was right.

Those cushions were a nice shock of color.

"Am I the only one who thinks they should have at it and leave a trail of blood and piles of bodies in their wake?" Mac asked the room at large.

"No," Jazz replied.

"Yes," Ian clipped.

Cassius sat in an armchair, pinching the bridge of his nose.

Elena sat on the arm of his chair, and it was unfortunate her arse in that gown was that close and he could not enjoy it by pulling it into his lap.

"This was not a good bird to go astray," Hera murmured.

"Otho was found?"

At Nero's quiet question, Cassius dropped his hand and looked to the Nadirii warrior, Peg.

"The bodies were preserved as best we could, boxed, and entered into the earth," Peg answered. "We did this because we did not have the warriors to spare to transport them here. And I am sorry, Your Grace," she aimed this at Cassius, "we do not know much of your gods, but we asked our goddess to bless them until this sacrament could be made by your own."

"We'll get them and return them to their families," Cassius muttered. "And thank you for your care of them."

She dipped her chin to him before she continued, her gaze moving to Elena, "Our trackers picked up a trail, it was hard to miss. Apparently, Zees enjoy leaving breadcrumbs. It was heading north. I know no more, my princess. I just know that Queen Ophelia led them that way."

"Do you find it odd we have received no raven since?" Cassius asked Elena's profile, for she was regarding Peg wearing a pensive expression.

She shook her head and looked down at him. "I find it hopeful."

Cassius nearly smiled.

Of course she did.

"She would send word if there was word to be sent," Elena finished.

"What did you do with the other bodies?" Ian asked Peg.

"We did not have time to make crates for all of them. There were too many," Peg answered, and Cassius winced. "But we shrouded them securely and buried them." She looked to Cass. "This is your way, is it not?"

Cassius nodded.

"Cass?" Rus prompted.

He expelled a heavy breath.

And then he decreed, "We cannot have Fern's army slaughtering citizens before a war has even officially broken out."

"Guess we're outvoted," Jasmine muttered to Mac.

Mac flung an arm around her shoulders.

She leaned into his frame.

"And we cannot have Silvanus and his Zees running amuck across Airen thinking he's helping, when he's not."

"I did not know you formed that deep of a bond with him, Cass," Elena remarked.

"I didn't either," Cassius replied, before he voiced his decision. "I need to make a proclamation, as soon as possible, that any unsanctioned aggression in this realm will be treated as the criminal act it is."

"Until it's sanctioned," Jasmine put in.

"*If* it is," Cassius retorted. He again looked to Ellie. "Your mother has my permission to proceed as she will to liberate Fern. That is all."

"Then we must get to parchment and gather the heralds," Elena said quietly.

He had hoped for a different end to this day.

Wine. Food. Their friends around.

And if they could, retiring early, if just so he could lie abed with Elena and hold her.

This being after he divested her of that fetching gown.

But this would clearly not be happening.

"I'll order dinner sent to your stu—" Ellie started to say.

She did not finish, for a soldier entered the room.

His rank was high, a marshal, and if Cass remembered his name correctly, it was Angus.

"Sire," he said on a smart bow. "A communication from the Nadirii squadron."

He lifted his hand and in it was a message from a raven.

"Shite," Cass muttered, pushing up.

He and the man met in between, Cassius walking with Elena close to his side.

The message was passed off, the marshal bowed, turned smartly and left the room.

Cassius unwound the missive and instantly made the decision any communications from anyone would be delivered to him in private.

For the message said,

Night Heights. Southeast Range. Bring Elena immediately. The queen is dying.

"No," Elena whispered.

He shoved the ribbon of parchment to the person nearest, this being Rus, and turned to take her in his arms before he took her from the room.

But she moved first, taking a step away.

"My darling," he said gently. "Come with me."

He heard a gasp, he knew not from who, but he knew it meant the news was traveling the chamber.

"Ellie, please, come with me."

"No," she whispered again.

"Ellie—"

"*No!*" she shrieked, the pain in that one word clawing at his heart.

And with that, Cassius went to her.

Cassius met his men in the Great Hall next to the table now sporting spikes of deep purple and shocking blue gladiolus.

"Report," he ordered when he stopped at their huddle.

"Scouts sent," Mac told him. "Those to find the location of the Nadirii squadron, those to assess our path is clear in getting to her." He paused and then said, "Cass, after the siege was defeated, we know they're holding back, waiting for any excuse to start the war. But you've just sentenced their king to twenty-five years in prison. And with your attention divided, this would be the perfect excuse."

"Yes, it would," Cassius replied. "And until this news from the Nadirii, I would relish it starting so it could be over. But we need to hold off their hostility for the now as my priority is to get my woman to her mother."

Mac nodded.

"Birds and riders sent," Ian entered the conversation. "To True so he knows and can tell Serena. To Mars and Aramus, not to the Go'Doan."

Cassius inclined his head.

"A battalion is readying," Tone put in. "As are the Nadirii who traveled with Elena. We will be ready to ride out in no more than half an hour."

Cassius tipped his head to Antonius and looked back to Ian. "I will need you to stay. The proclamation must be made, and the Bay kept secure. Also, send reinforcements to the Bailey. King Gallienus does not breathe a free breath until he serves his twenty-five years."

"Of course," Ian replied.

His gaze went through them all. "Rus stays with Ian. The rest of you ride with me and my princess."

He received gestures of assent.

"This does not seem important now, but who knows what is important in times like these with all manner of things happening," Rus spoke up. "The unicorns are restless."

"It is my understanding they are bonded with Elena and I, and thus, probably sense her agitation," Cassius told him.

"Do you wish for them to ride with you?" Rus asked.

"I wish for them to be free to make that decision," Cass answered.

Rus nodded. "I'll see to it that that their paddock is opened."

Cassius held a moment in case there was more to report.

When no one spoke, he commanded, "Those of you going, get ready to ride. Ian, Rus, stay strong."

He then turned and moved swiftly to the stairs, and once on them, took them two at a time.

In the upper hall, he made haste to his and Elena's bedchamber, and upon entering it, saw her weapons littered the coverlet of their bed with her at the sofa, shoving things in her saddle bags.

Her gown was a pool of tulle on the floor.

Her body was now covered in her Nadirii gear.

Her face was harsh.

"All is ready, we ride out in half an hour," he shared.

She did naught but grunt, flipping over the flap on her bag and tying the fastenings tighter than necessary.

He got close and called softly, "My lamb."

"I suppose, soon, I will be joining you and Dora and Aelia and True and Farah's family," she stated.

He was surprised she said these words, for he did not know she knew of his conversation with Theodora.

Perhaps Dora told her.

"Ellie, cease a moment and come let me hold you," he urged.

She ceased, only to turn woodenly to him and look up in his eyes.

And then, even in her dread, preparing for the onslaught of grief, she spoke words that completed her self-appointed task of coloring his world.

"I was certain my love for True was genuine. I longed for nothing but a life with him. But at one look at you, I did not think of it again. But now, Cass, in this time since that message was received, it is all I can think about."

His words sounded choked when he asked, "The life you would have had with True?"

"No. The life I could have with *you* if we had been naught but *us*. Not prince. Or princess. A Dellish maiden and shepherd. A Firenz nomad and the girl who caught his eye. A Mar-el pirate and a bar wench. I do not care what we were, except, no offense, but I have not considered a life in Airen."

"No offense taken," he murmured.

"What would it be if that was us?" she asked. "What would be our lives if we were just man and woman who could meet and marry and make children? We could grumble about the decisions of kings and queens at night in our bed by a fire under a thatched roof, but their machinations had very little to do with the next day's toil or the love shared when it was done."

"Ellie," he whispered.

"If we were that, when my mother got sick, she would be down the lane, resting in bed, cared for by her daughters, with those who loved her close at hand when—"

Her voice cracked, the harshness dissolved from her face, and it was then Cass took the step separating them and drew her tight in his arms.

Her body bucked once with a muted sob.

After that, she settled into heartbreaking shakes.

He put his lips to the top of her hair.

"We will get to her."

"Serena—"

"A raven and rider have been sent."

She held onto him, and his clever future wife, she allowed herself the time to feel what she was feeling and express it, before he heard her sniff and give his waist a squeeze.

He took his cue, let her go but lifted both hands to her jaws and swept his thumbs over her wet cheeks, dipping his face so it was in hers.

Her violet eyes shone with love and anguish.

I love you, he thought.

"Are you ready?" he asked.

She nodded.

Cass kissed her forehead.

Then he looked again in her eyes and said, "Let us go."

IIO
THE DISTRACTION

Princess Serena
The Shanty, Notting Thicket
WODELL

Serena careened down the alley unsteadily, the only sure thing about her was her hold on the jug of grog.

She approached the spent bottles of whiskey farthest from the troll and did not waste much time assessing if they had a taste left (none) or if they were entirely empty (all).

Things had, of late, hit a critical stage.

The cases of liquor stacked in the doorframe of the building the troll guarded had run low.

And she had noted the troll not once, but several times, eyeing and even sometimes moving to the lock on the door and tugging on it or flicking it in frustration.

She also had noted that he seemed to be on the lookout for something.

This, she suspected, being his benefactor, who he did not know would never be returning.

The troll was growing restless.

Fortunately, True had sent word that it was time for her crew to move.

She could only assume the arrests had been made, that blow delivered to The Goddess-Damned Bloody Rising.

Now, she hoped she and Gal and Brix would deliver another.

There were ten of True's men as well as Tor in their little room through the maze of alleyways, waiting for Serena, Gal and Brix to get into the building. They could have overcome the troll, but if the coin wasn't behind that locked door, they didn't want a big hullabaloo to indicate they were in search of it and had homed in on the Shanty.

However, if what they thought was inside was indeed inside, the soldiers and Tor would secure it until troops could be sent in to reclaim what was in it.

The time was nigh.

And this was it.

Serena moved closer to the troll, already noting she had his attention.

It was not the first time she had assessed his spent bottles. In fact, it was not the first time she had assessed the spent bottles she was now assessing.

This did not matter.

All the troll knew was that she was a drunkard. As such, she would not remember what she had done five minutes ago, much less the day before.

She got closer but stopped and looked at him with blinking eyes, squatting but still swaying.

She shuffled ever closer, but he did not move, just kept watching her.

She picked up some bottles, held them to the sun, set them down. More, she held up, sniffed at their mouths, set them aside, shuffled closer, all the while dragging her jug.

She came ever closer, and he pushed away from his lounge against the wall.

He did not arise, but he wanted her to know he was alert.

She scuttled back and eyed the lone crate behind him that had been at least five stacked when she had discovered him and the building he guarded.

Cautiously, she waddled closer.

"Fanshy a shag?" she slurred.

His deep-set black eyes at the sides of his pronounced nose looked around the matted locks falling in his face, this look aimed at her body.

"Mm?" she asked, shuffling closer. "Wanna have shum fun?"

His fangs moved against his upper lip.

Serena came ever closer, securing her grip on the jug.

"C'mon, big boy, les 'af shum fun."

He sniffed her way, slightly recoiled.

And she moved.

Fast.

Coming up and swinging around, she brained him with the heavy, earthenware jug.

He fell sideways, and she threw the crock at him with all her might.

It hit him in the jaw, and he slammed down to his side.

With that, she dashed around him, took hold of his last crate, dragged it from its alcove and gripped it.

She then lifted it, turned and ran.

The troll snorted his fury, she sensed him shifting, and she prayed to the goddess he would leave his post and give chase.

She did not go fast, she did not go slow, and she did not move with coordination.

She was a drunken wench in the Shanty stealing whiskey from a troll, struggling against her inebriation and the weight of the crate.

She needed to be this, take him elsewhere and find ways to keep him occupied, for Gal told her if the lock on the door of that building was easy, it would take less than a minute to open. If it was difficult, it would take more akin to five.

And at what was found inside, it would take another five for Brix to swing rooftop to rooftop to get whatever the word was to Tor.

But they would not be able to get to it if she could not distract the troll.

She nearly cried out her relief when she heard him lumbering behind her.

As she had never dealt with trolls, she did not, regrettably, know how fast they moved.

So, when he caught her with his claws in the back of her tattered gown and took her off her feet, she was surprised.

She tossed the crate up and out, and it crashed to the cobbles.

Glass could be heard breaking.

Then *she* was tossed, and she grunted in pain when she landed hard against a wall right before the troll roared his fury so loud, if there was any glass in the panes of the dwellings around her, it would have shaken.

She landed in a crouch on her feet, got herself in hand, and watched the troll tear off the top of the crate.

Apparently, what was inside was not salvageable for his head turned her way, and his large mouth opened to emit another roar.

Oh, shite.

He was enraged.

How long had they been gone?

Two minutes?

Three?

She surged up to make a getaway at the same time lead him away from where Gal and Brix were doing their work.

But she got not a step in before she was grabbed again by her gown at the back. She heard a rending of fabric but ignored it, endeavoring to twist her body out of his hold to gain her feet.

She could fight on her feet.

She could run on her feet.

She could not do either dangling in the air.

Alas, she was not that way for long for she again was thrown with some power against a wall.

She felt the impact throughout her body.

However, she was prepared this time. Thus, she landed light, head up, aware, and was able to duck a swipe of the troll's large hand. A swipe, that if it had landed, would likely have sent her staggering several feet and who knew what damage it would have done to her body.

Serena ducked again when he swiped the other way, this time scuttling out from between him and the wall.

She did not have time to get a hand on the dagger in her boot. She only had time to dodge two more blows before, when his torso was twisted, she raced beyond him at his other side, doing this away from the building he had guarded for so long.

He gave chase, and in the now, Serena did not bother to appear inebriated and ungainly.

She could not go so fast she would escape, and he would give up and return.

She absolutely did not go slow.

She shunted into an alleyway she knew was a wynd.

But he surprised her again by catching up with her, nearly grabbing hold on her, so she was forced to make a quick turn.

Sadly, doing this took her down a close.

And at the dead end of it, she knew she'd have to turn, stand and fight.

This she did.

Doing a whirl with her arm and fist in position, she caught him in his starkly protruding jaw.

She did not know if he felt pain, though his head snapped around.

She did know *she* felt pain, as his jaw felt like it was made of iron.

She ignored that and landed another blow to his jaw, but he was ready for it this time and shook it off instantly.

Serena then switched tactics, pivoted to her side, putting her weight in her left leg, and kicking out with her right, into his stomach.

He did not even expel air at her strike, and when she adjusted her aim to kick him in the groin, he caught her ankle and twisted it viciously.

In order for him not to break it, she flung her body in the direction her ankle was going, which meant she hit the ground on her shoulder with a body-wracking thud.

But she immediately swung about with her left leg, landing a whack to his temple.

He grunted at that.

She was heartened by that.

Thus, she drew back her left leg and caught him full in the nose with her heel.

He fell back, still with a hold on her ankle, so she was dragged back when he went.

She engaged her stomach muscles to reach to her left boot for her dagger when he made it plain that he'd had enough.

She knew this when he used her ankle to shake her bodily, his strength such she lost control of her frame and her head cracked on the cobbles.

As she blinked away stars, he let go of her ankle to grasp onto her hips and tow her to him.

She was up.

He was up.

And then she was slammed to the wall at the end of the close so hard, her breath left her.

Holding her there with his body, he was clawing at her skirts, thin streams of saliva dribbling through his fangs.

Well then.

Apparently, he'd picked now to have some fun.

However, that would not be happening.

She landed as many blows as she could as powerfully as she could in this position, at his jaw, temple, cheekbone, neck and throat.

He grew impatient with her endeavors and shared this when he snapped at her with his teeth, bursts of slobber slapping her in the face.

Her legs were astride his hips, she yanked up her left knee, reaching for her dagger, and screaming in his face, "*Bloody no!*"

And then something else splattered her face so violently, she blinked against it.

When she opened her eyes, the body that had her pinned to the wall started listing.

This was because it had no head.

She fell to her feet as it thudded to the ground and that was when she saw Tor in the alley, two of True's guard behind him.

Both Tor's hands were wound about the hilt of his broadsword.

Through the blood and drool streaming down her face, she looked down at the body of the troll, its head resting, mouth still in full sneer, some four feet away.

She lifted her hands, swiped the wet from about her eyes, and looked back to Tor.

"Well, that was expedient," she drawled.

"We don't have such creatures in my land," he told her. "And I did not fancy figuring out what it would take to subdue him."

She studied the Valerian king, and at what she saw, she said quietly, "He does not leave behind a wife and children who depend on him, Tor."

It took him a moment before he jerked up his chin, took out a handkerchief and offered the snowy cloth to her.

She shook her head, bent double and used her tatty skirts to clear her face.

As she straightened, she saw Tor wipe the blood from his blade before scabbarded it, dropping the cloth to the cobbles and looking to her.

"Right," he stated shortly. "Do you wish to see what a very large stash of coin looks like?"

"It's there?" she whispered.

He nodded. "It's there."

She could not stop it. Suddenly it was affixed to her face.

A large smile.

Tor's eyes flashed with humor as his lips twitched then he tipped his head toward the alley behind him.

They made haste back to the building where that troll had spent much of his time, perhaps unwittingly (though it mattered not now if it was willful or other) a conspirator in treason.

The closed door was now guarded by two of True's soldiers, two more patrolled the alley (that she could see) and one had his bow at the ready on the roof.

She and Tor walked directly to the door.

Serena opened it and stepped inside.

There were several lanterns lit, but they didn't do much to dispel the dim of the place.

Regardless, there were small and large trunks scattered everywhere, some of their lids opened, these exposing the contents within, and on the edge of one, Brix sat, flipping and catching a coin in one hand.

"We were remiss in not asking True if there was a reward," he joked.

"I need no money," Gal stated, strolling to the chest on which Brix sat, leaning against it and crossing his feet at the ankle. "I will simply gorge on the heaps of gnomish fanny that is going to be thrown at me as the Great Gnome Hero who saved the realm's treasury."

"Oh right, there is that," Brix muttered.

"What's mixed with the blood all over your face?" Gal asked her.

Apparently, she hadn't been thorough with her skirts.

"Slobber," Serena answered.

"Blimey," Gal muttered, making a face.

"It appears our jobs were much more fun," Brix remarked, then he flipped the gold coin he was tossing across the space her way.

She flashed out a hand and caught it.

Serena then looked to her crew, her boys...

Her friends.

And she burst out laughing.

THE FIRST THING she wanted to do when she entered Birchlire Castle was go direct to a bath.

What she did not want to do (until perhaps later), was be summoned to the king's informal study to receive True's gratitude for recovering what was left of Wodell's treasury that Carrington had stolen (and it was not all that had been stolen, obviously, but it was quite a lot *and* came with large tomes in which an accounting of the expenditures had been made, with coded notes, which, decoded, could lead to evidence of treason and more arrests).

But this, it would seem, was what she had no choice but to do when she, Gal, Brix and Tor arrived at the castle after half a battalion had appeared in the Shanty to transport the coin back where it belonged.

They had not only been summoned.

They were told to attend him immediately.

Thus, Serena revised her plans.

She would hear True's words, these words likely of gratitude, however, the moment he got a whiff of her, she had no doubt he'd make them short. She would then have a very long bath. After, she would put on her tunic and casings. Then she would find Gal and Brix.

And they would go out and get extremely drunk.

While doing so, she would hope there were gnome wenches they could find with whom her boys could celebrate properly.

And maybe, she would be drunk enough to drown her memories of Chu in the taking of another man's cock.

She did not hold hope for that last.

Once she sobered and had a good meal, she would pack and journey to meet up with Heloise, Genia and Darma, grab her squad in The Enchantments then ride out to assist her mother.

And, finally...

Even though she would not want it, Serena would give it...

Do what she could to make Airen safe for her sister.

These were her plans. These were the only thoughts on her mind.

That was, these were the only thoughts on her mind until she walked through the door to True's study, saw True resting his arse at the front of his desk, arms crossed on his chest, gaze on Farah who sat before him at the edge of a chair, leaned forward, her hand curled around his forearm.

The moment they entered, however, True's gaze jumped to her, and Farah rose from the chair, turning toward the newcomers.

But her eyes were only for Serena.

And at seeing what was in them, an arrow pierced her heart.

"Serena—" True began.

"Is she dead?" Serena croaked.

"Not yet," he said gently. "Not that we know. We just received the bird but an hour ago."

"I must go," she stated.

"What's happening?" Tor asked.

"Queen Ophelia. She has been ill," Farah said quietly. "And she is..." She clearly could not say the words, so she finished, "Now much more ill."

"We go with you."

These words came from around her thighs.

She looked down to Galdor and Welbrix standing in front of her.

"I ride alone."

"We go with you," Brix declared firmly.

She opened her mouth, but she did not have time to speak.

"You do not ride alone. I send you with a troop, Serena," True decreed. "You would not be safe on your own. But I will see to it that you're safe on your journey to Ophelia. You will ride under the Dellish standard. If things are as we think in Airen, they would attack a Nadirii riding on her own. They would think twice about engaging a Dellish guard."

"And we will ride with them," Gal added.

"That is your choice," True said.

"I do not think—" Serena began.

"Get a bath," Gal ordered. "We will have a meal ready when you are bathed, dressed and packed. We will eat well, but swiftly. And once we do, we will go."

"Can you have her guard prepared by then?" Brix asked True.

"They are already prepared to ride when you are," True replied.

That was True...

Always so....

True.

At a thought in her head, another arrow pierced her heart.

"Does Elena know?" she queried.

True shook his head but said, "I do not know, but I assume she received the same message we did."

Serena drew in a deep breath.

"Go," True urged. "Tell your mother when you see her that she is in our thoughts and it is an honor to know her."

"Thank you," Serena whispered.

She meant the guard. She meant his care in sharing this information.

And she meant him referring to her mother in present tense.

True quickly masked the surprise these words coming from Serena caused before he replied, "It is I who should be thanking you."

"Thank you," she repeated.

He let that go and inclined his head.

Then he urged softly, "Go, Serena."

She nodded.

She looked to Farah, who actually blew her a kiss with tears trembling in her eyes, to Tor, who looked down at her with such a gentle expression, she had to tip her chin to him quickly before the witnessing of it unraveled her...

And finally, down to Gal and Brix.

"Let's go," she said.

They nodded.

She walked out of the room and her friends followed.

She bathed.

Quickly packed.

Wolfed down some food.

And with her crew of gnomes on horses on either side of her, a troop of Dellish soldiers at her back, Princess Serena, a Dellish hero, bolted down the lane that led away from Birchlire Castle, and then she raced over the cobbles of Notting Thicket on her way to her mother.

On her way home.

III

THE HOLIDAY

King Mars

Bedchamber of the King, Catrame Palace, Fire City

FIRENZE

Mars licked his way up his queen's belly, between her breasts, along her throat, over her chin to her mouth, where he said, "I will pierce you tonight while our company stumbles from cock to cunt in the garden celebrating *Miet*."

Silence giggled.

Then she grasped his cock and tried to guide it to her sex.

"This sounds fine, but I would wish to watch," she murmured.

"The piercing?" he asked.

"The celebrations," she said on a tug of his shaft that earned her a grunt and a stroke through her hand, this bringing him nearly inside her, but his body stilled when a heavy knock sounded at the door.

"Not now!" he bellowed.

"My king! Urgent news from Wodell and the Nadirii."

Gods dammit.

When Mars did not move, his wife's hand left his shaft to alight on his cheek.

"You must go," she said.

"*We* must go," he returned. "I'll put on your chain, you shall link mine, and then you don something accessible. After I hear this news, I'll finish fucking you on my desk."

Her eyes went molten and her cheeks turned pink.

Thus, he kept his eyes open as he kissed her so he could enjoy both.

When he was done, he dragged her up the bed onto his lap, reached for his wedding chain on his night table and handed it to her.

She threaded it through his hoops and linked it, kissing the hoop by his lip when her task was complete. She then reached for hers and he did the same.

After his kiss, which was full on her lips, they left the bed.

They met again outside their dressing rooms.

And holding her hand, he led his queen to his study.

MARS SAT BEHIND HIS DESK, Silence sat on his side atop it, but at an angle and twisted at the waist, so she could regard Chu as he sat in the chair opposite them, his face perfectly composed.

Nyx sat in the chair next to him.

Her face was *not* perfectly composed.

Lorenz, agitated as he had been for some days now, was pacing beside his desk.

"This is your choice," Mars said to Chu. "Basil oversees the removal of the Go'Doan. Those priests having been arrested can be interrogated by Lorenz, Guard, Kyril and I. You do not have to be present when they're executed. Thus, you are free to ride."

"And the recovery of this asset that the priest G'Fenn took direct from one of our own homes?" Chu asked, an edge to his deep voice that belied the utter unconcern on his face.

"He is not an *asset*, he is *my friend*," Lorenz bit out.

Chu turned coolly to his captain. "I refer to him as such in order not to make rise emotion that is already skating the surface, my brother."

"There is no chance of that," Nyx spat. "For this emotion is not buried in the slightest. In *either* of us."

"We will get to you both in a moment," Mars murmured.

Nyx sat back and drummed her fingers on the arm of her chair, shooting daggers from her gaze wherever it landed, indicating she was not angry at any of them, just angry in general.

She had a right, with what had befallen her, and what was now lost that they all hoped would be found.

Indeed, the black was still under her eye, and Mars could not look at it for very long, or the emotion he was burying at the sight of it would rise in him as well and that would help nobody.

Mars sighed and turned back to Chu.

"I know how it started. I also know that since you left Serena behind, you have not been yourself. You have been removed to the point you've been withdrawn. And I know that since you left her, Princess Serena has acted honorably. We have all worked in our ways to put an end to this uprising. But outside the agent Tedrey, she is the one amongst our inner circle who has been the most in danger."

Mars allowed Chu a moment to experience the emotion he did not hide flashing in his eyes.

Then he went on.

"She did not have to do what she did, Chu. She did not do it for peace amongst realms or diplomatic relations. She did it because she could, and it was the right thing to do. I don't know what passed between you when you were together. But I do know what the two of you had changed from what it was when you started. And Serena having it, it changed *who* she was. Therefore, I encourage you," he glanced at Silence before he moved his attention back to Chu, "*strongly* to consider going after her and healing this rift so you can attend her as she loses her mother."

"This is a critical juncture with The Rising," Chu replied.

"They have no coin, fifty-seven key operatives in two different realms have been or will soon be put out of commission, and within weeks, they will be entirely removed from Firenz soil," Mars returned. "You can go."

Chu said nothing.

"Chu, what I am trying to express is that you not only have my permission, you have my blessing," Mars encouraged. "You can *go.*"

"And you *should* go," Silence said quietly. She then twisted more fully to his Trusted. "Her mother is dying, Chu. When that happens, she will need you."

Chu stared at Silence for but a second.

Then he rose and strode from the room.

As the door latched behind him, Silence asked, "Does that mean he's going?"

"That means he's going," Mars answered.

He looked from the door to her and grinned.

She grinned back.

"My brother," Lorenz growled.

Mars gave his attention to Lorenz.

"Faunus has a team—" he began to remind his captain.

"I wish to catch up and ride with them."

"Your emotion is too deeply stirred," Mars said.

"And Faunus's isn't?" Nyx demanded.

"Faunus is searching for his lover, and as such, his determination will be resolute," Mars said to Nyx. "Lorenz would be hunting the man who took his friend from his home, a home this man invaded after the guard assigned to it was assassinated, in it a servant with Lorenz's protection was murdered, also in it the wife who is his life was struck repeatedly and her life threatened. His emotion...is too deeply...*stirred*."

Nyx could not argue that and didn't.

Lorenz, however, changed tactics.

"Faunus is too young to lead such a—"

"Faunus is skilled, clever and determined," Mars interrupted Lorenz to say. "He will bring the villain back here with your friend," Mars promised quietly. "And when he does, that villain will be given to you to do with as you will."

Lorenz visibly clenched his teeth.

"Faunus will find him, my brother," Mars assured and looked to Nyx. "He will find your friend and bring him home."

Nyx looked away, her lips thin with the effort to stop them from trembling.

"Go home, my friends, have a quiet *Miet*," Mars encouraged. "For tomorrow, we have prisoners to interview and executions to plan. Chu was correct, there is much to be done to finish with this Rising. He just does not need to be here to do it."

"And Queen Ophelia?" Lorenz asked.

"She will be a great loss," Mars answered. "But I would wager now, with this shift in Serena, whoever she names as her successor, we will continue to enjoy good relations. Thus, if things are enough in hand, Silence and I will journey up to the Great Wohd, take it to the Seil and make Sky Bay for Elena and Cassius's wedding, which I am certain, considering recent communications, will soon be pending."

"And the Beast?" Lorenz persisted.

"It is my understanding we are stronger together, so to be in the Bay with Elena and Cassius, closer to True and Farah, Aramus and Ha-Lah, should he surface, we will be in a more advantageous position."

Lorenz said nothing.

"I cannot imagine, if one dear to me, say...*you*," Mars began, "was taken by the enemy, your location, their intention, your condition unknown, how I would feel. Except I would feel fury at my powerlessness. So, I urge you to do things you have power over, Lorenz, until we can find Tedrey, bring him home and beset those who took him with your vengeance."

"I should have had more than one guard on my home," Lorenz gritted.

"This is not your fault," Mars replied.

"He did not only take Teddy, he almost killed my wife."

"I am right here, *amore*," Nyx murmured.

"Do something you have power over," Mars urged.

"We will call Persephone," Nyx said.

"I don't want to *fuck*," he bit at his wife. "I want to *hurt something*."

"Then we will go to the District, find someone who likes to be hurt, and *then* we will fuck," Nyx returned.

Lorenz scowled at his love.

Nyx rose. "The District at *Miet* is the best place to be." She looked to Mars. "My apologies, my king. Elpis always hosted a very good orgy. But the District..."

She did not finish that, and she did not have to.

For obvious reasons, from the time he'd come of age to participate in them, he'd always avoided his mother's orgies and celebrated *Miet* in the District.

"I'm going to Heden, do you go with me?" Nyx asked her husband.

Lorenz made a noise.

And then he approached his wife, took hold, and with but a dip of his chin to his king and queen, he hauled her out of the room.

When the door latched behind them, Mars took hold on his own wife, dragging her arse across the desk so she sat in front of him.

Before he could do more, however, she caught his wrists, and he looked up at her.

"I find all this talk of the District intriguing," she murmured.

Mars felt his face softening before he shared, "On a normal day, I fear it would be too much for you, *piccolina*. So on *Miet*, it would be overwhelming."

"If it is, would my king not take me away?" she asked.

"There is much smoke, *ashesh*, *taibac*, *koekah*, spirits, women and men, women and women, men and men."

"Mars."

"Tethers, instruments."

Her brows rose. "Instruments?"

Yes, this would be too overwhelming for her.

"You have great passion, *mio ardente*, but I fear you are not prepared for the District at *Miet*. Perhaps next year," he decided.

"It is your holiday."

"And I will share it with you, piercing your navel, claiming your body as mine."

"It already is yours, Mars," she pointed out. "The Rising and the threat of the Beast and journeys and losses and wedding and quarrels and fathers who are not fathers and friends abducted from homes. Soon, we will prepare to leave for Sky Bay. And after that, we cannot know. But there is always something. There will always be something. In all this, I am your queen. I am the Queen of Firenze. We are here now. This is my land, my home. When it is all done, this will *still* be my land, my home. Should I not know it? Experience it? Share in it with you?"

He examined her face then noted, "You very much wish to go."

That pink he adored hit her cheeks again, and she nodded.

She had much passion, his queen. Such spirit.

His brazen wanton.

He nearly smiled.

He did not.

"You will say if it is too much?" he demanded.

"I will always be honest with you, my darling king," she replied.

"Come here," he ordered.

She bent to him and offered him what he wished.

Thus, Mars took her mouth.

Then he took her hand as he straightened from his chair and pulled her off the desk before him.

"Do you wish to bathe, arrange your hair?" he queried.

"Do people turn themselves out extravagantly for *Miet*?

"Most wear nothing at all."

She grinned. "Then I think I am fine. We can bathe later, together, after we return, before you pierce me."

"This will be our deal," he murmured.

She smiled up at him.

He smiled down at her.

Then he guided her from the room and called for their mounts.

The People of Firenze
Heden District, Fire City
FIRENZE

IT WAS COMING to be no surprise to the citizens of Fire City when they saw their queen as she was with their king during their celebrations.

They were much attuned to each other, King Mars and his Silence.

And although she looked on curiously, a natural reserve in her demeanor, she by no means looked on with disgust or distaste or any such reactions what they thought a Dellish would have.

Indeed, she seemed quite taken with the proceedings.

And as ever, her husband seemed quite taken with her.

She wore a lovely gown that caressed her body, hiding most from view, but nevertheless enhancing it.

It was much like the gowns many of the other women had made especially for the celebrations and were wearing, or partly wearing or were littering the floors and halls and rooms and stairwells and pavements.

There was one thing many noted was not reserved about their new Queen Silence.

The smiles she shared with their king.

She was openly just as smitten with him as he was with her.

And indeed, she partook of wine and puffs of smoke and witnessing (though not participating in, but that was no matter, there were many who did not do as such) the activities of the celebrations, doing this entirely unashamedly.

Many who observed their king and queen in the District were not in any shape to think much on it at the time.

But as the next day dawned—and as tales were told, the days after and the weeks, those who did witness her there, or her riding to attend her friend, or her about the marketplaces with her guard, would come to the same conclusion.

Silence of Wodell, nay, Silence, Queen of Firenze would do for their King Mars.

Yes, she would do.

Very well, indeed.

~

King Mars
At the Entrance to Catrame Palace, Fire City
FIRENZE

"QUICKLY," she urged as Mars pulled her from her steed.

It was not he who needed to be told that.

It was she, with her shorter legs who would have to rush to keep up.

Her skirts sailed out behind her, exposing her beautiful legs, as he practically dragged her up the palace steps.

It would be in the entryway that he tugged on her hand so hard, she cried out and flew through the air, only for him to catch her in his arms, turn right, and stride swiftly down the hall toward his study.

He locked the door behind them.

He did not kiss her.

He did not embrace her.

He positioned her bent over his desk, shoved her skirts up about her waist, and allowed himself a moment to enjoy the pale flesh of her arse as he released his cock.

He then buried himself in his wife's drenched cunt.

She moaned and arched into her forearms before him, straining into his thrusts.

One could say, the activities in full bore in Heden was not overwhelming to his Silence.

Though, unable to participate in them with her at that location, it was obviously overwhelming to him.

Having to wait, however, was perfection.

He watched her take him, felt her take him, listened to her take him, and knew it would go fast for her.

He was correct.

"*Mars,*" she breathed and then bucked against him.

He pulled out, turned her to her back, she lifted her eyes dazedly, raising her legs and pressing them to his sides as he drove back in bent over her, now watching her face in climax.

That was, until he planted himself deep and experienced his own.

He had his forehead resting against his desk, his breath stirring her hair, and his cock still buried in his wife when the orgasm released him, only then hearing the familiar whisper of the muted explosions of fire all about them disappearing.

He also had her arms tight about him.

She turned her head his way.

"Can we watch again?"

He lifted his head. "Yes."

"It is proved. I *am* brazen," she mumbled.

He smiled.

Largely.

"Yes," he repeated.

She took in his smile and giggled.

When she was done, she decreed, "I think I like *Miet*."

He pulsed into her, enjoyed watching her lips part at the feel of him and remarked, "I noticed."

She wrapped her legs around his hips but shifted one hand to his throat.

"This is our lesson," she whispered.

"What?" he whispered in return.

"That it will always be too much. There will always be something to do. A decision to be made. A responsibility to fulfill. An obligation to be borne. So, when we have the time, be it moments or more, we must enjoy our lives together. Yes?"

"Yes, *amore*," he agreed.

His Silence's beautiful face gentled before it grew impish.

"I liked watching the men," she shared.

He had not missed this.

"I liked watching the women," he retorted.

Her expression turned pensive when she said, "I do not understand this."

He grinned at her. "And I do not understand your preference."

"We will enjoy variety when we watch," she decided.

When he agreed with that, he did it with a kiss.

~

Much later, Mars had closed the windows to shut away any noises that might come from the city.

Though he had ordered his servants to clear out the garden some time ago.

Thus, for Mars and his queen, there was dark and quiet in their chamber.

Or for his Silence, there was naught but dreams, as she was asleep.

And for Mars, the same thing, even if his were in the awake.

For he lay with his wife tucked into the curve of him, his hand open, the cool of the hoop with it's perfect, brilliant Firenz ruby affixed to her navel resting against his palm.

And he settled into the knowledge that this day, her piercing, that very moment would be one he would call up again and again in the time to come.

For Silence had told him that the tremor of the earth they had experienced some time past had not been of the Beast, not something to fear, but a moment of goodness and joy, even if she could not say what that goodness was. She did feel, quite strongly, that she was learning to read these omens correctly, as the couples fell deeper into the prophecy.

And that day had been full of goodness and joy.

But Mars had a feeling in all they had experienced...

The worst was yet to come.

112

THE EXODUS

King Aramus
Throne Room, Keel Castle, Nautilus
Mar-el

It was safe to say Aramus was sitting on his ostentatious throne in his castle watching a slew of pirates sulk out of the room in an actual *snit*.

He was the Sea King.

He was also the pirate king.

Pirates did not have *snits*.

However, the ones leaving did.

"They will go to the Mystics."

He looked down at the lone man who stood before him.

He was a pirate named Magnus. An exceptional sailor, a fearsome buccaneer, and although he had not spent a great deal of time with him, Aramus could call him a friend.

"They will not be told what to do, or what not to do," Magnus carried on, sharing information Aramus knew at the start, but had been reminded repeatedly of very recently.

"Considering weeks of discussion just broke down irretrievably, I have realized that," Aramus replied on a sigh.

"I know it is not lost on you, my king, that your decisions are rocking the very foundation of who we are," Magnus declared. "No whaling? No pirating?"

"We have vast fleets of ships we've seized over decades, Magnus. And I have arranged to sell some of these...*with* crews...to Airen, Wodell, Firenze. I have further offered our pirates opportunities only a fool would turn his back on. Our wares will more freely be sold there, their wares sold here. There is work to be had. There is money to be made. For the men who just left this room, there are opportunities to make enormous amounts of it. There is even employment on offer my citizens know how to do. It is not as vast a change as people wish to think. It is only change. I understand people do not like change. And yet, it is the only constant throughout the millennia. You simply have to come to understand that and navigate it."

"Yes, but in an attempt to avoid it, they will go to the Mystics," Magnus repeated.

"As you heard me remind them repeatedly, Magnus, telling them something they very much know, Mar-el pirates are not welcome in the Mystics. They also do not have the might of the Mar-el kingdom behind them there. Thus, they will not find the freedom to do as they will. The journey will be long, and in the end, fruitless at best, disastrous at worst. They would be better to shift their pursuits at home. But that is not my choice. My choices have been made and My Will be done. Now, they make theirs."

Magnus nodded before twisting at the waist and looking over his shoulder at the long doors.

He studied them for some time while Aramus waited.

He then turned back and took the offer that Aramus had given them all.

"I'll have a captaincy of a fleet of our merchant ships."

Aramus smiled. "Considering you are the only one, I can be rather generous with the number in your fleet. However, whatever number you choose, you'll need to manage it."

"Twenty-five ships," Magnus said.

"It will be done," Aramus replied. He dipped his voice when he went on, "A fool fights the future, the wise man embraces it. I always knew you were wise, Magnus. But I am glad for further proof of it."

Magnus looked him direct in the eye. "I do not know if it matters whether there is a fight or an embrace. The quakes have stopped, my king, and with them the tidals. But my sense is that the future is more unclear now than it usually is, and it is usually entirely unknown. I take this decision in order to make great amounts of money. I also make it to be close to defend my realm if needed."

One of the reasons why Aramus could call Magnus a friend was that he admired the man's crafty mind.

But mostly, his loyalty to Mar-el.

And this was another indication of all of that, not only Magnus choosing the right path, but understanding the depths of murkiness it held that had nothing to do with managing a fleet of merchant ships as they traded wares on three continents.

"We will persevere, Magnus, we always do," Aramus said with more conviction than he felt.

"I hope so, Aramus, I really do."

On that, Aramus rose and moved behind his throne to walk down the steps and meet his friend face to face.

They shook, their fingers grasping the other's forearm, before Magnus dipped his chin, released his arm, turned and strode from the room.

As he did, Aramus saw Bond entering it.

His other men gathered around him.

However, as they started discussing the breakdown in relations and what it would mean, Aramus kept his gaze to Bond as he made his journey across the long chamber.

Or more accurately, his gaze was on trying to decipher the expression on his lieutenant's face.

Thus, the men also fell silent as Bond approached.

"Another uprising?" Tint asked when Bondi met them.

"No," Bond answered. "A ship has arrived with a messenger from Wodell. They've discovered the location of the treasury of that Rising. This discovery came with carefully kept accounts. It is in code, but they are at work breaking that code and feel, once they do, all operatives, not just the higher-ups, will be identified. Once this is so, they will arrest them in their lands, and if these men are in residence in the Dome City, demand they are extradited to Wodell to sit tribunal for conspiracy to wage war."

Finally, some good news.

"This is a great victory," Aramus noted.

"It is indeed," Bond agreed. "However, King True also shared that Princess Serena, who was instrumental in discovering the location of their purloined coin, is away to Airen in hopes of seeing her mother before the queen passes."

Aramus felt his lips thin.

He had received the ravens that shared Ophelia had taken a turn, and that Cassius and Elena were riding to her.

He could not help but think, after his meeting with the seer, with issues finding resolution—right or wrong, onerous or easy—this simply paved the way to the need to confront new ones.

Ophelia was thoughtful, decisive, honorable and stalwart, and her loss would be a grave one at any time.

In times like these, Aramus was concerned it would be a cataclysmic one.

"True has shared he's growing concerned," Bondi continued. "Ophelia, Serena *and* Elena all on enemy soil as Ophelia slips into the veil. This with Cassius distracted by Elena's impending loss. He does not foresee good things. He is considering leaving the Rising situation in the hands of Alfie and riding to Cassius's aid."

"Alfie?" Aramus inquired with open surprise.

"He has made Alfie his royal counsel."

Aramus almost smiled.

His friend True was a good man.

He was also a smart one.

"And Mars?" Aramus queried.

"We've had no word from Mars. Though, as far as we know, his men continue to be at the Airenzian border in case they are needed."

"Our ships still sit in Sky Bay?" Aramus asked.

"Yes. But there are only three," Bondi answered.

Aramus nodded decisively. "Send seven to Sky Bay, ten to Abhainn Mouth and ten to Dunlyn. We shall start there." He looked about his men. "Tint, you command the ships in the Bay. Ore, the ships at the Mouth. And Nav, the ones sent to Dunlyn. If aggression starts in Airen, send word to me, and until I can engage, take orders from Cassius."

"You wish for us to go now?" Ore asked.

Aramus nodded.

Those men headed out.

The others gathered closer.

"I am assuming the wedding is postponed indefinitely," Nis remarked.

"Ophelia would not make it known she is not long for this world if she was not actually long for this world," Aramus replied, his tone grave. "And Cass and Elena know they are the final couple to ally to fulfill the prophecy, thus they will not delay. With the change afoot in Mar-el, we need to bolster here as best we can, men. Thus, Ha-Lah and I will not leave until we must. But my gut tells me we cannot be too far from the others. Not for much longer."

The men nodded.

Aramus looked to the door, unable to shake the thought that, his best seamen headed to the Mystics and uprisings, no matter how puny and easily quelled, would be the kind of problems he very soon would long to have.

ARAMUS HEARD his queen's pleasured mew as he tasted her climax in his mouth, this before Aramus slid out from under her, positioned behind her and took a moment to enjoy her beauty as she gripped the tall, wide half-helm that formed the headboard of their bed.

He then rested a hand on her hip, took hold of his cock with his other, found her, and glided inside.

Her curls hit his shoulder as her head fell back.

His hips moved, thrusting in and out, in order to return her to where she was now floating away.

"Love you, my king," she whispered.

"And I you, my queen," he replied.

"I could have you inside me an eternity," she said.

"I could be inside you an eternity," he returned with feeling.

"We are one," she breathed.

He very much liked that.

"One," he growled, filling her with his cock and moving his head in order that his lips could find hers.

But he did not kiss her.

For she murmured, "But I am prettier."

Thus, when he finally kissed her, and began again to move inside her, he did it laughing.

As she had already found release once, he had to engage his fingers at her nipple and nub to take her there again.

It was an agony holding back until he was able to give it to her.

But it was worth it as her head pressed into his shoulder, her luscious body made an arc, thrusting her sex into his, her breast into his hand, and her beautiful face went vague with her moistened lips parted, her eyes drifting shut.

Watching her, only then did he allow himself to follow her.

When their breathing again became normal, Ha-Lah's forehead was tucked into the side of his neck.

He could smell her, feel her, see her beauty from face to knees, in their bed, in their home, in their land.

And in that moment, he knew he would die for her.

He would die for her to have life.

He would die for her to be safe.

He would leave this earth so she could carry on in it.

But if she was not in it, he did not know if he would have the will to carry on.

Thus, in that moment, he understood the dread that had, more and more each day, begun to plague him.

"I will go clean up," she said softly.

"You will not move a muscle," he replied gruffly.

Her head came off his shoulder, but he evaded her eyes by kissing her shoulder as he gently slid from the heat between her legs.

"Aramus?" she called.

"I will return," he said and finally looked into her eyes. "Do not move, Ha-Lah."

"All right, my darling," she whispered.

Aramus left their bed and walked across the thick ocean-colored rugs over mosaic tiles in the colors of turquoise and sea glass to his valet chamber.

There, he wet a cloth and returned.

As he did, he drank in the vision of his wife in their bed, her fingers wound around the symbol of their realm, her skin perfection, her hair an emblem of her spirit, her eyes on him warm, thoughtful and concerned, a shining reminder of her intelligence and the depth of her ability to feel.

He entered the bed and held her about her waist with one arm as he gently cleaned his seed from between her legs, his gaze cast down her body as his hand went about its ministrations.

"Why do I sense this is not sexual?" she asked quietly.

"I am simply taking care of my queen," he muttered.

"It is more."

He said nothing.

"Aramus, look at me."

His eyes went to hers.

"Did something happen that you did not tell me in your discussions with the pirates?"

He did not want his hand between her legs with anything on his mind but his Ha-Lah.

Thus, he kissed her shoulder again, moved from her, the bed, to his valet chamber, where he tossed the cloth.

She was no longer holding her position for him but seated cross-legged in their bed with eyes on him when he returned to their bedchamber.

"You didn't answer me," she noted.

He entered the bed, and she cried out in surprise as he positioned them, Aramus with his back to the helm, Ha-Lah astride him on her knees.

He pulled up the bedclothes so their legs and hips were covered and then he looked into her eyes.

"Outside of Magnus, it was an exodus. They leave for the Mystics, or to attempt to wreak havoc in the Northlands and Southlands. Now knowing Tor, Lahn and Apollo as well as Frey, I do not think, if they choose east, it will go well for them. I know from experience, if they choose west, it will go worse."

"I do too," his wife replied softly.

And she did. Her grandfather, a pirate who tried his hand in the Mystics, met his end there.

"My best captains are gone, Ha-Lah. Which weakens our armada."

"Oh no," she murmured.

"All is not lost," he assured. "My navy is always strong. But with them here, if the time came it was needed, and the time might be coming it is needed, it would have been unbeatable."

"Whatever comes our way, we will prevail."

He did not hold that hope.

"You worry," she remarked.

"Yes," he admitted.

"Aramus—"

"You said that tremor, the one felt recently, was one we had no need to fear," he noted.

She nodded. "I do not know what it was, but it was not like the others. Not in the slightest."

"I have a gnawing dread."

These words came out in a burst.

His wife blinked at him.

And he felt a fool.

"Do not consider what I say. I simply—" he began.

"Shh," she hushed, her fingers to his lips. "My love, you can tell me anything." She slid her hand along the beard at his jaw. "Anything, darling."

"It is that...I understand happiness."

Her body gave a slight twitch that made her curls bounce, but she said nothing.

"It is the headache of hearing of a revolt against the King's Will, and sending men to quell it, and going to the dinner table where you sit, and what happened in the day means nothing, for I dine with you. It is listening to pirates grouse, understanding I ask for great change, but feeling frustrated they, in turn, do not understand the valid reasons I am asking it, and coming to my bed with you here, and their complaints lose all significance. In other words, it is knowing each day will dawn, and it might be good, it might be bad, but it will end happy, for I have you."

"My king," she breathed, her forehead falling to his, her fingers curling tight around the sides of his neck.

He slid his hands from her hips to wrap his arms around her waist, and he held on.

"Now that I have this happiness, I understand it, I do not wish to lose it," he whispered.

"Of course, you don't," she whispered in return. "I do not either. But we will prevail."

"I fear the other possibility, that we will not."

She lifted her head slightly and erroneously surmised, "And you've never feared anything and now do not understand how to cope with this feeling."

"I have known fear, Ha-Lah. I have fled *angmostros*. I have battled ibex-whales. But it pales to nothing at the thought of losing you."

Her face, already tender, became more so as she repeated, "We will prevail."

"What if we do not?"

"We will."

"How do you know?"

"I don't," she shared. "I just refuse to consider it will happen the other way."

"I see the wisdom of this," he muttered.

"I cannot guide you into that place," she replied gently. "Even if I very much wish I could. But I can encourage you to seek it as best you can. And as always, be here to listen to you when you are in need."

He nodded to let his queen know her words were heard, and they had meaning to him.

But he did not feel better.

"I should seek my people," she declared.

The arms Aramus had about her tightened.

"Ha-Lah," he said.

"If they are needed, I can ask them to come to our aid, but they should know, and prepare for that time."

"And you think they would help those who did hideous things to them? Things that sent them into self-imposed exile?"

"I do not know, but I will not know unless I ask."

"Is this dangerous for you?" he queried.

"No."

He studied her closely. "You are sure."

She relaxed against him. "I am."

"We will endeavor to do this, and soon, if you wish to attend Elena and Cassius's wedding."

"I do," she confirmed.

"We will talk later and plan," he murmured, beginning to move them to put them in bed, though he was doing this wondering if he wished to sleep, or if he wished to recommence other activities with his wife.

Ha-Lah clamping her thighs on his hips and calling, "Aramus," made him stop. She then announced, "I have something to tell you."

Oh shite.

"Something to tell me or something to admit to me?" he asked.

The knowledge his wife was Mer was not given to him by his wife.

Thus, he would be gladdened she had something to share and she was the one who shared it.

Nevertheless, if it was something she should have shared some time ago, this would not gladden him at all.

"Not to admit, or even share," she answered confusingly. "I do not know, and I am troubled for I do not think it is mine to give. I still feel deeply you should know it."

This was not a stellar preamble.

"What is it?"

"You must promise not to say anything, not to anybody. Not anybody at all."

And this was not much better.

"What is it, Ha-Lah?"

"I cannot tell you unless you promise that."

"You will tell me," he returned.

"I really cannot. Not unless you promise."

"Ha-Lah," he said in warning.

"Really, Aramus." She gave his neck a squeeze. "You will know when I share, so now, please, just promise."

He scowled at her.

Then he growled at her.

"I promise."

She smiled at him.

Then she spoke.

"Silence is a mermaid."

He did a slow blink.

"I'm sorry?"

"Silence, she is Mer."

"Mars's Silence," he stated, but it was a question.

Ha-Lah nodded.

"The Queen of Firenze."

She smiled again. "The Queen of Firenze."

"She is of the Arbor," he pointed out. "And the Arbor is landlocked."

His wife shrugged. "I do not know how she is Mer. I just know she's Mer." She then tipped her head. "But I sense she either does not know, or like me, she fears sharing."

"Not only to you, but to Mars."

She bit her full lower lip, knowing how a husband would take this news when it was not freely given to him.

"Shite," he muttered, on his side of the matter, knowing precisely how he felt about his wife not sharing.

He sensed with the affection growing between Mars and Silence that Mars would not care his queen was Mer. Aramus did not know this, but he sensed it.

However, he knew exactly how it felt that his wife kept something crucial from him.

And he had good reason to believe Mars would feel the same way.

"This is not a bad thing," Ha-Lah declared. "This is possibly a good thing. It is just that I need to speak to her about it as soon as I can when I am with her again."

At this, Aramus thought he understood.

"Which would expose you as a mermaid to her if you did."

"No, for if she knows she is Mer, she will know I am. Though if she does not..."

It was only then Aramus relaxed.

Silence, he could trust, and not only because he could trust Mars, for if Silence knew something, she would share it with her husband, and if anyone needed to know his wife's secrets, it was the couples of the prophecy.

But she was Silence and her name did not entirely define her, but it was not far off.

And of all the women, he had noted that Silence had a deep affinity for and with his wife.

Not to mention, she wrote to Ha-Lah with great consistency and it was clear their friendship meant much to both women.

"Then we will endeavor to find you some time to discuss this with Silence and what it might mean to this Sisterhood of the Beast when we are with her again."

His wife pressed into his body at the same time she pressed her lips to his.

As she did so, Aramus slid them fully into their bed, pulling the bedclothes over them and rolling her to her back, with him atop her, making the decision on his earlier conundrum, when her soft body was under his, thus taking the kiss deeper.

His queen pressed closer.

When he broke the kiss to slide his lips down her neck, she said in his ear, "You are right, my king. This is happiness."

He knew he was right.

He still took her mouth yet again to show his gratitude that she agreed.

II3
THE CONNECTION

Tedrey
Journey to the Ancient Ritual Ground
WODELL

They rode under the cover of night.

They slept in hiding during the day.

They gave him food and water, and fortunately were so determined to get where they were going, they paid him little mind except to secure him when the time had come to rest.

However, Tedrey had a feeling things were going to change when, before the fall of twilight, he heard the hoot of a bird which caused a milling within the cave where they had holed up for the day.

At the sound, one of Fenn's brethren, wearing the clothing of a Dellish, not the robes of a Go'Doan priest, went to the cave's mouth.

There was then a muted commotion and torches were lit as several men who had not been traveling with them moved into the cave.

Fenn walked directly to the man at the front.

Fenn studied that man closely.

He was much older, but he still had soft, golden hair and a good deal of it that grew all the way down to brush the shoulders of his fine coat.

He also had an air of authority, and it was clear all those with him, and the others in the cave, regarded him deferentially.

"Thom," Fenn greeted, bowing his head respectfully as he made it to the man.

Thom?

G'Thom?

Golden Thomas?

Tedrey, his wrists bound to his feet, focused closer on the new arrivals.

"We were to meet you, not the other way around," Fenn continued.

"It is no longer safe for us in the Dome City," Thom replied.

It was no longer safe—for *priests*—in the Dome City?

Fenn looked as shocked as Tedrey felt.

"How could that be?" Fenn asked.

"They located our funds before we could discover where Carrington had them hidden. And Carrington proved himself more of a buffoon than his detection and capture showed him to be. He kept the records *with* the funds, rather than elsewhere."

"They have our records?" Fenn asked in disbelief.

"They have everything," Thom confirmed. "However, in my case, that mattered not. Some of Carrington's communications were uncovered. He referred to me within them."

Thom lifted a hand and rested it on Fenn's shoulder before he shared further.

"There is great dissension in our home, my brother. A door was opened, and a tidal wave poured through it. Priests turning against priests. The more reprisals against our own in Wodell and Firenze, and now even Airen, the expulsion of our priests from Firenze, the more anger our brotherhood is treated to by those who refused to follow our ways. Anger will obviate fear, and now we no longer hold the upper hand with those who knew of us but knew not to speak of us. Thus, when the Go'En called for me to attend them with urgency, I had to escape my sacred city in the strictest of secret. I could not even give word to our brothers that they needed to take measures to protect themselves."

Fenn's shock faded as anger replaced it.

"So we are ruined," he stated flatly.

"Perhaps not, though we have had need to abandon our current strategy."

Thank the gods.

Though he had said "current," thus abandoning it meant creating another and that might give them time to end this altogether.

"Jell?" Fenn inquired.

Jell?

The priest G'Thom, clearly the leader of The Rising, shook his head.

"We have not heard from him for months. I do not know if he fled or if something befell him. But it is worse."

Tedrey noted that Fenn's expression shared he did not think there could be much worse.

However, what Thom said next proved there could.

"All the men who do the blessed work at the Ritual Ground have disappeared," Thom declared.

"*All* of them?" Fenn asked.

"All. They, with Jell, have vanished."

"But, not long ago, we felt a tremor," Fenn said.

"It has been shared with me by sorcerers it was not of the Beast," Thom informed him.

The Beast?

The Beast?

"So, the Beast has gone unstirred for *months*?" Fenn demanded. "*Again?*" he went on as if this was catastrophic.

"Yes. And we've suffered a number of blows, my friend," Thom stated. "Thus, we must restructure our strategy. This, I have discussed with the Society, and we have done."

There it was again.

What Faunus had mentioned.

The Society.

But, what Society?

Who were they and what had all this to do with the Beast?

They could not possibly be referring to the Beast of yore. The creature that assailed the earth, nearly wiping out humankind.

They could not possibly wish to stir *that* Beast.

For what good would come of surfacing such a creature?

"We had hoped to weaken the realms, establish a firm foothold of leaders and followers, and use him when we had him with us, under our control, to finish cowing them should they protest the righteous worship of the true gods. Now, we will have to use him to bring down the royal houses, eliminate the royal lines, and then we shall install our brothers in their castles, tear down their temples, and build up our own."

They did.

They intended to stir *that* Beast but not for good.

To complete The Rising.

From what Tedrey knew, from what all knew from the last earthly tenure of the Beast, it was unconquerable.

Mars was mighty, Cassius was clever, True was steadfast, and Aramus commanded the seas.

But they would stand no chance against the Beast.

Lorenz must know this.

Mars must know this.

They *all* needed to *know this.*

Which meant Tedrey needed to find his way free, find his way back, and share *this.*

"We must make haste to the ritual grounds and resume the sacrifices," Thom stated.

By the gods.

With every word uttered, it simply became worse.

Sacrifices?

He did not wish to hope (but he did) that they were speaking of sheep.

He, however, had a feeling, with their determination, and what Tedrey knew about the Beast, that they were not.

"One each night until we lure him to the surface," Thom finished.

Gods.

"I have your first," Fenn told him, sweeping an arm to where Tedrey lay, silent and watching.

"This is the traitor?" Thom queried, beginning to walk in Tedrey's direction.

Tedrey did not move, not even to shift his regard from Thom.

They had not gagged him, for he had not fought them or given any indication he was going to try to escape.

He hoped, if he remained passive and resigned to his fate, they would not send word to harm Nyx or Lorenz or Faunus or anyone he held in his heart.

So with them, he would remain.

But now, he could not.

Thom stood above him and stared down at Tedrey.

"Most handsome," he murmured. "I understand your fascination with him."

"I am fascinated no more," Fenn spat, glaring at Tedrey.

Thom crouched beside where he lay.

"I think we shall keep you special," he whispered to Tedrey. "When the Beast finally surfaces, he will be most hungry. You will slake his craving."

Tedrey stared into Thom's eyes and said not a word.

He did not wish to slake the Beast's craving, obviously.

But that was not why it was imperative he found his way away from this band and made his swift return home.

He had to warn them.

He had to warn them all.

II4
THE HOPE

Princess Elena
Night Heights Mountain Range
AIREN

In the dilapidated, abandoned cottage my sisters had cleaned, the roof and chimney they had made makeshift repairs to in order for them to serve their purpose, I sat on a rickety stool next to the narrow bed that swung low on its moorings, making it appear like a cozy hammock.

However, with my mother's thin, frail body ensconced in it, cozy seemed almost a profane word to use to describe it.

She had her eyes closed, but I knew she was not asleep.

"I would have you talk with me, in the time I have for you to talk with me, if you have the strength to do so," I requested softly.

Her eyes opened and focused steadily on me.

Her gaze might have been steady, but her voice was as thin as her body, and the sound of it clawed at my ears.

"I lie here thinking of all the things I would wish to say to you, at the same time praying to the goddess that I have already shared all the things you need to know."

I reached for her hand, curling my fingers around, and she did not pull away.

This did not rend my heart. She had not been overtly affectionate throughout my life, but if we were alone, she could find ways to be thus.

And we were now alone.

"Please know, I am equipped with what I need," I assured her stiltedly, just as I had been the days since we'd arrived. Uncertain how to speak, how to say words that needed to be said in order to give her the peace I wished her to have. "You are a good and beloved mother, and you have shared great bounty with me."

"I was as good a mother as I could be, still being queen," she returned.

"Yes, and your mention of it makes me think you have issue with it," I replied. "You are queen. I am your daughter, thus you are also my mother. You could not be less of one and more of the other. Who would that have served?"

Her hand squeezed mine.

"I made a grave mistake with you and your sister," she whispered.

I did not wish to talk of Serena.

I said nothing.

"I did not know, you were so young, but if I had taken more time with the both of you—"

It was with that, I squeezed her hand. "Mum, don't do this. It serves no purpose."

"You don't lie abed in an abandoned cottage in the mountains of bloody Airen, of all places, dying, Elena. You do not know what purpose I need served."

I pressed my lips together, and I did this in order not to smile.

That was my mother.

That was also my mum.

"You find this amusing?" she demanded.

"I hate to bear these sad tidings, but sometimes I found you funny when you were being arrogant."

"This was not lost on me," she replied.

I shrugged, trying very hard not to grin at her.

"May I say what I wanted to say now?" she inquired.

"Of course," I murmured.

"I have spoken with Julia, Agnes and Lucinda, other elders, healers, teachers, captains. It is known my will. And that is, you will be named Queen of the Nadirii at my passing."

With that, my fingers around hers automatically curled so strongly, I had to force my grip to relax.

"Mother," I whispered.

"It is the right choice, even if it was a difficult one. I sense change in your sister, but I have not had time to assess it. Something has thrown her off the course of the life I expected her to lead, and I do not know where this new wind will take her. Though at my end, I am glad of the knowing of it, for it gives me hope. However, I cannot let my sisters lie in those hands. I need to know they will have someone who can balance strength with diplomacy. Who understands the heart is in tune with the head and which way to lean with both guiding you when it is time to make decisions. And that is you."

"But I will be Queen of Airen and Cass does not wish that to be in name only." I bent closer to her. "Mum, it is not that I would not wish this. It is the highest of honors. It is just that the fates have taken me elsewhere."

"Cassius knows of my decision, and he knows that compromises will need to be made in your marriage and in your realms in order for you both to give all you have to all your responsibilities."

I had sat back on her first words, and I remained focused on them when I spoke.

"Cassius knows this?"

Her hand then gripped mine, the grip was meager, but it was felt.

"You will not be angry with him. It was mine to share, not his. It was mine to find the time I wished to share it, not his. And this is my time. However, it was crucial to discuss it with him for I had to know he would be at your side, when needed, at your back, when needed, and lifting you up, when that was needed."

I had no doubt Cassius had assured her he would do all of these things as I had no doubt, when needed, he would indeed do all of these things.

But I would deal with Cassius later.

For the now, I nodded.

"As I was saying," she went on, "I made a grave mistake with you and your sister. And as things will be how they will be, it is important, daughter, for you to understand what it was. For you to know. And so, if the same should come to pass in your future, you will know the right thing to do."

My silence was her prompt to carry on.

This she did.

"I offered you and your sister mentors that corresponded with your strengths, I did not offer you mentors that challenged your natures. You have the spirit of the goddess in you, meditative, patient. Your sister had the spirit of the warrior, combative, assertive. Melisse did not enhance what you had, she simply guided the way to bring it out. The same with Darma in her teachings with Serena. In giving you what you already had, I did not offer you a different point of view."

"We both have done well," I lied.

"*You* have, because you always would. Serena did not, because she needed to be taught how. And once I realized my mistake, it was too late."

I drew in breath as I came to understand what she was saying.

And then she spoke her true message in a quiet voice filled with yearning.

"You need to be patient with her, Elena."

"Mother—"

"That is not your mother who requests that of you, Ellie. It is your mum."

My eyes started stinging.

"She is your sister, my glorious daughter," she whispered.

I turned my head away.

"I would have Dora here," she said, changing the subject.

I turned back, the words on my lips to offer to send a bird, bring the girls to her immediately (or as immediately as was possible), however, she carried on before I could.

"But that is selfish. She would not benefit from seeing me thus. But if I had my wish, she would be at my side, as well as the buoyancy of Cassius's girl. Aelia knows no other way than the one you will soon endure. If Aelia were here, she'd lift you up."

"I will be fine," I assured her.

"You will be lost, and you will be sad and then you will be angry and after that you will be sad again. And maybe later, you will be fine. It will be a different manner of fine to what you are used to, but trust me, my daughter, you will find your way to it."

I did not know if that was true, but I did not argue it.

I bent to her again, lifting her hand to hold it close to my heart.

But she pulled it away in order to lift it farther and touch my cheek.

"You will make a magnificent queen, Elena," she said quietly. "I've had much time to think on it these past days, and I have realized I envy Wilmer. He will be alive to watch his son thrive. I will not have that gift, but I wish you to know, I die understanding it."

"Perhaps I was wrong, and I did not wish for you to talk with me."

Her mouth curled up at the ends.

I took up her hand again in both my own and held her fingers to my lips.

I cast my eyes down, filling my vision with her fingers, still looking so capable, and I memorized the sight of them.

And with those fingers pressed to my mouth, I spoke against them.

"I love you, Mum."

"And I you, my glorious Elena," she replied. "I love you to the sun and every star beyond and I have from the moment I sensed you in my womb."

I closed my eyes.

"You do not know," she said.

I opened my eyes and looked at her, replying fiercely, "I *do* know."

She gave me a soft smile. "I know you know of my love, or at least I hope so. That is not of which I speak."

I moved her hand back to my heart. "Of what do you speak?"

"You embody the hope," she shared. "The hope of our sisters those centuries ago, before it was lost, and they had to do their worst to gain their liberty. The hope of Airenzian women now, when they look at you, or simply know you are amongst them. Indeed, the hope of all women everywhere. That you can be you, the strength of you, the magic of you, the skills of you, the nurture of you, the compassion of you, the thoughtfulness of you, the love of you, even the flaws of you. You can be that, and just be free to be that. All of it. All the magnificence of you."

I stared down at her, feeling the tears trembling in my eyes.

She was not finished, however.

"And you can be that and have him," she said, her voice softer. "And he returns all of it, and this is the way it can be. The way it *should* be. That you are free to be all of you, give all of you, and receive it in return."

I swallowed, for this was what I had, what Cassius had, and what we gave each other.

"Do you love him?" she whispered.

"He is a third of my world, the other two are you and Dora."

"And Aelia," she stated.

"All right, so he's a quarter of my world," I muttered.

"And Melisse."

I narrowed my eyes at her.

"And Jasmine and Hera," she continued.

At that, those eyes rolled.

"And Serena," her hand shook mine, "and don't pretend you do not have love in your heart for your sister. I know you do."

"This makes what I feel for Cassius sound less dramatic than it actually is," I complained.

"This is the problem of the world," my mother declared grandly, her voice stronger than it had been our entire conversation, as it always became when she was offering wisdom. "There is this idea that love has limits. You can love many with all of your heart, Elena. It does not come in pieces. It is not a well you dip into and deplete. It is not a sword you wield to give and then take away to cause injury. It is a muscle that, the more you use it, the stronger it gets."

"I am now torn between annoyance that you are always so very right, and agony, knowing..."

I did not complete my thought.

I did not need to.

"You will have Melisse," she said gently. "You will have my lieutenants. Cassius. You will find strength. You will gain wisdom. You, my Ellie," her eyes began to shine brightly, and at seeing this, I again had to swallow, "will be all right."

"Yes, I will," I assured.

It was a lie in that moment.

But it was a lie that needed to be spoken.

"Do you need water?" I asked. "Some broth?"

"I need to rest," she replied. "Perhaps you can read to me?"

I looked to the floor where her book lay.

I put her hand to her chest, took up the book, opened it at the ribbon and began reading.

I continued to do so when I sensed she was asleep.

I only stopped when there was a quiet knock on the door.

Whoever was behind it did not wait for me to open it.

It opened, albeit slowly, and I saw Cassius's head come around its edge.

I opened my mouth to tell him Mother was asleep, but he looked to me and to her too quickly.

Thus, he fully opened the door and came in as I stood from my seat.

And then I froze when, from behind him, came Serena, then Melisse, and after, a Go'Doan priest. The one I had met some time ago in Firenze who had given me tinctures to offer Mother.

I did not like the priest being there, but I had no time for that.

I went directly to Melisse.

But it was she who pulled me in her arms.

"You look robust," I said into her ear.

"You lie. I need meat on my bones and the ride to this place was more than I was ready for, so I also need a nap."

I leaned away from her, still in her arms, as she was in mine, and I looked down at her.

"But I am here," she finished.

She was there. Pale. Worn.

But alive.

I pulled her into my arms again.

"How did I know you would not stay away?"

My mother's voice made me turn.

And when I did, I saw Serena standing at the foot of the bed, her arms crossed on her chest, her eyes locked to our mother.

But the Go'Doan priest was at Mum's bedside, he had her wrist in his hand, and it was he to whom she was speaking.

He then placed her hand on her stomach and moved his to her forehead.

I opened my mouth to ask who the bloody hell he thought he was when he asked his own question to my mum, though it came out more as an accusation.

"You're in pain?"

"A little."

"I gave you draughts for this," he stated.

He did?

"I thought I would wait—" Mother began.

"The time is now," he stated smartly and then turned to the door and called, "Saira?"

A woman in a Dellish gown and cloak, ones of fine quality that were rather charming, bustled in carrying a leather satchel.

"Allo, Saira," Mother greeted her warmly.

"You did not send a raven for Liam when the time came, Ophelia," she replied. "He's most cross with you."

"He will survive this," Mum sighed.

I felt something, looked in the direction from whence it was coming, and saw my sister's eyes on me.

I also heard my mother's earlier words in my head.

"I will give you time with her," I said.

She jerked up her chin.

I gave Liam and Saira a glance, a smile to Melisse, a frown to Cassius, and I walked out.

The sky was night. The air smelled of dirt and pine and chill. The pointed tops of the trees seemed an imperative to tip your head back and study the stars.

I did not do this.

I stomped several feet away and whirled on the man I knew followed me.

"So, I have news," I shared. "Apparently, I will be queen to the Sisterhood and my man knew this *well* before me."

"Ellie," he murmured.

"She said it was hers to give at the time she wished to give it," I went on.

"It was, and you cannot argue that."

I drattedly could not.

I looked away.

And because I loved him so, not to mention felt the odd sensation that my body might fly apart at any moment, when he took me in his arms, I did not pull away.

"Melisse is here, as is Serena," he murmured. "This is good."

He was very right.

I relaxed into his tall frame and laid my cheek to his chest.

We spoke no words for some time, but Cassius did not move or give the slightest inclination he would wish to do this as we stood on a mountain in his realm, surrounded by soldiers who were keeping us safe from possible attack.

And because he gave me this, I loved him all the more.

Mother was right, as ever.

The heart, if you used it, just grew in its capacity to give.

"She says I'll be fine," I told him quietly.

"She is not right, but you will go on," he replied.

"Cass?" I called, tipping my head back.

"Yes, Ellie," he answered, dipping his chin down.

"To the sun and every star beyond," I whispered.

He dipped even farther, and in a return whisper against my lips, he said, "To the sun and every star beyond, my darling."

~

Prince Cassius
Night Heights Mountain Range
Airen

Three days hence, Cassius entered the cottage at the queen's behest.

He moved to stand by her bed.

She stared up at him.

"You do?" she asked, her voice a memory of what it once was.

"I do," he answered, his voice strong as granite.

"You will?" she asked.

"With my all, with my life," he answered.

"Take my hand," she ordered.

He bent to take her hand.

She closed her eyes.

He waited.

Then he felt a curious sensation, like a feather was brushing his palm.

She opened her eyes, he let her go and straightened.

"When they come, as you first hold them to you, their heads cradled in your palm, whisper in their ears, 'Your grandmother loves you,' and they will know."

He felt his jaw flex as he clenched his teeth.

"Promise me, son," she urged.

"It will be done," he gritted.

"You were loved," she shared.

His voice was thick when he replied, "I know."

Her head made a slight movement against its pillow, like a nod.

"I must rest."

He bowed to her and moved to the door.

Before he opened it, he turned back.

"You were loved," he told her.

"I know," she replied.

～

The Squad of the Sisterhood of the Nadirii and the Airenzian Battalion
Night Heights Mountain Range
AIREN

FOUR DAYS HENCE, the Sisterhood of the Nadirii formed circles around a platform made of piled stones, pinecones and dirt.

These circles of sisters started small and tight to the altar atop which lay the body shrouded in coral and purple. Close to the backs of the circle at the altar formed the next. And close behind them, the next. And so on.

The Airenzian soldiers stood at the back, not in circles, amongst them The Drakkar and his princess.

All except for the crowned prince of Airen, and his lieutenants Macrinus, Antonius and Nero.

These men stood in the circle at the front along with G'Liam of the Go'Doan and his chosen one, Saira.

The queen's lieutenants moved silently around the edges of the altar, placing candles on the ground and in the stones and lighting them.

The hums began when Melisse, Lucinda, Agnes and Julia joined the circle closest to the altar and everyone amongst all the rings held hands.

The hum sifted through the sisters, rising higher, as bodies swayed side to side.

The Nadirii kept their gazes focused on the remains of their queen, their thoughts on her, or in prayer, as their mournful hum drifted through the pines.

The soldiers at the back began to shuffle and mill when the breeze came, the needles of the pines rustling, as if attempting to join in with the hum.

The united sound of the Sisterhood grew louder as the swaying broke its cadence. Some sisters rounding their torsos, some swinging front to back, some moving faster, some slower, as all tilted their heads back and stared into the heavens.

Clasped hands were raised, two by two, front, back, middle, all around, until all those joined had lifted fists to the skies along with their voices.

And then, after this had gone on for much time, suddenly, startling the soldiers, as one, all of the Nadirii drew their arms down and bent their knees, and a gust so great it could be seen whooshed over the body, extinguishing the candles.

The Airenzian soldiers crept away as this wind soared through the Nadirii, wafting their hair, billowing their cloaks.

But it halted at the end of its sisters and drew back with great speed toward the altar.

And as it retreated to its origin, it dragged the Sisterhood with it so they were crowded against each other, their arms lifted to the sky.

A great Nadirii yell soared from hundreds of throats, rending the air as the pines around them swayed violently and the moon and stars grew blurry.

Then suddenly, it was gone, as was the body atop the altar.

And Queen Ophelia of the Nadirii had become one with the veil.

King Aramus
Bedchamber of the King, Keel Castle, Nautilus
Mar-el

Aramus jerked awake when his wife did the same.

He turned direct to her, and for a moment, his heart stopped as Ha-Lah stared, motionless and unseeing into the moonlit room.

She then turned into his body, burrowing in, sobbing.

"Ha-Lah," he whispered into her hair.

"Ophelia," she hiccupped into his chest.

He held her tighter and closed his eyes.

The loss was great.

But as ever, it was indication time marched on.

Just as it was an indication he could not ignore that it was also time to prepare.

He set thoughts of that aside for the now and focused on soothing his queen.

Hold her tight in your embrace, he prayed to Medusa.

King Mars
On the Journey to the Great Wohd
Wodell

He heard the flap to their tent slap open, and Mars was up from his seat on the log about the fire where he was with his men, discussing the message they'd just received from a bird.

He turned to his wife, who was dashing across to them through the chill of the night in naught but her nightgown.

Silence was wee, but the force of her impact when she made it to him took him back on a foot.

She then clutched his shirt into her fists, buried her face in his chest, and dissolved into tears.

He wrapped his arms around her.

"What on earth, *piccolina*?" he asked, torn between concern at her state, and fury at whatever might have caused it.

"Ophelia," she answered.

Shite.

He drew in breath, and with it, her body deeper into his.

Accept her with mercy, he prayed to The Spirit.

King True
One Hundred Miles over the Border
Airen

It was not True who woke that night with a start in their tent, it was Farah.

And she sat bolt upright when she did so.

He came up with her, blinking away sleep, and trying to focus on his queen in the shadows.

"Darling," he murmured.

"They are all gone, save one," she whispered, before her frame began to shake with her tears.

He pulled her into his arms, asking gently, "What do you speak of, Farah?"

"Ophelia," she told him.

Gods.

He shut his eyes tight and held her closer.

May she walk in the sun forever, he prayed to Alabasta.

Marian and Jellan
Underground Lair of the Beast
WODELL

MARIAN FELT ONLY a tremor in the veil, though a strong one, for she knew of the veil, just not how to read it.

And she grew wary, for this seemed to be happening far too often of late.

But she had other things on her mind.

Precisely, stopping what was happening just above them, at the surface.

JELLAN KNEW of the veil *and* how to read it.

Thus, he felt the tremor, and his eyes went direct to the Beast.

The creature had felt it too.

"It is time," he mouthed soundlessly.

The Beast nodded.

Princess Elena
Night Heights Mountain Range
A*iren*

I FOUND her sitting atop a slab of stone at the side of a cliff, the dark shadows of mountains and valleys before her with a backdrop of taller rises in the distance, their black shapes cutting into the night sky.

The two gnomes who had traveled with her, males who had introduced themselves to me some days earlier as Galbdor and Welbrix, were loitering about the top of the slab, strangely as if they were guarding my sister.

They let me pass, however, with courteous tips of their bearded chins.

I dropped down beside her to sit as she was on the slab. Arse to stone, knees up, but Serena had her wrists resting on her knees.

I pulled my thighs closer to my chest and hugged my shins.

I studied the landscape.

She spoke.

"Trust it to be you who was the one who sought me."

"I can just as easily leave," I replied.

She turned her head to look at me. "No, you can't. It would wound you to leave me to my grief, no matter the anger you hold toward me, no matter the spites I have inflicted on you. That is you. That is my sister Elena."

My sister Elena.

If I was not wrong, that was an olive branch, as best Serena could extend it.

"Serena, we must—" I began.

She turned back to the view and stated, "I know she has named you queen. She told me."

"And I know it is soon after she's joined the veil, but perhaps, before feelings can dig in, we should talk about it."

She again gave me her attention. "Why?"

I blinked at her. "Why?"

"It is her wish. And there is one thing I am certain you know about me. I can follow orders."

"Are you disappointed?" I asked.

She shook her head. "No. I plan to sail to the Southlands. I liked the look of that warrior from there, and if there are more of them as such, they would be an appealing challenge to me, as both a warrior and a woman."

"I, well…yes," I stammered. "It is my understanding that they are all like that there."

"Hmm," she hummed, again looking away.

"There is much change in you," I whispered.

"Yes," she agreed.

I braved leaning an inch her way and saying under my breath, "Who are the gnomes?"

"They are my friends," she told the view.

Friends?

"What about Darma, and Heloise and Genia?" I asked.

"They have sent me ravens. They have returned from Firenze to The Enchantments. I have ordered them to stay there. It still needs guarding and patrolling, especially on the Airenzian border."

"Of course," I muttered.

She looked at me. "If you wish, while this is happening, with your marriage, and the Beast, I will act in your stead in The Enchantments," she offered.

I had intended to ask Lucinda to do that.

"Right," she mumbled, reading my face.

"Serena—"

"Then I would wish to be at your side."

My chin jerked in my neck at the shock of this.

She thought she read that too.

"As you do not wish that either, I will need your orders, my queen."

"I will always be your sister," I corrected her.

"Then I will need your orders, my sister."

"I meant *sister* sister."

"So did I."

I could not continue to be startled by everything she said, thus I quickly moved beyond that one.

"Cassius fears there is going to be a war," I informed her.

She nodded shortly. "There will be. They will not accept a Nadirii as their queen. Not without a fight."

"Then if he and you are correct, we will need all the skilled warriors and experienced generals we can have."

Serena did not move or speak.

I did.

"And when it is over, if you wish to travel to the Southlands, so be it. If that is what you want, I want it for you. But in the meantime, I will need your help. I will need your counsel. And I might continue to need your sword."

"I have behaved—" she started softly.

But I couldn't bear it.

I couldn't bear my Serena soft.

She was the hard edge of stone breaking through my dirt.

The world needed the dirt to nurture it.

But it also needed the stone to support it.

"You have, and that is done. We no longer have Mum, but we have each other. And I will tell you that Lahn has brought a number of his warriors here. They are in Sky Bay, and I sense they would greatly enjoy a dalliance with a woman such as you. I have not noted they are fond of what is on offer in Airen. They go to the docks often. They return appearing in bad moods."

"Well then, let us hope our journey to the Bay is a swift one," she muttered.

I did not smile. It was not the time for smiles. My heart was heavy, and my limbs felt numb, but my mind was awash with too many thoughts.

And thus, I did not think one that I should have before I also turned to face the view and stated, "I am glad of this quest for a Korwahk warrior for you. And I am glad of your gnome friends. He was handsome, but I never was fond of the bent of Cassius's decision to remove your attention from me, using that Trusted. Chu."

"Chu?" she asked, her voice odd, croaky, but then again, perhaps not so odd as our mother had joined the veil not an hour ago.

"I hope you enjoyed him, my sister, before you were rid of him," I said and turned back to her to see her gaze on me. "And it is good that his shenanigans necessarily meant he taught you how to be an apparently very successful spy."

"Shenanigans," she muttered.

"Indeed, and I will say now what I should have said earlier, but with Mum, and the fact we weren't speaking, I did not. Well done in Notting Thicket, Serena. That was brilliant."

"Yes," she said as if it was not.

Then again, it was not the time to get effusive over compliments, or the accepting of them.

And Serena had changed, but she'd never been effusive over anything, and I had the feeling she did not change that much.

I returned to the topic. "But those games are over for us. Yes?"

"Games," she said, and I started to get concerned due to her one-word answers.

"Yes. And they are over." I turned fully to her, letting go of my shins to wrap my fingers around her forearm. "Because this is what we have decided. Though I will share the warning that this also is because Cassius won't abide it. He's ridiculously protective and it bothers me he has these worries or upsets. So, I am doubly glad we will not upset him."

"I would not wish to upset Cassius. By the goddess, I have learned not to do that," she said to the view.

Although, with that, she spoke more words, they did not give me a good feeling.

"Serena?" I called.

"I fell in love with him," she told the night sky before a burst of sharp, humorless laughter came from her, a sound that alarmed me all the more.

"Who?" I asked, perplexed.

"Chu," she answered, and my stomach clenched.

"Serena," I whispered, having had no idea, wishing I had talked Cassius away from this idea before it took root, and scooting closer to her. "Oh goddess," I breathed. "What have I said?"

"You have told me the truth." Her gaze came to me. "It is high time for that between us, Elena, and it will be necessary in the future. You will need to trust me, and I you. Not that you ever did anything that would make me not trust you, but I need to earn that in return. I will endeavor to do that in our time ahead. But as you said, what is done is done. And Chu and I are done."

I did not like the rock-solid manner in which she said that.

"I could have stopped this," I admitted.

"Oh, but I am glad you did not. For I would not have met Gal and Brix and dealt a crushing blow to a pack of insidious malcontents if you hadn't," she replied, sounding partly serious, and partly caustic.

"Still, I—"

"And had a number of mind-scattering orgasms."

I decided to leave it at that and move on to something more important.

"Did he...also, with you?" I asked.

She shook her head. "No. He did not fall in love with me. He followed orders. He is a Trusted One after all."

"I fear what should have been a much different conversation between us, I have ruined," I stated miserably.

"No," she disagreed. "It is the first time you have spoken unguarded to me since we were girls. It is all now gone. There is nothing between us. No intrigues, no lies. And as it was only me who pushed these things between us, I feel relief that they are gone. Thus, here we start."

"Here we start," I said uncertainly.

"I have learned to be a friend, Elena. It is new to me, as it is not to you." She tipped her head to the side. "Perhaps you will help to continue to guide the way?"

"I would...that would be..." I drew in breath to pull myself together. "That would make me happy."

She nodded briskly and turned her attention to the view.

I followed suit.

I gave it time before I said, "Thank you for bringing Melisse."

"Mother needed her, Melisse needed to see Mum, and you needed Melisse."

A triple win in thoughtfulness for my sister.

Yes, she had changed.

We fell silent again.

Not long later, the gnomes joined us.

One walked to the very edge of the cliff and sat there with his back to us.

The other one, to my shock, dropped down by Serena. She straightened her legs when he did, and thus, when he fell to his back, his head was resting on her ankle.

By the goddess, she had very much *changed*.

"All right, you're going to have to share about Galbdor and Welbrix," I declared, even if they were both right there.

"Gal and Brix," she corrected me. "And all you need to know is that both of them will stiff you on the tally when you're out drinking if you're not careful."

"That is untrue," Brix, at the edge, called irritably.

"It is very true," Gal, at Serena's ankle, stated good-naturedly. "Never start a tally with a gnome. You'll be paying."

Brix twisted to glare at Gal. "You need to stop telling these Nadirii all our secrets, Galbdor."

"I told you when he had a drink with you, or twelve, he would stiff you," Gal said to Serena.

"I never buy drinks. I have breasts. I press them together, and some fool male slobbers over himself in order to throw coin at my tankard," Serena returned.

"This is the only time in my life I wished I had breasts," Brix muttered.

I couldn't believe it, I let out a little laugh.

I then took a chance and bumped my shoulder to my sister's.

She did not bump back.

But she also did not draw away.

Prince Cassius
Night Heights Mountain Range
*A*IREN

CASSIUS MOVED to where Mac was standing on the ridge, regarding the slope below.

He stopped beside his captain.

"How many of them are there?" he asked Mac.

"Ten thousand, give or take a few hundred...or thousand," Mac replied drily.

Cass felt his heart squeeze and his mouth get tight.

He also felt Mac's regard.

"We have cliffs to the north. Cliffs to the east. Cliffs to the west. The Nadirii selected an excellent place in which their queen could die, it is not easy to get to. But now, the enemy blocks the only way out," Mac told him.

Cassius said nothing.

"One way or another, we're going to have to fight our way out of here, brother," Mac shared. "And the numbers aren't in our favor."

Cassius stared down the dark, quiet slope.

No rustling.

No fires.

Well hidden.

Ready for an ambush.

"We attack in the morning," he decreed.

Mac shifted and Cass knew he was turning fully to his prince.

"Have you lost your mind?" he asked.

He gave his eyes to his friend. "No."

"We're outnumbered, likely ten to one."

"Yes."

"Frey is with us. Do you intend to use the dragons?"

"No."

"We need more time to create a strategy."

"I already have a strategy."

"Cass—"

"You can come out," Cass called.

Mac jerked around, his hand going to the hilt of his sword.

"No need for that, soldier. Good gods, you Airenzian blokes are sword-happy," the man forming from the shadows said to Mac.

He took shape as much as he could lit only by moonlight.

"Hello, Silvanus," Cassius greeted.

The Zee doffed his hat, bent low at the waist in a mock tribute, then straightened, returning his hat to its jaunty angle.

"Howzit, Your Grace," the Zee replied.

And with that, Silvanus's mouth split into a smile that was blinding, even in the moonlight.

Cassius did not smile back.

He looked to Mac and answered his unasked question.

"As you can see, we will not be calling the dragons, not yet. For we'll be using the Zees."

He glanced to Silvanus and caught a bloody sparkle in the man's eye before he turned back to Mac and finished.

"And Fern's army."

II5

THE MER

Queen Ha-Lah
Nautilus Beach, Strait of Medusa
Mar-el

"I do not like this," my husband shared something that I was in no doubt about, considering his expression and the way he held his body.

We stood in the sand on the empty beach, the pre-dawn wind whipping about us, and we did this holding hands.

"I will be fine," I assured.

"You could catch a chill," he returned. "It is coming on winter and that water—"

I squeezed his hand. "Aramus, I am Mer, my darling. I do not feel it."

He glowered down at me.

I leaned into him and gave him a reassuring smile.

"We are here while all are still abed. No one can see us. I will go, then I will return, hopefully with new allies in the seas."

Close to the end of my words, I noted I was losing his attention as his gaze drifted to the ocean.

It was then I felt it, so intent on assuring my king, its coming did not register with me.

Thus, I whirled and but only glanced at the waters before my hand tightened in his and I shouted, "Run!"

Aramus did not need me to share this warning, he was already bracing to drag me up the beach.

Thus, together, we bolted up the shore.

His boots sunk in the sand, and I lost a slipper before I'd taken two steps, the other one on the third, but the both of us knew it was useless as the roar of the water filled our ears.

This was why Aramus tossed me to the sand. And I had barely hit before he was throwing himself bodily over me.

He wrapped his arms around me tightly, just as the tidal landed on his back.

Being dragged uncontrollably into the sea, I wrapped an arm around him too, cupping the back of his head with my other hand and pulling his mouth to mine.

I opened my lips, he opened his, thus our lips were sealed, and we held to each other tightly as the power of the seas drug us deep.

I felt my legs knitting, the scales pressing through the skin as they formed, my gills opening, while the water twisted us and towed us, flipped us and twirled us.

I knew only one thing in the tumult, I had to keep hold of my husband, and I had to keep his mouth to mine, breathing air into him, until it was over.

For if I did this, no matter how deep it swept us out to sea, I could take him with me as I swam back.

I simply had to keep him alive until the furor was over, and we could surface.

Aramus knew this was my strategy, thus he held my head to his as I did the same and locked his long legs around my scaly hips.

We could do this, together.

I could help him survive.

I *would* help him survive.

All we had to do was hold on.

On this thought, he was ripped from my arms.

My underwater scream formed large bubbles as I began to flip my fin to regain my hold on my king, but I got nowhere, and not only because I froze at what I saw before me.

Hands had seized me under my arms.

I turned my head to the side and looked angrily at one of the mermales who had a hold on me and was drawing me deeper into the sea.

My watery words I knew he could hear.

"He cannot breathe!" I screamed, violently trying to pull at his hold.

The mermale remained facing forward, his grip on me unbreakable as we swam deeper.

"*The pressure!*" I shrieked.

The male just glanced at me and carried on swimming.

I tugged and fought as we followed the males dragging my husband into the depths of the ocean, my heart beating a fierce tattoo, my mind sending messages to my friends to come and save me.

Save me.

And my husband.

Save us...

From *my people*.

I saw the dolphins, and the octopi, even a few whales in the distance.

But I did not think to call out to them as I also saw the manner in which Aramus's body floated in the hold of the mermales before us.

"*No!*" I screeched.

He could not be dead.

Please, no.

He could not be dead.

My mind scrambled.

How long had he been separated from me?

Too long.

Oh, Medusa.

He could not be dead!

I struggled with all I had against the hold on me.

"You will calm, maid," the mermale on my other side demanded.

"You will let me go!" I shouted.

"You are not queen here, Ha-Lah," he told me.

No, I was not.

Sirens dammit.

"By the gods, by Medusa, by the sirens," I chanted, so fraught, I paid no heed to the dim light I could now see shining from below.

Where we were heading.

All right.

I had to think.

My beloved was the Sea King.

The Mer would not kill the Sea King. His line was chosen by the gods. Triton and Medusa would be furious.

My people would do naught to anger the gods. Especially not Triton and Medusa, whose love created the Mer. Mer revered Triton and Medusa almost past reasoning.

I knew, for I was Mer and I did too.

Thus, they must be taking him to air, and doing it swiftly, for they swam much faster than us.

These thoughts assailing me, it was only vaguely I noted the ocean floor as it became awash with bright blooms of sea anemone, not as if they grew naturally, but as if we were entering a garden.

Ahead of us, the males dragged Aramus's body through a slim opening which was the source of the light. This opening being a slit in a great cavern.

There would be air there, I prayed.

There had to be air there.

My captors and I entered behind them.

We swam through a tunnel, me trying to make them do it faster, the light becoming brighter and brighter, before I noticed, my heart slamming in my chest, Aramus and his abductors dipping low, apparently entering a larger section.

Going down was not good.

They must endeavor to go *up*.

All right.

They had to know what they were doing.

He would be fine.

They would keep him alive.

He was the Sea King.

They were surely taking him to a bubble of air.

I knew there were pockets of air under the surface. They were how, in times millennia ago, the Mer had adapted to being able to breathe outside the water, as well as in it.

I was pulled into the larger section, a mammoth cavern that went down stories upon stories of what would be human buildings, and up the same. Not to mention, it was so vast across, it could fit half a dozen of the coliseums of Fire City within it.

And I stopped.

I reared back as the massive space around me could be seen, mermaids and males swimming amongst other sea life, anemones sprouting from below and along the tall walls of the vast space, sea lettuce and kelp drifting lazily.

And all around, from the bottom to a top that went so high up, I could not see its end, there appeared to be doors or windows, the latter with lights shining through. Some even had what appeared to be window boxes tucked with sea lettuce and anemone and trailing vines of seaweed.

These were dwellings.

But I could pay very little mind to that.

Or to where they took my husband.

For right before me floated a mermale, the largest I'd ever seen who also had the longest, most powerful fin I'd ever beheld. His tail had to be at least fifteen feet long, curling behind him.

I didn't even know merfins could get that long.

His chest was wide. His muscles pronounced. The definition of his stomach indented. The veins along his forearms distended.

His hair was long and jet black.

His beard was thick and distinct, the swoop of whiskers guiding from his beard up to the bottom edge of his lower lip something, in other circumstances, I might find fascinating.

His thick, dark eyebrows were drawn.

His eyes were a startling silver I had seen before.

He was carrying a fearsome trident in one fist.

He scowled at me before he growled, "Welcome, Ha-Lah."

And then he turned on a supple swell and swam ahead of us.

We followed, straight to another sea wall, swimming down, to and through a tall, arched doorway that was adorned with floating anemone and set with seashells and pearls in an extraordinary pattern I did not have it within me to appreciate at that time.

Beyond the arch, we swam through another tunnel into another open underwater pool, and then we swam upwards.

My gills closed instantly as we made a glassy surface that only broke with the most gentle of ripples at our emergence.

Here, I saw we were in a grotto that had an island in the middle on which was built a magnificent half dome, the opening pointed my way, that seemed to shine with an ethereal bright pearly light.

And on the smooth rocks that formed the island's base, beyond the opening to the dome, lay my husband.

I also saw the merman who had met us had formed legs and he was walking, nude, up the rocks of the island, his trident still in his hand.

I pulled viciously at the hold on me, and I did not pause to register surprise when they easily released me.

I also did not look at the variety of Mer bobbing about in the pool around me, or the ones that milled about on the island, including the mermaid who was handing the silver-eyed, raven-haired mermale a pair of trousers.

I struck out toward my husband.

I ignored the pain of the split I felt as I closed in on the island and formed legs.

I just found my feet on the rocks in the shallows and ran through them, my sodden gown slapping against my skin.

Aramus was on his side, his back to me, and I fell to my knees when I reached him, pressing him to his back, battling fear and hysteria and a pain so overwhelming, it threatened to consume me.

His eyes were closed.

My king looked to be asleep.

Oh, Medusa.

Maybe he had not survived that swim.

Or maybe the weight of the sea had crushed his innards, made pulp of his brain.

Regardless of these thoughts, I pressed against his chest, holding to hope that it was just water in his lungs, thinking fast about how, once I revived him, I could get him back to the surface. Back to the beach.

Back home.

As I pumped, I lifted my accusatory gaze to the silver-eyed male who stood, now wearing trousers that appeared to be subtly gilded leathers, the shine against the gray material shimmering a light aqua and silver.

He was leaning negligently on his bloody trident.

"You sent that tidal!" I bit.

"If you spent time amongst your people, Ha-Lah," his deep voice returned to me, "you would know, with the magic of a Mer, if a human has the touch of one of our own, we can take him or her anywhere we wish, even to the bottom of the deepest depths of the sea."

I stopped pressing against Aramus's chest as relief flooded through me, and with it came the ability to gather my wits enough to look down upon my husband and see he was breathing.

This was joyous.

And I felt that joy.

But our abduction was anything but.

And thus, I felt fury.

I lifted squinty eyes at the male.

He shook his head, muttering with disgust, "The land Mer. So intent on passing, they forget who they are."

"The decision to remain on land was not made by me, male," I snapped. "It was made generations before my existence was even a hope."

"But have you visited us?" he asked, opening a hand and using it to indicate our surroundings. "Have you come to be amongst your people?"

"No," I spat. "And it would appear it was a smart decision, as I am not feeling much delight at the manner of my first invitation here."

The male glowered at me, and I assumed, quite rightly in my mind, that meant my point was taken.

"And I *was* amongst my people on the surface," I went on. "Or have you forsaken us as it's clear you feel I have forsaken you?"

He had no answer to that either.

I decided not to pursue that line of questioning any longer, for something vastly more important took precedence.

"Why does my husband sleep?" I demanded.

"He was struggling. If his guards lost hold on him, he would die. Necessity urged he lose consciousness. Thus…" he trailed off on a shrug and an indication with a tip of his head to Aramus.

"When will he wake?" I asked.

The male shrugged. "He will be fine."

With some difficulty (it must be said, my husband was bulky), I pulled Aramus's torso up and held him to me as I kept my gaze pinned on the mermale.

"Why did you send the tidal?"

"You were coming to us, were you not?" he asked.

I did not request to know how he knew this.

"*I* was," I amended. "My husband was *not*."

"But I wished to speak to the king of the sea."

"Well, you can't speak to him if he's *unconscious*," I pointed out.

"Settle, maid," he rumbled. "You are amongst your own here."

"I thought he was dead," I spat, hearing my husband breathe steadily, feeling the warmth return to his skin now that he was no longer in the chill of the sea, neither of these wiping away the fear and misery of the last ten minutes.

"Did you think to come and demand an audience, and aid in correcting the ruin you made of the surface, at your whim?" he asked.

Belatedly, important things were dawning on me.

Starting with the fact he knew much that I did not understand how he knew.

But onward from that, and the priority in the moment, something else.

Thus, I adjusted my tone when I noted, "I see you're angry with me."

"You?" he returned. "No. Him?" He jerked his trident toward my husband. "Yes."

Oh no.

I held Aramus closer.

"He knows I am Mer, and he accepts this," I shared.

"Bully for him," he clipped.

Hmm.

I decided to begin again.

"You know I am Ha-Lah, Queen of Mar-el. But I do not know you."

"I am Jorie, King of the Mer."

Well, it was advantageous to know I'd been directed right to the top.

Except if the one at the top wasn't terribly thrilled to see you.

"There is much happening on the surface," I shared.

"There is always much happening there."

"It may be the end of Triton."

"And this concerns us how?" he demanded.

This was not going well.

"We have reason to believe the Beast wakes," I informed him. "My husband feels—"

"Oh, he wakes. And he will make the surface," Jorie confirmed. Finishing ominously, "Soon."

I had no response to that, partially because Jorie seemed so unconcerned, but I, on the other hand, was very much the opposite.

He explained this presently.

"We took care of this the last time for the humans of Triton, and where did it get us?"

I knew very well where it got my people.

At first, I had no response to this either.

And then I asked, "If you are so angry, if you wish to remain detached, if you do not wish to come to the aid of Triton, then why do you want to speak to my husband? Why did you pull him and I under? Why are we here?"

He scowled at me.
He did this for quite some time.
And then he said words that seemed dragged from him.
But they were words that gave me hope.
"I wish to meet my sister."

116

THE DAWN OF THE END

King True
One Hundred Miles over the Border
AIREN

"Sire, a bird," a corporal said, handing True the ribbon of parchment. True nodded to him as the soldier saluted and then walked away.

True unrolled the ribbon, and by the still-moonlit, pre-dawn sky, he read the message from one of his scouts.

12,000. Base of Heights. Blocked in. Riders unable to get through. Ravens down. Enemy preparing to attack.

"BRAM!" True shouted, crumbling the missive in a fist and marching in the direction where he'd seen his friend disappear some minutes before. "Bram!" he repeated, men he passed looking to him, some breaking from huddles, he knew, to find Bram for True.

Thus, in half a minute, he saw Bram jogging his way.

"The men need to prepare to ride, *now*," True ordered. "We're going to the Heights, not the Bay, and we need to make haste. Find Wally and Luther. They escort Farah back to Notting Thicket."

"What the hell is going on?" Bram asked.

"Twelve thousand of the allied gentry militia surround Cassius and Elena at the base of the Heights. We lost riders trying to get them warning. They're shooting down ravens that would do the same. They're blocked in and the enemy is poised to attack."

"Fuck," Bram bit, turned and started to sprint away, when True stopped him.

"Bird to Alfie. I want reinforcements from Wodell. A regiment to bolster the Bay, a regiment making haste, following us. Also, a bird to Mars. He must send his men in from the south. And get messages to Aramus and the Citadel. They need to know if they don't already."

Bram nodded shortly and resumed his sprint.

True turned on his boot and strode to his tent.

By the time he arrived, he saw it had been struck, and Farah, dressed and cloaked, ready to ride, was standing by her mount, Regina, stroking her neck, talking to Helga.

He went direct to her, but she noted him before his arrival, and he noted she did not miss the expression on his face.

"*Caro,*" she whispered. "What more could have happened?"

They had lost Ophelia to the veil in the night.

Now he was too far away to make certain they would not lose Elena and Cassius in the day.

And this knowledge that his friends were in danger and he was too far away to help was eating him from the inside.

"We've had a message. If the war has not already begun, it will soon. You need to return to the Thicket," he told her.

She dropped her hands from her horse and turned to fully face him.

"True," she said softly.

"You will make haste. Wallace and Luther will be your guard."

"I go with you."

For a moment, he was thrown.

"You can't ride into battle with me, Farah."

"I can't leave you," she returned.

"You don't know of what you speak," he shot back. "Airen is now dangerous. We ride intent to engage and thus now are officially the enemy. We are too far away from the Bay to get you to Cassius's stronghold safely, and regardless, that detour would take time we do not have. Thus, I need you home immediately."

"I cannot leave you."

"Farah, you cannot go," he clipped.

"I can be of help. My magic—"

"You can barely control your magic," he gritted, his legendary patience waning.

For reason.

He needed her on her horse.

He needed to know she was headed to safety.

And he needed to get to their friends.

She looked to Helga and something passed between them he would find in Farah's next words that he did not like.

For she lifted her chin, straightened her spine and decreed, "I ride with my husband."

"I will never, not ever, order you to do something, or forbid you from doing something," he retorted. "Except in times like this."

"I ride with my husband," she repeated.

"Gods dammit, Farah," he bit.

"I ride," she lifted her hands and swept them to her side, and with them up came the fallen leaves all around. They formed a funnel about them with a wind that whipped her cloak, his mantle, and both their hair. This, before she finished, "With *my husband*!"

For the first time in their marriage...

Nay.

For the first time of their acquaintance, True Axelsson, King of Wodell, and Farah Magos Axelsson, Queen of Wodell, stood staring at each other, locked in a battle of wills.

"True!" a voice could be heard through the wind and angry rustling of leaves that swirled about he and his wife's bodies. It was Wallace. "We don't have time for this."

"This is the dawn of the end, *mia vita*," she said. "And whatever shape that end takes, I will face it at your side."

True frowned at her.

Then he said, "Gods dammit," before he yelled, "We ride!"

The leaves about them instantly stopped swirling.

And they floated to the ground.

～

King Mars
On the Journey to the Great Wohd
WODELL

"NOT GOOD," Basil grunted, handing Mars a ribbon from a raven.

Mars unwound it and read in Firenzii,

Ambush planned. Night Heights. 12,000. They're clearing skies. No way in for scouts. Orders?

Mars let the ribbon fall to the ground and looked to Basil.

"Send a raven to the Airenzian border. They ride. Another to Lorenz, I want Firenz warriors guarding The Enchantments. Tell him to send more to the Bay. Another raven to Aramus. He must engage. Find Kyril. He will take some men and escort my queen back to the palace."

Basil nodded and asked, "Ride or ship?"

"I cannot control the passage of a ship, but I can control the hooves of Hephaestus."

Basil appeared relieved.

Not a surprise. Firenz were not seamen.

Not a one of them, including Mars, had been looking forward to the journey up the Wohd to the Bay.

"Go," Mars commanded, turned on his boot and moved to the tent where his wife was dressing.

When he slapped aside the flaps and entered, he saw her sitting a stool, Tril dressing her hair.

"May I have a moment with my wife, Tril?" he requested.

The maid took in his face, bobbed a curtsy, touched her queen's shoulder and scuttled out.

Silence slowly rose, her gaze riveted to him, and when she had her feet, she asked, "Oh no, my love, what new is amiss?"

"The war begins in Airen. In earnest. I am certain Cassius knows this could happen at any time. I am not certain he knows it is going to happen imminently. My scouts have seen the traitors preparing for an ambush, but there is no way to get word to Cass to warn him, and they're clearing birds from the sky in his direction. He's outnumbered. Significantly."

"Oh no," she said again, this time in a whisper.

"I have but scouts in that land, no help to him and he needs reinforcements. I ride to him. You ride back to Fire City."

Her head twitched as if this idea confused her.

"I must go with you," she declared.

Had she gone mad?

"Silence, I ride to war. You will not be going with me."

"But, I must," she returned.

"This is not the Beast, my queen. There is naught you can do but be in danger. We are declaring our intentions, meaning our allegiance. When we set foot on Airen soil, for some there, we are the enemy."

"I can't leave you."

He loved her very much, thus he loved she did not think she could leave his side.

But in this instance, that was not happening.

"I adore you, and as I do, I will have you safe," he told her.

"And I adore you, and as I do, *I* will have *you* safe," she told him.

His patience was waning.

Quickly.

"I will not belittle your work with your dagger, with Kyril, the strength of your will, the intelligence of your mind, but Silence, this is *war*."

"And I will ride with you."

"You will be naught but a blight on my mind."

It was not the right thing to say, but it was true.

She did not get angry at his words.

She remained true to her theme.

"I cannot leave you."

"You will not be going with me."

"I *will* not leave you."

"Why?" he bit.

"I do not know, but I cannot, Mars. I just simply cannot," she returned.

"This is wasting time we do not have," he ground out. "Cass and Elena are in danger and we're bloody weeks away."

"Then we should ride. Immediately."

"We will. Me northeast, and you south."

"Mars, I—"

"This conversation is over."

"Mars! I—"

He was done.

"*This conversation is over!*" he roared.

"*It is not!*" she thundered back, lifting both fists over her head and thrusting them forward, her hands opening, and from them fired two balls of flame that made him duck, even if they sailed well over his head and would not have hit him.

They dissipated before they struck the wall of the tent, as if she had willed their vanishing before they caused destruction.

Mars straightened slowly, all the while gazing at his wife in disbelief.

But she was gazing where the flames had disappeared and doing it in wonder.

Before he could say another word, her attention jumped to him.

"I ride *with you*," she decreed. And then she bustled to her trunk, yelling, "Tril! I need a saddlebag, my warmest cloak and a sturdy gown! And my dagger!"

Tril hurried in.

Mars drew a breath into his nose, turned and strode out of the tent, nearly slamming into Kyril upon exiting it.

"Does the queen prepare to leave?" Kyril asked.

"Yes," Mars answered. "And she rides with me."

Prince Cassius
Night Heights Mountain Range
AIREN

CASSIUS SAT ASTRIDE CAELUS, Elena to his right side, sitting her mount, Diana.

Caelus shifted restlessly under him.

Diana stood solid as stone.

He, and his princess, stared down into the trees.

"I am sorry so soon after—" he began.

"It is clever, attacking when they think we hunker down in mourning."

He turned his head and studied her beautiful profile.

That was, he did this until she faced him.

It was then he studied her beautiful face.

He saw the sadness in her eyes.

And the determination.

And last, that something he treasured so very much.

"What was your card this morning?" he asked quietly.

She scrunched her nose, and by the gods, he started smiling at the sight.

"The mermaid," she answered.

He stopped smiling as he was now perplexed.

"What does that mean?" he inquired.

"Storms, in life or from the sky. Magic afoot." She paused then finished, "Revenge. In other words, nothing useful."

"Revenge? Fern's army?" he asked.

She shook her head but said, "Perhaps. Or perhaps its literal and somehow the Mer will alight from where they've hidden for centuries and swim to our aid."

"In a mountain range?" he asked drily.

She shrugged.

He grinned at her.

She grinned back.

Mac rode up to his left side and asked, "Are you two going to flirt until dawn? Or are we going to ride down this mountain so I can gut something?"

Jazz rode up to Mac's left side and concurred with, "Yes. What he said."

Cassius turned his head when he sensed movement at Elena's other side, and he saw her sister line up there, Hera beyond her, Rosehana beyond Hera.

Serena did not appear in a joking mood.

She was gazing down the mountain with sheer focus.

It would be good to finally fight alongside that formidable warrior, instead of against her.

He looked behind him to see Nero and Tone at his back.

Behind them, Airenzian and Nadirii, all mounted, all ready to seek their fates on the battlefield.

Nero jerked up his chin.

Cassius dipped his.

He then looked again to his princess.

She was watching him.

"Are you ready?" he asked.

She nodded, and as if to assert this, she hunkered over Diana's neck, her eyes straight ahead, her heels lifting, ready to dig into her steed's sides.

Serena, Hera and Rosehana assumed this position.

Cass looked left and saw Mac and Jasmine the same.

So he bent over Caelus, thrust his forearm into the bands at the back of his shield hanging at his side and lifted his heels.

But he turned his head one more time.

"Elena."

She looked to him.

"I love you," he said.

He caught only the shock and warmth suffusing her exquisite features before he dug his heels into his mount and shot forward.

AND AS THE hundreds of Nadirii and Airenzian horses with their riders were tearing through the pines...

None of them felt the earth shuddering violently beneath them from something else altogether.

The prophecy was now complete.

Love was sealed.

It was the dawn of the end.

However that would be.

But the warriors could not miss it when the heavens opened.

And poured down rain.

117

THE SURFACING

Tedrey
Ancient Ritual Ground
WODELL

Tedrey was tied to a tree, his face averted, his hands busy, his ears feeling like they were bleeding, his eyes behind closed lids feeling like they were scalding.

There was a huddle of women close beside him, gagged, but not blindfolded, tied together, fretting, moaning, but they'd learned in difficult ways not to struggle or try to escape.

The screams of the last one that had been tied to the ground, used in base and vile manners, cut and bled into the dirt, had long faded, along with her life.

But Tedrey could not look.

He had already seen too much.

Too many.

Their spent, lifeless bodies were piled behind the tree at his back, and thus he could not look that way either. He could not again look into those staring, vacant eyes that still held the stark remnants of fear and degradation and pain.

However, in the diligent frenzy of ritual and sacrifice that had now gone on, one after the other, for two days, Fenn had even gotten caught up in it and took his turn with the others, using and dispatching the women.

They were animals.

Monsters.

Tedrey had known cruelty in his life, but he could not...

He would not...

His mind simply would never be able to reconcile *this*.

And thus, he focused.

As they were so very involved in their endeavors, and thus paid him little mind, Tedrey focused on the ropes binding his hands, which he hoped to free and then he could see to the ones binding his ankles.

And then he would flee.

He would want to save the ones at his side, the ones taken by Fenn, Thom and their brethren. The ones agonizing beside him, dreading their turn.

But he could not.

There was Golden Thomas, and Fenn, and nine others had come with Thom, to join the eleven with Fenn.

Tedrey had to manage to escape them all and get to Birchlire, which was closest, and warn King True.

Unless he could somehow find a loft and get ravens dispatched, not having a single coin to pay an aviast to send them.

But to save this land and all others, he had to leave the women behind.

He had to leave them to this fate.

And he had to ignore the burn in his gut at the fury he had to swallow at what had befallen the pile at his back, what would befall the terrified at his side, what he had seen that he knew he could never erase from his brain, what had been lost by all of them for this maniacal crusade.

He felt the rope at his wrists loosening and took heart, only to stop when he felt something else.

The beginnings of a quake was coming from under them, the loose dirt about him shimmying.

And then he braced, for it started slow, but it came fast and strong.

"He rises!" one of the men shouted jubilantly.

"It's working! Quick, release her and discard the body. Bring another," Fenn demanded.

"She is not drained yet," another man said.

"Do what I say!" Fenn ordered zealously.

The quake shuddered to a halt, and as they went about their business much more enthusiastically, Tedrey dismissed the turn in his stomach and took advantage of their diverted attention, picking with great care at the knot at his wrists.

When a woman was selected, they divested her of her gag, thus her screams rent the air, and the men fed on them as this time, Tedrey forced himself to watch.

Forced himself to study them each in turn. Forced his focus to them to make certain they were tuned to what they were doing, and none of them turned to Tedrey.

Forced his memory to carve their visages in his brain, for he hoped one day to find them all again and make them pay for this desecration.

It took some time, the clouds covering the dawning sun, before the rains came.

Tedrey worked at his wrists.

The men brutalized.

The knot slipped free. His hands fell free. And Tedrey almost did not catch his cry of joy before the next quake came.

Thus, Tedrey did not move a muscle.

For this one felt different.

It felt unlike the other, which had been a powerful shudder. Like the earth below them seemed to be speaking and very much wished those who walked it to listen to its message.

This had another meaning.

A sinister one.

And as the men before him ambled about excitedly, the man at work on the miserable girl tethered to the dirt cried out his release, right before, suddenly, he cried out for a different reason as the earth underneath them broke open.

The man was tossed one way.

She rolled the other.

And Tedrey stared as it seemed beings were forming from the mud.

With the stakes she'd been tied to no longer stuck in the ground, the woman who had been being used struggled to her feet and raced into the forest with ropes and rods dangling from wrists and ankles.

No one paid her mind at what seemed to be happening in the clearing.

The women at his side started scuffling on their behinds to get away, as the men who had wrought this catastrophe milled about with wonder and jubilation, watching the breaking of the earth with zealotry awash on their faces.

And then Tedrey saw two men and a number of women form from the sludge as if erupting from a swell at the center of the earth.

The rain pelted them as they stood in the mire, gazing about.

And as the rain cleaned the mud from them, Thom cried joyously, "Jell!" Thom rushed forward.

"No!" the man wearing filthy robes of what Tedrey thought was a Go'Doan priest cried. "He is my—!"

"*Kill him!*" the woman, standing closest to the man between her and the priest, a priest that was G'Jell, shrieked.

But that man was already moving.

And then there was naught in that clearing but the sound of the driving rain as all went immobile when the man took Thom's head in his two hands, and with a terrible crunching noise, crushed it in an explosion of gore with no apparent effort.

Tedrey blinked against the rain as the man released Thom, and he fell lifeless to the muck.

Good *gods*.

"You were saying?" the woman asked Jell.

"But Thom was my—" Jell began.

"Release those girls," the woman commanded.

The man who had killed Thom did not move.

"And do not let them flee!" she shouted, and the other women scurried after Fenn and the retreating Rising priests. "I said, release those girls," she repeated her order.

And as the man who killed Thom looked side to side, carefully, Tedrey moved the hands that he'd left held behind him, forgotten in the spectacle, to his ankles, where, trying to mask his movements, he worked on the ropes at his feet.

"Did you hear me!" she snapped to the man. "Release those girls!"

When no one did her bidding, she turned to Jell.

"You do it," she bit out. "He's always like this when he makes the surface. Like he's never seen trees before."

"Daemon?" Jell called tentatively.

The ropes at Tedrey's ankles fell loose.

He thus poised to take flight.

"Daemon?" the woman asked snidely.

"Daemon? Look at me," Jell bid to the unmoving man.

"What do you speak of? *Daemon?*" she spat.

Tedrey did not take flight.

With their attention on each other, and the Rising contingent gone, he took his chance.

He crawled swiftly to the women who were all scooting, but not as one, willy-nilly, to get away in all directions, which would get them nowhere.

He put his fingers to the ropes at the wrists of one, these ropes also tied to two others, with a line leading down to bind their feet.

"I let you go, you help me release the others," he whispered to her.

She shook her head, tears of panic escaping her eyes, spittle mixing with rain dripping from her gag as she panted behind it.

"You help me get as many loose as we can," he pushed.

Her head kept moving frenziedly in denial.

He loosened her.

She immediately tugged the binds from her feet and bolted.

Gods dammit.

"He has given you *a name?*" Tedrey heard the woman demand.

"I will help you," he heard whispered.

He looked to another woman who had somehow nudged her gag free and moved to her.

"Daemon, we must find the others. We must find them, for they are our friends, and then be away from this place," he heard Jell say.

"When did he give you a name?" the woman asked.

Working as swiftly he could with wet fingers on slick ropes, Tedrey released the girl. She freed her feet and instantly shifted around, her hands going to the ropes on the next.

"Run west when you are released," he instructed. "Take cover and call to any that race after you. We will meet up, move as one, it will be safer."

The girl he was working on nodded to him.

He released her.

However she did not bolt, and she did not do as he said.

Once she had her feet free, she turned and put her fingers to the ropes of another.

"Have you two, the both of you, been *conniving?*" the woman's tone was becoming shrill. "Against *me?*"

"You will be quiet."

This was a new voice, a smooth one. A calm one.

An attractive one.

Even an alluring one.

Tedrey chanced a glance to the clearing to see the three of them facing off against each other.

Paying he and the women no mind.

They had time.

But they had to work quickly.

"Hurry," he encouraged, loosening the binds of another, who in turn moved to help.

"You do not tell me what to do. I am your mistress," she retorted, and Tedrey heard a pained cry and a thudding splash.

He'd struck her.

Tedrey did not look to see if he was correct.

They only had three women left to go.

He turned to the second he'd released who had stayed. The others he sensed, but did not chance to look, were huddled behind them and waiting.

"Draw them away, quiet, but quick," he ordered.

She nodded, stood and moved.

"We found one," he heard called and glanced up to see four of the women who had emerged from the earth shoving Fenn into the clearing, his hands tied behind his back.

Tedrey's fingers slipped on the wet ropes.

Gods be with me, gods be with me, he chanted in his head. *Just get this done. Just get it done.*

He let her loose.

"Go, go," he hissed at her.

She fumbled with the ties that bound her feet, got free, but slipped as she tried to stand, took the hand another was holding out to her, and then they were away.

It was he and the first he'd released who had stayed to help now working on the last two girls.

"You take them. I will follow slowly, so if they notice, I can distract them from your leaving," he instructed before warning, "I do not think the new is any better than the old."

"You must go with us," she urged.

He opened his mouth to reply but did not as more words came from the clearing.

"Put him to his knees," the woman, clearly having recovered, demanded.

"He keeps his feet," Jell ordered.

"Knees!" she shouted.

"Feet!" Jell bit.

"*He* is not yours!" she yelled.

"*He* has always been mine!" Jell yelled in return.

Tedrey looked up, the end of the rope beginning to slide free as Daemon roared, "*Enough!*"

"As we planned, we will—" Jell began, looking to Daemon.

"*You* planned?" the woman countered. "We came to the surface to save those girls."

"Oh, gods, no, only two more," his mate whispered in the same terror he had, for they were mentioned, and that might gain attention.

"I said...*enough!*" Daemon snarled.

"Just get them to their feet and go," Tedrey demanded, forcing the hoops of the ropes over the heels of the woman he was working on.

"But—" his comrade began.

"There are only two of them. They can run connected. Untie their hands later, get them to their feet and *go!*" he nearly yelled as the earth beneath them began to shake.

She took his cue, slid the ropes over the heels of the woman she was assisting, and Tedrey and she got the girls up.

They started away, the last two still connected, and Tedrey followed them, backing away slowly, watching the clearing, his arms out to either side like they could fend off an attack, giving them a head start just in case those in the clearing noticed him, waiting for his chance to turn and run.

But as he did this, his eyes riveted to the man in the middle.

Daemon.

He had bent with a shoulder dipped, as if he was going low to gather momentum to swing up and strike.

But when he swung up, he did not strike.

He *emerged*.

The women holding Fenn all screamed.

Fenn barked a shout of shock and staggered back into them.

Jell and the woman froze.

And Tedrey's blood turned to ice and his feet stopped moving.

For now, there was no man.

There was only...

A Beast.

He was twice his original height.

He had a hump on his back.

The entirety of his body had short, coarse fur, except around his neck, where there was a long, thick mane. His legs were painfully thin with long cloven feet. But his arms were beefy, with enormous hands that had long, lethally-clawed fingers.

Tedrey could not see his face, for it was turned from him, but he saw the head had short fur above that mane, it sloped forward in a flattish way, and now it turned toward the women, who took one look at it and scattered like mice.

But Fenn stood still, as if he was stunned, staring up at the creature, his face a study of amazement.

Or repulsion.

And then Fenn's body jolted as the creature struck out with its claws, opening four lines of gore across Fenn's chest.

Fenn's knees gave out, and he began to fall, only to be struck by another swipe, this opening up more of his body, including his throat in a gash so deep, his head began to list backwards off his neck.

It did not.

For the creature tore it free, lifted it over his head with the neck pointed down, and tipped his own head back, allowing Fenn's blood to seep into its open mouth.

Abruptly, however, he tossed Fenn's head to the side, turned, and in a mighty sweep, he caught up the woman and Jell, both of whom had been preparing to run away.

He did this in the thin, overlong fingers of only one of his huge hands.

He lifted them up with not an ounce of apparent effort and tossed them across the clearing, away from Tedrey.

The woman slammed, back against the tree, and Tedrey heard the break.

Jell went rolling between some trees.

And the creature followed them, with each step transforming from the Beast he was back to the man he used to be.

"Oh no you don't," he said, standing, now naked, and human, hands on his narrow hips, looking down at the groaning woman then into the trees toward Jell. "I'm not done with you yet. No, no. We're just beginning. And to be certain things are straight, you both are *mine*."

And on those words, Tedrey unfroze.

He turned.

And he raced into the woods.

He did it knowing it was the end of The Rising.

But it was the beginning of *The Rising*.

He also knew one more thing.
At all costs.
He had to get to King True.

The End of Part Three.
The Rising Series continues with The Rising.

THE RISING SERIES GLOSSARY

Terms, Words, Places

Abhainn Mouth – (AH-been) (n/place): Harbor city in the north of Airen located at the mouth of the Dunleth Abhainn (river).

Abyss (the) – (n/place): Large "bottomless" hole in the rock of a cliff on the coast of Mar-el fifteen miles down the coast from Nautilus, the capital city of Mar-el.

Airen – (Air-EN) (n/place): Country of Airen located in the northeast of the Triton mainland. The northernmost area is barren and craggy and made up of great boulders of black rock. The rest is mountainous or fertile and green, mostly pastureland, forests and rolling hills.

Airenzian – (Air-EN-zee-an) (adj.): Of Airen.

Alabasta – (Al-ah-BASS-tah) (goddess): Of Wodell. Goddess of Wisdom and the Earth. A goddess shared with Lunwyn in The Northlands.

Amphite – (Am-FITE) (n/place): Underwater capital of the Mer. Location of royal palace of King of the Mer.

Ancient Ritual Ground – (n/place): Area in the Lesser Thicket Forest of the country of Wodell where rituals were (are) conducted, including human sacrifice.

Argyll Forest – (n/place): Forest on the western border of Airen, butting The Enchantments, the city-state of Go'Doan and Wodell. The parts of it in Wodell are known as the Lesser Thicket Forest. Location of the Silbury Henge.

Ashesh – (Ash-EHSH) (n): Drug akin to opium. Available throughout Triton. Grown in Firenze.

Angmostros – (Aing-MO-stros) (n/creature): Sea creatures in the shape of enormous eels, some one hundred yards long, with two heads with long necks, very large mouths and very sharp teeth.

Aviast – (Ay-VEE-ast) (n): Keeper of a loft of ravens used for sending messages.

Bayzian – (Bay-ZEE-an) (n): Citizens of Sky Bay, the capital of Airen.

Birchlire Castle – (Birch-LEER) (n/place): Home of the King of Wodell. Located in Notting Thicket.

Bishop Cross – (n/island): Island off the southeast coast of the country of Airen. Temperate, but barren and very remote.

Bloody Boy Cove – (n/place): Deep cove to the north, across the wide bay (and hidden from sight) from Nautilus, in Mar-el.

Body stocking – (n): Worn by the Nadirii under tunics. More like a leotard or bathing suit. Can be tank/spaghetti strap/long-sleeved/strapless at top. Regular cut or high cut at the hips.

Bounden (The) – (n): Those taken into service on Mar-el as punishment for sailing the Triton seas without permission from the Mar-el king. This punishment is known and anyone who sails the seas risks it if caught doing so. The service of the bounden lasts a specified amount of time and those taken into it are guarded under significant strictures as by law as to their treatment. Once service is done, many of the bounden remain on Mar-el to make their lives there.

Cairngorn Lake – (KAREN-gorn) (n/lake): Very large lake located in the southeast of the country of Airen.

Carleigh Manor – (Car-LAY) (n/place): Royal manor house about thirty-five kilometers south of Sky Bay in the country of Airen.

Catrame Palace – (Cah-TRAME) (n/place): Royal palace of the King of Firenze. Located in Fire City.

Cells – (n): The room or rooms of a Go'Doan priest. In Go'Doan, they are quarters, with more than one room. For new priests or those in Go'Doan temples in other countries, the cell could be one room. However, they are not spartan, ranging from very comfortable (for a Go'Tish, a new priest) to luxurious (for a Go'En, a high priest).

Close – (n): A narrow, dead-end alleyway in a city. Mostly a footpath and not used for carriages or horses, etc. Opposite of "wynd" [see below].

Collected (The) – (n): Old or ancient books gathered and translated by the Go'Doan from all the realms of Triton. These were protected and kept safe in the Narration Hall (main library) of the Dome City.

Crittich Keep – (Crid-ITCH) (n/place): Royal prison and dungeons of Wodell, located in the capital of Notting Thicket. Also contains administration offices of the constabulary, prison and guard system in Wodell, interrogation rooms, cells for those held for questioning, and in the bowels of its depths, ancient torture chambers. Outside the Keep is the Lawn, where executions take place.

Cyrus – (SEAR-us) (n/place): Large merchant town to the northeast of Silbury Henge on the outskirts of the Argyll Forest.

Dahksahna – (Dahk-SAH-nah) (n/title): Means "queen" in Korwahkian, the language of Korwahk in The Southlands.

Dahlia Rooms – (n/place): Sex palace in the Heden District of Fire City in Firenze.

Dax – (n/title): Means "king" in Korwahkian, the language of Korwahk in The Southlands.

Dellish – (Del-ISH) (adj): Of Wodell (akin to English, Spanish, etc.).

Dome City – (n/place): Another name for the city-state of Go'Doan, named as such as it's known for its plentiful gold domes.

Doors (The) – (n/place): A magical gnome settlement in the Great Thicket Forest of Wodell where the gnomes live in the trees, the name referring to the many doors carved into the trunks.

Dune Desert – (n/place): Desert north of the Sheeonee Mountain range in Firenze.

Dunleth Abhainn – (DONE-leth AH-been) (n/river): Long, wide river running from an inlet in the northern shore of the country of Airen, southeast all the way to Cairngorn Lake. At the town of Kilcree Break, the Dunleth forks into Westfork River, which runs southwest to the Argyll Forest. (Abhainn means "river" in Gaelic).

Emerald Oil Asps – (n): Snakes in Firenze. Black with emerald-colored eyes. Highly venomous.

Enchantments (The) – (n/place): Forest in the center of the mainland of Triton with trees made magically tall and stout in order to house the Nadirii Sisterhood in their treehouses. Protected by fierce magic, The Enchantments cannot be breached by anyone other than one of the Sisterhood or unless given Nadirii permission. Regardless of the intensity of magic that protects it, it is patrolled constantly by Nadirii warriors.

Fire City – (n/place): Capital city of Firenze. Located to the north of the Sheeonee Mountain range that takes up the center of Firenze. Fire City is close to Fire Lake, the largest lake in Firenze.

Fire Lake – (n/lake): Very large lake to the east of Fire City in the country of Firenze formed by runoff of melted snow from the Sheeonee Mountains.

Firenz – (Fir-EHNZ) (adj): Meaning, of the country of Firenze.

Firenze – (Fir-ehn-ZAY) (n/place): Country of Firenze situated across the south of the Triton mainland. The largest country in Triton. Most of the country is desert or sand dunes with the middle of the country having a very large mountain range with high peaks that get great amounts of snow. When this snow melts, it floods Fire Lake, close to Fire City, and leads off into a large number of rivers and tributaries that cut through the desert and dunes with strips of fertile oases.

Firenzii – (Fir-ehn-ZEE) (n): Language of Firenze (much like Italian).

Fotiá Sea – (Foh-SHAH) (n/ocean): Body of water to the south of the continent of Triton.

Fumeria – (Foo-mare-EE-ah) (n): Water pipe. Akin to a marijuana bong but much more elegant and ornate.

Gairn Plain – (n/place): A stretch of plain southeast of Sky Bay and west of the Dunleth Abhainn in the country of Airen.

Go'Doan – (Go'Dōn) (n/place/religion):
  (1) City-state of priests, scholars and healers with temples, archives of the history Triton and a university. Also known as Dome City.
  a.   Go'Da (Go'DAH) (n): University in Go'Doan

  (2) Religion in Triton with temples across the continent where people worship:
  a.   Go'Bedi (Go'bed-EE) (god of obedience)
  b.   Go'Vicee (Go'vee-SEE) (god of service)
  c.   Go'Chas (god of faithfulness)

  (3) Orders of Go'Doan:
  a.   Go'Fell (order of priests as a whole)
  b.   Go'En (high priests)

    c.   Go'Ar (Advanced priests, often are sent to do missionary work or teach in Go'Doan schools across Triton)
    d.   Go'Tish (new priests/trainee priests)
    e.   Go'Tec (priests who teach/scholars in the city-state)
    f.   Go'Nis ("Keepers of the Records," priests who record history)
    g.   Go'Ella (female acolytes that serve priests and the city-state)

Great Thicket Forest – (n/place): Massive forest in the middle of the country of Wodell, to the east of which is Notting Thicket, the capital city of Wodell.

Great Wohd (River) – (n/river): A very wide, very long river separating from the River Dorian in the north which runs from the Seil Sea. The Great Wohd cuts through the eastern part of Wodell, meeting the River Fae at Notting Thicket, the capital of Wodell, and continuing westerly nearly to the border of Wodell.

Green Sea – (n/ocean): Body of water to the east of the continent of Triton.

Gulliver – (n/place): Town in the south of Wodell located seventy-five miles from the Firenz boarder.

Hawkvale – (n/place): Country in the middle of The Northlands, south of Lunwyn, north of Fleuridia, ruled by King Noctorno and Queen Cora.

Heden District – (HEE-den) (n/place): Red light district of Fire City, Firenze. Where to find prostitutes (male and female), participate in orgies or other sexual games and play, consume smoke or *ashesh* or *koekah* and other forms of decadence.

Highgate – (n/place): Large gate at the top of the cliffs protecting Sky Bay, the capital city of Airen. Situated slightly to the southeast at the highest heights of the mountains that surround the capital city.

Ibex-whales – (EYE-bex whales) (n): Whales of which the bulls have enormous, ridged tusks that look like that of an ibex.

Irons – (n): Used in fireplaces or freestanding in rooms in Airen, Mar-el and Wodell, wood or other burning fuel in them or piled on them to heat them in order to heat a room.

kah rahna fauna – (n): Loosely means "my golden doe" in Korwahkian, the language of Korwahk in The Southlands.

Keel Castle – (n/place): Home of the king of Mar-el. Located in Nautilus, the capital city.

Keeper of The Lights – (group): A group of fairies who oversee and protect the area where The Lights (see: Lights (The)) can be viewed in the Greater Thicket Forest of Wodell.

Keerian Name – (description): The way Lunwynians (people of Lunwyn in the Northlands) describe a given name or as we know it Christian or first name.

Kilcree Break – (Kill-KREE Break) (n/place): Town in the middle of the country of Airen located at the break of the Dunleth Abhainn (river) where the Dunleth continues on to Cairngorn Lake and the Westfork River begins, running toward the Argyll Forest. A gentry seat.

Koekah – (koe-KAH) (n): Drug akin to cocaine. Available throughout Triton. Grown and manufactured in Firenze.

Korwahk – (n/place): Country taking up the northern part of the continent, The Southlands. Ruled by *Dax* (King) Lahn and *Dahksahna* (Queen) Circe of the Golden Dynasty.

Korwahn – (n/place): Capital city of Korwahk in The Southlands.

Lawn (The) – (n/place): Grassy area outside Crittich Keep, the royal prison and dungeons of Wodell, where executions take place. Located in Notting Thicket.

Lesser Thicket Forest – (n/place): Forest on the east border of the country of Wodell, west border of Airen. The parts of it in Airen are known as the Argyll Forest. Within it in Wodell is the Ancient Ritual Ground.

Leuthea – (LOU-thee-ah) (n): Sea goddess of sailors in distress. Worshiped by Mar-el.

Lights (The) (n/place): Atop the highest hill in the center of the Great Thicket Forest of Wodell where, on occasion, the sky illuminates with colored lights (akin to the Northern Lights). The reason for the phenomenon is unknown.

Lotus Den – (n/place): Bar and drug den with rooms for rent for a variety of hedonistic activities in the Heden District of Fire City in Firenze.

Lowgate – (n/place): Large gate in the downslope of the cliffs that protect Sky Bay, the capital city of Airen. Situated to the northwest in the lowest area where the cliffs meets the sea at Twilight Harbor.

Lunwyn – (n/place): Country taking up the northern part of The Northlands. Ruled by Queen Aurora.

Mar-el – (n/place): Country of Mar-el, island nation situated to the northeast of Triton (off the coast of Airen). Made up of dark rock around the shores, beaches, fertile land inland. Most of population works in some form of sea trade.

Marital Chain – (n): Firenz form of a wedding ring. It starts at upper ear, threads down to the lobe, across to the nostril and down to end at a hoop at the side of the mouth. In most cases, if it indicates marriage, it's worn on the right side. It's meant to signify listening to your mate, keeping them in mind, and communicating honestly with them.

McGarrity's Teahouse – (n/place): A brothel in Wodell.

Medusa – (n): Goddess of the sea. Worshipped by Mar-el.

Medusa's Gate – (n): Large, ornate monument to the goddess Medusa in which is the gate to the lane to Keel Castle in Nautilus, the home of the King of Mar-el.

Mer (The) – (n/people): Race of underwater charmed folk, including mermaids and mermales. Their fins split into legs and their gills disappear when they swim close to land so they can "pass" as human and move about on land.

Miet – (n/celebration/holiday): The celebration of the crop yield in Firenze, held as autumn subsides to winter. Celebrations mostly center around planned orgies, but they also include copious intake of liquor, food and drugs.

Mystics (The/the) – (n/place/spiritual practice):
(1) The continent to the west of Triton across the Triton Sea. Referred to with capitalized "The."

(2) Spiritual practice that includes personal reflection, transcendent study and deep training in various physical skills of defense and attack. Referred to with a lowercase "the."

Nadirii – (Nah-DEER-ee) (n): Sisterhood of warriors who live in an enchanted forest (The Enchantments) with no men. The veil around this forest was raised after the women of Airen revolted against their oppressors, magicking them to sleep, slitting their throats and escaping by stealing into the night to the newly established enchanted forest. No one can enter without Nadirii permission.
(1) "Nadirii" means "oppressed" in the old tongue.
(2) "Nadirii" means "sisterhood" in the ancient tongue.

Narration Hall – (n/building): Very large library that is very tall as well as built down deep in the earth in the Dome City where the tomes of history are recorded and kept, as well as all other books the Go'Doan have collected.

Nautilus – (n/place): Capital city of Mar-el, located on the southwest coast.

Night Heights – (n/mountain range): Range of mountains to the east of Sky Bay, the capital city of the country of Airen.

Nippenlas – (n/festival/holiday): A festival held midwinter in Wodell for the sole purpose of drawing the citizens out of their homes and to break the monotony of long nights and cold winters.

Northlands (The) – (n/place): One of two continents to the east of Triton across the Green Sea.

Notting Thicket – (n/place): Capital city of the country of Wodell, located to the east of the Great Thicket Forest.

Our Lady the Queen's Orphanage – (n/place): National orphanage in Notting Thicket, Wodell. Under patronage of the Queen of Wodell.

Pennyrium – (Pen-EER-ee-um) (n): A drug a woman can take through dissolving a powder in water in order to protect against conception.

Piercing Ceremony – (event): Done at age thirteen to boys and girls in Firenze, it is the ceremony where the right ear is pierced at the top and lobe, as well as the nostril and the side of the top lip. It is where the marital chain is threaded after a Firenz is wedded. Small hoops are worn in these piercings until a person is married and takes their chain.

Rayloo – (command): A Korwahkian word meaning [as it is in the imperative conjunction] "be quiet."

River Dorian – (n/river): Long, wide river running from Seil Sea through the eastern region of the country of Wodell, through the Lesser Thicket Forest, to the city-state of Go'Doan.

River Fae – (n/river): A river running from mountains to the north of the country of Wodell, through the mid-eastern part of the country to join with the Great Wohd at Notting Thicket, the capital of Wodell.

Royal Service Infirmary – (n/place): National hospital in Notting Thicket, the capital of Wodell, that treats all, but was created and caters to Dellish soldiers.

Seil Sea – (n/ocean): Body of water north of the continent of Triton.

Sheeonee Mountain Range – (SHE-oh-nee) (n/place): Large mountain range that makes up most of the central part of the country of Firenze. Very high peaks that get a great deal of snow. Snow melt feeds Fire Lake (outside Fire City) and five large rivers that run through the country, including the widest that flows north toward Wodell, the Tebes River.

Smoke – (n): Marijuana. Used mostly in Firenze but available throughout Triton.

Silbury Henge – (n/place): Standing stone henge in the forest on the western border of Airen where it meets The Enchantments and the city-state of Go'Doan. Made up of five standing stones and a sacrificial/ritual slab.

Sky Bay – (n/place): Capital city of Airen, located in a northwesternmost bay of Airen, close to the border of Wodell.

Sky Citadel – (n/place): Home of the King of Airen. Located in Sky Bay.

Slán Bailey – (SLAHN) (n/place): Royal prison in Airen, the building of which takes up a full, small island off the coast of Twilight Harbor in Sky Bay.

Soldier's Poison – (ritual): If a soldier is wounded gravely in the service of Airen or Wodell, he can request to be relieved of his life. This request is made of his commanding officer, and that officer can grant or refuse it. The ritual allows for a farewell from any loved one the soldier selects and making peace with his gods, before he's given a fast-acting, painless poison of a dense concentration of undiluted *taibac* to take, or if he's unable to drink it himself, it is administered to him by his commanding officer.

Southlands (The) – (n/place): One of two continents to the east of Triton across the Green Sea.

Strait of Medusa – (n/waterway): Narrow body of water that separates Mar-el from Airen.

Sparkles – (n): (When referring to a beverage) Champagne.

Taibac – (TIE-back) (n): Tobacco. Not smoked. Used as a poison to induce cardiac arrest. Can go undetected if poison is administered in small doses for a long time.

Tebes River – (TEH-behz) (n/river): Large river that flows from the Sheeonee Mountain range in Firenze, north toward the country of Wodell.

Temple to Wohden – (WOE-den) (n/place): National cathedral in Notting Thicket, Wodell where parishioners worship the god Wohden, the Dellish god of power and war. Also, where all royals are wed.

Trevor's Gorge – (n/place):

(1) A gorge south of Notting Thicket in Wodell that runs through a small, ancient mountain range (thus not high). It was formed by a narrow, but strong tributary that breaks off the Great Wohd River in Wodell.

(2) Also, the name of the large town situated at the west end of the gorge. This town is known for the making of sharp, but rich, goat's cheese that is renown throughout Triton.
    a.   Trevor cheese (n/food): Cheese from this region.

Triton – (n/place):

(1) The continent to the west of the Northlands and Southlands, and to the east of The Mystics. It is surrounded by the Green Sea to the east, the Triton Sea to the west, Seil Sea to the north and Fotiá Sea to the south. It consists of one large land mass about the size of Australia and one large island (Mar-el) to the northeast. Countries include Airen, The Enchantments, Firenze, Mar-el, Wodell and the city-state of the Go'Doan.

(2) (n/god): God of the sea, worshiped by Mar-el.

Triton Sea – (n/ocean): Body of water to the west of the continent of Triton.

Trusted Ones (The) – (n): The elite guard that is commissioned with the safety of the King and Queen of Firenze. Also known as "The Trusted."

Twilight Harbor – (n/place): Wharf/dock in Sky Bay, the capital city of Airen.

Westfork River – (n/river): Short, narrow river in the country of Airen running from a break in the great Dunleth Abhainn at the town of Kilcree Break. The Westfork River runs southwest to the Argyll Forest.

Wodell – (n/place): Country of Wodell situated at the northwest of the Triton mainland. Very fertile and green, consisting of mainly farmland, forests, hills, dells and moors.

Wynd – (pronounced like "to wind your way") (n): A narrow, open-ended alley. Mostly a footpath and not used for carriages or horses, etc. Opposite of "close" [see above].

Zees – (people): A race of wanderers. Mostly in Wodell, but also some would travel around the westernmost border of Airen.

Full glossary, including character lists, tarot meanings, and gods and goddesses can be found on The Rising Series page at KristenAshley.net

KEEP READING FOR MORE OF THE RISING

The Rising

Once upon a time, in a parallel universe, there existed the continent of Triton...

The Beast has risen!

Airen is at war. The queen is dead. The coven is incomplete. And things are uncertain under the sea.

Now, the unicorns and mermaids and witches and warriors and the strangers from other lands all must band together to face The Beast and save Triton.

The unions have been realized. Silence and Mars, True and Farah, Cassius and Elena and Aramus and Ha-Lah are at their fullest powers.

But the gods require sacrifice. The sacrifice of pure love. If it isn't given, the Beast will prevail, and Triton will fall.

It cannot be escaped; they must use all their might and magic...

The Rising is nigh!

Keep reading for more of The Rising.

THE RISING
CHAPTER 118 - THE WORK

Marian

Farm Six Miles West of the Ancient Ritual Ground
Wodell

She was beginning to feel the pain in her back becoming an ache in her entire body, which was good.

Everything else was bad.

She lay on her side on the floor in the farmstead, peering into the lifeless eyes of the dead child not five feet from her as she heard the screams of the mother coming from the other room.

The father had already been consumed.

Consumed.

The screams stopped but worse started as she heard the noises of sobs and pleas.

And then noises of something else.

What have I done? she thought.

After some time, she heard the familiar sound of the Beast's release and the crying and moaning of the woman abruptly halted.

Marian tried to move her legs, and they moved, but it made the pain in her back excruciating, thus she was forced to stop.

She needed a draught for the pain.

She needed to rest.

She'd have neither.

Where is that bloody priest? she thought.

"We must be away, Daemon," Jellan stated in a voice of genuine obsequiousness, false calm, but still managing to convey not a small amount of urgency.

"Fetch me some of the man's clothes," the Beast ordered.

"Of course," Jellan murmured.

"You don some too," the Beast went on.

"As you wish."

"Pack more, and I want my female bathed. She is dirty. I do not like her dirty. Bathe her and dress her in the woman's clothes," the Beast finished.

"It will be done," Jellan, the arsehole, the fool, the duplicitous sycophantic *cretin* assured.

She heard steps ascending stairs as she heard others approaching her.

She also heard the rain coming down in sheets and sheets.

She saw his feet, filthy with mud and grass, before he crouched and she saw his member hanging between his thighs, large even flaccid, and now tainted with blood.

Marian's mouth filled with bile.

She then felt his gentle touch as her hair was pulled away from her face.

"Do not be angry at me, my witch," he clucked.

Don't be angry?

Her mind reeled for ways to play this.

Jellan could shove his nose right up the creature's arse.

She would be who she was.

"You might have broken my back," she snapped.

"You could have a broken back, but you would still have your magic."

She lifted her eyes to his and saw what she did not see all these months she had been with him.

He was still beautiful.

In this form.

But he was not innocent and docile and misunderstood. He was not simple and easily led.

He was devious and crafty.

She had been played.

By her Beast *and* Jellan.

"You connived with him against me," she accused.

He shrugged.

She turned her eyes away.

"I needed you both," he shared. "I could not ascend without your power, and his. But when I ascended, I needed a meal. And such it was."

"Will you do me like you did that woman in the kitchens?" she demanded.

"I like you willing. You have much exuberance."

Her gaze shot to his handsome visage again.

The new definition of twofaced.

"I can hardly be of service to you in that manner if my spine is snapped," she spat.

He fell to his arse, and Marian gritted her teeth against the moan welling up her throat wrought by the pain in her body as he pulled her into his lap.

He then smoothed her hair again before he chucked her under the chin.

"I will not hurt you if you do not earn it. You are too important to me," he told her.

"Important how?" she asked.

"There is more work to be done, important work, and I need you and our friend to do it."

Marian was not feeling joyous about this news.

"What work is to be done?" she inquired.

"I fear it would be foolhardy to tell you of this at this juncture," he shared.

She opened her mouth to speak but was interrupted when Jellan appeared at their sides, stating, "I have your clothing, Daemon."

Marian glared up at the fallen priest.

He was dressed in the dead Dellish farmer's clothing.

It was too big on him.

However, as fate would have it, it would fit *Daemon* perfectly.

"Heat water for Marian's bath," Daemon commanded. "We must soothe her aches. And see if this dwelling has medicine. She is in pain."

Jellan's eyes flashed his displeasure at his service, but he said nothing against it, nodded, set the clothing on the floor beside Daemon and moved away.

"And get these bodies out of here," Daemon added.

"I am but one man, Daemon," Jellan reminded him.

Daemon twisted his head to look at the priest. "Then we shall have to find you some assistance. But for now, it's just you, and your standing there, glaring at me is not seeing to the things I've asked you to see to."

No, this Beast was not simple, docile, innocent and easily led.

Jellan bowed his head and scurried off.

Marian would have smirked, but such was the direness of the situation, she could not even take enjoyment in Jellan's subjugation.

"He, well he..." Daemon began, stroking her cheek. "Black of soul, is he."

Marian lay still in his arms, held to his body, seated in his lap, and stared at his face for she felt something had changed about him and she'd experienced enough change from him that morn, she could take no more.

"You," he whispered, still stroking her cheek. "I regret you. You were guided to your darkness."

"I don't..." She swallowed. "What do you speak of, Daemon?"

"If I did not need you for what must be done for me to succeed this time, kill the gods, claim their kingdom, I would have used you like the one in the kitchen and then put you out of your misery."

Kill the gods?

What gods?

"Daemon," she whispered, "what do you intend to do?"

"They created us; they cannot forsake us. They will learn this time."

Us? she wondered.

Who was *us*?

"But you could have veered away from the darkness. You did not," he murmured, studying her face. "This was your mistake."

Oh, *Gods*.

"Daemon—"

"Thank you for releasing me, my witch."

The Rising is available now.

ABOUT THE AUTHOR

Kristen Ashley is the *New York Times* bestselling author of over eighty romance novels including the *Rock Chick, Colorado Mountain, Dream Man, Chaos, Unfinished Heroes, The 'Burg, Magdalene, Fantasyland, The Three, Ghost and Reincarnation, The Rising, Dream Team, Moonlight and Motor Oil, River Rain, Wild West MC, Misted Pines* and *Honey* series along with several stand-alone novels. She's a hybrid author, publishing titles both independently and traditionally, her books have been translated in fourteen languages and she's sold over five million books.

Kristen's novel, *Law Man*, won the *RT Book Reviews* Reviewer's Choice Award for best Romantic Suspense, her independently published title *Hold On* was nominated for *RT Book Reviews* best Independent Contemporary Romance and her traditionally published title *Breathe* was nominated for best Contemporary Romance. Kristen's titles *Motorcycle Man, The Will*, and *Ride Steady* (which won the Reader's Choice award from *Romance Reviews*) all made the final rounds for Goodreads Choice Awards in the Romance category.

Kristen, born in Gary and raised in Brownsburg, Indiana, is a fourth-generation graduate of Purdue University. Since, she's lived in Denver, the West Country of England, and she now resides in Phoenix. She worked as a charity executive for eighteen years prior to beginning her independent publishing career. She now writes full-time.

Although romance is her genre, the prevailing themes running through all of Kristen's novels are friendship, family and a strong sisterhood. To this end, and as a way to thank her readers for their support, Kristen has created the Rock Chick Nation, a series of programs that are designed to give back to her readers and promote a strong female community.

The mission of the Rock Chick Nation is to live your best life, be true to your true self, recognize your beauty, and take your sister's back whether they're at your side as friends and family or if they're thousands of miles away and you don't know who they are.

The programs of the RC Nation include Rock Chick Rendezvous, weekends Kristen organizes full of parties and get-togethers to bring the sisterhood together, Rock Chick Recharges, evenings Kristen arranges for women who have been nominated to receive a special night, and Rock Chick Rewards, an ongoing program that raises funds for nonprofit women's organizations Kristen's readers nominate. Kristen's Rock Chick Rewards have donated hundreds of thousands of dollars to charity and this number continues to rise.

You can read more about Kristen, her titles and the Rock Chick Nation at KristenAshley.net.

facebook.com/kristenashleybooks

twitter.com/KristenAshley68

instagram.com/kristenashleybooks

pinterest.com/KristenAshleyBooks

goodreads.com/kristenashleybooks

bookbub.com/authors/kristen-ashley

Also by Kristen Ashley

Rock Chick Series:

Rock Chick

Rock Chick Rescue

Rock Chick Redemption

Rock Chick Renegade

Rock Chick Revenge

Rock Chick Reckoning

Rock Chick Regret

Rock Chick Revolution

Rock Chick Reawakening

Rock Chick Reborn

The 'Burg Series:

For You

At Peace

Golden Trail

Games of the Heart

The Promise

Hold On

The Chaos Series:

Own the Wind

Fire Inside

Ride Steady

Walk Through Fire

A Christmas to Remember

Rough Ride

Wild Like the Wind

Free

Wild Fire

Wild Wind

The Colorado Mountain Series:

The Gamble

Sweet Dreams

Lady Luck

Breathe

Jagged

Kaleidoscope

Bounty

Dream Man Series:

Mystery Man

Wild Man

Law Man

Motorcycle Man

Quiet Man

Dream Team Series:

Dream Maker

Dream Chaser

Dream Bites Cookbook

Dream Spinner

Dream Keeper

The Fantasyland Series:

Wildest Dreams

The Golden Dynasty

Fantastical

Broken Dove

Midnight Soul

Gossamer in the Darkness

Ghosts and Reincarnation Series:

Sommersgate House

Lacybourne Manor

Penmort Castle

Fairytale Come Alive

Lucky Stars

The Honey Series:

The Deep End

The Farthest Edge

The Greatest Risk

The Magdalene Series:

The Will

Soaring

The Time in Between

Mathilda, SuperWitch:

Mathilda's Book of Shadows

Mathilda The Rise of the Dark Lord

Misted Pines Series

The Girl in the Mist

The Girl in the Woods

Moonlight and Motor Oil Series:

The Hookup

The Slow Burn

The Rising Series:

The Beginning of Everything

The Plan Commences

The Dawn of the End

The Rising

The River Rain Series:

After the Climb

After the Climb Special Edition

Chasing Serenity

Taking the Leap

Making the Match

The Three Series:

Until the Sun Falls from the Sky

With Everything I Am

Wild and Free

The Unfinished Hero Series:

Knight

Creed

Raid

Deacon

Sebring

Wild West MC Series:

Still Standing

Smoke and Steel

Other Titles by Kristen Ashley:

Heaven and Hell

Play It Safe

Three Wishes

Complicated

Loose Ends

Fast Lane

Perfect Together

Too Good To Be True